"Hunter's world continu[es]... highly original fantasy with lively chara[cters] where nothing can ever be taken for granted."   —*Publishers Weekly*

"Hunter has created a remarkable interpretation of the aftermath of Armageddon in which angels and devils once again walk the earth and humans struggle to find a place. Stylish storytelling and gripping drama make this a good addition to most fantasy collections."   —*Library Journal*

"Readers will admire [Thorn's] sacrifice [in] placing others before herself.... Fans will enjoy reading about the continuing end of days."   —*Midwest Book Review*

"With fast-paced action and the possibility of more romance, this is an enjoyable read with an alluring magical touch."
                                                            —Darque Reviews

Seraphs

"The world [Hunter] has created is unique and bleak.... [An] exciting science fiction thriller."
                                                            —*Midwest Book Review*

"Continuing the story begun in *Bloodring*, Hunter expands on her darkly alluring vision of a future in which the armies of good and evil wage their eternal struggle in the world of flesh and blood. Strong characters and a compelling story."
                                                            —*Library Journal*

"This thrilling dark fantasy has elements of danger, adventure, and religious fanaticism, plus sexual overtones. Hunter's impressive narrative skills vividly describe a changed world, and she artfully weaves in social commentary ... a well-written, exciting novel."   —*Romantic Times*

continued ...

Other Novels by Faith Hunter

Seraphs
Bloodring

HOST

A Rogue Mage Novel

FAITH HUNTER

A ROC BOOK

ROC
Published by New American Library, a division of
Penguin Group (USA) Inc., 375 Hudson Street,
New York, New York 10014, USA
Penguin Group (Canada), 90 Eglinton Avenue East, Suite 700, Toronto,
Ontario M4P 2Y3, Canada (a division of Pearson Penguin Canada Inc.)
Penguin Books Ltd., 80 Strand, London WC2R 0RL, England
Penguin Ireland, 25 St. Stephen's Green, Dublin 2,
Ireland (a division of Penguin Books Ltd.)
Penguin Group (Australia), 250 Camberwell Road, Camberwell, Victoria 3124,
Australia (a division of Pearson Australia Group Pty. Ltd.)
Penguin Books India Pvt. Ltd., 11 Community Centre, Panchsheel Park,
New Delhi - 110 017, India
Penguin Group (NZ), 67 Apollo Drive, Rosedale, North Shore 0632,
New Zealand (a division of Pearson New Zealand Ltd.)
Penguin Books (South Africa) (Pty.) Ltd., 24 Sturdee Avenue,
Rosebank, Johannesburg 2196, South Africa

Penguin Books Ltd., Registered Offices:
80 Strand, London WC2R 0RL, England

Published by Roc, an imprint of New American Library, a division of Penguin
Group (USA) Inc. Previously published in a Roc trade paperback edition.

First Roc Mass Market Printing, January 2009
10 9 8 7 6 5 4 3 2 1

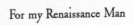

For my Renaissance Man

Acknowledgments

Many thanks to:

My Renaissance Man, for rubbing my tired feet.

Kim, for the tea breaks and your friendship.

My agent, Lucienne Diver, for believing in
the world of the Rogue Mage.

Finally, my editor, Liz Scheier. This has been *fun*!

3 *And there appeared another wonder in heaven; . . . a great red dragon, having seven heads and ten horns, and seven crowns upon his heads.*

4 *And his tail drew the third part of the stars of heaven, and did cast them to the earth . . .*

7 *And there was war in heaven: Michael and his angels fought against the dragon; and the dragon fought and his angels,*

8 *And prevailed not; neither was their place found any more in heaven.*

9 *And the great dragon was cast out, that old serpent, called the Devil, and Satan, which deceiveth the whole world: he was cast out into the earth, and his angels were cast out with him. . . .*

12 *Therefore rejoice, ye heavens, and ye that dwell in them. Woe to the inhabiters of the earth and of the sea! for the devil is come down unto you, having great wrath. . . .*

—Revelation 12

Prologue

HISTORY OF THE WORLD, POST-AP (POST-APOCALYPSE)

The three plagues heralded the beginning of the Battle of Armageddon; the seraphim, led by the Angels of Punishment, ravaged the earth with weapons of genocide, killing more than five-sixths of the population; Darkness rose from the depths, its minions attacking humans and the seraphim alike, bringing warfare between the High Host and the Fallen, between mankind and evil, between man and man. Most great cities were reduced to rubble; communications were devastated; trade was totally disrupted. The year was 2011.

In the aftermath of the apocalypse, the United States still stood—those parts that survived the blast of Light and earthquakes that took out much of the southwest coast. Washington, DC, remained a place of human political power. Large-scale food production was protected under seraphic domes in the Napa Valley and Kansas. Hollywood reinvented itself in northern California, far from an angry sea. New York was usurped by seraphs as their own, becoming a Realm of Light.

Africa became a wasteland where bleached bones were scoured by winds bringing death to any who trespassed on its soil. Europe survived as small pockets of modern life, some slipping back into superstition, a new Dark Age. The China Sea grew devoid of life; the East went silent for over sixty years, and is only now, in the year 105 Post-Apocalypse, beginning to regenerate its fabled technology and industrialization, creating a shipping industry unrivaled in the Post-Ap world. South America was largely untouched by warfare. Or so they say. And an ice age commenced, glaciers creeping quickly from the poles.

Into the chaos of the end of the Last War were born the few babies who were conceived just prior to the first plague, and who had survived in vivo through the Last Days—the plague of blood, the plague of sores, and the plague of insanity and judgment. They were born perfect in mind and body, beautiful beings who carried the hope of mankind within them. Until they reached puberty. Then their gifts blossomed and they discovered their abilities to manipulate leftover creation energies—the powers of earth, air, stone, sea, fire, metals, or water. Soulless beings who understood the mathematics of energy and matter and could wield them, shape them, use them. They were wild mages with no one to teach them, and they brought a second devastation upon an earth still reeling from the horrors of spiritual warfare. Humans looked upon them with fear and the neomages were slaughtered by the thousands until the seraphs intervened and set places aside for them—places sacrosanct, under holy protection. The Enclaves.

A new society developed in the Enclaves, where today the neomages experiment and train, breed and grow, though breeding is difficult as the females must achieve mage-heat in order to produce viable ova. Only the overflight of seraphs, or the rare permitted visitation of one, can bring on such a heat with ease, and because the rut is uncontrolled, it is looked upon with moral and righteous horror by humankind.

Over the next decades, trade began between humans and the Enclaves. Permanent diplomatic missions opened in Atlanta and in Washington, DC, and consulates were licensed. The Administration of the ArchSeraph began regulating the presence of neomages in the human world, and because of their vigilance, mages have begun to be accepted by humans, with the exception of the fundamental orthodoxy of the kirk.

With the permission of the AAS, this religious minority hunts down and kills any unlicensed neomage. The punishment is grisly and horrific and approved by the High Host of Seraphim and the Most High—God the Victorious.

I am Thorn St. Croix, once a maker of stone trinkets and jewelry. Now that I am a licensed neomage, my life has been turned upside down by the things I have learned. Things about the nature of evil and good. Things about myself.

I learned that evil has a personal interest in me. I learned that the Administration of the ArchSeraph and its enemies, the Earth Invasion Heretics, may be secret allies. I learned that my own past is not as simple as it seemed. My parents were killed by a Prince of the Dark. My sister may be a captive of the same beast. May be. A world of possibility in those two words.

Me? I am a stone mage, a soulless being, one whom the religious call a mistake of the Most High. I think perhaps I am also a battle mage. I have fought against the Darkness living under the triple peaks of the Trine, a mountain north of Mineral City, Carolina, in the Appalachian Mountains. Using my gifts, I have fought beside seraphs, and though mage-heat threatened, it was held at bay by the fighting-lust that comes upon me in warfare.

But time is running out. One of the Powers and Principalities of Darkness that was bound at the end of the Last War has been loosed and will soon be free. And there is nothing in this world I can do about it.

Chapter 1

I'd been feeling itchy all day, like something was about to happen. As if the lynx—my personal portent—was about to howl. As if the skies were trying to drop down a mega-omen with the destructive potential of a nuclear warhead. As if my life was about to change. Again. So I picked up on his presence nearly a mile away, and my teeth were aching from grinding my jaws together long before he walked into the shop.

In stereotypical mage style, he was contemptuous of everything he saw: the retail shops, the grocery, the kirk, the dour fashions of the local citizens, the dented and rusted el-cars whizzing up and down the ice-covered street, even the town meeting hall in the old Central Baptist Church. If he'd worn a sign that said he was too good for Mineral City—and for me—he couldn't have been any more onerous. And like most of the mages I remembered from my first fourteen years in Enclave, he walked with his nose in the air. Quite literally. When he appeared in the front windows and entered the shop, I nearly shuddered.

He was midthirties and stood about five-five, with mousy brown hair and nondescript features. Except for his clothes, he was totally forgettable. A mage-style fashion plate, he was dressed for the dance floor and the mating floor, wearing a velvet cloak that covered him from head to toe. Gold-foiled leather boots peeked from under its hem. And his hat, the latest trend in Hollywood, was bright pink, with an honest-to-God feather in it. To further endear himself, he grimaced when he looked around Thorn's Gems, the jewelry shop owned by me and my best friends. It was the prissy, looking-down-his-nose expression that ticked me off most; that is, until he spotted Rupert, one of my business partners, and sneered, letting me see he had a mean streak a half mile long.

He was violently, lethally homophobic. His mind open and clear as a faceted gem. He envisioned spitting Rupert on a spike, and when his hand twitched toward the sword at his hip, I lifted my longsword and advanced with mage-speed. In two strides, I reached him.

Before I could complete the opening form of the lion rising, he had drawn his sword, swatted my blade aside with contemptuous ease, and completed two counterstrikes I almost didn't block. Either of the moves would have been fatal, and had Audric not advanced and thrust a sword point under the mage's raised left arm, stopping a third, I would have been toast.

My champard's quick reaction ended with his blade lightly touching the mage's skin, sliced deep through his fancy velvet cloak. That effectively halted the fight. We stood in the center of the shop, the stranger's sword point under my chin, Audric's poised to pierce his heart, and my blade hovering for a thrust through his lungs. I was boiling mad, but I waited for his next move.

No fear showed in his chocolate brown eyes as they measured me, and his back to Audric was a screaming insult. "You're a sloppy swordswoman," he said. "You broadcast your intent before you drew your weapon. And your mule is useless."

My rage flared at the insult to Audric, but I kept it off my face and out of my voice. "You have sloppy thoughts," I said. "You broadcast your intent when you were still on the train, and your insults as you sauntered up the street. And violence when you walked in the door. I knew you intended to test me, and wondered if you were as good as your ego claimed. Look down."

When the mage spotted my new kogatana, a gift from Audric, pressed between his ribs, his brows went up. I suspected that was high praise. The kogatana, a long-bladed dagger, was poised in a killing strike. I elected not to tell the mage he'd have killed me if I hadn't been privy to his thoughts.

"Whoever you are," I said, "get out of Thorn's Gems and out of my life. No one who thinks insulting thoughts about this town, my shop, or my friends is welcome here."

"So." With a fancy flourish, he batted Audric's heavy battle sword away and sheathed his slim-bladed weapon. It went along his hip and down the length of his leg, which was clad in winter-weight black wool and cashmere, elegantly tailored as a tuxedo. "They were right. You can read my mind."

"Yeah. Lucky me," I deadpanned. I kept my blades out and in play. So did Audric, his face impassive, even after the mule slur, but he'd nicked the mage through the velvet and several underlayers, which he'd never do by accident. I could smell the blood and wanted to grin.

"Then"—the neomage swirled back his emerald cape and stepped away from Audric—"you'll be needing this." With his left hand, he tossed an amulet into the air. I glimpsed a blur of snowflake obsidian strung on a cord. Still moving fast, I set the dagger on the glass display case and snatched the leather thong. I could sense his intention to pull his sword when I was distracted, so I never took my gaze off him. My longsword never wavered from his chest.

The nugget bumped against my hand and his thoughts disappeared. As it swung away, I sensed his curiosity. When the stone hit my hand again, his thoughts were gone. The stone swinging away on the leather cord brought his thoughts flooding back, and his interest grew at whatever showed on my face. I gripped the nugget. My temper and his violent tendencies washed away as blessed silence filled my head.

"Audric," I said, backing away. He stepped close and disarmed the petite mage, the big half-breed towering over the smaller supernat as he removed the sword and two throwing blades. They clanked on the case near my kogatana, the pile growing to include a small long-barreled semiautomatic pistol, which the mage carried in a holster strapped at the small of his back, a Pre-Ap-style cellular satellite phone with a built-in camera, and a belt made of metal rings and discs on leather. The metal was charged with incantations

I could see in mage-sight. Audric was familiar with mages, having grown up in an Enclave on the west coast, and knew not to touch them in case they were spelled.

Several cleverly hidden throwing stars clinked to the glass, the kind of steel stars ninjas used in old Pre-Ap movies. These looked nasty, all sharp edges and points. When he was as disarmed as Audric could make him without stripping him naked and probing body cavities, I sheathed my longsword in its walking-stick sheath and backed away, keeping a hand on the prime amulet that composed its hilt. "Watch him," I said. "He's more than he appears."

Audric nodded and pulled a vicious-looking knife designed for close-in fighting. "Hands on the case," he directed. The velvet-cloaked man sighed and placed his palms on the counter. My champard slipped a beefy, dark-skinned arm around the thin neck, pressing the knifepoint against the mage's carotid artery and esophagus.

I inspected the amulet. It was an Apache Tear, a teardrop-shaped, obsidian nugget naturally rounded and smoothed by wind and water. Undrilled, it had been wrapped in copper and sterling silver wire and strung on a fancy, dyed, knotted leather thong.

I'm a stone mage, able to manipulate creation energies through the crystalline matrix of stone and minerals, but stones corrupted by eons of contact with the lighter elements weren't something I could usually use, not without a lot of prep time. And obsidian was beyond the scope of most stone mages. This Apache Tear was different in a lot of ways.

Obsidian is produced by volcanoes, the heat creating a type of glass when felsic lava cools too quickly for crystals to grow. Crystals in lava make gems and various minerals, while obsidian is mineral-like, but not a true mineral because it's not crystalline, hence not stone. Yet, I had discovered in my teens that I could manipulate some obsidian, a fairly rare trait in stone mages.

It contained a powerful conjure.

It felt greasy against my fingertips, practically vibrating with power. Audric, poised over the deadly mage, his blade ready to rip out the intruder's throat, asked, "What is he?" The mage bristled at the blunt query, but it was an appropriate question for my champard—my half-human, half-mage bodyguard cum teacher cum friend, among other things. The friend was the most important part, though he took the other duties seriously. Perhaps too much so; Audric had once nearly died taking them seriously.

I looked at the mage, at his belt, his weapons, and his expressionless face. "I think he's a metal mage, but that's not all he is." The mage's eyes didn't exactly flicker, but I knew I had surprised him. "I don't know what else, but I'd sooner trust a starving devil spawn at my back than him." Though it was intended as a gross insult, the mage smiled. I really, really didn't like that smile.

As if to prove me right, the mage seemed to go limp. He slid down, almost out of Audric's grip. It was a boneless move, fluid, like water from a pitcher, and so fast he seemed to blur with mage-speed.

Almost as if expecting it, Audric caught him and yanked him up, slamming the mage against the display case and crushing his face into the wood that braced the glass. I heard the old wood creak. And I managed not to blink.

I sharpened my mage-sight and looked the mage over. His aura glowed a clear blue that fractured into a scintillating fire like rainbow fluorite. He wore an amulet ring, a conjure encapsulated in the sterling band, the stone an empty vessel. A metal ring on a gold chain hung around his neck, glowing with the steady power of his legally required mage visa. The GPS locator device embedded in the gold bracelet on his left wrist shone with both technology and a conjure, and a fourth talisman, probably a chain, encircled his ankle, clasped beneath his boot.

That talisman made me pause. It glowed with peculiar energies, like a link to a mega-strong energy sink. It was way too much power to carry around safely. Unless he had great control, he could go blooey, scattering bits and pieces of himself around the environment. Backing up until I touched the wall, I leaned into it for balance. Stabilized, I opened a mindskim, blending the two senses into a single scan, a trick that caused vertigo and made me want to toss my cookies. Not the impression I wanted to make. In the scan, the anklet was a horrid smear of brown and yellow enwrapping his lower leg. And his eyes, passionless brown, were shadowy holes, giving nothing away, even in the scan. This guy was scary.

"What are you doing?" he asked, voice sharp.

Fairly certain I wouldn't pass out, fall down, or get embarrassingly sick, I levered my weight away from the wall and onto my feet. "Looking you over."

"I got that. But with what?" He pushed with his hands and Audric let him up, slowly. The mage rocked his head, as if the threat of Audric's knife wasn't real, or as if it didn't matter, and that meant he was either very stupid or a lot more deadly than I thought. And I didn't think the visiting mage was stupid. His eyes narrowed with interest. "I saw the sight for an instant and then I thought I saw a skim, but it disappeared."

Audric glanced a warning at me. "My mistrend is uninterested in answering questions."

"Yeah. But we have a few," Rupert said from my left. "Let's start with who you are, and why you're here. And let's see your visa."

I had questions of my own, like—*you mean you've never blended senses? Why not?* And for Audric, the obvious ones—*this isn't normal for mages?* And, *Why didn't you tell me I was doing something weird?* And, *How did he know what I was doing at all?* But I kept the questions to myself.

"Cheran Jones, metal mage, at your service. I'd bow, but circumstances prevent grand gestures," he said with a hard, acerbic edge that promised retribution. "My visa, papers, and tickets are inside my vest. I would present it as requested, but I'd like to keep my throat, so perhaps we'll forgo the diplomatic niceties for a more auspicious moment; perhaps when I'm no longer being threatened at knifepoint. I'm here as an emissary from the New Orleans Enclave. Name, rank, and mission specifications, as requested."

"My mistrend said you were something more," Audric said. "What more?"

I wanted to cringe at the use of the formal word. Mistrend—mistress, friend—miss, as in error, and *end*, as in life. Too many champards died in the course of their sworn duties and I was still getting used to the idea of being responsible for two sentient beings who wanted to serve me and fight with me, and who would die for me. It gave me the willies.

"The fine points of diplomacy do not require me to discuss my personal life. However, I will say that I am here to discuss the Flames and the prophecy." Without turning his head, he raised a hand off the case and pointed over the doorway of the stairs to my loft. Above it was a framed needlepoint of the prophecy proclaimed by the Enclave priestess when my twin and I were born. *A Rose by any Other Name will still draw Blood.*

Seraph stones. He was here to rake me over the coals and meddle in my life. And how did he know where the prophecy was hung? He hadn't looked that way when he entered.

Cheran glanced at my left cheek and I didn't need my unique mage gift to read his slur. He thought the crosshatch scars on my cheek were ugly. Well, so did I, but there wasn't much I could do about them. I had a lot of scars I couldn't do anything about.

Rupert had opened the papers and tickets, and said, "He originated in New Orleans Enclave, stopped for a rest and change of trains in Birmingham, and came on straight here." He rustled papers and read, "Cheran Jones, litter of four, metal mage of the New Orleans Enclave, licensed to visit the consulate general in Mineral City in the mountains of Carolina. Hail to Adonai." Rupert looked up at me. "Blow it out Gabriel's horn. What's all that mean?"

The door to the shop opened and a dry, thin voice asked, "Something going on here I need to know about, Miz Thorn?" Shamus Waldroup, the town kirk's senior elder and the highest-ranking of the town fathers, owned the bakery across the street. He kept an eye on me, which, at the best of times, like now, could be comforting. Of course, the feeling of being spied on was always there too. "Is this another mage come a-visitin'?" His bald, dark-skinned head caught the light as he shuffled inside, his brown robe of office dragging the floor. He was followed by a second wizened man, also in kirk robes, who closed the door behind them.

Waldroup indicated the other man and said, "Ernest Waldroup, my brother and the chief bishop of the Atlanta kirk." Seeing no threats in the newcomers, I dropped the blended scan and tucked the sheathed walking-stick sword through my belt, drawing on the prime amulet of its hilt to steady myself. The kogatana went beside the longsword.

The new elder was mostly Caucasian and seemed to share not a single genetic or ethnic trait with Shamus except for the bald head, but after the end of the world and the deaths of nearly six billion humans, ethnic traits had become pretty intertwined as men and women formed alliances for survival. Families often looked nothing alike. Or too much alike, which was another kind of problem entirely.

The elders inspected the tableau of the shop: Rupert and me, armed and silent, the pile of weapons on the counter; and Audric holding a velvet-cloaked stranger at knifepoint. Ernest seemed amused at the scene, and Shamus was grinning ear to ear. I suppose I was high entertainment in Mineral City. It made me want to wring Jones' neck.

The new elder, a chief in the largest kirk on the Atlantic seaboard, could be construed as an additional threat to my security in Mineral City, but he merely nodded to me as he looked Cheran over. He said, "You mages wear the most gosh-awful clothes a man ever did see." I converted a laugh at Cheran's reaction into an unconvincing cough. Elder Ernest poked Cheran in the side with his walking stick as if Audric, holding a knife to the mage's throat, didn't exist. "You got a visa, pretty boy?"

Audric didn't budge. Silently, I set the Apache Tear on the counter. Cheran saw the movement and glanced at me as his thoughts flooded into my mind. Rage. Fury. Visions of disemboweling Audric. And deeper, muddy thoughts I couldn't follow, thoughts his temper obscured as he tried to control it. Thoughts he didn't want me to see.

But the anger was real. Fury at the *mule* holding the knife. Wrath that he had been embarrassed in front of the locals on his first independent mission. Hatred at the gay men. Rage directed at me because it was all my fault. I wanted to say *Bite me*. Instead, I blew out a resigned breath. "Let him go," I said to Audric. "Yes, Elders Waldroup, he's a neomage and he has a visa." *More's the pity*. Without one, he'd be quickly dispatched; not to jail, but dispatched as in dead. Unlicensed mages were killed on sight.

Not happy, but unable to do anything about it, Audric stepped away, and Cheran shook himself to settle his cloak. I could smell his blood from the nick under his arm as anger made his pulse race faster. He executed a mage-fast martial-art move as he turned, which positioned him neatly to pick up his weapons. Before bowing to the Elders Waldroup, he chose the small gun, which he stuck in his waistband. It was a good defensive ploy, but a terrible one for making friends. The town officials backed up fast.

Too angry now to notice their reactions, the visiting mage went through his intro again, and held out the GPS bracelet and the visa as required by international law. But I had to wonder at his tactics. I didn't know much about consulate etiquette, but picking up a gun didn't seem real conducive to achieving peace and harmony between races. Cheran Jones was either sloppy or devious. Or he wasn't a visiting consulate at all. My blood chilled at the thought. Was he an imposter? What was he? That was part of what I couldn't read in his mind and I didn't like it. Not at all.

Shamus, stooped and irascible as ever, recovered quickly and winked at me. Though he couldn't exactly be called a good buddy, he was more than fair where I was concerned. He watched as his brother inspected the visa and read the purpose of the visit on the metal disc. Shamus said to me, "That says he's a teacher. What is he here to teach?"

"I am to be Thorn St. Croix's instructor in swordplay, diplomatic protocol for humans and seraphs, media relations, and whatever else I discover she needs to know as a mage living in this town. She is thought to be woefully lacking in the necessary skills and diplomatic procedure. And she won't be stuck in a backwater like this for long," Cheran said, his lip curling. "She needs schooling."

"Backwater? Humph."

At the tone, Jones' face and thoughts cleared of anger and he seemed to realize he had made a mistake. I read, clear as a seraph-bell, that he was here on probation. After all, how much trouble could a quick-tempered man make in an unimportant place like Mineral City? But this was his last chance to make good.

"Manners ain't a problem for our Thorn. She's been doing all right without your help the last decade or so," Shamus said. "Miz Thorn, you willing to take responsibility for anything else stupid he does?" I could have hugged the old man. Rupert chuckled under his breath. Cheran's mind went coldly quiet.

"I'll take care of him," I said, following the mage's thoughts.

The baker's brother added, "And get him into some decent clothes, not this girly rag he's got on." Elder Ernest jerked on the emerald velvet cloak, released the visa, and hobbled to the door, rudely turning his back on the visitor.

Shamus followed, saying, "Some orthodox factions are difficult enough these days without another catamite prancing around. Your pardon, Rupert, Audric."

Cheran drew himself up and I gleaned from his mind that this time it was honest insult. "I'm not a catamite, you—"

"Careful there, son," Waldroup said over his shoulder as he opened the door into the cold. "You got to teach all that diplomatic stuff to our town mage. You don't want to be deported from a *backwater posting* following a diplomatic incident before you get it all taught." Chuckling, the two elders shuffled out and closed the door.

"Our town mage?" Cheran repeated softly, obviously surprised. He'd been painstakingly prepped for this mission, tutored to deal with recalcitrant humans and instructed on how to pull my butt out of almost any fire. He had expected to find me in danger and up to my armpits in diplomatic troubles, but nothing was going like he'd expected. I wasn't what he'd expected. And that fact affected his secondary mission. I caught that before it disappeared beneath other thoughts.

He studied me closely. "What's 'our town mage' supposed to mean?" When no one answered, he looked from my hand to the Apache Tear, still on the counter. His mind went quickly blank as he envisioned a candle flame, one of the first mind-clearing meditation techniques taught to a neomage child. It was the last clear thought I got from him. Below that it was all a cloudy muddle, shadowed by the flame. As a hint, it was pretty direct. I picked up the obsidian and looped it around my neck. His thoughts died away.

When we all continued to stare, silent and assessing, he said, "Our town mage, huh? Fine. I'm adaptable. What's wrong with my clothes? They were made according to the cut and style of the official neomage emissary to Atlanta. They're modest and suitable to this miserable cold, and yet still have a certain flair." He flipped the hem of the cloak in example.

"The elders didn't kill him, so it looks like we have to keep him," Rupert said, deliberately boorish, crossing his arms over his chest and leaning over a glass display cabinet. "But you do have to get him properly dressed. That hat has to go. Even *I* wouldn't wear it, and I'm pretty gutsy with my wardrobe." That was an understatement. Rupert was a fashion queen.

Cheran reached up and touched his hat, running his hand along the foot-long feather regretfully. "I can leave the hat. And the cloak. What else?"

"I can find you some suitable clothes. Something wool. Maybe a mustard brown tweed coat and a bowler hat in that green that Miz Abernathy came up with."

"Mustard brown tweed? A bowler?" Cheran turned faintly pale at the description of local clothing.

Rupert grinned happily. Audric was smiling, undoubtedly at the mental image of Cheran Jones in local garb, and was picking his fingernails with the gigantic knife. No one could look equally amused and deadly like my champards. Far too casually Audric said, "Ernest Waldroup, Atlanta's elder, came in today's train. Did you not see him en route?"

Cheran said, "I traveled on the train by private coach, as befits a fully licensed mage, the same way I'll return to civili—to Enclave," he corrected, "when this assignment is over."

Audric looked at me, pointedly. I pressed my lips into a thin line. It was clear that Cheran Jones wouldn't fit seamlessly into the life of the town. I had the feeling that the mage wouldn't fit in anywhere outside of Enclave, and getting him deported before he accomplished his secondary, covert mission, was high on my to-do list at the moment. Silently, I thanked the senior elders for the idea. Yet, part of me, admittedly a small part, hoped that Cheran was really here to teach me. There was a lot I needed to learn about the visa I wore. Like how to use the darn thing as more than an elaborate megaphone.

It was clear Cheran was finally getting a clue what to expect from this assignment and the culture shock was intense. I was about to make it worse. "Where is the coach now?"

"I left orders that it be stored behind the consulate and

my bags be deposited by the bellman in an appropriate
suite—" He stopped abruptly as if a frightening possibility
had just penetrated his mind.

"Mineral City...doesn't have a consulate," Rupert said
with wicked delight.

The mage stared at me, dread warring with suspicion in
his gaze. "He's joking."

I shook my head. "No consulate."

He recovered quickly, I'll give him that. "As Mineral
Town is deficient in that regard, it would be appropriate for
you to put me up. I'll stay here. Your servant and mule can
care for both of us without undue difficulty."

Audric's mouth narrowed. I knew he had endured the
last insult. Before he could bonk the mage on the head with
a brawny fist or stick him through with the fingernail blade,
I said, "It's Mineral City. And you can get a room in the
hotel across the street and down the next block, or you can
ask Miz Essie if you can rent a room. She sometimes takes
boarders."

Rupert said, "Essie has three guest rooms with a bath
down the hall, and serves two meals a day. Oatmeal for
breakfast and a mystery meat stew for supper. You take
your turn at cleaning the communal toilet and change your
own sheets."

The look on Cheran's face was priceless. It was suddenly
occurring to the unexpected visitor that he might have been
sent to the backside of a hellhole with insufficient recon.
"Down the hall," he repeated.

My friends looked at one another and grinned happily.
Sometimes the best weapon is the tongue. "The mattress is
only twenty-four years old," Audric said.

"Clean sheets once a month," Rupert added.

"Whether they need washing or not," Audric said.

"Once a month," Cheran repeated faintly. "A communal
toilet. Not here?"

I shook my head no and tried to ignore the gleeful
expressions on my champards' faces. "No guest room,"
Rupert said. "Just a loft my mistrend has no intention of
sharing with anyone."

"And who will be paying for this five-star service?" he
asked.

"Beats me," I said, feeling almost sorry for him. "I was never given a diplomatic stipend. And if the Enclave didn't send funds with you, you'll need to hop a train back south or figure out how to pay your way."

A dozen thoughts crossed his face in an instant. I had only a moment to recognize surprise, cunning, and, lastly, horror. "Tears of Taharial," he swore softly. "I'm in hell."

My champards thought that was hilarious. The bad part was, it might be true.

Chapter 2

B ecause I didn't want the mage in my loft upstairs, I
bought him takeout from the Chinese place down the
street and led him to the workroom behind the shop.
Unconsciously, Cheran moved mage-fast when he entered
the workroom, eyes darting to the far corners, as if for possible threat. His speed made my heart ache with something
akin to loneliness. I didn't want to look too closely at that
emotion. Fortunately, he grimaced at the food and that
restored my antipathy to him.

He set the ridiculous hat and cloak to the side and we
perched in ugly, mismatched, but really comfortable cast-
off chairs, paper plates on makeshift tables Rupert had
knocked together out of discarded lumber years ago, the
gas logs turned on high to heat the frozen room. In an
uncomfortable silence, we ate heaping portions of three
mostly vegetarian dishes with chopsticks.

The fare wasn't up to a visiting mage's palette. He'd
probably expected state dinners or something. I hid
a smile as he inspected a chunk of meat. Even with a
mage's increased need for calories and protein, I don't
eat meat. It tends to disagree with my digestion. Eggs—
costly in midwinter, in a mini ice age—and dairy provide
some of my protein, but the bulk of it comes from soy
and other beans, which I didn't try to foist off on him.
The town citizens eat a lot of pork year-round, and I figured the nibblets in the fried rice were chopped, spiced

pork, which should have made him happy from a strictly caloric viewpoint. It didn't. Fortunately, we ate in silence and he didn't complain.

However, he did seem to like the Dancing Bear Brew, which he complimented by drinking three. The Appalachian Mountains are famous for guns, quilts, pottery, and especially beer, and are infamous for moonshine, not that I had any on hand or even knew where to purchase it. Kirk elders tend to punish hard drinkers by branding. I had enough scars without adding to them.

When the meal was finished, he sighed and relaxed in the padded wingback chair. Cheran Jones, like most mages, was smaller than an average human man, standing about five feet five and weighing less than a hundred twenty pounds. He should have looked innocent and childlike in the big chair. He didn't. There was something calculating about him, and it set my teeth on edge.

I'm a bit shy of five feet and haven't weighed myself in years. My size usually doesn't bother me, but in the presence of the mage, I really wished I was bigger. Which meant that, on some level, I was afraid of him. Being afraid ticked me off.

I'd have been a lot more afraid if he had been a stone mage instead of a metal mage and whatever else he was, the parts of himself he had kept hidden when I searched through his mind. A stone mage would have felt the pull of the special amethyst kept in metal boxes in the stockroom.

I had a moment of discomfort. I hadn't thought about the possibility that the stone could charge the metal. If it had, then a metal mage might be able to sense the power so close by, even power so drained. And Cheran was awfully close to the metal boxes. *Stupid* to have put him so close to that much power. I wondered what else I was overlooking about my unwanted visitor. But Cheran hadn't looked toward the stockroom even once.

The amethyst hidden there had broken off from the wheels belonging to the cherub, Holy Amethyst, and though the living ship had been healed, or repaired, or whatever had been done to it to make it whole, the pieces had been left to me. They were bound to me on a psychic level, and just the thought of the large purple crystals sent a soft crooning into my mind. I was really glad the stones were in the stockroom down the hall, the distance adding more protection from the mage before me.

"Tell me about the Dragon," Cheran said.

"So much for segues," I said, fear making me snarky. "Thanks for the meal. It was tasty. You're welcome, it was my pleasure. The weather's awfully nasty out. Indeed it is. I'm so glad we've cozied up here by the fire."

"Cozied. You and me." His lips twitched. He laced his fingers across his chest.

"It means sitting with ease and comfort."

"I'm familiar with the term. But I've never 'cozied' with a consulate general on such sort acquaintance. In fact I can't say as I've *ever* cozied with a consulate general."

"Fine. So let's toss the fine points of manners out the window and be frank. I don't like you. You don't like me, this town, this assignment, or much of anything at the moment. This is the first time you've been on a mission alone, and the last time you were let out of Enclave, you screwed up something important."

Cheran's eyelid twitched the tiniest bit. Bull's-eye.

I plowed on. "I'm betting the reason you were charged with this one has to do with the secondary clandestine mission you carry in the back of your thoughts. How's that for frank?"

Cheran tilted his head in a "Good for you" gesture, but he didn't reply.

"What about the Dragon?" I almost snarled.

"That I can talk about." Cheran slouched deeper in the chair and tucked one foot under the opposite thigh, looking relaxed. As befitted a self-styled fashionista, he looked elegant in the black, well-tailored suit, even while sprawling out comfortably. Suits costing more than I make in a month can have that effect on a man. "I know you're aware that there was a major battle in the heavens a few weeks ago."

I nodded.

"It's come to the attention of the Enclaves that you know more about it than the rest of us. I'd like to hear your story."

"Is this an official request?" I asked, meaning, *Is my butt in the wringer?*

"It could be someday, but isn't now."

"Audric," I said, without raising my voice. My champard stuck his head around the corner so fast I knew he had been listening, keeping tabs on me. And so did my guest. *Good.* "In your official capacity as my champard, I require your legal counsel."

Cheran rolled his eyes and sat up in the chair. "Fine. Everything you say here today is off the record. It was never spoken and will not result in legalities."

"This is acceptable," Audric said, invading the emissary's space and seating himself on a tall stool. Cheran ignored him. The man claiming to be here to teach me diplomatic etiquette needed a serious lesson in common manners. I was tempted to teach him one, but I already knew he was faster and a better swordsman than I. The tutorial could wait for another time. Like when I had the drop on him again.

"Tell me what happened," he said to me. "The Dragon started to break his chains and then was halted. How and why?"

I had wondered when someone would find a way to blame me for the Dragon's partial freedom and I was pretty sure Cheran was here to prove that the Dragon's escape attempt was my fault. Which it was and wasn't.

Dragons are Major Darkness. In the hierarchy of evil, they rank right up there beneath the chief bad guy—if such really existed—the beast called the Lord of the Dark, the Great Red Dragon, or Satan, a name never spoken aloud for fear it might call him. He hadn't been seen in the Last War, but then neither had the Most High God. Smart people didn't mention that. Fools who did sometimes died on the spot.

Some theologians label Dragons *satanels.* According to scripture, they had been chief angels or seraphs in heaven until they followed Lucifer's lead and rebelled against the Most High. The First Battle recorded in the Revelation of John between the ArchSeraph Michael and the followers of the Light, and the Great Red Dragon and his followers—the Powers and Principalities of the Dark—was near mythic. In it, the Red Dragon and a third of those who had followed him had been swept away. They had landed on Earth back before humans started to keep written records, and continued the fight.

The battleground of Earth got a lot more bloody in the Last War between the Dark and Light, which took place a little over a hundred years ago. Some scholars say there were twenty Dragons rechained back then. Some say a hundred. But everyone agreed they were bad business, impossible to kill, and almost as difficult to imprison. The total followers of Darkness, counting spawn, still number in the hundreds of thousands, if not the low millions. Not that there's any kind of intel to back that up.

I opened a beer and studied the label. On it was a big bear, standing on a hind leg in the midst of a jig, a foaming mug in his paw and a big grin on his face. "The binding of a Dragon sometimes requires blood," I said. Cheran nodded. I turned the beer, inspecting the bottle, putting my thoughts together.

I could have told the story with all the dramatic wiles at a mage's beck and call. Instead I said baldly, "In the campaign of the Last Battle, a key skirmish was fought here in the mountains. The ArchSeraph's lieutenant, Zadkiel, was losing to a Dragon, and was nearly drained unto emptiness"—the correct wording for the deathlike state suffered by an immortal being. "Several of his winged warriors had already been drained to husks.

"Benaiah Stanhope, the several-times-great-grandfather of my partner, Rupert Stanhope, and my ex-husband, Lucas, went underground with the winged warriors and gave his life saving Zadkiel. His blood coated the chain that bound the beast. The locals called him Mole Man."

Cheran made a little rolling motion with his hand to indicate I should continue. I put down the beer and locked eyes with the slouching, elegant, bored mage. "The Dragon's second in command took over his territory when the Dragon was bound, and spent the following century creating new beasts and gathering power. You saw some of his handiwork on SNN a couple of weeks back when the skirmish in Mineral City was filmed by a news crew and went out live."

Cheran nodded, his expression steady. "Spawn, of course. But some of the beasts were like nothing we'd ever seen before," he said, finally sounding like the emissary he purported to be. "The light was bad and they moved faster than the camera could follow, but they looked like they were composed of body parts of various creatures."

My eyes went hot and dry, my throat ached. "Dragonets. They were hard as heck to destroy. The Darkness who made them was called Forcas," I said. "The attack you saw, I think, had a threefold purpose. It was a trial, an assessment, to test its handiwork in battle. And it sent them into town to get the blood of Mole Man's progeny. And it hoped to free its master." It also came to get me, but I didn't say that. "Forcas had somehow acquired a link from the chain that bound the Dragon with Benaiah Stanhope's blood. Using that, it made a counterconjure, an anticonjure," I clarified, "and was using the blood of Stanhope progeny to empower it."

The air burned my dry throat and I put a hand to the swath of ugly white scar tissue there. My throat had been ripped away in the fight and been regenerated by the application of kylen blood. I had survived, but the disfigurement wasn't pretty. Not that I was complaining. So many had died in the battles that followed.

Audric popped the top from a cold beer and passed it to me. I drank several sips, the moisture softening my dry throat. "A succubus queen had laid eggs in the Trine and a few of us went underground to wipe out the nest. We were too late, but we did manage to free a Watcher, Barak, one allied with the Light."

Cheran twitched slightly before his face hardened, hiding his reaction. A man with lesser self-control might have sat up straight in his chair, kicking over the table, making a mess.

Watchers were seraphs who had left heaven willingly and acquired sublunary bodies in order to mate with human women. Their pre-historical sin had left them without the ability to transmogrify or to return to heaven. Some had been grievously punished. Many, like Barak, had allied with the Light, while others joined the Dark.

Bluntly, I added, "And we also freed the seraph Zadkiel and his cherub."

Cheran wasn't able to disguise his reaction to that. Shock

widened his pupils. I was pretty sure he had stopped breathing. My own eyes went hard and dry.

Only a few local humans, the Administration of the Arch-Seraph, and I knew that a seraph and his cherub had been trapped in a lair of Darkness. No one else even grasped that the capture of a Major Prince of the Light was possible, and I didn't know what it might mean in the ongoing war. Over the last century, a list had been compiled of seraphs missing from Regions of Light. How many more were in the clutches of Darkness? And why hadn't the seraphs gone to rescue them? Questions I had no answers for, and the AAS certainly wasn't going to enlighten *me*.

I watched Cheran, who was once again giving nothing away. "We made it back to the surface," I said, my voice painfully hoarse, my eyes dry as bone. "I was injured. The seraph Raziel joined us battling Forcas at the opening to the hellhole on the Trine. The combat in the heavens took place at the same time as ours. I'm pretty sure it was all tied to the Dragon being set free. I felt something coming." I blinked, looking at Audric, whom I had left in the town with battles of his own, and who had nearly died following my orders.

"With the combined assets of a cherub's wheels and seraphic help, we drained Forcas to a husk. In the heavens, even with multiple winged warriors, they were losing to the Dragon. It was getting free. To stop it, the humans with me went back into the hellhole carrying a shoulder-mounted weapon with a bunker-busting nuclear warhead, something new and lightweight the US Army and mages developed. They used it to help close up the entrance and stop the Dragon. They didn't come back out."

Audric said, "Only the deaths of two brave human males, multiple beings of Light, the use of a nuclear warhead, and my mistrend's valiant warfare prevented the Dragon's freedom. That warfare resulted in Thorn's grave physical injury and the appreciation of the Council of the Seraphim."

Cheran looked at my cheek, and at the whiter expanse of scar tissue on my throat, curiosity finally showing on his face. "We heard that humans died saving you," Cheran said.

"Saving Thorn and the town," Audric said softly.

"Nearly four thousand people would have died to feed that thing if it got free."

"If I'd killed Forcas on the first try they wouldn't have died," I said. "I screwed up."

Audric said nothing. He hadn't been there. He'd been fighting the succubus queen I had accidentally bound to me and left temporarily imprisoned in a conjured circle. He'd nearly died keeping the newly hatched succubus queen away from Mineral City. Mistake piled on mistake. Maybe I did need a teacher from Enclave. I had done pretty poorly on my own.

"Let me see if I understand this," Cheran said slowly, his tone a clarification. "You went underground—*underground*—to fight Darkness."

"Twice," Audric answered for me.

Cheran kept his eyes on me. "The Enclave masters, the ones who made the amulet that keeps you out of my head," he said with a wry tilt of his mouth, "knew something was happening. They figured out that a beast, a Major Darkness, was trying to get free and they tracked its movements from its prison. They were prepared to send battle mages to the fight, but it ended suddenly. It's still trapped, no longer bound, but not free either. According to them, it's in a sort of spiritual and dimensional stasis. You might say it has one foot in this world and one foot in another. But it won't be frozen in place long. We need a plan before it gets free."

"Battle mages would take weeks to get here in winter. If it gets free, we run," Audric said.

Cheran finally looked at him. "Spoken like a true coward."

Audric seemed to shift, to blur, and a knife thunked into the chair, pinning Cheran's oh-so-expensive pants to the wood beneath the upholstery and padding. The hilt quivered along Cheran's inner thigh, a micron from his privates. He went deathly still, his fingertips bloodless.

I drank a long swallow of beer, hiding a smile. Some of my tension eased away. "I suggest you show my champard the respect due a master of both savage-chi and savage-blade," I said, my voice sounding casual once again. "When you insult him, you insult me. And you don't want to take us both on, no matter what else you are besides a traveling Enclave emissary."

"Even a fool does his homework before he travels," Audric said. "You assumed your unexpected arrival, your speed, and a visa would provide you with protection from the humans and answers to your questions. Your teachers in Enclave will be disappointed when I report to them your . . . sloppy"—he used the mage's own word—"work." He rested a hand on the hilt of a second throwing knife in his belt.

Cheran scratched his chin, fighting a grin. "My speed and skills haven't gained me much, true. But what about the visa? I'm alive and still have my skin."

"The orthodox in this town are sharply divided over my mistrend's presence. Another mage, especially one with so few survival instincts and the wardrobe of a court jester, may not fare so well and may, furthermore, place her in greater danger. I will not permit this. If you endanger her, I'll hand you over to them."

Cheran's brows lifted and he finally looked at Audric. "The orthodox would violate the legal sanctity of a diplomatic visa? *You* would violate it?"

"Anger the people in this town and they will leave you in tiny pieces in the snow," Audric said, his strong teeth bared. "A mage lived among them in hiding for a decade. Many want her dead. Prejudice and emotions run high here, and most of the town fathers aren't overly impressed with mages."

Cheran worked the throwing blade back and forth until it eased from the chair frame. A tuft of stuffing came out with the tip, which he held up to the light. "Mule, I've known you less than an hour and you've sliced two holes in my clothes." He flicked the stuffing away and tested the edge with the pad of his thumb. It was a vaguely threatening gesture; Audric gave him a "Try it and I'll eat your guts for supper" grin. Territorial play by two males, one an alpha, one a wannabe.

"He's a sweetheart," I said. "Hand him the pretty knife like a gentleman. Hilt first."

"Spoilsport." He reversed the knife and offered it to Audric. "Since it seems I need an income, and your champard's blades need work, do you mind if I set up my equipment in the corner there? I can put on new edges," he said to me. Which told me what kind of mage he was. Not *just* a metal mage. But one of the few, very specialized, steel mages.

The thought flashed through my mind that I could put him in contact with the Schuberts, who owned Blue Tick Hound Guns. But I didn't trust him enough to provide mage-steel for the family business, not when the guns they made would be used to fight Darkness in defense of the town. Our blades, however, needed attention, and giving them new edges couldn't negatively affect their fighting power. Or I didn't think it could.

"Okay by me," I said, standing. "But you'll have to ask Rupert and Jacey."

He looked horrified. "You let humans make decisions for you? *Humans?*"

If this idiot didn't watch his tone, I'd save the orthodox the trouble and run him through with a sword myself.

Chapter 3

I climbed into a restorative bath and settled into the bottom of the tub with a sigh of purely human pleasure. In the nearest window, the lunar curve brightened a snaking mist that rested along the ground and above the hollows, the black shadows of trees following the hump of hills against the night sky. It was beautiful, almost surreal; no artist's rendition of nighttime could come close to the reality of the mountain sky at midnight.

Not even the moon over the Gulf of Mexico was as lovely. Though I was certain no one at the New Orleans Enclave, where I had been born and raised—where I had spent the first fourteen years of my life, ten of them in stone mage training, and savage-chi and savage-blade training (the martial arts developed by the first neomages)—would agree. I would never see a Louisiana moon rise again. I was forever barred from Enclave due to the unlucky perversity of being mentally open to all the mage-minds present—

The thought vanished. I saw in memory a nugget of snowflake obsidian tossed at me, its leather cord flipping through the air. I hadn't realized it when I removed my necklace for the bath, but Cheran hadn't jumped back into my mind when the nugget of volcanic glass was no longer in contact with my flesh. Just having it near me now shut Cheran out of my mind. Was the amulet's conjure spreading through me? And if so, what else might it be doing to me?

Dripping bathwater, I reached for the steel necklace of

chain-mail links that secured my amulets. I had several new ones, conjures as yet untried, dangerous things I hoped I would never need. With wet fingers, I shifted through them all and lifted the rounded obsidian nugget Cheran had brought. Though I had looked into the incantation with my mage-senses, studying both the internal composition of the glass and as much of the conjure it contained as I could, I wasn't sure yet exactly what it could do.

The amulet contained a conjure crafted just for me, a sort of semiprime amulet, one created by my old teachers at Enclave without access to my genetic material; I knew it was powerful, and that it was still settling into my psyche with far greater ease than I would have liked. That ease demonstrated that I was open and very vulnerable to certain types of incantations. That part I didn't like. But the part about keeping other mages out of my mind...

A shiver raced over my skin, half fear, half unhealthy excitement. If the amulet held true to keeping one mage out of my mind, could it, just maybe, keep out all twelve hundred mages at the New Orleans Enclave that had sent Cheran? I turned the wire-wrapped bauble I had tied to my necklace. Drops plinked from my fingers to the bathwater. Could I, maybe, go home again? The word echoed in the silence of my mind.

Home. To Enclave? If that warm, muggy, sultry place *was* home. *Or is home here, in the life I've built?*

I could go ... home. I tested the word on my tongue.

I dropped the Apache Tear to the table and it rattled softly on the old wood where I kept my oils and unguents and bath salts. Apache Tear. It seemed an apt name.

Releasing control over my mage-attributes, I relaxed totally, my skin glowing in the bathwater, pinkish and coral, warm tints. My scars glowed brighter, a fierce white tracery. Fingers drawn to the one wound that hadn't completely healed, I traced the site on my left side where the spur of Darkness had pierced me. It was better. Almost gone. In human vision it was a dull bruise, in mage-sight, it was worse, but healing. Definitely healing. And the spur itself was safe in a pocket of my battle cloak. My throat, I couldn't see except in a mirror. It was all new tissue, blazing white when my mage-attributes were set free.

I slipped deeper into the water, looking around at the loft where I had lived for so many years. I had moved here soon after my foster father died, his estate leaving me just enough money to buy the old, decrepit two-story building. It had been bare stone and brick walls three feet thick, splintered boards underfoot. The loft had rough beams overhead, empty windows, abandoned birds' nests in the rafters. Downstairs, in the shop, it had been worse, the floor rotten in places, the pressed tin ceiling rusted, the walls filthy and covered in graffiti.

I'd had washerwoman's hands for the entire year it took my friends and me to renovate the building. It was mine, in every sense of the word. Going back to Enclave would mean leaving…home. The bath was suddenly less than restful and I stood, splashing water as I stepped from the antique, claw-footed tub to the turquoise tile and threw a robe on. I had laid the tile myself. Rupert had restored the tub for me. It had been a birthday present. There was no way I could take it with me.…

The soft velvet reminded me of Cheran's cloak. And reminded me that he wasn't the only hedonistic mage in the area. The robe was new, a gift left at the shop's front door, folded in a brown bag. There hadn't been a tag, but the scent of seraph had proven it a gift from Raziel. The smell of chocolate still clung to the iridescent teal fabric, and it added conflict to the emotions sparring in my heart. I stroked the velvet. Mage-heat quivered low in my belly each time I wore it. I wondered if the seraph had thought about the fabric against my naked skin when he picked it out. Unholy thoughts. Wicked feelings. Ideas and hopes I would surely never have a chance to work through—or possibly experience—if I returned to Enclave, to my people. I would never see the seraph again.

Eyes closed, I breathed in the scent and sighed as the pleasure increased. And more than merely pleasure. Thoughts of naked carousing with one of the angelic Host were never far from the surface of my mind these days, though most times I could control the images. Most times. Well, when I wanted to. Which wasn't often enough.

I set the amulets over my head. Though thoughts were relatively safe, acting on them could get me into trouble, like being dragged before the town fathers or the seraphic high council—and death by various means, all of them protracted and painful. But they could only kill me once, as I had grown fond of reminding myself.

Of course, unlike humans, neomages had no souls, so perhaps I had more to lose than most folk. For us, death was permanent, no hope of resurrection, paradise, and better things to come. However, such wonderful scents as my robe reminded me that the adverse was also true. There was no hell or damnation for us either.

Religion and politics, sex and death. "Lovely bedtime thoughts," I murmured as I looked around the teal and cream bower I had made for myself. I had chosen the antique kitchen table, had handpicked each of the old wooden chairs that surrounded it. Had sanded the floors and refinished them. Had hung each of the tapestries. And I loved my sofa and the carved, upholstered rocker.

Unsettled, I lifted the marble sphere by my bed and set the ward on the loft and shop, drawing stored power from the energy sink at the spring out back. Like magic. But neomages don't use magic as humans understand it. We use the leftover energies of creation, the particles Einstein postulated about in his famous equations. Which meant that mages are bound in many ways to the laws of physics.

Even back before neomages, humans knew that mass and energy are inseparably linked to each other, both having the luxon impulse as the base of their definition. They knew that each "matter with rest mass" consists of particles with light velocity. That means: every particle of matter and every particle of energy consists of luxons. Matter and energy are one thing in different stages. Humans used this knowledge to create weapons, atomic bombs whose explosions blast atoms apart. Mages draw upon luxons to create safety, health, and beauty. Most of the time. Not always. But the luxons that made up the incantation protecting my home were a good thing. A very good thing.

I drank a glass of spring water, turned down the gas flames on the fireplaces, put on warm pajamas with pink hearts on them, turned out the lights, and went to bed early.

Deep in the night, the lynx screamed, drawing me back from a dream of dying at seraph hands. I woke, shattering the images of death and destruction as the cry echoed, rocking across the hills, a deep vibrato of warning. I lay in the dark, breathing fast, mage-sight on, searching out the cause of the alarm. My ward was still on, the loft was safe, walls glowing with protective power. I didn't smell smoke, or hear people screaming, or scent blood.

The predator cat had entered my life only weeks ago, but had instantly become an omen, a portent, issuing a warning whenever trouble was headed my way. I closed down my sight and opened a mind-skim, drawing air and sensation into my lungs. Still nothing. Maybe the blasted cat was wrong this time. Or maybe it was finally reacting to whatever mage properties made animals go seriously wacko when in the vicinity of neomages for too long.

I eased the amulet necklace over my head and gripped my tanto—a long-bladed knife with a simple hilt and cross-guard. I was small enough that it worked as a shortsword. Skin prickling, I stole from the bed on sock-covered feet and padded through the loft, checking each window and door, staring out the window where the moon had shone. The sky was now deep black, full of stars, the hills below a murky, smudged shadow.

Behind me, the door sprang open, banging hard. I whirled and rushed it, tanto swinging up. I recognized the shadow in the last instant and whipped aside the blade before I stabbed Rupert. He stood in the opening, chest naked, black hair standing up on one side. He was wild-eyed, his skin sheet-creased. "Thorn," he said, his tone peculiar.

"I nearly killed you!"

"In the street," he said, his words sleep-slurred. "It's Gramma."

Mage-fast, I pivoted and raced through the loft, shutting off the protective ward, grabbing my longsword, and leaving the walking-stick sheath behind as I sprinted to the front of the apartment and out onto the frozen porch over the side-walk. The sickle moon rode high in the sky, throwing cold light on the old woman in the ice-slick street. Dressed in a summer frock, lilacs on white, wattles of flesh hanging from her bare arms. One clenched a child tight against her, and she held a blade at the girl's throat.

"Cissy," I whispered. It was Jacey's nine-year-old daughter, hair loose on her shoulders, nightgown fluttering in the cold breeze. In the dark of the night, Gramma's crazed eyes met mine. Mage-sight slammed on, and I saw a flash of dull orange flecked with shards of glowing black in her irises, like coals banked beneath ashes. The blade she held was demon-iron, and it wasn't burning her hand. *Bloody plagues.*

"Gramma," Rupert said softly at my back, the word slurred.

"It's not her," I said. I hoped he knew it, because I was about to have to kill the old witch. "It's a glamour," I said, one that looked like the Stanhope matriarch.

"Gramma," he whispered, joining me at the rail, his flesh tight with goose bumps.

"No!" I insisted. Leaving him on the porch, I sped down the stairs and unlocked the door. I ran into the street. Silently, Audric appeared at my side and followed me into the still night. The cold bit into my feet, my socks sticking and ripping from the ice with each step. *Stupid, stupid, stupid to not stop for shoes.*

I drew on my two prime amulets, the bloodstone hilt and the seven-layered stone prime ring, to warm my feet. To fight the cold, I allowed my mage attributes to blaze on, my flesh glowing a pearly roseate hue. It was easier for the beast to see me, but it would also help keep me warm. Taking my lead, Audric's less-vibrant glow brightened the night.

The smell of decaying leaves, rotting roses, and stagnant water filled the air, sour and cloying. I knew that scent. It was a succubus, a sexual demon that appeared in the form of a woman, enticed human males, had sex with them, and then ate them. From the privates up. And I knew this scent. It was specific to the succubus queen, the mother of all unholy sexual desires. It enticed by conjure.

Gramma, though not my idea of a sexually alluring female, was having an effect on Rupert, who watched from the porch; he was panting in fear and need. The beast saw me across ten yards of rutted snow. For a moment, scales slid over its skin like foam on the beach, the glamour of the old woman giving way to the true form beneath. It cackled, and when it spoke, it talked in Gramma's voice. "Little mage. This child is mine to kill or save, yet her life is in your hands. A boon, and she will be set free."

The last time I was this close to the succubus queen, it was newly born, only a month old, cocky and bragging with a teenager's fragile ego, easy to manipulate. Now it looked deadly. The succubus pressed the edge of the blade against the girl's throat. Cissy stared at me in horror, gasping. Her skin darkened at the touch of the demon-iron as the metal burned into living flesh.

Audric moved counterclockwise, placing his bare feet firmly with each step, his blades in the swan. This was the beast that had nearly killed him, the thing I had left him to fight alone. He still hadn't told me about that fight. There were lots of secrets resting uneasily between us, unspoken. "The entrance to the hellhole was sealed," he said. "How did it get out?"

I shook my head. I didn't know. I moved clockwise, away from the shop, feet freezing.

"You bound it once," Audric said softly, his face hard. "Can you use that?"

Gramma ignored him, eyes locked on mine. "Send a child of Mole Man to me and I will release her. My word. You may even choose the one you would sacrifice."

"I don't know," I said just as softly. I wasn't going to bet on it. The partial binding hadn't held for long last time.

All succubi were dangerous, but the adolescent queen was doubly so. It could reason and make independent decisions, and it was capable of breeding other succubi. Once, it had taken orders from Forcas, the Power who lived on the Trine, but that beast had been burned in battle dire, meaning the big ugly sucker was the next best thing to dead. Its boss, the Dragon, was stuck between realities, but maybe the Dragon had found another beast willing to risk everything in return for a bit of Dragon power and appreciation. Unless things had changed, the Dragon's freedom required Stanhope blood to finish the job.

As I watched, the creature seemed to grow, its form expanding, its glamour slipping and slithering across its body. The smell of sex-demon blossomed out, fetid and cloying. While not able to transmogrify—to restructure their energies into almost any physical body—powerful minions of the Dark often appeared physically attractive to humans. Not so this Darkness. Though once it had been able to assume and maintain the shape of its victims, it seemed to have lost that ability. Or maybe it felt it no longer needed camouflage. The queen was all about being a BBU, which could mean she would be bigger and badder and uglier in the future, as she matured. That was a scary thought.

Cissy straddled its thigh, her feet kicking, tendons in her neck straining as she tried to take the weight off her throat to breathe. To the succubus, I said, "Better deal. I kill you and no one gets handed over." A thin rivulet of blood, near black in the scant light, rolled down Cissy's throat, into her collar. The blade cauterized the wound even as it cut her.

"Call mage in dire," Audric demanded as we circled the queen, feet icy in the snow.

"Can't. Cissy isn't close enough to death for me to summon seraphic warriors."

"I say she is," he said.

Uncertainty snaked through me. My breath puffed in tiny, rapid clouds. If I called mage in dire, every adult in town could die. When seraphs came to fight evil, humans died. Always.

Gramma smiled, drawing its lips back to reveal sharp teeth, jaw stretching forward, squaring off. I had seen this transformation before. It wasn't pretty. The succubus drew its illusion back around itself like a cloak, smile narrowing and teeth reshaping into human-molar bluntness. But Cissy's blood and burned skin were no illusion. She mewled like a kitten in the grip of a hawk. Gramma kissed the top of her head, snuggling her close. "Not to worry, poppet. It won't hurt much. And not for long."

"Cissy?"

It was Ciana, my stepchild, above and behind me, on the porch of Rupert's loft. Gramma's nostrils flared as she scent-searched, but her eyes never rose to the girl. Ciana possessed a pin with camouflage properties. She didn't become invisible, exactly, but it did seem really hard for evil to find and focus on her.

"No seraphs," I warned. I didn't have to explain what could, what *would*, happen if she called the High Host for help. She had seen humans die in the presence of the holy ones. But I wasn't sure we could save Cissy without help. The beast bulked larger as I watched. It had grown in power since I'd seen it last. I didn't think I could use verbal ploys against it this time. "Not yet," I added.

"All right," the young girl said, sounding far calmer than I felt. Her trust in me had always been terrifying.

Use the binding, Audric had suggested. Okay. An icy wind blew against my body and I shivered in reaction. "You are mine," I said to the beast, "bound to me. Let the child go."

The thing that no longer resembled Gramma cocked its head, the movement human-slow. Its shoulders rose and fell, an almost pensive shift of muscles.

"Let the child go. You are mine. You must obey," I said, drawing on the mage visa, the one function I had mastered, to instill my voice with command.

The glamour quivered across its features again, revealing patches of alabaster skin, blond hair, and one vivid eye in a mishmash of features, the beautiful Jane Hilton on one half, Gramma on the other. The new face, the face Lucas had left me for, looked startled, then astonished, and said, "You!" The lovely half snarled in anger and rippled, and the human visages vanished, leaving only succubus in its wake. The beast smiled, canines longer and razor sharp. Cissy fell silent. I wasn't sure she was breathing.

I rushed it, blades flashing. It snapped back a dozen steps, demon-fast. "No, no, no, mageling." A shield snapped open just in front of my toes, the energies throwing me back, feet burning like lightning. In mage-sight, the shield was an ocher-yellow dome seething with earth energies. It was a mage construct, which meant there were mages nearby, Dark mages, helping this beast. Whether willing or under compulsion, it was bad on all sorts of levels. "You constrained me once," it said. "My master's master freed me of your lowly incantation."

My master's master? Death and plagues. Is she talking about the Dragon? Audric and I circled the shield, reversing midway, back and forth. My socks stuck and pulled free of the ice beneath my aching feet with each careful step. Gramma sniffed, head raised, searching for a whiff of the Stanhope genetic strain, but was unable to locate Ciana. I looked around for Rupert or Ciana's father—my ex-husband, Lucas—or Thaddeus Bartholomew, their cousin, all descendents of Mole Man. I would have prayed they'd all remain indoors, but I knew they wouldn't. I knew they hadn't. That would be too easy and men never made anything easy. The succubus's eyes glowed brightly as it located prey off to my right. *Seraph stones.* What was I going to do?

From my angle, I could see Ciana standing on the high porch, her nightgown fluttering in the rising breeze. She was watching me, and in her hand was the pin gifted her by the seraph Raziel as protection from evil; it glowed a brilliant gold, as if she held a star in her fist, shielding her. The succubus was looking away from the girl and down, on street level, at Rupert.

My best friend was standing in the doorway of the shop, sleep-creased, half-naked. His face was blank, empty. *Seraph stones.* He was spelled. So was Lucas. In my side vision, I saw Ciana's father walk onto Upper Street; he stared at the beast as if it held his heart in one hand. On his neck, smudges of Dark energies glowed, old scars left from imprisonment beneath the Trine, activated by the growing power of the beast. But the queen hadn't seen him. Yet.

"Audric," I warned. Cold wind tore through my pajamas. My calves cramped as my feet froze. Cissy had gone limp. Above me, Ciana watched, her face serene, waiting.

"I see them." Face blank, Rupert reached toward the beast. Audric stepped to block him, arms out wide. "Now might be a good time to try the anticonjures you've been working on."

My mind cleared, taking on the crisp clarity of incipient battle. I lifted one of the small, drilled, and polished Dalmatian jasper nuggets, the opaque black-and-white stones hanging from thin string loops on my necklace. I had made a batch of the anticonjures—supposed to disable most lower to midlevel incantations—but hadn't tested them. I had no idea if they would diminish the lure of a succubus or make things worse. If the succubus' allure was a higher level conjure, they probably wouldn't work at all.

I ripped a nugget from its temporary loop and tossed it to the ice at Rupert's feet. It bounced. Exploded. Time slid sideways, a slow-motion vision, a dozen things happening at once and I saw/felt them in overlays of sensation.

Snow and ice blasted over Rupert, the concussion throwing him backward. Audric and I hit the snow, my skin abrading in a wide patch along calf and lower arm as I slid. My ears popped painfully. The succubus' shield fell and she howled, sharp canines reflecting moonlight. The knife at Cissy's throat bit down. Blood drenched her nightgown. Snow and ice tumbled from the air like hail. As ice-shrapnel fell, the beast changed its grip and reached for Rupert, lying prone, stunned. The beast smiled in a parody of lust and delight. Lucas stepped closer, his expression hungry, arms out in entreaty. Wordless, I rolled to my knees. I couldn't reach them in time.

A thunk sounded over the ringing in my ears. The succubus shuddered and dropped its arm. A knife hilt protruded from its neck below the clavicle. Snarling, it almost let Cissy fall.

From the street, I threw the remaining two amulets at the queen. They exploded at her clawed feet, ripping into the rutted ice. The smell of succubus, of dead things, stagnant water, and rotting flowers vanished in a blast of sulfur and brimstone, the scent of Darkness. Lucas was knocked to the earth and rose shaking his head as if waking from a nightmare. I had a single glimpse of his horrified face. The anticonjure had worked. Sort of. Its shield was gone and its conjure of allure was nullified, but it wasn't dead. Another knife appeared in the body of the creature, the sound lost in the concussion of the blasts.

"Audric?" I shouted. I was deaf but needed information. Who'd thrown the knives? I rolled to my feet and raced forward.

"Not mine," he shouted, the words muffled in my damaged ears.

My longsword and tanto slashed in the lion rising, aiming along the succubus's torso beside and below the child held against its breast. I cut the beast deeply, leaving four wounds in its hide, and danced back when it slashed out with claws that hadn't been there before. Cissy, who I had thought unconscious, whimpered in pain, her tears bright pink in mage-sight. She inhaled, the sound harsh in the night.

The succubus pulled one knife from its chest and dropped

it to the street. It fell slowly, time still out of sync, to the rutted snow. The blood-covered blade glowed Dark in magesight. I sliced through the beast's right Achilles tendon and it staggered. So I severed its left, leaving it flatfooted and immobile for a moment. Darkness healed fast. The succubus wasn't a fallen seraph or demon, not in the scriptural sense of the word; it wasn't a spirit being; it wasn't immortal. Like spawn and other minor Darkness, it could be killed.

"Crap in a bucket," a tinny voice called from across the street. "Thorn?" I shook my head to clear the fear and the dregs of the blast away and saw Eli standing in an open doorway, his slight form backlit by lamplight, night-vision goggles on his face, a bulbous weapon slung across his body.

"Can you burn it?" I asked, my ears popping, adapting to the pressure changes.

He looked down at his weapons and back to the succubus and shook his head. "Not dead. Not something that powerful. We're gonna need help with this big sucker."

"I was afraid of that," I said. Eli's flamethrower was effective against smaller creatures, and had once burned Forcas' eyes to slow it down, but to kill the bigger baddies, I would need more firepower. Which was scary on top of scary. It limited our options, because I didn't know how to use my visa to call for seraphic support, and the succubus hadn't given us an opening to call for help in the traditional manner. So far. When it did, that help probably wouldn't come in time. Someone would die. Then lots of someones. Save the town to let it die by holy salvation; a catch-22.

Another knife hit the succubus and it roared, bulking huge, its body nearly six feet tall, its energy patterns swarming nearly two feet higher. Its transformation from Gramma to Big Bad Ugly was complete: a square jaw filled with jagged teeth, black lips and white gums, upper and lower tusks, unblinking slit-eyes like a snake's, and skin banded in orange and black scales. And it had claws that a full-grown lion would envy. It had evolved since I'd last seen it unglamoured. It was huge, far more powerful. Yet it hadn't seen Lucas or Ciana. Why not? That was probably important.

The answer opened out before me almost like a response to prayer. Lucas had been exposed to seraphic forces. So

had Ciana. The queen could only locate Rupert, and until I
turned off the ward on the loft, it hadn't even been able to
smell him well. Though I knew the outcome would not have
been different, guilt slithered through my mind.

The succubus looked at me and shook Cissy. "Give me
one of Mole Man's blood or this one will feed me," the
queen said. "Others will follow."

"Oh, merciful savior," a voice echoed through the dark.
"My baby." Jacey emerged from her doorway, nightgown
showing beneath a drab shift. She held knitting needles like
weapons in one hand, a blue-coned acetylene torch flaming
in the other. A mother come to do battle for her child. But
she wasn't a warrior. "Thorn?" Fear coated her voice.

Dancing to avoid its flailing free arm, I cut the succubus
again, aiming for its hamstring. Even moving with mage-
speed I barely avoided an immense, swiping fist. The beast
was slowing, but not enough. Unless it fell, I couldn't take
its head. It could heal from most anything else. And a queen
might heal from that too for all I knew. I stabbed its groin
and raced back. The fight had lasted only moments but it
felt like hours. I was growing clumsy with cold.

Lights flashed on along the street, throwing rectangles of
brightness onto the snow. Rupert moaned, pushing himself
into a sitting position, touching his head as if his ears hurt.
"What—" he stopped, staring at the scaled beast clutch-
ing his godchild in its arms. "Cissy," he breathed. Scantily
clad humans poured from doorways, drawn by the anticonjure explosions. Some carried axes, others shotguns and
long-bladed knives. Moments passed, fractions of seconds
that felt like days. Like Ciana, Jacey stood, waiting on me.
Trusting me. I was breathing hard, the frigid air burning
my lungs.

A third knife slammed into the beast, catching it in the
hip joint with deadly accuracy, missing Cissy by a quarter
of an inch. It shrieked, an agonized sound, and I feared the
queen would crush Cissy in anger, but the succubus held
the girl high, staring at the black blood pumping from its
femoral artery.

A fourth knife thunked into the base of its spine, hilt
quivering. I whipped my head, scanning the night. Like
me, the attacker was circling the succubus, but even with

mage-sight open, I wasn't seeing him. Cheran was shielding himself.

To my left and right, the Steins appeared out of the night, automatic weapons at the ready. Unlike the rest of us, the town's only Jewish family was dressed for war, in padded clothes, coats, gloves, and boots. At the sight, pure agony arched through my feet. The man to the left wore a yarmulke instead of a battle helmet, as if battling Darkness was a holy act. Maybe it was. The woman to my right had knotted her hair into a tight fighting queue, her face rigid with resolve, fear nowhere to be seen.

Her confidence restored my own. All minor Darkness could be destroyed. The succubus could be killed. The Steins' people had been battling Darkness for six thousand years. I took a breath, settling myself.

Lucas stepped close, buttoning a flannel shirt against the freezing night, black hair loose in the breeze. He accepted a shotgun from the woman.

"It's loaded with Dead Sea salt ammo," she said. Which meant the pellets in each shell were encased in a capsule of salt mined from the Dead Sea and shipped over at dreadful cost. It was worth more than gold or diamonds, but it was one thing that would kill Darkness as well as a blade. She acknowledged me, a sharp nod. I remembered her name. Gloria. Gloria Stein. She had two kids and a husband, the man locked in fighting stance beside her.

"Thanks," Lucas said. "Can you get Cissy free?" he asked me, placing his feet carefully to either side of a rut in the snow. "If you can, maybe I can disable it with this."

"And we can finish it off," the woman said, her weapon making a smooth ratcheting sound, metal on metal.

I took a second breath to answer yes. "Smoke," I said instead.

Audric looked around and up. "The roofs. Spawn."

"Jesus," Lucas prayed.

Reddish creatures scampered across the roof of my loft. They carried brands glowing with fire. Farther down the street, flames shot from the roof of the library. *Seraph stones.* They were burning the town.

Ciana mumbled. It sounded like, "I can do this. I can."

"Ciana, no!" I shouted. Whatever it was, it would be dangerous. Stanhopes always found self-destructive, sacrificial methods to help others. Lucas looked from his daughter to the beast, started to speak, and closed his mouth on the words, his face going cold and expressionless as he studied the queen. I had never seen that look before.

"Thorn?" Jacey said again.

"Shut off the torch," I said to her, turning from my ex-husband. "Fire can't hurt that thing." At her stricken reaction, I said, "We'll rescue Cissy. I promise." *Stupid, stupid, stupid. Never promise the life of another.* But I had. The determination on Gloria's and Lucas' faces convinced me we could.

Ciana held the shining seraph pin straight-armed over her other palm, as she leaned perilously out over the street. She stabbed down. The smell of Stanhope blood filled the night and the succubus whipped up its head, searching for the source. Ciana extended her wounded hand, bloody palm down. In some small part of my mind, I was startled. I had expected Ciana to place the pin in her bloody palm, which I figured would have called Raziel to protect her.

Her voice floated down. "Y'hee . . ." With each syllable, a drop of her blood hit the snow, landing in a rectangle of light from a window. *Stanhope blood.* The permutations and consequences of what she was doing were beyond me. I was only a half-trained mage. ". . . ore. Y'hee ore. Ore."

"Hebrew," the woman beside me said, tilting her head toward the porch and Ciana. "She's speaking Hebrew. Genesis one. Let there be light."

Saints' balls. Time snapped, a dizzying, fast-forward dislocation. Audric raced in and stabbed the beast, cutting across its abdomen, down, and across in a Zorro, to disembowel it. Ichor ruptured into the street and the half-breed wrenched away from the putrid mess.

"The kid speaks Hebrew?" Eli asked, his voice tight.

"No," I said. "She doesn't."

The beast hit the ground with a meaty fist. "Stones and blood," Cheran swore from the shadows, foolishly, stupidly, giving power to the Dark. The succubus raised its head and roared in victory at the might of the blasphemy. I heard the mage hiss as he realized what he'd done. Cheran had clearly never been to war.

Lucas stood flatfooted, his face etched with sorrow, looking from the beast to his only child. I didn't know why he grieved, but my breath caught in my throat as the lynx howled again. "God in heaven," he said softly, in the echo of the roar. "What are we?"

What are who? Stanhopes? There wasn't time to consider that question. The succubus dangled Cissy by the neck like a broken doll, her face ashen, her tongue swollen and protruding. She was unconscious. Close to death. I opened my mouth to call mage in dire, permitted when a child or another innocent was near death at the hands of Darkness. Shots rang out, echoing down the street. The succubus roared, shaking the child.

In the same instant, fire shot from the roof of Shamus Waldroup's bakery across the street. Four knives landed in the Darkness, centered between its ribs, a small compensation for the control Cheran had given it.

"Y'hee ore." On the ice below Ciana, her blood began to brighten, seven crimson drops lightening to a ruby glow. As if ignited by the energies of her blood, a circular grid below the snow and ice of the street began to brighten. A sigil had been placed there, perhaps below the asphalt, by a seraph. It had lain, inert, invisible to all but me, or so I thought. Now I realized that Ciana had to have seen it, somehow, with her human eyes. *Impossible.* Yet, the sigil was being called to life. The sigil of the seraph Cheriour, an Angel of Punishment and Judgment.

In the street, humans jumped aside, to the left or the right of the spreading, glowing lines. The succubus roared, shouting my name as it stepped away, as if the lines beneath its feet burned. A human raced in brandishing an ax, and buried it in the beast's thigh. It swatted him away, leaving a bloody trail. Other humans raced in to fight; blades landed in the tough flesh and shots rang out. Warriors screamed and I smelled blood, but I didn't watch the combat. I watched the child of my heart. I watched Ciana as she closed her fist against the flow of blood. I didn't know what she had done, but the call of mage in dire died in my throat.

Below Ciana, the golden streaks moved together, finishing the sigil's outline. When they met, the sigil was complete. Seven spots of ruby light shot up from the snow, one spot for each drop of sacrificed blood. Within each beam of light, fingers of flame rose, tickling the night air, changing from ruby to purple to deepest blue, bluer than a burning torch. Fire swayed in the breeze a moment before popping free of the ground and forming round globes of Flame.

Ciana laughed delightedly, blue eyes sparkling. My breath stopped. Ciana had called for help from the High Host. She had called Minor Flames. No human should be able to summon them, especially not an eight-year-old girl. Even I didn't know how.

Two of the Flames danced close to me and away, almost in greeting. I wondered fleetingly if they were the two Flames I had rescued after a battle. They had been wounded, drained of power. And I had kept them safe, mixing them in with my amulets. Later, following another battle, I had discovered that the Flames were gone. Were these two the same? Either way, I knew what to do with them.

The faint sense of paralysis sluiced from me like water across a boulder. Time, elastic and supple, snapped back and settled. Always a liquid construct in battle, time made seconds seem like hours or hours seconds. I took a breath of the frigid air. "Thorn?" Jacey asked, her voice desperate.

On feet that were numb with cold, I moved away from the succubus, studying the scene: the gathering fighters circling the beast, shooting and cutting, darting in and back out. Some of the warriors were bleeding badly. Cissy. The Flames hovered in the air, seven balls of plasma. My night vision was consumed by them, and I slipped in the slick blood and ichor of the Darkness. I caught myself, expecting to feel the burn of acid on my soles. I felt nothing from the body fluids of the Dark, which was bad. I had no idea how long I had been standing in the snow, paralyzed by indecision, but it was too long. There was no time for the cold or for wounds. If I lived, I could worry about injury later. I focused to the side of the beings dancing on the air.

"Three and three and one, I greet thee," I said with the formality of mage to the High Host. "If you will, three to demolish spawn, three to harass the beast, and one to me."

From down the street voices called out, "Fire brigade!"

"Buckets!" A siren sounded, a long wail. "Get the truck!"

Before my face, the Flames rose and twirled, leaving plasma trails in the night, blue-bright on my retinas. They divided and spun away in groups of three, one group to the rooftops where spawn chittered, another to attack the succubus, darting toward it in an arrow shape. One lone Flame hovered near me. It worked. They had done what I asked.

Out of the shadows, Cheran hissed again, this time a single word. "Omega." But that was for another time as well.

Still looking to the side so my vision wouldn't be affected, I asked the Flame, "Can you coat my blade with your power? Is it possible?"

It dashed along the mage-steel of the longsword, touching it once. A shock zapped through the prime amulet hilt, stinging my palm, and the Flame swept away with a tremor, as if pained. "I guess not," I said, shaking my hand. My gaze raked the street.

The succubus shrieked as an arrow of Flames stabbed beneath its arm, pierced its side, and disappeared within. The reek of the blood of Darkness, rancid and sulfurous, was joined by the scent of scorched, rotting meat, and the cleaner smell of burning wood. Screams echoed up and down the street and up into the hills.

Audric and Rupert danced into the illumination and back into the night, part of the struggle, swords flashing in savage-blade.

Fire brightened the night, sputtering yellow, throwing smoke from the housetops in choking clouds. In the fitful light, two humans, Gloria and her husband, aimed carefully, their weapons set for single-shot. They rang out, the smell of cordite adding to the stench. Eli moved almost as gracefully as a supernat, darting in to recut the tendons on the beast's ankles. I smelled Thadd in the night, far off, not coming close. It wasn't fear of the beast, I knew, but he had to have heard about the new mage in town, and was protecting himself.

I extended the tanto to the Flame. "How about this one?" This blade was also mage-made steel, but not the highest quality, not made especially for me, and not attached to a prime amulet like the hilt of the longsword. Gingerly, it

touched the edge, singing a single note, like a silver bell
pealing. There was no shock. The Flame elongated, drawing itself into a narrow beam of light, and settled onto the
edge of the blade.

"Holy light sabers, Batman," Eli said from my side. "It's
Luke Skywalker."

I didn't always know what he was talking about, but it
was usually irreverent. I also knew that to use the weapon
I had just been given, I'd have to get close to the succubus. Real close. Mage-in-dire close. How dumb was that? I
handed my longsword to Eli.

"I take it you're going to do something stupid," he said.

With a daunting sense of déjà vu, I asked, "Can you get
me next to it?"

Most men, even my champards, would have tried to stop
me. Eli just blew out a breath and said, "I may not be able
to kill it, but I can give it a hurtin'."

I liked him a lot in that moment. He stuck my sword in
his belt and brandished the flamethrower, checking the fluid
levels in the bulbous bag. "Don't get yourself killed," he said
as he worked. "We have unfinished business." When I looked
the question at him, he said, "A saddle, whipped cream,
maybe a pair of handcuffs? And silk. Yeah." He twirled a
handgun like a western gunslinger and pumped the bag of
the flamethrower. "Red silk. A teddy."

I laughed, the sound a surprised huff of breath.

"Follow me," he said, winking an amber eye. He adjusted
a black wire that arched from his mouth to his ear, a high-
tech radio. "Alpha to my four o'clock," Eli said into the
mike, a command. "Beta to twelve," he shouted. "On my
mark!" And he rushed forward, racing to the feet of the
succubus.

Chapter 4

E li aimed the barrel of the flamethrower up at the
queen's face and pulled the trigger. A ten-foot-long
burst of fire shot into the night and hit the beast's face,
scenting the air with hyssop, rosemary, and scorched meat.
The queen's high-pitched squeal echoed between the buildings. The fire went out and Eli ducked under an ungainly
swipe. He had blinded the succubus. It dropped Cissy. Jacey
screamed. I saw the girl tumble to our left. *Dead, surely
dead.* I heard a thump and grunt.

"Got her," Rupert shouted. Relief swept through me.

"Inside!" Audric said to his partner. "Set the ward."

I had a quick impression of Rupert, still half-naked, carrying the child, running through the frozen street, Jacey at
his heels. Humans attacked, slashing at the beast, leaping
back.

Three Flames arrowed in, hitting soft tissue in the queen's
underarms, its groin, its ripped belly, retreating, hitting again
like pulsars. Each site flamed blue before darkening with
a puff of acrid smoke. Well-fed Darkness healed fast, but
these wounds gaped and seeped. As I watched, the Flames
darted into an open wound and disappeared inside, burned,
sliced, and reappeared as the Darkness wailed and raged
and beat its own body, trying to rid itself of the pain.

Shots rang in the night. Blood splattered. Humans
shouted. It looked like we were winning, yet, as I watched,
one eye formed into an orb and the beast's face healed.

To compensate, the Flames grew in size, from basketball-sized to globe-sized, three feet across and too bright to look at, dazzling as small suns. The entire street was lit by their glory.

In mage-sight, the beast's energies reached nearly twice my height, its physical form bulked with prehistoric musculature. If it struck me, it would shatter my mage-brittle bones. If it scored a direct hit, it would kill me. I was still going in. How stupid was that? I carefully placed my feet in the proper positions, unable to feel the uneven ground beneath me. Nausea from the stress of battle gripped me; I shuddered with cold, waiting for Eli's order.

A second arc of fire shot through the night, hitting its face. "Now!" Eli shouted. "Now!"

I attacked the Darkness. Mage-fast, trusting my balance on unsteady, numb feet, I dashed in, cutting, cutting, thrusting into the succubus' belly with the blue-glowing tanto. I flew from the sleeping cat to the dolphin, through all three forms of the crab, abridged versions used by a mage with only one blade.

With each strike, the tanto sang against my palm, long bell-like tones of pleasure and fury. The smell of holiness, if there was one, had to be the scent of the burning blade. Roses, lilies, herbs, and wildflowers. The scent of sunlight and the ozone of lightning. The dust of fresh-mined stone. Guns boomed, aiming higher at the queen, hitting its shoulders and chest. The succubus shrieked, an earsplitting howl.

Screams went up around me—terror and pain. I whirled away from the beast. Devil-spawn swarmed in. I executed the whirlwind, a slashing figure eight, a wild move, suitable for dispatching numbers of the small reddish creatures at once. Black blood flew, a wide spray of acidic droplets that burned through my pajamas like fire on my flesh.

Instead of driving the spawn back, instead of granting a respite, my move triggered an unexpected response: the usually mindless creatures regrouped and darted in, their symmetry and organization distinctly unspawnlike. One took a bite out of my calf, ripping my pajamas, bloody gouges from razor-sharp teeth and three-fingered, clawed hands. I felt a conjure sizzle over my skin and the spawn dropped away, lifeless on the snow. Cheran, I knew. I was losing blood but at least I was no longer cold or paralyzed with uncertainty. I dashed in, striking, wishing I was stronger, taller, a lot taller.

The queen was thrashing, roaring, head back, a man held in its left fist, his limbs whipping bonelessly. Its right hand made a sweeping motion, as if drawing in threads of yarn. The spawn followed in its wake, attacking a grouping of humans at its feet.

"It's directing spawn," Eli said of the queen. He pulled me beneath the porch of Rupert's loft for a moment, our backs to a brick wall. Breath heaving, I lowered the tanto with its blue-light blade. My muscles protested the sudden stillness, my back tight, threatening to spasm. My left side ached, the old injury that had never quite healed. My feet were numb. I ignored them all.

The queen gestured. Too far away to help, we watched as a group of spawn attacked with military precision, taking down three humans who were erecting a barricade. The attack was quick and brutal, and they began to feed on flesh while it still quivered with life. The beast devoured the man it had been holding, energy for healing. "It's in charge," Eli said, knocking over a stack of firewood, creating a makeshift fence between us and the fight in the street.

"Looks like," Audric replied, ducking into our temporary haven. He was slicked with sweat, which was freezing in the cold wind, a white, rimming crust on his dark skin, which glowed with the mage energies of his half-breed heritage. He was smeared with black and red blood. His skin was scorched and blistered from the acid, but he seemed not to notice. "Shield," he instructed me. With a single thought I activated a shield I had devised. It allowed in beings of Light, people I liked, and necessities like air, but kept out bad guys and bullets. Or had, once.

"What do they want?" I asked, winded. "Besides Stanhope blood?"

"That's not enough?" Eli asked, breathing harder. He handed me my longsword and bent over, trying to catch his breath.

"Their strategy is structured, which is unheard of," Audric said, sinking into teacher mode, the tone he used when training me in savage-chi. "Watch them. With this kind of organization, they could have taken a Stanhope with no fight at all."

"They couldn't find them," I said. "Rupert and Ciana were behind the ward until I turned it off, and Lucas ate something when he was a prisoner on the Trine. I think it changed the way he smells." And Thadd smells like kylen, but I didn't say that and no one asked.

"It could have taken a Stanhope since. So what else do they want?" Audric asked.

"Chaos and—" Eli cut himself off as a new thought formed. He stood and leaned over the pile of wood, so close to the shield he was nearly touching it, watching the bedlam as a score of humans circled the succubus, firing shotguns up at it, the sound of four-aught buck incredible. Bodies littered the snow. "This is the third time they've attacked the town itself," he mused, his voice growing steady, his breath evening out. "Each attack has utilized different methodology, tactics, and combatants. And this time they're firing the roofs, so this time, maybe they came prepared to finish us off, to take out the town after they get their blood donor. A two-fer."

"More aims than those, perhaps," Audric said.

"Collect Stanhope blood, wipe out the town or damage it substantially, kill or capture our mage," Eli said, twisting his back and delts in a series of stretches. "And it could have sensed the presence of a second mage."

Audric nodded and finished the thought. "And felt the time was propitious for taking both." *Propitious*. I wanted to laugh, but didn't have the energy. Only a second unforeseen, a half-breed, a master of savage-chi, would use a ten-dollar word during a prolonged battle.

"Or maybe it's been training troops just for tonight," Eli said, repositioning his weapons and the night-vision goggles hanging on his chest. "Maybe the previous assaults were sorties to train and get the layout of the place." Audric lit up as the thought found a home in his mind. The men shared one of those chest-beating manly looks that always excluded women. *Ugh. Big trouble. Protect the women and children. Blood, guts, and glory. Ugh.*

I was too drained to comment. All I wanted to do was fall

to the snow and sleep. Unlike Eli, I couldn't seem to catch my breath.

"Time for the big guns," Eli said. This time when he spoke into the ear wire, it was sotto voce, but mages have a broad audible range, and I heard what he said. "Deploy the W-T-seven, asap." He looked at Audric, a wide grin splitting his face. "A big-ass gun. Big enough to take out Godzilla."

I hoped the WT7 was all he claimed, as the succubus had drawn in a thunderhead of energy. In mage-sight its aura was flashing with black lightning, a big, ugly monster. Like the ugly paintings in ancient Pre-Ap cathedrals and museums.

Rupert, dressed now in flannel, jeans, and a jacket and carrying an armful of clothing and weapons, dashed from the doorway. To avoid an energy backlash, I flicked the shield off as he entered the shelter. He tossed me the green marble sphere that set the ward over the shop and loft. I fumbled the catch, which thankfully no one saw or I'd have been the victim of ribbing. Mages were supposed to be so much faster than humans. Gesturing the men away from the wall at our backs, I thumbed on the ward, protecting Ciana, Cissy, and Jacey. A weight seemed to lift off me. Careful to keep the differing energy patterns separate, I opened the shield again.

"Cissy's alive," he said when I focused on him. I closed my eyes in gratitude. Maybe it was true that God the Victorious didn't listen to mages, but he had heard somebody's prayer. "Put these on." Rupert dropped my battle boots in the snow and draped my battle cloak around my shoulders. The warmth trapped in the lining was like a furnace to my skin. I realized how cold I was. I had gotten dangerously hypothermic. Stupid, stupid, *stupid*. My champard had noted my condition and acted to correct it, but that didn't negate my stupidity.

I smiled my thanks at him as I thumbed on an amulet for heating water and dropped it at my feet. Immediately the snow and ice melted, the puddle warming to steam. My feet felt like they were in boiling water, but the conjure was for bathwater, a maximum of one hundred four degrees. The water tinged red as blood softened and melted. Muscles and

tendons ached, and my soles felt as if I had sliced them with
knives and walked through salt.

I dropped in a healing amulet and dipped my hands in,
sliding the ripped socks off and tossing them away as I
massaged my toes and scrubbed my feet. Snowmelt wasn't
beneficial water for stone mages, but any port in a storm.
My ring-shaped prime amulet and the hilt-prime flared
brighter, offering me protection from the snowmelt, the loss
of power that came from contact with unpurified water, as
they had from frostbite. Blood flowed freely, but I could
deal with that later. My neomage attributes brightened,
my skin closer to its normal pearly hue, and I realized how
stupid—and lucky—I had been. On my necklace, various
amulets were emitting a sort of hum as they responded to
the state of my stressed body.

In the street, two snow-el-mobiles whizzed up, sling-
ing snow and ice from the runners. Half a dozen ragged
men jumped from them and spread into formation, joining
the attackers from the front and sides. I looked away long
enough to pull the boots on over my wet and bleeding feet.
When I looked back up, a third snow-el-mobile scattered
the combatants and hissed to a halt. Mounted on the back
was a four-foot-long black metal pipe attached to a black
box about eighteen inches on a side. A magazine coiled
from a spindle on one side. The WT7. Eli was right. It was
a big-ass gun.

"Sixty-six caliber, loaded with shells designed to explode
a millisecond after contact, composed of standard ammo
and salt mined from the shores of the Dead Sea," Eli said.
"Mixed with a few atoms of seraph-steel."

I looked up from securing my cloak. Audric stared at
him as well. "Seraph-steel?" he asked. "Where did the EIH
obtain seraph-steel?"

"Some unallied Watchers are a little less fastidious than
the High Host would like." Into the mike he said, "Fire at
will."

The Earth Invasion Heretics believed that seraphs and
Darkness alike were invaders from another planet, here to
continue a conflict that destroyed their home world and to
claim Earth for their own. It was a conspiracy theory of the

lowest order. I thought it was a bunch of hooey, but I was willing to be proved wrong. There was a lot I didn't know about the High Host.

The kirk actively sought out EIH operatives for punishment, which varied from branding to death—very messy death, with lots of blood and gore. The operatives fighting the succubus didn't seem very concerned with that at the moment, however. All were men, all dressed in layers of rags, from their ratty knit caps to the strips of old car tires bound to their feet in lieu of boots. Their pants were tattered, coats were full of holes, but their pockets were bulging and each carried assault rifles, holstered handguns, and myriad knives. One had an ax strapped to his back. What they did without in terms of personal comfort, they made up for in weaponry. It was impressive. And I had seen them fight. They seemed to know little in the way of fear.

These were stone-hard mountain men, bred to war from generations of hardscrabble survivalists. There was no way they had gotten here this fast from their homes high in the surrounding hills. They had been nearby. Waiting. Another question to ask later, when there was time. If there was time.

The gunner leaped to the back of the el-mobile and cradled his weapon like a lover. The big gun boomed. In the back-flash of fire, I caught sight of an amulet on his chest, a ring of shells sewn onto his coat, a mage-made talisman. On the snow-el-mobile was another, this one made of fish bones shaped in a rune of protection. *Spawn balls. The EIH are working with a sea mage.*

"Ready?" Eli asked. The men with me nodded, checking their weapons. "Let's boogie."

I flicked off the shield as swarms of spawn scampered down the sides of buildings and out of alleys, pursued by Flames with a diameter of three feet. They chased the spawn straight at a massive vehicle racing down the street with a horrid roar, spitting smoke. It was the town's old fire truck, usually stored in an old barn on Lower Street, and powered by rare and expensive gasoline. The truck barreled into the swarms, scattering the midsized reddish creatures as if the Flames had planned the move. The men with me shouted war cries and raced into the night behind the truck, joining the fight, leaving me alone as the vehicle careened around a corner.

A mage-conjure whispered across my skin and spawn stragglers fell smoking to the street. Other spawn shrieked and slowed, stumbling. I had to learn that conjure. Above me, in the wake of the truck, I heard a whir. In the night sky were two beasts with dozens of wings, dragonets, darting down. If it had been safe to curse, I would have let out a string of them. Instead, I pulled an amulet I had created just for such creatures and tore after them. I had to be close for the incantation stored in the amulets to work. Real close.

In the middle of the street, the succubus queen was on one knee, blackened and scored, so badly wounded it no longer screamed, but fought for life. If it fell, the fighters would behead it.

The orthodox had joined the fight, their black clothing making them hard to spot. They were fearless warriors, believing that their place beside the Most High was assured if they fell fighting his enemies. The sound of their prayers resonated in a continuous burr of scripture as they called on God the Victorious to grant them success. In mage-sight, they gleamed as I raced past, their faith and zealotry adding energy to bland human flesh. Or maybe, as they believed, it was the spirit of God the Victorious filling them with his holy presence. I didn't know. Soulless beings like me had no way to confirm or deny the claims of the religious. But part of me wanted them to be right, wanted the Most High to have a continued interest in humanity and the world all claimed he'd created.

One man looked up as the dragonets whirred overhead and fired a dozen shots into the air. The dragonets soared in the night sky and seemed to home in on one form in the melee below. They dropped into the midst of the skirmish, ten feet long and sinuous, exoskeletons bristling with dagger-sharp spines and barbs, legs with multiple joints, spikes at each bend.

At the sight, battle-lust pulsed into my bloodstream, and I swung both blades in perfect arcs, powerful strikes that took off spawn limbs and heads with ease as I raced toward the fight, cutting my way through the Minor Darkness in mindless bloodlust. With the walking horse, I dispatched three spawn that had hemmed two men into a doorway, one severely wounded.

I didn't feel a moment's shame at taking the spawn from behind. Fighting minions of Darkness required no honor. The spawn fell in a dozen pieces, my tanto singing in victory. I shouted my battle cry, "Jehovah sabaoth!" as spawn blood drenched the snow. The man still standing tipped his hat at me while cleaning a blade on his pant leg. He was an orthodox, his black suit ripped, torn, bloody. I recognized him but couldn't place his name. I nodded back and stepped to the side, into the leaping cat form, blades in graceful arcs, ripping another group of spawn to pieces before they could regroup and fight me.

Ahead, my two champards fought back-to-back against both dragonets. I didn't have time to wonder why they fought alone, without the help of other townspeople. I gauged my incline on the run and leaped high, landing on a wide leg joint, slicing backhanded to sever the poisoned stinger of its descending tail. At the taste of dragonet blood, the tanto belled a paean of triumph and joy. Planting my feet in the angles where legs met body, I raced up the dragonet, slicing through legs and wings, temporarily disabling the appendages, but knowing the beast was able to regenerate with supernatural speed. I had to get to its head.

Just as I climbed within striking distance, the dragonet reared straight up, roaring, throwing me back. My feet slipped. I bounced once on my backside, spun, and slid toward the ground. I caught myself one-handed in the notch of a missing leg, swaying wide and back, wedging both feet into crevices in the steel-hard shell.

The dragonet's head rotated on overlapping ridges and it snapped at me, fangs flashing. Six inches of ichor-coated teeth grazed my arm. It drew away, mouth opening for another strike. I whirled the tanto and thrust up, into its open mouth and through its palate, into its brain—if it had a brain—a kill strike.

The tanto blazed cerulean blue and an electric pulse surged up my arm as I twisted the blade and ripped it free. A gush of blood followed, drenching up my arm, eating away the pajama sleeve, searing my skin, splashing from

the battle cloak. With a simple flick of my wrist, I tossed a
stone into its maw. The shard of amethyst bounced and fell
down its throat.

"Audric!" I shouted. I didn't look, I simply jumped, trusting the big man to catch me if he could. If he was occupied,
if he missed, landing on the hard street was still a better
choice than staying up here. An arm snatched me out of the
air and set me down in a dancer's stance.

"Took you long enough!" Audric shouted at me. The joy
of battle lit his eyes in a mad gleam and he laughed. Rupert
ripped the air with his master's blade, holding off the other
dragonet, detaching several many-jointed legs. Above me,
the dragonet I had ridden coiled into an S to strike.

The effect of the amethyst wasn't as spectacular as the
anti-conjure amulet, but it worked just as well. Lavender
light blazed up its throat and burst from every joint. The
dragonet squealed like a hog on a spike and fell to a writhing heap on the ice.

"One down," I said, meeting Audric's fierce glare with
battle glee of my own.

He raised his head and shouted his battle cry, "Raziel!
By blood and fire!" He stooped, making a staircase out of
his body. It was a move we hadn't practiced, but I remembered it from savage-chi lessons as a child. I pulled a second
amethyst and ran at him. Placed a foot on his calf, a foot
on his thigh, his back, his shoulder, racing up his body. He
thrust straight up, throwing me into the air, the move created to scale the walls of a fortified compound. He timed
it perfectly, and I plunged the tanto down at the remaining
dragonet, directly into one of its six eyes. The same pulse
of the Flame-enhanced blade prickled up the tanto and
through my blood.

The dragonet howled, its hinged jaw open to the moon. I
threw the crystal of amethyst down its maw and wrenched
my body, removing the blade. Eye fluid splattered me as
I dropped. Again Audric caught me, this time like a baby
falling from a bough, a bloody lullaby of war.

Lavender light ripped through the beast. It fell atop the
body of the first, whipping back and forth. Shouting my battle cry, I whirled to the succubus, but it was down, a dozen

humans hacking into it, working at its scaled throat with swords and hoes and kitchen knives. It was bleeding out on the street. It looked like we were winning. I should have stifled the thought unborn. Murphy's Law kicked in.

In arrowhead formation, dragonets overflew the town. There were at least six, and these babies were furred, with large leathery wings and lobster claws that looked as if they were formed of demon-iron. Two elders in brown robes fell to their knees at the sight, praying aloud, spiritual warfare. In mage-sight, I recognized the Elders Waldroup praying back-to-back, their bodies glowing with the bright light of their faith, blades in both hands.

Audric, Rupert, and I spread into a triangle to cover as much of the street as we could. Eli raced to join us. "You see 'em? These things just keep getting uglier. How many are there?" I shook my head. I didn't know.

Jasper, one of the town's youngest elders, appeared out of the night. He wore wool pants, boots, and a coat, with pajama bottoms peeking out the pants' legs. His bare chest was puckered with cold and he was heaving for breath, his face drawn and white except for the blood frozen or dried in his hair. He'd taken a nasty blow. His desperate black eyes met mine.

"Call mage in dire," he said. "You have to."

"My mistrend has considered and rejected the call," Audric said, his face implacable. "Last time thirty-seven died from the raised sword of judgment. What if she can't get the holy one to sheathe the weapon? The whole town could die. It has happened before."

When seraphs are called, they fight evil to a standstill. But after the fight, the naked swords sometimes take on a different function, the role of swords of judgment, and humans die as punishment for their sins. It was why I hadn't called for help.

Ignoring Audric in his position of my legal spokesperson, Jasper again spoke directly to me. "They've disabled the town's satellite terminus and cut the phone lines. They set off avalanches that blocked the roads and trails to the east and west and both sides of the Toe," he said, speaking of the Toe River, which bisected the town. "We have no way to call for help. No way to get out. It looks like this time they mean to destroy the town."

As if to emphasize his words, a wood building in the middle of the block between Upper and Lower Streets fell with a thunderous roar, sparks shooting into the sky.

Chapter 5

Ⱨ

Over the sulfur and brimstone stench of dying succubus and hacked-to-death dragonets and spawn, over
the odor of burning wood, I smelled caramel and
brown sugar and felt my body react to the pull of kylen. The
low-level mage-heat I lived with day and night flamed high
and I turned in a circle, skimming for Thadd.

"Thorn." Eli grabbed my elbow. I shook him away.

From out of the shadows, I heard a hiss of indrawn
breath. Even through the protection of the amulet he had
brought me, I felt Cheran's body clench. He too smelled
kylen. His heat was instantaneous, and if Thadd didn't ease
back into the shadows and away from us, Cheran's mating instinct would intensify, driving him into near madness
until he found someone to satisfy his lust. I was fighting, my
blood flooded with endorphins that cooled ardor, and I'd
had better practice at resisting the mating urge brought on
by seraphs and kylen, but the other mage clearly had not.
Not actively part of the melee, surrounded by the lure-scent
of succubus, his visa and primes weren't keeping the uncontrollable sexual arousal of mage-heat at bay.

With mage-sight, I now saw the other mage, breathing too
hard, too fast, a blur of warmth and need, the high temperature of passion overriding his glamour as mage-heat took
over—the animal rut that came over mages and seraphs in
close company. If someone wasn't willing, Cheran would
attack and mate by force. The town fathers would flay him

alive for rape—and he would deserve it, even if sexual violence didn't bring seraphic judgment down on the town.

I spotted Thadd hunched over in shadow. In mage-sight, he blazed with kylen light, his long coat clutched closed in one fist, pale feathers peeking from the back. Had he removed the conjured ring that kept his kylen attributes in check? Either that or something had happened that allowed me to see his energies as they really were.

Toes touching the outstretched claw of a hand, he bent forward, his fingers tracing the length of the succubus' scaled forearm. The dying beast twitched, claw scraping on the ice. Stepping closer, Thadd caressed its armored chest as if it were a woman's perfect breast.

The queen had been built from mage and Stanhope genetic material, and enhanced with the stolen essence of Barak, the captured Watcher I had freed. The succubus scent was tantalizing to human males, to seraphs, and to kylen, who were the result of matings between mage, seraph, and later, humans. Cheriour, the Angel of Punishment who'd left his sigil on the roadway, once went into violent sexual arousal at the scent.

If I called mage in dire and a seraph answered my call, would it go into heat rather than to war? Had that been part of the Darkness's plan all along? My own heat was growing, a warm pulsation low in my belly. Battle dire was supposed to stop mage-heat. Something was very wrong. What should I do?

Eli whirled me around and shook me. My teeth clacked together with the force. "What's wrong with you?"

I lifted a hand, traced the length of his jaw with my knuckles, my longsword trailing behind the caress. His mouth opened in surprise and I leaned against him. It was hard to find words but the visa pulsed once and my mind cleared enough to say, "The dragonets and the succubus were made with Mole Man's blood, which confuses the Host. The succubus was created to make seraphs go into heat. Dangerous, deadly heat. It's already begun. Don't you feel it?" I pressed my body against his.

His eyes widened but he didn't pull away. "There're no seraphs here," he said.

I breathed in, smelling kylen, and wrapped my arms

around Eli, my blades clinking together at his back. His body was warm, sweat-drenched, and I melded mine around him, breathing in his scent, musky with battle. "It wants me to mate. It wants me to call mage in dire. The smell of succubus and mage will make answering seraphs go into a mating fury. I don't know what would happen or how bad it could get. I—"

The ground shook beneath us, and Eli spread his feet for balance. The itchy feeling I had been suppressing all week intensified, enticing me from the hypnotic heat. Something was coming. Something big. The shaking of the ground increased. The visa pulsed again and I shook myself, trying to think, to reason. Earthquake.

Jasper, his face tight with fear and revulsion at the way I was grinding myself into Eli, seized a porch column and held on. Thadd looked up from the queen's carcass and licked his lips. My heat-rating went from battle-controlled to orgy-hot. I unwound from Eli and stepped toward Thadd. From my left, Cheran appeared. He was peeling out of the velvet cloak, the jacket and shirt beneath falling to the ground. I dropped the tanto and the longsword and pulled at the fastenings of my cloak. I could have a mage and kylen at once. I could—

Eli slapped my face so hard my head whipped back. Thadd watched, his eyes hot with desire. The ground shook, knocking me flat. Eli crouched over me, supporting himself on his arms. His body smelled of human pheromones, blood, and that strange form of lust soldiers experience during combat. I slid a hand into his jeans, grasping him with tight fingers. He sucked in a startled breath. From Cheran, I heard an excited growl and I laughed. A human, a mage, and a kylen. I could have all three. "Yessss," I hissed. "All three. Now."

"Much as I like having your hand in my britches, lady, this ain't exactly the time or the place," Eli said, squirming away. "What's got into you? Three what?" Danger forgotten, I gripped his shoulders and arched up into him, sweeping the streets for Thadd and Cheran.

In a blur of speed, Audric raced from the dark and barreled into Thadd. They bowled away, into the shadows. My head cleared. I jerked my hand free of Eli's jeans and

shook my head. "Seraph st—" I stopped myself, feeling a
flush cover me in a different kind of heat as embarrassment
swept through me.

Eli, who had my wrist in his hand and a probing but interested look on his face, dropped his grip, stood, and stepped
back. The ground was still shaking, a low, slow rumble as if
the earth was purring. Or growling.

"Thorn?" Rupert asked from nearby. His voice grew formal. "Mistrend. What's that?"

I snapped my mouth closed and followed his pointing
finger. The streetlights had burned out nearly a century ago,
and the smoke-filled street, lit only by the flickering light
of multiple fires, had darkened. A wash of gray filled in the
already dark spaces between snatches of light.

"Something evil this way comes," a voice out of the night
said, as if quoting.

"A big powerful evil," a second voice said.

"Yeah. A big, honking, evil mofo," Eli said. He pulled me
to my feet. Above us was a cloud of Darkness.

I looked toward the Trine, its peaks lost in the night.
Someone had asked how the succubus got to town with
the hellhole closed. "The Dragon trapped between planes
of reality is using the earthquake, or generating the earthquake, to get free. Its minions burrowed new openings
and came looking for human deaths to provide the energy
needed for its release."

"This little war here," Eli said, understanding. "The
Dragon was using it, siphoning off our energies to power
the earthquake. Getting you and a Stanhope, while important, were secondary to the first part of the plan."

"Yeah," I said. "That feels right."

Dragonets whipped through the cloud, writhing in pleasure, brushing against one another in sensuous abandon.
Whatever dragonets liked couldn't be good for the rest
of us. It wasn't easy, but I pushed away the residual heat,
picked up my weapons, and stepped into the cat.

Near me, Cheran was fastening his clothes. "Powers and
high-level Principalities of Darkness once could assume
any form they wished, including the form of a cloud," he
said, his voice sounding dazed. "They had full seraphic

gifts. But God the Victorious stripped them of most such abilities at the Fall. Some can still assume one shape that's more than a glamour, but not a true transmogrification, like the succubus queen." He indicated the cloud with a jut of his head. "*That* looks like true transmogrification, a true seraphic gift."

The cloud rolled low, taking with it the little bit of light that came from windows, doors, and fires. I took a tentative breath. It smelled of dying lilies.

"What makes a Darkness with seraphic gifts so special?" Rupert asked, his voice thick.

"Something happened in the *otherness*," I said, remembering the sensation of being beneath the ground, trapped, fighting for my life and the lives of others. My scars blazed with white light and remembered pain as the cloud descended over us.

"What's an otherness?" Rupert asked. He rubbed his face, and then stared at his hand, which trembled with exhaustion.

"I think it's the same thing as the heavens. Or part of the heavens," I said. "I think this means that Darkness found a victory there and gained back a foothold."

"Enough to give it power to transmogrify?" Eli asked. "If so, it's got honking big mojo."

"Whatever it is," Rupert said, "I think it's poisonous." He fell forward, landing face-first on the hard ice. My heart wrenched and I stepped over him, shielding him as I turned in a slow circle, watching. The cloud of Darkness rolled up the street like a wave. Men and women fell as if poleaxed, all except Eli, Cheran, and the EIH, who pulled gas masks over their faces. I saw Eli hand a spare mask to Lucas.

I had no incantation for clean air. I had no way to help Rupert. He was breathing, however, and that meant he was alive. Audric's half-mage genetic structure would provide him some protection from the gaseous Dark. I didn't know about Thadd. Whatever the cloud was, it seemed to have been designed to affect only humans. Cheran and I were still upright.

A voice whispered, and I turned, searching for its source. "Little mage. I have tasted of you." My heart rate sped up, an uneven riff of fear as I pivoted, placing my feet to either side of my friend. Cheran stepped slowly away from me, body relaxed, throwing-blades held loosely.

"Friend of yours?" he asked.

"No. Not a friend."

"That's what I was afraid of," Eli said, his voice muffled behind the mask.

Tendrils of the cloud brushed my face, slid along my seared, scraped arm, as cold and wintery as the fingers of death. I searched the deeper night, blades curling up and around in the egret. I glanced up. The moon and the stars were gone.

"I have placed a drop of your blood between my lips," the voice said. "I claim you. Come to me."

"Moving in beside you, Thorn," Eli said, "at your four o'clock. Try not to cut off my head." I chuckled, and the tone was dead, as if all sound stopped inches from my mouth. "Lucas is at your eight," he finished.

"Yeah. Okay," I said. I stopped turning. I felt light-headed and the back of my throat was tickling, so there was some effect.

The cloud slid inside my battle cloak, and I felt it moving against my skin. My flesh quivered and I wanted to throw up as it brushed my belly. It felt like claws, a conjure to render me weaponless and filled with terror. The world wavered beneath me, and I thought again, *earthquake*, but this time it was only vertigo. Burning acid rose in the back of my throat.

"You are the Thorn," it whispered. "I have waited long for you."

"You can wait a lot longer," Eli said to the night.

My cloak billowed out as if a strong wind swirled beneath it. The tanto in my hand blazed bright blue and sang a note of warning that hurt my ears.

"I desired a child of your body, through the Mole Man's lineage." Claws scraped down my sides, curious, possessive.

I swallowed the acid down, a convulsive spasm. "Fancy that," I said, bravado the only weapon I had left. Weakness leached into my bones from the night air, freezing. The Dragon was close enough to draw on our energies. Death was coming to the town and I didn't know how to stop it.

I clamped my arms tight to my sides, my useless blades crossed at my waist.

The thing in the air chuckled, the sound of a lover, amused. "Come. I desire you."

Muscles weak, I slid to my knees, straddling Rupert. His body was warm beneath me, my shins and knees cold on the ice. Up and down the street the elders who had prayed, shouting scripture in spiritual warfare, lay silent and still. I missed the continuous sound of their litany, a background to the warfare of steel and explosives.

"You *will* be mine. You carry my talisman," it said, its voice a sibilant hiss.

Blue light blazed like a torch in the darkness, trilling a piercing cry. I saw my hand setting the tanto on the street. I placed the longsword beside it. My hand went into a pocket.

"What the flying f—heck is she doing?" Eli said, barely avoiding swearing in the presence of the Dark. I wanted to laugh. As if the cloud surrounding us needed any help at all. "What's she holding?" he asked no one in particular.

It was a six-inch-long claw from the underside of a drag-onet leg. A spur. A *thorn*. I stroked the talisman, feeling the power thrum within it. I had carried it with me, in the pocket of my cloak, since it pierced my side. "Forcas used it to try to claim me," I said.

"Forcas was my errand boy," the Darkness breathed, "delivering the thorn of binding." The spur hummed in my hand. Not the empty vessel I had thought, the spur had been waiting for this moment, this Darkness. In mage-sight, it glowed like a black opal with fire at its heart.

In some small, rational part of my brain, I knew I had been stupid to keep it, a keepsake of victory disguising a defeat postponed. *Stupid, stupid, stupid*, my mental voice condemned. I watched as my hand lifted, arm straight, pointing the barbed, razor-sharp spur at my left side. My scars blazed with a strange smoky light. The unhealed psy-chic wound on my side knotted tightly, the sensation more pleasure than pain. Something long and sinuous twisted through me.

"Come. You are mine."

I belong to someone? A gentle joy welled up in me, surging with the beat of my heart. I was no longer alone. I was so tired of being alone. So tired of fighting.

"Thorn?"

"Stop her!"

A hand grabbed my arm, ripped the spur from me, and threw it to the street. Another raised a battle-ax above the amulet. The steel blade smashed down, breaking the talisman, disrupting the conjure. A shaft of dark lightning shot into the sky. Audric fell away from the broken barb, grunting. Thunder echoed down the street. Pain wrenched through my scars and a single pulse of white light lit them, a terrible schema of old wounds and ancient pain. For an instant, my amulets shone bright as a Flame. In the retinal afterburn, the world was a negative reality, black snow and white sky.

"What was that thing?" Eli shouted through the muffling of the gas mask. Audric, lying on the snow, shook with a single epilepticlike tremor in the aftermath of the explosion.

I snatched up my blades and stood. The whir of wings sounded and I tried to dance over Rupert's body, but stumbled, falling to the side. A blow sent me sprawling. A stinger whipped by my ear. A second dragonet hovered over Rupert, barbed legs to either side, long snarled fur dragging the street. The flying beast slashed a long gash down my friend's back.

I leaped at the beast's head, changing my grip on the tanto, bringing the weapon forward along the plane of my body. I drew on the prime amulet in the hilt of the longsword, pulled on the prime ring and visa, drawing all the power at my disposal into me. Strength poured in.

Midstrike, the visa suggested a verse from Job and I shouted, my voice swelling through the tourmaline into a mighty roar as I cut. "His hand hath pierced the swift serpent!" In a death strike, I thrust up under its jaw with the last word, snapping its mouth shut, driving the blade up through the roof of its mouth. The final thud against the top of its skull was a satisfying finish, forcing back its head, but again the tanto missed its tiny brain.

In a ferocious flex of muscle, it rose into the air over me, wrenching my left arm up as I gripped the tanto hilt. It carried my body high and again I shouted the scripture. Below me, a second dragonet darted in. I caught a glimpse of gray metal, a shaped ring, demon-iron forged over human steel. The claw holding it slid the steel along my body, into the bite wound on my calf. I screamed as the frozen metal seared down to the bone.

With a supple twist, the beast then dipped the iron against Rupert's body, following the length of the bloody wound in his back. When it came away, Rupert's blood splattered over my shins, hot and human, mixed with mage-blood. Comprehension blossomed, wordless.

The dragonet I had pinned thrashed in a vicious whip. The tanto blade slipped free of it. I hung suspended a moment, the blade plasma-bright. And then I fell to the ice. I gasped as air slammed out of my body. Breathless, lungs empty, I lay on the street, arms outspread, watching the night sky reappear overhead as the cloud of blackness coalesced into a spiral, forming a black tornado of might over the town. *A true Darkness,* the visa proposed. *Leviathan.*

Fear tightened my body and set off sparks in my vision. I understood why it had suggested Job in warfare. This was the vision of true Darkness Job had seen and prophesied. "Let that day be darkness; Let not God from above seek for it, Neither let the light shine upon it. Let darkness and the shadow of death claim it. . . . Who are ready to rouse up leviathan."

Leviathan.

This was the opponent we faced, an evil who had played two roles in the rebellion against the High Host: as one who joined the Watchers, became their leader, and taught humans the arts of war before language had been recorded, and also as the left hand of Lucifer, taking part in that one's rebellion against heaven. Since the time of the Last War, Leviathan had been coupled with the name Azazel. Azazel was the left hand of Satan.

This Dragon had been bound three times, twice in prehistory, and once by Mole Man's sacrifice. The Dragon of Darkness was greater than we had guessed. I wondered if Mole Man had known the beast's name.

The coil of air tightened, growing darker, shot through with motes of emptiness like holes in the universe, a Darkness so intense it trailed afterimages of lightless tails. The spiral of power centered on the demon-iron in the claw of the small dragonet. A link three inches across, smeared in Rupert's blood. In my blood. "Oh, merciful seraphs," I breathed. The Dragon, partially unbound from Mole Man's chain, was manifesting.

The tornado of power slipped through the link like a finger gliding through a ring and carried it into the night air, swirling through it in a twisting, undulating snake of black cloud. Dragonets flew beside it, trumpeting in victory. The ground trembled as the earthquake shuddered through the ancient hills.

Audric and Eli were right. It was indeed much more than a two-fer. Layered intentions, incantations, and conjures, purposes that covered every possible contingency. The Dragon was using the death of the townsfolk, the mixed blood, its minions, and the link to break fully free. The Dark Wind whipped overhead, the spirit form of the Dragon.

Close by, the WT7 boomed. A dragonet split in two, spraying me with gore, its head tumbling into the night. The two-foot section between was vaporized. The big gun boomed again. Flames darted across my line of sight, zapping the dragonets. Where had they been, the Flames and the big weapon? Fighting what? I remembered to breathe, my ribs creaking with the motion. The cloud of Darkness hurt to inhale, bitter with the taste of failure.

Two more booms took out other dragonets and a chunk of a nearby building. A group of EIH soldiers hacked a beast into little pieces, too small to regenerate. Another creature was wounded when Gloria and her husband, legs wide and braced against the earth's shaking, walked it down the street, pumping rounds into its underbelly.

I saw a flash of the beast's face, and I could have sworn it was surprised. Bullets had never worked on Darkness. Until now. Humans had always been excellent at devising means of death, and they had finally discovered how to kill evil with Dead Sea salt ammo. Ironic that humans, who had been taught the arts of war by Azazel, were now able to destroy its followers.

Beneath me, the earth continued to roll and shift. Along the street, buildings buckled, walls giving way. Stones and chunks of brick fell. The cloud lifted, riding the night sky.

EIH warriors raced up and down the street in el-cars, weapons booming. Elders rose to their knees and resumed praying. Human soldiers stood, wobbly, and checked their weapons. The tornado continued to roar, pulling light and life through the link. I gripped my prime ring and mouthed the words to mage in dire, but the sound died unborn. It was too late. I was too late. I should have called long before now. *Stupid, stupid, stupid.*

Once more I crawled to my feet. Audric struggled upright on the unstable earth, his face hard as polished marble. He strode to Rupert's side, knelt, lifted him in a fireman's hold, and carried his partner to partial protection beneath the porch of Thorn's Gems. Its three-foot-thick walls still stood, though a crack ran along the mortar from a foundation stone to the roof.

Audric eased Rupert to the snow and sat beside him, holding the smaller man like a child. Windows and doors brightened. Snow on the street was a scorched white pelt running between the buildings. The Darkness was withdrawing. The remaining few dragonets flew away, north. The funnel cloud thrashed and tightened. In a flash, it dipped down and touched the succubus. The scaled body crumbled to dust, the particles sucked up by the roaring wind.

As if wrenched through a hole in the air, the tornado disappeared through the link. Black wind followed and vanished. Misty remnants dispersed. Silence was so loud my ears ached with the emptiness of it. Above me, the stars and moon shone white and pure onto the blood-splashed snow and ice. Wood smoke billowed in the wake of the Dark Wind. The dark tornado.

My parents had been killed by a tornado. A tornado was one of the Dragon's forms. Two vital facts. Crucially significant. That meant its plans had been in place for decades. But I was so tired it was hard to think it through logically, point by point. All I could think was that Lolo, who had raised me when my parents died, had perhaps been behind the whole thing.

A voice whispered up from the depths of my mind: *Or a dupe, led astray?*

Weariness ached through my shoulders and hips, pain throbbing up from lacerated, frostbitten feet. My soles had bled in the boots and stuck. I tore ruined flesh with each step. My fingers had gripped the hilts so long, they creaked when I opened my hands. Bodies lay in pools of blood. The cries of the injured resounded weakly in the vacuum of silence left by the wind. So many dead and wounded. And all for nothing. I couldn't help the single sob that welled up in me and echoed quietly down the street.

I wanted to believe that the retrieval of its succubus queen and the loss of so many dragonets was the reason the Dragon disappeared, but the Darkness said it wanted a child of mine through Mole Man's line. Even though trapped in a different reality, had it been aware I was married to Lucas, a Stanhope, a grandchild several times down the line from Mole Man, Benaiah Stanhope?

There was too much I didn't know, but I knew this—the reason for its departure. It had plenty of blood, mine and Rupert's, mage and Stanhope. Mixed. And Rose? Did it have her?

It was all starting to make a terrible kind of sense. After Forcas and the dragon killed my parents, after I had been rescued from the hellhole, it had waited for my blood, unable to sense me. Then, in a moment of jealous anger, I had accidentally damaged my prime amulet and it found me. It had learned I was here, within the reach of its minions, placed here by Lolo, as part of her Machiavellian plan to free Barak, her lover, trapped on the Trine. Lolo, my Lolo, had been part of the Dragon's plan. Knowingly or unknowingly. I shuddered.

I hadn't been smart enough to figure it out, not good enough, fast enough, or strong enough. And because of that, the Dragon had what it needed to break the chain and finish what it had started so long ago. The destruction of humanity, of the seraphs, of the heavens and the earth. If ignorance was bliss, I'd never be blissful again. Tears trickled down my cheeks, the salt stinging in cuts and burns. This was my fault.

Chapter 6

This town will not allow the heresy of the Earth Invasion Heretics to be spoken. We will remain pure, true to the Most High and his High Host," Elder Perkins shouted, his brown robe quivering along his body, both hands fisted.

"You don't speak for all the citizens of Mineral City," the small Cherokee woman said. "I say the EIH have every right to be heard. I'm the widow of Joseph Barefoot, who gave his life to save this misbegotten town."

"So you say," Perkins said. "We've seen no proof of his death."

"She saw him die." She pointed a finger at me. "Ask the town mage." It seemed the entire crowd sighed. So did I.

It was morning, after a night spent gathering the bodies of the fallen Darkness and burning them. A night putting out fires that still smoked. A night healing the wounded and finding makeshift homes for the dispossessed. A night spent in grief and what-might-have-beens. And guilt. And anger.

Cheran, his fancy suit in tatters, fought fires, devising incantations and making conjures to melt snow and to snuff flame. I needed to learn those, but I wasn't speaking to the flashy mage. He was working hard now, but he hadn't fought when Darkness attacked. Instead, he had hidden under a glamour, throwing knives from a distance, helping only when it was prudent. He had accused Audric of cowardice, and then had behaved like a coward himself.

He hadn't acknowledged me once since the conflict. He avoided Audric like the plagues. His shame was a harsh burden.

It was an hour after dawn, and most of the townsfolk were gathered in the Central Baptist Church, the building used for town meetings, and the rare worship service when the crowd was too large for the newer kirk building or when the kirk was under repair. Everyone was exhausted, frightened, irritable, and looking for someone to blame. I had a feeling it would be me.

The meeting was being shown on SNN live, because the reporter/cameraman—woman, rather—had found a way to rig up something through one of the few satellite phones in town. The broadcast wouldn't be delayed until the satellite dish could be repaired, though devil-spawn had done a number on it. Mineral City and its third fight with Major Darkness this winter was breaking news. Lucky me.

"Thorn St. Croix, you are called to the dais," Elder Waldroup intoned.

Maybe Romona Benson would film me only from the rear. Or not at all, and just focus on the crowd. Maybe pigs could dance and horses could play the tuba. Maybe I'd grow wings and fly out of here. I heaved another breath, stood, and walked to the front of the old church.

At least I had found time to shower and change clothes. I wasn't speaking before the town splattered in blood, wearing pink jammies with hearts on them. I was in my clean black battle dobok and was fully armed. Had I been wearing the fighting uniform the night before, I wouldn't have been so badly injured, as the leather was treated by mage masters to be impervious to the acid and ichor of the Dark, resistant to fire, and hardened to the cutting of claw and fang. Instead, I'd fought barefoot. In the snow. How dumb was that?

My feet ached and, like most of the audience, I had multiple bandages. I hadn't had enough amulets to heal my insignificant wounds when so many had been desperately injured. There were twenty-nine bodies; four townspeople were missing and presumed eaten; twelve others were grievously wounded, resting under seraphic healing domes in the fellowship room downstairs. The domes were thought to be mine. They weren't; they were Ciana's, but the town didn't know that and I wasn't telling.

Another twenty had minor wounds, and, when I ran out of both domes and healing amulets, I had forced Cheran to assist them. It had taken the threat of my sword through his testicles to make him comply, but he'd helped in the end. He didn't like humans and he wasn't a talented healer, but he was better than nothing.

Now, on no sleep, feet so sore it felt like I was walking on tacks, forearm and calf swathed in gauze, I was walking to the front of the room to address the town. Again. *Seraph stones.* The silent swear words made me smile. I actually owned a seraph stone.

The last time I had addressed the town, I had done so with all the flair of a mage storyteller. Now I made sure to dampen all my mage attributes as I climbed the seven steps to the dais, battle boots echoing in the silent church. My feet screamed with the torture and I felt a half-healed laceration break open. Great. More blood in my boots. Looking fully human, hurting, I turned slowly to face them.

Baldly, I said, "Joseph Barefoot and Tomas and Rickie Ernandez were EIH. Nazareth Durbarge was with the Administration of the ArchSeraph. Thaddeus Bartholomew is with Carolina law enforcement. Eli Walker is a miner with a claim in the mountains close by. They went with me to the hellhole on the Trine. Seven of us against the hordes beneath the mountain. We were outnumbered and outgunned." Every eye was riveted on me. So was the camera. "We went underground and fought the Darkness." The crowd gasped. No one, not even fools, went underground to meet the Dark.

"Inside the mountain, and later in front of the entrance, we fought a Darkness called Forcas. We won. But while we were fighting and dying, there was also a battle in the heavens. 'As above, so below,'" I said, quoting the adage theologians used to explain the unexplainable parallels between heaven and earth. "In the heavens, the chains drenched in Mole Man's blood, the chains that bound the Dragon, were weakened.

"We were injured and lost half our number. We could have given up and come back down the mountain. We could have done nothing; but that would have meant that you"—I looked across the room; it was packed to standing room only, people sitting in the aisles and lining the walls—"all of you, would have died to feed his release. He was so close to getting free."

Sudden tears filled my eyes and I batted them away, trying for composure, my throat tight, my hands gripping and regripping my swords for the comfort they brought. "Joseph and Durbarge went into the mouth of the hellhole carrying a weapon provided by, I don't know, maybe by the EIH. Maybe by the AAS. They died when they fired it."

I could see the men in my memory, stepping into the opening, bright forms against the yellowish energies radiating from the cave entrance. Tears overflowed and the crowd, a shadowy and sullen cluster of humanity, wavered in my vision. "They weren't sure they could stop it getting free, but they knew they could slow it down, and they did. The Dragon's escape was interrupted. I had hoped it would last for a long time. It didn't."

"Last night, I think it used the deaths of so many of us to take another step closer to freedom. And I think if it had gotten totally free, it would have destroyed the town and used our deaths to feed its hunger."

The crowd was silent. I took a composing breath and looked at Shamus and his brother sitting at the judgment table on the dais. They nodded for me to continue. For whatever reason, they had asked me to tell the town the whole bad news. A single bad dose, as if that would make it all go down easier. "You may as well know. The Darkness set off avalanches and cut communications. We're all trapped in this town, at its mercy, until spring thaw."

The crowd erupted. Yeah. That was pretty much how I felt about it all too. I held up a hand to quiet them. "We can't get away. There isn't time to evacuate the town by nightfall. You have to decide what you're going to do about the Dragon getting free. Fight or die." Having said my piece, I stepped to the edge of the dais.

"Why didn't you call for seraphs to save us last night?" a man's querulous voice called. "Some of us woulda died from its judgment, but the rest of us woulda lived, jist like last time."

I spotted the man, his face creased with hate and his own version of judgment. I didn't care if he liked me or not, but the question was a fair one. "Calling mage in dire is dangerous. When I called mage in dire during the last attack, we got lucky. The seraph put away its sword. But sometimes, when a seraph draws its weapon, every human within ten miles dies."

"Not the witchy-folk?" he asked, disbelieving. "You trying to say that mages don't die in judgment?" This was a dangerous question and it seemed calculated to feed the growing religious disharmony in the town. No way did I think he had come up with it on his own. He smoothed his black suit coat, darting a look once to the left. "Mages are better'n us?" I didn't follow his look but I would have bet the shop he was watching Elder Culpepper for approval.

Carefully, I said, "No. Not better. Some say that because we don't have souls we aren't worthy of the judgment of the Most High." Some say. Not all. In fact, not most. But I kept that to myself.

He pursed his lips. "So. Like the dogs and cats, chickens and goats, like the other animals, you live."

I couldn't keep the shock from my face and a low rumble of anger started in the old church. The camera was suddenly as big as a house, and I felt the focus tighten on me. "If you were trying to insult me, you succeeded," I said, abruptly too tired to care about cameras or the motives and intent of my enemies. I'd had enough, and I slowly descended two steps from the dais, speaking as my boots scuffed the worn boards. "But yes, that is what a lot of humans think. That mages are no better than dogs."

"Are the seraphs really members of the court of the creator of the universe?" another voice rang out. This one was clearly a member of the EIH.

I halted midway down. Before I spotted the speaker, another EIH voice called, "Are the things we call evil and good really only combatants in a war from another planet?"

"Blasphemy!" Elder Perkins bellowed.

"Tell us the truth! And not kirk lies," the first EIH man said angrily.

"This is an outrage!" a woman shouted. "Arrest the EIH!"

Men in rags stood quickly. All were heavily armed, scattered throughout the meetinghouse. They were positioned so they could cover the crowd without getting caught in a crossfire. Not a good sign. The elders stood as well, and the black-clad orthodox. Voices were raised, and someone cursed. A struggle broke out in the back of the room. Mothers pushed younger children to the floor. It was escalating. Fast.

Romona Benson moved the camera from person to person in the crowd, filming.

"Thorn," a soft voice said, "you have to stop this." I met Elder Jasper's stare from three rows back. I noticed that Jasper had washed the blood off his face, then I saw that he was armed to the teeth. *Tears of Taharial.* A spurt of adrenaline raced through me.

My champards swiftly ringed around me at the foot of the dais. All three of them. It seemed I had gained a new protector. Eli was armed for bear. Or for fighting his kindred. He leveled a deadly looking matte-black gun at the crowd. Jasper was right. Only I could stop it. If it could be stopped.

I threw open my cloak to reveal the black dobok beneath, and the amulets of my office. I gripped the visa and drew on it. "Stop!" Amplified by the visa, the word rang in the tall-ceilinged room. Yelling real loud was about the only thing I had learned to do with it. That and ask it for advice in diplomatic situations. Avoiding civil war seemed to have been left out of its library, however, as it was oddly silent. Releasing some of my pent-up anger, I shouted, "Stop!" A window shattered; children covered their ears. But the crowd went still, fearful eyes on me.

"Sit down," I snarled; then, softer, "All of you." The visa throbbed in my hand, insistent, and I added, gently, "Please." The near-mob slowly settled, all but the EIH, until Eli tilted his head a fraction. It could have been a coincidence that the operatives sat as one, but I doubted it.

I looked out over the crowd, the tears that had gathered gone, my eyes hot and painful in their aftermath. I had their attention. Now what? I drew on the visa for advice, my hand holding the four-inch-diameter pink tourmaline ring. *Family, community, history,* it suggested. Well, duh. I had that one figured out already.

"This town has fought in the war against Darkness for over a century. You have stood together, friends and neighbors, on the battlefield, when many others fled in fear." I saw some heads nod. People were settling into their seats, their weapons disappeared from sight. I nudged Audric, and he sheathed his sword. The two humans followed his lead. But they didn't sit down. Good. They could be a shield in front of me and hide my shaking knees from the camera.

"One hundred years ago, when the Darkness seemed to be defeated, when the rest of the world began to divide into religious factions, when the rest of humanity turned on itself, this town met together instead. In this very building." I let my voice mellow into a soft rhythm as I spoke. Mage storytelling cant. And if most of what I said was true, so much the better. As some Pre-Ap person had said, spin is everything.

"Your ancestors—Christian, both Protestant and the one Catholic family, Jewish, and the Cherokee—sat down together and worked out a system of kirk services that was fair to all. They built a new building that had no Pre-Ap religious symbols, and yet had room for all of them." I looked across the crowd, assessing. "It wasn't easy. But they did it. And they didn't fight among themselves. You never have fought against each other, from the very beginning."

That part wasn't the complete truth about the town history, but at least no one had died while the discussions took place, so it wasn't a total lie either. "In the kirk, you all meet, at different times and days, to worship in the forms you adhere to, all in one building, the kirk, the symbol of peace, just as the seraphs instituted in the rest of the world. What the seraphs had to impose on others, you figured out for yourselves." More heads bobbed as the history of Mineral City and their ancestors took place of pride.

"You had only just settled the matter of kirk when the battle of the Trine took place. I don't have to tell you about that struggle. You teach it in grade school. Your children learn of the heroism of their ancestors and the sacrifice of Benaiah Stanhope, the Mole Man. You know your own history, your own bravery and self-reliance. That conflict, fighting alongside the seraphs, a battle fought without army troops, without air support, without high-tech weapons, but fought with faith and sacrifice, was the turning point of the war on the North American coast. Your ancestors were peaceful people who did what had to be done.

"Now the orthodox are trying to convert the progressives and the reformed. The progressives and reformed are trying to shut out the orthodox. The three Christian groups are at odds because of styles of dress, because of the foods you eat and the clothes you wear. You're dividing over the inconsequential." Heads were nodding throughout the old church building now, a few looked abashed, some were defiant. I noted who they were, and wasn't surprised to find them mostly orthodox, the religious group who had stood up against me in the past. *Tears of Taharial. What do I have to do for them to like me? Die?* Not a happy thought.

"Neighbors have begun to turn away, to refuse to speak when they pass on the street." They refused to speak to me too, but I didn't add that. I was learning to keep my mouth shut. "The Cherokee have withdrawn to the nearby hills to practice their religion, and that saddens me, because they too have a place to worship in kirk."

Because I was getting ready to tread on quicksand, theologically speaking, I took hold of an amulet that contained a shield big enough to protect my champards and me. It seemed every time I came in here I was prepared for fighting. I centered myself, ready for an outburst at best, violence at worst. "Are seraphs and the High Host really the spiritual beings, the angels, depicted in the ancient scriptures? Is the Darkness really the devils who fought against them in the heavens? Were they really defeated on a spiritual plane and cast to Earth? Or are they invaders?" Dozens of shocked exclamations sounded as I said aloud what the EIH believed. The heresy. But I had timed it right. "I really don't know. None of us does." No one screamed or jumped up and down or started civil war. No one shot at me. That was the best part.

I let a smidgen of my neomage attributes shine through my skin. Mage showmanship. "My stepdaughter assures me that I have to have faith. Mages who have no souls. Have faith," I said, making a small, sad joke. A ripple of amusement followed. And pity. *Good. Pity me rather than fear me. It might keep me alive a day or two longer.*

"The Most High offers us no power, no help in times of trouble, save the use of his leftover creation power, which is there for the taking. Only seraphs, upon occasion, provide us power to draw upon, just as the seraph Mutuol allows us to call on him for exorcism of demons from the innocent."

I considered the assembled. "Maybe the seraphs are ready to allow humans to question where they come from. We've seen some evidence of change this winter. Maybe they're ready to be asked when the Most High will show his face. They've allowed other changes over the last hundred years. TV. Pre-Ap music." I smiled. "Rock and roll." The crowd laughed softly.

"But history tells us one thing absolutely. No matter who the seraphs are, they will not allow violence"—I paused—"*between us.* Between humans and mages. Nor between humans and humans in the name of religion." I set my face in stern lines. "They. Will. *Not.*" I let my skin glow a bit, a roseate hue. My scars shone, the one at my throat bright as the face of the moon.

Slowly, I drew my longsword from its walking-stick scabbard. In my other hand, I drew my tanto, its blade the blue glow of a Minor Flame. I held it up so the entire town could see the blue glow of the High Host. "During the fight last night, seven Minor Flames came to help us. I didn't call them," I said before the question could be asked. I didn't volunteer who did. "But they came. They fought beside us. With us. And one, of its own free will, joined to this blade and helped to kill dragonets.

"With the seven Flames, we of this town once again slowed and stopped the Major Darkness that was fighting free of its bonds. A Dragon that appeared in the form of a whirlwind. It vanished but it isn't defeated; it's just delayed. It will be completely free soon, and then it will come this way, to this town. You know that." I sheathed the longsword with a scritch of sound and lowered the tanto to my side as the crowd stirred uneasily at my words.

Obligingly, Audric and Rupert stepped away a bit.

Rupert was moving with noticeable stiffness. His back had been partially repaired, but he should be in bed. I hoped he didn't pass out before we got out of here.

"We can't get out of the mountains in time, not without seraphic help or a lot of government helicopters," I said. "We're trapped."

"Fat chance the government will help us," a voice shouted from the rear of the room. "The tax base here isn't big enough for them to bother." More laughter ensued.

I said, "A couple of satellite phones and some old Pre-Ap ham radios are the only way we can reach the outside world. I understand that the army has been called, but they can send only one small group of special forces, and none before night falls tomorrow. We're on our own. We need all of our warriors, the orthodox, the Jews, the reformed, the progressives, the Cherokee, and the EIH. Like your ancestors, we have to put aside matters of dogma and religious doctrine. We have to bury the mounting hatred. We have to pull together, all of us. Or we will fall prey and dinner to that thing on the Trine." Finally, I saw some speculation on faces, a wisp of what could have been shame. And a growing alarm.

"Will you prove yourselves to be the equal of your ancestors and fight together? Or will you prove they were an anomaly? Will you fight? Or will you hide?" I stepped between my champards and down to the floor as the human congregation craned around to see. "Whatever you do, do it together. As one. As your ancestors did. Make them proud."

A knobby hand reached out to me, veins blue and knotted, skin delicate and bruised. "Will you lead us?" a fragile old woman asked, holding me with watery eyes.

Shock zinged through me. *Blow it out Gabriel's horn. Me?* I managed to keep from giggling hysterically at the thought. "No. I'm not a general."

Jasper stood in the crowd and called out, "We have to ask who among us has such training. I believe that we will find such a person here in this room. Today." He walked to the dais and climbed two steps as I moved down the aisle toward the front doors. "After all," Jasper continued, raising his voice, "hasn't time proved that the Most High puts his people where he will, ready for his hand? People of faith have always found what was needed when the attack of Darkness was imminent. And yes, *people of faith* includes our town mage."

Shock rippled through me. Tears gathered again.

Our town mage. A person of faith. As Ciana might have said, how cool is that?

As the doors closed behind us, I had a glimpse of Eli, who had stayed behind. He slipped into an aisle seat beside an EIH fighter and an elder who was a leader of the progressives. Interesting. I heard Romona Benson say softly into her mike, "Who is this mage who speaks of faith, who fights alongside humans and seraphs, who carries a blade anointed by a member of the High Host? And when will the Most High show his face to the world? Will we ever see him?"

Wrath of angels, I thought with a spurt of real fear. Romona was questioning the Most High. The last reporter to do that on air had been struck down with a deadly aneurysm.

Another quandary came to mind. I was going to be famous. *Tears and blood.* Royally ticked off about that, I followed my champards into the winter morning. The doors to the old church closed behind us with a resounding thud.

Midway down the long steps, Rupert stumbled. A mindskim flashed on as a gust of wind blew in my face and I scented human blood. I reached out. Audric caught Rupert before he tumbled to the street.

Chapter 7

I threw my cloak aside and helped Audric settle Rupert on the leather sofa in his loft apartment across from mine. Blood had soaked through the bandages along his spine, through his clothes, and down his legs into his boots. Audric cut through his saturated shirt without ceremony. The half-breed was a competent battlefield medic when needed.

He pulled Rupert's pants and boots off, tossing them to the floor in a bloody heap. The bandage, a mound along the right side of Rupert's spine, was soggy with blood, half-clotted and gummy. He had lost a lot of blood.

As Audric worked, I turned up the gas fireplaces to heat the room. In the linen chest, I found old sheets and raced back to find Audric on his knees beside Rupert. My friend's breathing was fast and shallow, his skin tinged a pale ash. That couldn't be good. How had I stood at his back and talked for so long and not smelled it? I touched the visa hanging on my necklace and wondered at the way it steered my mind into channels of its own choosing. It seemed to have a lot of authority over me and I didn't like that at all. It gave me the willies.

"Do you have any healing amulets left?" Audric asked.

"No. I'll go fill some. Fast as I can." I raced for the door, but stopped at his next words.

"No time. Wake Ciana."

My mage attributes flared up and mage-sight snapped

on, battle-ready at his tone, grim and spare as death. Ciana, Rupert's niece, had worked through the night putting injured humans under seraphic healing domes, using the pin gifted her by Raziel. She had fallen asleep at dawn, so exhausted she hadn't waked when I carried her up the stairs, undressed her, and put her to bed in the nook where she slept when she visited her uncle.

I turned on my heel and raced across the room, pulled back the purple-flowered drape that provided the girl with privacy. I stopped fast, rocking on my toes, barking my knee on the bed frame, taking in the scene in a single heartbeat of time.

Cissy lay spooned against Ciana, both girls curled under a down comforter and lavender flannel sheets. They were bathed in sparkles of soft pink light, sparkles that shifted and moved as if with currents of their own, centering in two places: Cissy's throat, where purple bruises and a single healing laceration were all that remained of the succubus' damage, and Ciana's chest, on the pin shaped like seraph wings.

There were additional sparkles on the Pre-Ap ring Ciana wore on her thumb. Marla had found the Stanhope ring in her jewelry box—imagine that—and Rupert had sized it down to fit his niece. The chunky bloodstone in its plain setting didn't look like an amulet, but it appeared to be involved in whatever the seraph pin was doing to heal Cissy. No. Not just the pin. Ciana was drawing on seraph power herself, directing the pin's energies into the wounded child in her arms. Not even a mage had that ability. And certainly not while asleep.

I remembered Lucas' words in the heat of battle. *What are we?* He had known in that moment what I fully understood now, looking at the little girl, frozen in shock for two more heartbeats. Whatever the Stanhopes were, they weren't fully human. I touched the edge of the sparkly glow and it glimmered against my fingertips, a painless twinkle.

"Thorn?" Audric said, his tension grating like a buzz saw.

But I couldn't hurry. Rupert might need this . . . whatever Ciana was doing in her sleep. *In her sleep!* I closed off the sight and extended my mind in a skim, breathing in, smell-

ing-sensing-reading her. In a mind-skim, seraphs smell like
living things and really good food and sex. Darkness smells
of dying plants, mold, brimstone, and sulfur. Humans smell
like their perfumes, the dyes in their clothes, with the underlying musky odor of males and the ripe scent or fresh-yeast
bread fragrance of females. Half-breeds have their own
odor and mages smell like, well, like mages. Ciana smelled
like sunshine on spring grass—nothing like a human child.
I pressed my hand through the sparkles and I stroked her
hair. "Ciana? Baby? Wake up, darlin'." She blinked once,
focusing up at me.

She smiled as if she knew what I was sensing. I wanted
to go deeper, perform a concentrated search on her, but
Rupert groaned and I kneeled at the bedside instead, stuffing my worry into a convenient niche in my mind. "Ciana,
Rupert was injured in the fight. I know you're tired, but is
there—"

"He's bleeding, isn't he?" she said, sitting up. "I smell it.
Kinda salty and rank, like the venison steaks Daddy cooked
last week. He soaked them in milk." She made a face and
her blue eyes met mine, innocent and curious.

Contrary to mystery books and television, most humans
can't smell blood unless it's decaying. There's no coppery
scent, no salty scent, there's zilch to the typical human nose.
I struggled to keep my reaction off my face and my voice
calm. "Yes. He's hurt. I used a healing amulet on him and
it was able to repair most of the nerve and muscle damage, but I ran out before we could close the wound. Zeddy
stitched it up, but it reopened and he didn't tell us. He's in
bad shape."

Ciana sighed and said, "Men." Her tone was so world-
weary I actually laughed. She sounded like she was eight
going on thirty-three. She sounded like her mother, Marla.

"Yeah. Men," I echoed. My stepdaughter was growing up.

She touched the seraph-wing pin and the healing glow
seemed to withdraw, coalescing into a pinpoint of bright
light beneath her fingers. She eased out from the covers,
tucking them around Cissy to keep the other girl warm.

On sock-covered feet, the flounce of her nightgown
dragging the floor, she crossed the intervening space and
crawled up on the leather couch beside her uncle. His shirt

was off, the wound exposed, and I got a quick look at it
before Audric covered it with a clean pad and applied pressure, sopping up blood.

It was a foot-long gaping wound with muscles, blood
vessels, and ribs visible in the ragged, broken flesh. The
ruptured stitches looked like black spider legs splaying to
either side. His skin was a dangerous gray, the edges of the
wound white with blood loss. I would have shielded any
other child from the sight, but Ciana was inured to such
injuries. She had helped me following two previous raids on
the town, assisting to heal the wounded, calling on domes
of healing stored in the pin, seraphic incantations I had no
idea how to use. When I asked her how she knew what to
do, she had shrugged and claimed not to know. It was a heck
of a burden for an eight-year-old and I felt more than a
moment of discomfort at asking her. But I kept asking.

Ciana touched her pin with one hand and Rupert's back
with the other. Her uncle spasmed as if struck with an elec-
trical jolt. When he sucked in a breath, it sounded wet and
somehow sticky. She pushed the bandage away and bent
over the wound, tilting her head first to one side, then the
other. From the hand holding the pin, pink and blue sparkles flowed, pinpoints of glittery light that I could see with
human vision. Mage-sight clicked on with an almost audible
snap, and the sparkles became strings of light flowing into
Rupert. But they came from Ciana's fingers, not from the
pin, which was really weird. And scary.

"Does that hurt?" I asked her. "I mean, does it hurt you?"

"A little." She shrugged. "I get tired after. The domes are
easier, but it's all out of those."

Healing domes were seraph energy constructs shaped
like upside-down bowls, a type of curative conjure that
had been permanently stored in the pin. She had figured
out how to use them all on her own. Or maybe, like my
visa, the pin had suggested the domes, a kind of interactive relationship. I wasn't sure I liked Ciana being tied to
an artifact of seraphic origins, but that hadn't stopped me
from encouraging her to use it to help the town's injured.
And I wasn't sure where the energy that powered the pin's
conjures came from, but I was guessing it came from the
cosmos itself. A lot of guessing on my part. And guessing

could mean throwing Ciana to the wolves. I was turning into a wicked stepmother, something from a fairytale.

"Bad stepmama," Ciana said with a stifled giggle.

I felt myself go cold. She had heard my thoughts.

Ciana looked up at me, the gap where she had recently lost a baby tooth a black hole in her smile. "It's okay, Thorn. It won't hurt me. And I can only hear you sometimes. I tried to hear you in the fight, and you were just a buzz in my ears. No words."

"What does she mean?" Audric asked. "This one looks deep." He pointed to a place on Rupert's back where the muscle was twisted, wrapped around a blood vessel.

Ciana put her fingers directly on the spot and pressed. The glittery pink and blue strands of light merged into a tight, shining braid and poured into the ruptured flesh. Rupert sighed as his pain began to ease. She said, "When I'm using the pin, I can hear Thorn's thoughts. And I'm out of domes because the pin has to regen—regena— What's the word? Make more?"

"Regenerate," I said. "It has to regenerate itself, and draw more power."

"Yep. From the Most High. He gives Raziel the power to make it work." She looked up at me under tousled dark brown hair. "He likes you."

"Who?" I asked. Raziel?

"The Most High."

Before I could guard my thoughts Ciana giggled. "That's a bad word. Shame on you, Thorn." Her grin faded. "It's okay. Really. I wasn't human in the first place. None of us are."

Mage-sight was already open, so I gripped the couch and opened a mind-skim, drawing in air and sensation through my nose and into my mind, blending the senses into one scan. Under it, Ciana was ... changed. She no longer coursed with human energies; instead, her body coruscated with blue light that raced just under her skin. Her aura was pink, like the domes she could open, but whispering with the blue and pink sparkles that came from her fingers. Her eyes were bright blue flames.

And beneath her fingers, Rupert was changing too. Still human, in that his body was rich with life and with what I had come to associate with normal human energy patterns, normal human chi, but through his blood vessels coursed that same blue light. Seraphic light. The energy of the holy ones.

The world tilted, and nausea rose in the back of my throat as the vertigo that came with blending scans gripped me. I stepped back and went down, sitting hard on the wood floor and catching myself with both hands. I had looked at Lucas' aura, not long after he ate food provided by the cherub Amethyst, manna or something close to it, while they were both imprisoned by Forcas in the Trine. Lucas, Ciana, and now Rupert had all been exposed to seraphic influences. And all three were changing, which humans simply did not do. Ciana said they weren't entirely human, never had been. So what the heck were they? Not mage. Not half-breeds. Not seraphs, though Ciana could manipulate seraphic energies. And talk to someone she thought was the Most High God. Psychosis? Or spiritual reality?

Audric looked at me over the back of the couch, his mouth in a grim line and questions in his glance that he wouldn't ask aloud in front of Ciana. "I don't know," I said to the unasked questions. *I don't know what the Stanhopes are.*

In response, the big man bent nearly double and gripped my wrist. With an effortless tug, he pulled me to my feet and deposited me in a chair. His look warned me to guard my thoughts, and I quickly blanked my mind, envisioning a candle flame, unwavering in the night, the first meditation technique taught to all mage children. I let the first thing that came into my mind fill me, latched on to the first litany taught mage children. *Stone and fire, water and air, blood and kin prevail. Wings and shield, dagger and sword, blood and kin prevail.*

Rupert's eyes opened and he looked at me. "Cool," he croaked. "I like that."

Somehow, I was able to keep my reaction to myself, focusing hard on the verse with laserlike precision. Rupert stretched his neck and found Audric. "Where's Death of Dragonets? I need it."

His face impassive, Audric went to a low chest and brought back the tooled leather sheath and sword, the gift he'd had made especially for Rupert to celebrate the day when he reached master status in savage-blade. My best boy-pal had been the recipient of a battlefield promotion, and now he had named his sword. Men and their toys. I shook my head, amused.

"Yeah. We're pretty weird that way," Rupert said, reading my body language, taking hold of the sword hilt. Shaken, I stood and left the apartment, closing the door on the healing, the sight of Rupert holding a master's sword, of Ciana bent over his spine, manipulating the energies of the High Host, energies no mage could use, and the image of Audric watching them both, his face closed but his body tense with some strange and awful kind of mourning. Returning to my loft, I closed the door and leaned against it, feeling tears burn their way down my cheeks. In the distance, the lynx howled, lost and lonely and full of despair.

I knew I was dreaming, the vision slipping through my mind like the mist slips across the ground in fall, just before the first snow. I was fighting, drenched in sweat, shattered by fear, struggling into wakefulness. Afraid. Mortally afraid I was going to die. Without a soul, I would simply cease to exist. Death would be forever.

With a final thrust of will, I sat up, ripping myself from the nightmare with a massive effort of will. I was sitting in my bed, dull light pouring in through the windows, shadowing everything in shades of gray, making the familiar seem foreign and malevolent. I gasped, filling my air-starved lungs, sucking breath after breath. My limbs quivered with the shock of battle interrupted. It was a dream. Only a dream.

I was left with one image. A ring of seraphs hovering, wings spread, beating the air, creating a terrible wind. Swords drawn, their eyes blazed yellow-orange-red, not the clear blue light of the High Host, servants of Light. Raziel— my seraph—and Cheriour, an Angel of Punishment, Zadkiel and his mate, Amethyst. Three more with black wings. They were attacking me. Bell-toned words of the seraphic Host ran through my mind, fading even as I remembered them. *A mage, one of the foretold ones . . . She is near.*

Definitely not a good omen. Icy, breathing hard, I lay back and pulled the covers over me, staring into the loft, hear-

ing only the soft hiss of the gas-log flames in the fireplaces
and the ticking of the black pig clock in the kitchen, seeing
the furniture and the slow-turning fans overhead, and the
red light of the answering machine. Feeling only the frigid
sheets. I was as cold as if I hadn't been in the bed for hours.
As if I'd slept naked instead of wearing long johns.

Trying to get warm, I snuggled deeper and breathed,
calming my racing heart.

I'd had the dream before. I understood the warning. I was
an omega mage. I could command seraphs in battle and the
winged warriors would obey. But if I took a single misstep,
they would destroy me. They *wanted* to destroy me. And I
had no idea why they hadn't killed me already.

I woke hours later, the sun still shining, my loft banded
with dull light from the west-facing windows. My face
was creased into the folds of the pillows and my eyes
felt gritty. I touched them, and found the lashes full of
sleep-sand. Sand, I assured myself. Not dried tears. No
way. Stretching between the sheets, I pulled on aching
joints and rolled out of bed. Stiff, I turned up the gas-
log flames before dressing in jeans and a fuzzy sweater
over the long johns. Boots completed the attire, and I
glamoured my skin to look fresher than I felt, looping
my amulet necklace around my neck, outside my clothes.
Once I would have hidden it, but no more.

I was eating a bowl of oatmeal with a sprinkle of honey-
sugar crystals and fresh milk when I heard footsteps on the
stairs. The door opened. I could have stopped him. I could
have raced and locked the door. I could have pulled one of
the weapons that I'd dumped on the kitchen table for cleaning and oiling and cut his throat as he entered. I hadn't.
Still, he shouldn't have presumed and walked in without
knocking. I welcomed the spurt of fury that warmed my
blood. I set down my spoon. "Next time you want to talk to
me, knock," I said.

"I don't have to knock. I supersede you in terms of
authority, age, diplomatic rank, and mage-power." Cheran
closed the door and leaned a shoulder negligently against
the jamb. He was wearing jeans and a silk shirt under a
corduroy vest and a new down-filled jacket. He would have

looked the height of mountain fashion had the silk shirt not been ruffled and edged with lace. "If I want this apartment, I just have to snap my fingers and the elders will deed it to me. They've already said as much."

I settled back in my chair and the grin that crossed my face showed teeth. Even through the Apache Tear, I felt Cheran flinch. "You've been talking to the Culpeppers, the kirk elder and his fashion-challenged son."

"The younger man does need the talents of a good designer," Cheran agreed with a faint shudder. "What did you do to make them hate you so much?"

"I cost them a lot of money."

"Bad form, that. It could get you killed."

"Bad form to try to intimidate me."

"Implying that such attempts could get me killed? You aren't swordswoman enough to best me."

I actually laughed at that one, my tone caustic, and he was unable to mask his annoyance. It seemed I pushed Cheran Jones' buttons almost as much as he pushed mine. "If you want the place, go ahead and try to take it. I'll tie you up in so much red tape you'll be sticky for years. Meanwhile, you'll still be in a boardinghouse, sharing the bathroom with two or three humans, trying to find ways to stay warm. I give you one full winter here before you give up and head back to the Gulf and warmer temps. One full winter, ten months of snow and ice. Spent in a boardinghouse eating stew and listening to Miz Essie chatter."

"Ten months?" Cheran actually blanched.

It made me feel really good. I felt the meanness spread through me. "Yeah. And meanwhile you'll be trying to figure out how to explain to the townsfolk that while they were battling Darkness in the streets, you were glamoured and hiding. A coward." His hands clenched and I let the nasty grin spread over my face. "Because someone, somewhere, will eventually remember that you were nowhere in sight while humans died. You could have called for seraphic intervention on your visa—something I don't know how to do—and you didn't. You could have fought alongside humans and you didn't. You could have waged a war of shields, protecting them, but you didn't. And someone somewhere will call you on it. And name you coward."

Cheran forced his hands open as if he knew he was giving too much away. "I fought. You saw my knives hit that thing. I killed spawn, dozens of them, with conjures."

"But no one saw you, did they? And I have no intention of telling them."

"You fight dirty," he said, moving toward me across the loft.

"You fight from cover, saving your own skin."

"I'm not a battle mage."

"No. You're something creepier, I just don't know what, yet. What do you want, Cheran? Other than to waste my time with empty threats. I was trying to eat."

"I want to know what you did when you looked at me in the shop," he said. He reached the table, pulled out a chair, and sat, uninvited. "When you were doing a mind-skim and then it changed."

"You never saw that before?" When he shook his head, I asked, "What did it look like? In mage-sight?"

"Hot. Gold. The way liquid gold looks when you've melted down twenty-four-carat casting grains. It seemed to pour all over you, like you had bathed in it and it was alive." His face was lit with excitement and beneath the animation was something that looked colder and darker, avarice and greed.

Suddenly I knew it wouldn't be smart to tell him. Not smart at all. I had been hungry when I sat down. Now I felt slightly sick. I pushed the bowl of oatmeal away. "You know that I was judged by Cheriour, the Angel of Punishment?" Cheran nodded. "He did something to me. I don't know what." It wasn't a lie. It just wasn't the answer to his question.

Cheran's face fell. "You can't teach me?"

"Nope." Well, I could, but I wouldn't. I had learned some things about him in the short time I had known him. He was a coward, he was secretive, and he was more than the simple metal mage he claimed. His offer to put new edges on our blades had identified him as a steel mage. The gold comment had also given him away. Most metal mages have an affinity for one particular type of metal, yet Cheran Jones seemed to be both a steel mage and a gold mage. I'd have to research how unusual the affinity for both steel and gold was. "Since we're trading information, your turn again," I said. "Why didn't you call for seraphic assistance on your visa?"

"I was told to teach you what you needed to function as a fully licensed mage and to watch you fight, if the opportunity presented itself."

I felt cold settle in my bones and my fingers dropped to touch the placemat. The texture was coarse and tough and I stroked it once as if it might purr and comfort me. "You let people get wounded, you let them die, so you could watch me fight?"

Cheran made a little hand-flap motion to show its unimportance. "They're only humans. It was imperative that I learn what you are and report back to Enclave."

They're only humans. I kept my breathing steady, schooling my face to emptiness, not letting him see how I reacted to his statement. How much I wanted to kill him in that moment. Cheran didn't seem to notice. "And now that you've seen me fight?" I asked softly.

"You have a lovely grasp of the basics, and if you had received proper training you would likely be a first-rate battle mage by now. But you forget to draw on your amulets and stored conjures during fighting and rely too much on your blades. If you ever came face-to-face with a well-trained mage in combat, you'd lose, because you would depend on steel."

I didn't like it that he was so perceptive—and that I was so poorly trained. Audric had taken over my instruction in the martial arts, but I had a decade of training to catch up on and not enough time to devote to it. Unlike mages in Enclaves, who lived off the trade of mage artifacts and services, I had to work for a living in the human world. And Audric, who had no ability to twist and use creation energies, couldn't help me with that part of fighting. I was indeed depending on blades because that was what Audric depended on. Drat. Cheran was right.

"But your biggest flaw in combat is that you care too much what happens to humans and don't seem willing to use them as they're intended to be used in battle."

"Like pawns," I said, still soft, remembering Enclave lessons learned so long ago. Lessons where mages were the generals and humans the troops. And humans died.

"Correct. Humans are disposable. You've lived among them so long you've forgotten. And, in addition to all that, you haven't reported back to Enclave about the child. Big mistake."

Ciana. He meant Ciana. "What about her?"

"She has a seraph artifact. The brooch has to be turned over to the proper authorities once we're able to leave this misbegotten town. And she summoned Minor Flames. To keep her from falling into the hands of Darkness, she has to be taken into protective custody and studied."

Fear lifted the small hairs across my flesh. My breathing sped up as the terror morphed into fury. *Over my dead body. Over my dead, bled-out, chopped-up, desiccated, rotting body. And yours.* I didn't say it, though my hands were tightening for swords that weren't there. I'd have known this was coming if I had pulverized the Apache Tear. And I could have offered him some tea with rat poison in it.

Some small part of me shuddered at the images in my mind, violent and final, Cheran in a bloody heap or dying in a toxin-induced seizure. On some level I was appalled at myself. On another, it wasn't nearly enough. I'd kill Cheran in cold blood before I let him touch my stepchild.

Had so few days of battle, of pitched combat, changed me so much? This was the second time in as many weeks that I had been ready to kill, to murder. Was I truly willing to commit a capital crime to save someone I loved? Yeah. Hell, yeah. But I shoved those thoughts down deep inside where I didn't have to look at them. "It's my right to tell Enclave. Not yours," I stated, my voice sounding remarkably calm despite the fact that my blood was boiling. Before he could pin me down I said, "I'll handle it in the next twenty-four hours." He had to give me that. And he did, with a regal nod of his head. The fiend.

Chapter 8

Cheran left just like he came in, without a word, though he did drop a sheaf of lesson plans on the table. I'd sooner read books on demonology than anything he offered to teach me. Though the incantation to kill spawn at a distance would be handy. So would the one that put out fire. Temptation was a real pain in the butt.

I was no longer hungry but I forced myself to eat the cold oatmeal. My jeans were hanging on my hips and I needed protein to restore my depleted reserves and fluids to reduce the dehydration. After the oatmeal, I drank a quart of water and grilled a veggie patty, eating standing at the sink, staring at the wall, wishing I had a window there, overlooking a mountain view. Forcing myself, knowing protein would help me think better, I opened a jar of peanut butter, carrying the half-full jar and a spoon around the loft. I ate, I tidied, but mostly I thought, running through possible scenarios on how to save Ciana.

In a little running debate, I kept coming back to killing Cheran. I didn't like it that part of me chose violence before alternative possibilities were exhausted. And it wasn't like his dying was a clean and neat solution. There was that pesky GPS locator device he wore, and the visa. The seraphs would know the moment he died and would send someone to investigate, someone with wings and a sword and a bad temper, so if I gave in to this particular temptation, I would be blasted with holy fire when the seraphs caught me. Dead in a heartbeat.

The violent part of me noted that I was smart and fast. I could plan something and be long gone when he kicked the bucket. Wryly, I wondered how accurate seraph forensics were, or if God the Victorious would just tell his winged warriors who had killed Cheran and where the guilty culprit was hiding. The violent part shut up at that one. No wonder murder had all but vanished from the list of human sins. Having talked myself out of committing murder, I felt better about myself. I wasn't a raving battle mage with a terminal case of bloodlust and an uncontrollable desire to kill. I wasn't. And I was pretty sure I wasn't becoming one either.

Mental conversation ended, I was back to—nothing. But I had twenty-four hours to figure something out, which made me feel better about it all. The entire world could change in a day. It had happened at the end of the world and the start of the plagues. Maybe Cheran would keel over twitching and bleeding and just die. That was a vision that made me grin happily.

"Who are you planning to kill and do you need any help?"

Peanut butter jar in one hand, spoon in the other, I whirled to face the door. Eli was leaning a shoulder against the doorjamb, booted feet crossed at the ankles, arms crossed over his chest, and his hat shading his brow. He looked as if he'd been there a while. "I knocked. Three times. Interesting choice of weapons."

I looked from the jar to the spoon and back to him. He looked good standing there. Maybe too good. That new, violent part of me had additional novel visions, of a less bloody, but no less physical nature. I reined them in too. The last time I gave in to physical needs, I ended up in bed with my ex-husband and that had been a disaster. I had changed the locks since, but clearly I hadn't secured them before my nap.

"You going to smother someone in peanut butter or scoop them to death? If you go for the smothering I'll volunteer to be a test subject. Soft foods have all sorts of interesting possibilities"—his lips turned up at the corners—"especially if you add whipped cream and melted chocolate. And that saddle I've been wanting to try."

"The mental picture is interesting but messy. And I just know the girl would have to clean up afterward. Why do you think I want to kill someone?"

Eli chuckled, all basso notes deep in his chest. It made things low in my belly do a little flutter and shimmy. "Better than interesting." He pushed back the brim of his hat so I could see his remarkable eyes, warm amber and gold. "You can leave all the work to me, even the cleanup. All you have to do is wear red the color of your hair and moan. Real loud. Maybe scream a time or two." His voice went up an octave. " 'Oh, Eli, enough, enough. Don't. Stop. Don't stop!' "

Grinning, I dropped the spoon into the jar where it clattered in the empty bottom. I walked to the kitchen and put them in the sink.

"And," he said, "I saw Cheran Jones leaving. From the look on his face and now yours, it looks like slaughter brewing."

I turned from the sink and braced myself, both hands on the counter at my back. His eyes strayed from my face to my chest, but only for a moment. I gave him points for effort. "Who are you?" I asked. "EIH or AAS?"

He didn't answer, and I felt, more than saw, him evaluating. "May I come in?"

Earth Invasion Heretics were, in their own way, as dangerous to nonhumans as the AAS. As likely to be enemies. But there was something about Eli Walker that I liked. I gestured to the kitchen table and poured water into a teakettle, setting it on the stove to heat. Once, I would have used a match, but today I drew on a fire amulet and the flame ignited with a little puff of sound and the smell of gas.

"Nice trick. You pull rabbits out of a hat too? Because if you do, we need a rabbit big enough to kill and eat a Dragon."

Shaking my head, fighting a smile that was at all odds with my mood, I set out teacups and offered him a choice of teas. "Whatever you're having," he said. "I'm more of a beer man." From the fridge I pulled a bottle of Black Bear Brew, twisted off the top, and held it out. The Bear Brewery near Asheville had a short list of offerings but they were all good, and I kept a varied supply handy. Unlike hard liquor, beer wasn't proscribed by seraphs or kirk.

Eli took the beer, one hand wrapping around my wrist, the other around my hand on the bottle. With a gentle tug, he pulled me and the bottle to him. Human muscle mass beat mage any day, but his grip was loose enough to give me a choice. I let myself be dragged to him. Gaze locked with mine, he drank, his encircling fingers warm, the cold bottle condensing and wet in my grip. When the bottle was half drained, he eased it away, but kept one hand curled on mine. The other he slid around my hips and pulled me close. It was a graceful dancer's move, all controlled power, fluid and lissome. His arms went around me.

I was left holding the bottle as his mouth came down on mine, our eyes still fastened together. The little things doing somersaults in my belly began to do backflips and handsprings when his mouth touched, lips wet and chilled from the beer, searching and yeasty and delicious. He melded my body to his, and my free hand went to his shoulder. His tongue touched mine and I heard myself sigh. He chuckled again, that purely masculine sound that could make a woman's nether regions stand up and beg, and deepened the kiss.

I was evil, foolish, heartless, and uncaring. My stepdaughter had been threatened, yet I was standing only a few feet from her, kissing a man who might be an enemy.

Eli was only a little taller than I, maybe five and half feet, and we fit together perfectly, his yin to my yang. Or maybe it was the other way around. But his hardness fit into my softness in just the right places.

Guiding me, he drifted us into motion, and I let him lead, dance steps that brought our hips together, apart, together, my belly just brushing his. Tension gathered in my flesh, my knees weakened, and I sighed into his mouth, not thinking at all.

When we came up for air minutes later, the beer was on the counter and we were stretched out on the couch, his body beneath mine. "I like a woman who wants to be on top," he said with a laugh that vibrated through me. I really liked that laugh. Then he spoiled it totally. "Let's get naked and party," he said.

I dropped my forehead to his chest. "You really need to work on your pitch. And I don't think so. I don't know anything about you. Except you have amber eyes and really soft hair."

He nudged my head back up and nuzzled my nose with his smiling lips. "What? You want roses and declarations of love? All that romantic stuff? I have really soft hair all over. You know that too, if I remember that incident in the street in the middle of the fight last night."

I blushed hotly and he laughed again, the rumble vaguely catlike, like a lion's purr. It seemed to rub against all the warm things deep inside me that were aching to be touched. Okay. I really *really* liked his laugh. With me pressing against him, it was a rumble deep in his chest, a growl of desire and humor, and I had no doubt that he wanted me in the worst way. Or maybe the best way. To combat the need growing within me, I asked, "So. EIH or AAS?"

The laugh eased away but his smile didn't. At some point, he had loosened my hair, and it covered us in a tumbled snarl. He took a single strand and stroked it, curling it around his finger, the vibrant scarlet contrasting on his winter-white skin. "You want to talk about work when things are going so well? Wouldn't you rather—" I rolled away from him, sat up, and he finished with, "Guess not."

I wriggled my bottom between his thigh and the couch back, my legs across his, feeling the hard shape of a gun strapped on his thigh, like a wild west gunslinger's. There was something about hard steel jabbing me that was strangely exciting, but I kept my reaction off my face. Getting turned on by close contact with guns was downright disturbing. "I don't sleep with men I don't know." I could have added that I had only slept with one man, and had married him, and that I didn't intend to sleep with another human, not ever, but that sounded a bit like a challenge and I had a feeling that Eli didn't turn away from a challenge. "EIH or AAS?" I repeated.

Eli had lost the hat and his coat somewhere and, wearing only two layered shirts, stretched up an arm, tucking his hand behind his neck. The position stretched out his chest, giving him a long, lean line. He grinned lazily when he saw the direction of my gaze, but I shook my head. "No way. Answer the question."

His amusement evaporated and he considered me, sitting beside him, my legs draping him, our thighs in intimate contact. "What do you know about the heretics' organization and the asseys? Do you know the difference?"

"Between the EIH and the AAS?" It sounded like a school question, a compare and contrast assignment. I crossed my arms over my chest. "I'll bite. One is an antigovernment, antiseraph organization at odds with every religious group on the planet, composed of poor, disenfranchised members of society, who advocate anarchy. The other is government to the core, working hand-in-hand with the Realms of Light, doing whatever the seraphs want, including tracking down and killing any unlicensed witchy-women, turning over EIH operatives to the local kirks, fighting demons and Darkness wherever they can, providing covert intelligence about the movements of Darkness to the military, and coordinating military action during conflict. And the biggest difference—asseys' salaries are paid by tax money."

"Well, there is that," he said.

I rolled my eyes. Only a little, but it got the point across.

"That's been the standard line for decades," he conceded. "But what if the EIH had evidence, real evidence, that the seraphs and demons, Light and Darkness, were really aliens from another planet, who, when their own solar system or galaxy or whatever was decimated by war, brought that conflict here."

"Solar system or galaxy. Far, far away," I quoted a Pre-Ap *Star Wars* movie line. It reminded me suddenly of the reference Eli had made about my tanto, the blade stretched with blue light. The minisword had reminded him of Luke Skywalker. How weird was that.

"Make fun if you want. Maybe they come from another dimension. But it isn't heaven or hell. Have you ever heard of the river of *time*?" I don't know what he saw in my expression, but his face went hard. "Talk to me," he said. "You've heard of it."

Actually, I had seen it. Had been there, sort of. In a series of out-of-body encounters that were more surreal than reality, experiences that kept slipping from my conscious memory like dreams. I had gone there during a kind of warfare that seemed to be fought in two places at once, on the earth as I knew it, and in another place that was all spiritual energy centered around this stream of lava-energy that the seraphs called the river of *time*. They talked about it a lot but they weren't exactly forthcoming on what it really was, or where it was, or what it did. All I knew for sure was that when I stood on its bank and joined with a seraph spiritually, in a mind-altering mystical mating, it changed the course of a battle. Because of it, Forcas had been drained and the Dragon was stopped in its tracks. I nearly died there too. I still wasn't sure why I hadn't.

I had a theory on what the river of *time* was. I guessed it was a fourth dimension, with time being the fourth. Meaning that the river of *time* could give seraphic beings access to all of time throughout the history of the universe. It was here, not here. It was Earth, not Earth. It was heaven and not heaven. It was a reality all its own.

Eli watched me. Could I trust him with what I had seen? "Assey or EIH?" I asked again. And subsequently, in one of those intuitive leaps that defied logic, my breath stopped in my chest. I asked, "Or both?"

One hand reached for my arm, the other went for the weapon along his thigh. Faster than humans can follow, mage-fast, I ripped my arm from his fingers in a corkscrew break, leaped from the couch, and tumbled across the floor, thumbing on a shield. In mage-sight, it was thousands of interlocking, overlapping purple feathers of energy. Unlike most mage-shields, this one moved with me, the feathers rippling as I dove for my blades on the end of the kitchen table.

His hand reached the holster and snapped it open. I whipped up the tanto and the kogatana, racing back to the couch, and flowed into the walking horse. Eli was still drawing the gun when his slow human eyes found me and he stopped cold. My blade was poised to cut through his liver. All it would take was a single thrust as I snapped off the shield.

Cold chills danced along my arms, raising the tiny hairs there in delayed reaction. "You're both, aren't you?" I said. "You're an assey, undercover, and you've infiltrated the EIH. Only you got sucked in with their blasphemy, their dogma, and you changed sides. You saw or heard something that made you believe them."

"Not quite," he said, holding very, very still.

Like a flower opening in time-lapse photography, it all fell together, all the things he had done and said and all the people he had spoken with. I understood. "You're supposed to bring the two groups together." He was a spy. And a freaking diplomat.

"You want to save Ciana from the AAS and the mages?" he asked, speaking at a pitiless clip, his fingers gripping the hilt of his gun, knuckles white. "You want to keep her living here, with you and her father and her uncle? Or you want her turned over to them and experimented on, tested, kept in a cell until she dies and they cut her open to see what made her tick?"

Shock flooded my system, trapping me in indecision. I wavered between flight or fight, pulled apart by opposing forces. My hands started sweating, my breathing sped.

"That's what the AAS will do, and you know it. If the neomages get her first, they'll do the same thing, except they'll kill her faster when they see what she can do. If you want Ciana alive and safe, you'll keep me alive. And you'll talk to me. You'll tell me everything you know."

"Seduction as an interrogation technique," I mocked, hating myself for having fallen for it even for a moment. Was I that lonely? "Get the sex-starved mage all hot and bothered and she'll tell you everything. Nice work."

He had the grace to look abashed for an instant before his face hardened over whatever he was feeling. "That wasn't the way it was supposed to go."

"Clarify," I said, whipping the steel to his throat. The tanto hummed softly at the nearness of the shield, the blade a fluctuating sky blue.

The shield tickled over his flesh and he pressed back into the couch cushion, but he had nowhere else to go. "Mages need sex. We all know that. And I'm not saying seduction wasn't attempted on mages in the past, but it never worked like anticipated."

"Go on."

"The human either ran like a bat out of hell or got snared and converted. Every time. Human version of mage-heat. Why do you think so few humans admitted to Enclave ever leave?"

I hadn't thought about it. I had been transported out of Enclave before I was old enough to spend time with humans or experience a full, seraph-induced, mage-heat rut myself. There was a lot about my own race I didn't know. I went for acerbic, hiding my thoughts. "I thought the rumor was that mages used them up sexually and then ate them."

"Tales to scare kids into obeying their parents and to keep teenage humans from experimenting. Like the boo-geyman." He watched my face. The clock ticked in the silence. "You don't know about the relationship between mages and humans," he said slowly. I said nothing, waiting, my blade and the shield so close they tickled his skin.

"Neomages can be . . ." He groped for words, his mouth opening and closing once before he started over. "They cause weird reactions in humans. Some humans feel anger or revulsion in the presence of mages. In others, it's this . . . this . . . weird kind of joy, maybe. They call it mage bliss. A kind of contentment just being around you. And for the humans who feel bliss, sex intensifies it. Once you're with a mage sexually for any length of time"—he stopped and swallowed, glanced down at the sword edge before continuing—"you're hooked. Not addicted exactly, but you don't want to leave."

"And for the ones who feel the negative things?" I asked, remembering people pulling away from me when I was growing up, people I wanted to be my friends, who just seemed to draw away. Remembering the recent revulsion on the faces of so many of the orthodox.

"Sex for them is always"—he groped again for words and I wondered what he hadn't said—"forceful. The AAS attracts a lot of that kind."

I remembered a comment made to me by an investigator for the Administration of the ArchSeraph when I was under arrest for a short time as an unlicensed mage. He had offered to take me for a ride as part of my intake interview. I had known what he meant. And every mage knew rape was likely to be a part of the torture if asseys ever held us prisoner. *Saints' balls.* It all fit. "So when they have a mage in their custody those are the ones who resort to rape," I said. Eli nodded, bumping his chin on the shield with a little sizzle of power, bringing it dangerously close to the blade. The Flame-augmented tanto's hum changed tone with the shift, almost as if it was reacting to Eli's movement. "And the ones who feel the good things are addicted. No wonder humans hate mages."

"It's not a true addiction," he said. "You won't die if you leave them, but you kind of . . . grieve. I've seen a guy grieving. After. It's said that when a human actually falls in love with a mage, they never leave."

Something sharp and cutting twisted inside. "Lucas did." The statement was out before I could stop it; I could have bitten off my tongue. The two little words exposed all the hurt I still kept inside, trapped like a tiger in a cage.

Eli's expression softened, and I stiffened at the emotion there. I didn't want his pity. "Ciana isn't human," he said. "Not anymore. Lucas may not be either. It may not work quite the same with them, whatever they are."

It wasn't a complete answer but it felt like the truth, or truth as he knew it, a truth that was a weighted shroud around me. Careful to keep my inflections neutral, I asked my second-biggest question. "How do you know that? That Ciana isn't human?"

"There's a little black box in my jacket. A device reverse engineered by the R and D Department of the Administration of the ArchSeraph. It's based on the sigils provided by the Realms of Light to the agency when they instituted us back in early Post-Ap times."

I didn't miss the *us* pronoun, but I stayed focused on his story. I had seen an assey's sigil up close and personal when I first met Captain Durbarge. Etched into clear crystal, glittering with seraph energies, were wings and a halo. Such sigils had been known to sparkle or glisten when mage-conjures were used nearby.

"The black box is used by the AAS to detect energy use, mage energies and seraph energies. Durbarge gave me his when we were on the Trine and he knew he wasn't coming back. I was supposed to watch you and the Stanhopes and the local EIH group and report back. But the EIH had one too, and they approached me. They wanted a parley. I set it up. My superiors met with their emissary in Asheville five days ago."

Okay, he was a spy first, a spy turned diplomat. "And Ciana?"

"With the box, I can see that thing on her chest. I saw what she did during the battle. She's manipulating seraphic energies. It's interactive with her. No human can do that."

"Mages can't either."

I saw the speculation on his face and knew I had corroborated some intel for the AAS. Me and my big mouth. Thinking about Lolo and the decades-long plan to put me in Mineral City and to free the trapped Watcher, Barak, I asked, "Your superiors in general or your superiors in a splinter group of the AAS?"

When Eli didn't answer, I said, "Hands behind your head, fingers laced together." He almost argued with me. I saw it flit through his thoughts before it was replaced with something else. Grinning that insouciant grin, daring me to watch him stretch, Eli extended his arms up, following my directions.

"I'm faster than you," I said. "You try to draw your gun again and I'll spit you like a frog on a gig." Backing slowly away from him, I let the shield slide over the hat and jacket on the floor. Blue light glimmered from the cloth when the shield energies encompassed it. With a toe I nudged the jacket open to expose a black box, three or four inches long, maybe two wide, and an inch thick. The blue light emanated from a screen on it. There were buttons and what might be an eyepiece.

Had he been around Thadd? Did he also know about the kylen or did the seraph ring Thadd wore protect him from detection? I didn't know how to ask without giving away the cop's secret so I abandoned that one for now. I sheathed the smaller blade and reached down to the coat, half expecting Eli to try to shoot me. I pocketed the device and his eyebrows went up. "Yeah, I'm stealing your little toy. Sue me." Of course if he wanted me to steal it, hoping to use it to listen to my conversations or to booby-trap me or something, then I was falling into his little assey trap. Am I a conspiracy theorist or what? But when you've been a pawn in a real conspiracy, you tend to anticipate more of them.

"Okay," I said. "We've made some progress. Not much but some." I clicked off the shield before it went off by itself. I had to recharge my amulets or they were all going to go blank. "I still don't know where you stand, with or against the seraphs, with or against mages, with or against the heretics, or somewhere in the middle of all of them."

Eli lowered his hands and levered himself upright, moving slowly, intent on my blades, careful to keep his hand away from his gun. He watched me for a long moment and seemed to make up his mind. "I'm gonna give you my weapon. I'm gonna use my left hand to reach across and pull the gun with two fingers. Then I'll put it on the floor and kick it to you. Okay?"

Not sure where he was going with this, I inclined my head. Carefully, he did just as he'd said, placing the gun on the floor and toeing it toward me. Just as slowly, he leaned back into the couch and slouched, legs splayed. "I'm with the seraphs," he said folding his fingers together in his lap, "at least until we help them defeat the Darkness. Like the Dark, they're invaders, but unlike them, the seraphs aren't currently killing us off, and they don't eat us. Other than that, there ain't that much to choose between them. Once their war is won, all bets are off.

"I'm neutral regarding the EIH, at least until I see the evidence they have to support the blasphemy. They think the seraphs will leave Earth if the Darkness is defeated. If they're right, and can prove it, and if they have a plan to defeat the Dark and make the Light leave Earth forever, then I'm on their side. And to answer your earlier accusation, no, I didn't go over to them. I was in communication with them and we've joined forces a couple times, worked together in the street fight. That's it."

I didn't believe that was the whole truth but I didn't say so. Big mouth staying shut now. When I didn't reply, Eli went on.

"And just so you know, I'm for little girls who have funky gifts and powers, and against anyone who might want to steal them away from their families or hurt them. I'm against the mages until I know what they want, but I'm for you. I think. Unless and until I learn you have an agenda against humanity. If I discover that, I'll kill you, bliss or no bliss, even if I give in to temptation first, jump your bones, and get obsessed with you. And by the way, that idiot man you married? He's hooked. Not like a human man, but he's"—Eli paused again as if searching for the exact word —

"besotted. Yeah. He's besotted. You want him, you can have him."

"He had an affair when we were married," I said, this time keeping my emotions in tight check.

"He was lured by a succubus. He was stupid and weak, but not many men could refuse one-a them fine mamas when they come calling. You may not be able to forgive him, but forgiveness is your choice, not something forced on you."

One-a them fine mamas? Forgiveness is your choice? If he wanted to disarm me with candor and his impressions of Lucas he had succeeded. I set the tanto aside, but I didn't sit down. I stood over him, watching him, feeling there was more he wanted to say.

"But there's one thing you might keep in mind. Lucas had you when he didn't know you were a mage. He had you when you didn't know you were binding him to you, if I'm reading you right. He's affected, to some extent, by mage bliss."

He didn't have to say it. I would never know if Lucas loved me for me or because of mage bliss. Because no matter what they called it, bliss sounded like addiction to me. Inexorably, as if he didn't know he was tearing my heart out, Eli went on.

"Any seraph or a mage would want you, in the right circumstances, and would take you in the street, a mass orgy you wouldn't be able to resist or refuse. The two-edged sword of true compulsion. Me? I'm not under compulsion. I know what you are. I know what would happen if I slept with you. I know it's likely that I'd give up everything I have and everything I am to be with you. I know all that and I want you anyway." His amber eyes studied me as carefully as I did him. "I knew you were something different when I saw you at early thaw, at the sun-day dance. I watched you for weeks before I made contact with you. I knew what you were from day one. I made a conscious choice to get to know you. I knew what I was doing. Something to think about. And hey. That's why no romance and roses and courting gestures. You want me, it's for me, and not for what I *make* you feel with overtures."

"And what do you want from me? Other than wild hot monkey sex?"

"I want you to ask your seraph what he's doing here, what they want, and where they came from. I want you to work with me, with the AAS, and with the EIH to defeat the Dark, and then work with us to defeat the seraphs and get them to leave Earth. And the hot monkey sex sounds like a great deal too."

I couldn't help my disbelieving chuckle. The man didn't want much. No. Not much at all. "And if there really is a Most High, and if he is the creator of the universe, and if he really does love humans, and if he really did kill off *six billion humans* as part of a cleansing and rebirth of the earth and a new age and all that? If the apocalypse was the event prophesied in every religion in history and not a takeover attempt to seize the earth? Then what?"

"If the Most High appears, or a messiah, or if evil is really defeated and paradise on earth results, then I'll lay down all resistance. If he really is God almighty, I'll bow down and worship him like the rest of humanity.

"Now, I got a question for you. Why do you think the big bad uglies are always ugly? What if they looked and smelled just like seraphs? The biggest BBUs used to be seraphs, right? Did the seraphs put an incantation on their enemies to make 'em look that way?"

I said nothing, just let the syllables flow over me. It wasn't anything the EIH hadn't been saying for years. It wasn't anything I hadn't thought before.

"What if they were beautiful like the seraphs? Which side would we go for? The side that killed six bil' of us right up front? Or the side that likes us for dinner? If one side decided to save us—really save our asses—would we care which side it was?"

Heresy. Profane sacrilege.

Truth? Finally, I looked away.

Chapter 9

And Azazel taught men to make swords, and knives, and shields, and breastplates, and made known to them the metals and the working of them ... and the use of antimony ... and all kinds of costly stones ... And there arose much godlessness ... And again the Lord said to Raphael, "Bind Azazel hand and foot, and cast him into the darkness: make an opening in the desert ... and cast him therein. And place upon him rough and jagged rocks, and cover him with darkness, and let him abide there forever. And on the Day of Judgment he shall be cast into the fire ... To him ascribe all sin."

Drinking cinnamon and vanilla tea, I reread the notes I had made not so long ago on the history of the one I now thought was the Dragon of the Trine, Azazel. I made additional notes on what I needed to ask Lolo, the priestess of the New Orleans Enclave. I had a lot of questions.

My parents had died when Rose and I were children and the priestess had taken us under her wing. She hadn't raised us, exactly, but she had overseen all aspects of our education. We had spent a lot of time in her house, being tutored by special teachers, listening to envoys from other Enclaves and to humans who came to barter or purchase services, and we hadn't spent as much time with other mage children

as we might have had our parents lived. Yet nothing I had
learned as a child had prepared me for the horror of my gift
when it came upon me.

For mage children, the ability to see and manipulate
leftover creation energies comes upon them at the onset of
puberty. Like all mage girls, I started my menses and my gift
descended, but for me it had an unintended, unexpected
consequence. My mind opened to every mage in Enclave, all
twelve hundred supernats. Every thought, hurt, fear, hope,
petty jealousy, hatred, desire, love, and need descended on
me at once. I nearly went mad. I was drugged and shipped to
Mineral City. Rose remained in Enclave until she was eighteen, when she was licensed and went to work in the Atlanta
consulate. Whatever we had been expected to become had
been lost when I nearly lost my mind. *A Rose by any Other
Name will still draw Blood*. Enigmatic to the point of use-
lessness. No one knew what the prophecy meant.

My special education hadn't prepared me for the past
winter either. I hadn't kept up my lessons in the ten years
I had been banished. I wasn't ready to fight Darkness any
more now than when I first went under the Trine. Not that
I had much of a choice.

I finished my tea and shoved the kitchen table against
the cabinets, exposing the tile floor. The tiles were stone-
ware from clay collected in Mexico, from a site near a battlefield where seraphs, humans, and Darkness had once
fought an earth-rending war. The glaze was composed
of mineral pigments Lolo had charged to my protection
before shipping them to me on a summer train. Taking
up a bag of unused salt, I poured a heavy ring in a six-
foot-diameter circle, leaving a foot of space open for me
to enter.

Around the outside of the ring, I positioned candles
scented with bayberry and juniper, to cleanse the air and
my spirit. I filled my sterling silver scrying bowl at the
sink and set it in the exact center of the salt ring, spring-
water sloshing gently. Stone amulets I tumbled at its side,
a pile all drained and needing to be charged. A shard
from the amethyst downstairs went with them, one too
small to have a fully formed eye, but still a part of the
wheels of the cherub. My ceremonial knife, in plain view

in the cutting block, I set to the side of the stones. Lastly, I pulled the *Book of Workings* from the shelf beside my bed, placing the book on the floor by the bowl in case I needed it. Into the bowl went three polished marble spheres, empty stones that could accept and store whatever energies I needed. The water lapped to its top.

I sat within the circle, at the open space in the salt ring, crossed my legs yogi-fashion, and closed my eyes. Spine erect, I blew out tension-filled breaths and drew in calming ones, again and again. There were several kinds of circles and several ways to open channels to the power left over from the creation of the universe. Because I was tired and my amulets were so drained, I was using the safest method to open one.

I'd been removed from Enclave long before I would have learned how to scry—a basic skill, but one a young neomage could learn only after her gift came upon her. I'd never practiced a skill I thought I'd never need. After all, scrying was a way to contact another neomage, and I couldn't do that. I was in hiding, so why bother? I had scried successfully only a time or two.

As I breathed, the silence of the loft settled about me. My breath smoothed. My heart beat a slow, methodical fifty beats a minute, beats I timed against the ticking of the black pig clock, the sound becoming one with the stillness I sought. All glamour fell from me. Behind my closed lids, my own flesh was a gentle radiance, the brighter glow of my scars a terrible tracery down my legs and arms. I opened my eyes, seeing now with mage-sight.

The loft pulsed with power, the bower of neomage safety I had created in the humans' world. Stones were everywhere, at bath and bed and gas fireplaces, every window and doorway, the floor. From them, every aspect of my home glowed with pale energy, subtle harmonious shades of lavender, green, rose, red, and vibrant yellow. Mage-sight saw the power of mass and energy in everything, luxons, the building blocks of the universe.

My skin burned brighter than the apartment, a pale pearl sheen, a soft roseate coral, the glow traced with the hotter glow of scars. I closed the circle with two handfuls of salt. As it closed, power seized me. Power from the beginning of time, heard as much as felt. It hummed through me, a drone, an echo of the first Word ever spoken. The first Word of Creation. The reverberation was captured in the core of the earth for me to draw upon, a constant, unvarying power of stone and mineral, the destructive potency of liquid rock and heat. I trembled as vibrations rolled through my bones and pulsed into my flesh. I could *see* the thrum of strength, the force, the raw, raging might of the earth, a molten mantle seeking outlet. Finding me, rising within me. I was a crucible for incandescent energy, mine to use. *Power.*

Because I was tired, perhaps because I was lonely, the need for power, the lust for it, rose in me, higher than ever before, calling to me, promising me everything I wanted. Promising me safety, happiness, a way to fight all Darkness and destroy the humans who wanted to hurt me, who wanted to hurt Ciana. For the first time in a long time, I had trouble fighting off the fulfillment it offered. *I could take what I wanted.* The might of the earth burned below me, writhed inside me, welding me to it. I *was* the strength of the earth, the might of the core, the power of the creation of the Most High. Temptation. To be as God is. . .

I forced my hand up. With a single motion, I slid the necklace of amulets over my head. The need receded, fled. Died. Acid churning in my belly and rising in the back of my throat, I returned to myself, gasping,

The loft was unchanged, the world unchanged, but now the power pulsing through the room was sharp and focused to my mage-eye. I swallowed reflexively, not knowing why it had been so hard this time to harness and control the stone-energy of creation. Something was wrong, I could feel it, but I didn't know what it was. The circle I had drawn looked fine, the loft looked okay. I was normal. But something didn't feel right. Exhaustion? The effect of low-level, prolonged mage-heat? I shook it off, concentrating on my breathing to settle myself.

Before I tried to scry, I drew on the creation energies I had harnessed, and dropped a shard of amethyst from the stockroom into the silver bowl. As it fell through the water, I sent out a mental call to the wheels of the cherub Amethyst. I had done this before, and the wheels made working with energies so much faster and easier. It was a shortcut, and I knew I probably shouldn't do it, and it was probably dangerous to contact and use a cherub's power base without her permission, but I was just so tired.

The wheels answered with a drone of joy and a gush of power so personal and tender that it felt like the love and affection of a mother's hands. A small smile curved my mouth and I sighed as the wheels poured power out on me, into me, filling my flesh with energy so gentle it was almost like a sedative. For a long moment, the wheels and I communed, and though they were far away, I could sense the wheels' eyes gazing at me tenderly.

As if knowing what I needed, the ship offered control of the power conversion properties of its living engine. Steadier now, I used the wheels to manipulate the energy of the molten heart of the earth, directing them and filling all the amulets on my necklace. Without the wheels, it would take hours to fill my amulets, but now, bonded as they were to cherubs' wheels, it took only minutes.

The speed was a blessing, but the payback would be a pure horror if Holy Amethyst noticed what I was doing. I had tried this after a previous battle when I needed healing from battle injuries, when I needed to fill my amulets and I was too tired and injured to do it. But I had been careless, and Amethyst had noticed. The backlash when she closed the power circuit had knocked me unconscious.

The ship crooned, its voice mellow and tender, vibrating along my nervous system, through my bones and marrow. "Little mage," it sang. "My little mage." Mentally, I caressed the wheels as I would a cat, if mages could keep pets without them eventually going feral and killing anything that moved.

The wheels increased the power flow, and when the amulets were all full, I transferred the surging energy to the empty household amulets. Utilizing the underground viaduct, I topped off the energy sink at the ring of stones around my spring out back. The wheels seemed to ripple and surge in my mind, though I knew it was probably impossible for a ship the size of a football field, one made of living amethyst stone filled with eyes, to move in the way I sensed.

"Enough," I told it softly, feeling warm and full and

slightly drunk on the might of the wheels. "Your mistress will see."

"Yours," it hummed, so softly in my mind. But it constricted the flow of power into a fine strand that twisted to a delicate point and pulled away.

"Thank you," I whispered as it withdrew, as grateful for the might it offered as for the secrecy we shared. When it was gone, even to the echo of its voice, I gathered the creation energies and my will and breathed myself into a meditative state again. Content, tranquil, I began the process of scrying.

Into the bowl, I dropped a stone, a small shard of unpolished bloodstone, a mineral I had a close affinity for. It clanged softly when it hit bottom. I added another. They settled gently into the bowl between the larger spheres of white and gray marble. When the third dropped in, a soft resonance of energy gathered, as crystalline matrix touched matrix. A faint sheen shimmered on the surface, mutable and chatoyant like liquid kyanite.

I had tried this several times before, without success. But I was not giving up. "Rose?" I whispered the incantation. "Can you hear me? Rose, hear your Thorn." The water mottled, darkened, as if light warped in lumps and bulges. The vision rippled at the bottom of the bowl, like a current in a creek, with sunlight dappling over smooth sand. I heard a roar, like howling wind in a storm. It lasted only a moment. A single heartbeat of time. The surface cleared.

Disappointment scoured my heart like steel wool. I had seen moments of visions in the last weeks, while trying to scry for my twin, and like this one, they had been out of focus, blurry, confused. But I kept trying, and had promised myself that I wouldn't give up, my hope bolstered by the memory of both Light and Dark claiming my twin was alive. Forcing away the frustration, I settled myself again and, when calm, began to scry for Lolo.

"Sea and shore, jazz and dance, I search for the priestess of Enclave," I said, repeating the incantation several times. It was a simple mantra as conjuring went, and the lack of scripture made it less powerful, but more focused. Simple seemed best. With my pitiful level of training, I was less likely to mess up and do a truth read or some other conjure

by accident. I had done that before and it wasn't fun. On the
seventh repetition of the verse, the water in the silver bowl
began to glisten. It thickened, forming a dark, mirrored surface. It didn't cloud or become opaque, but it was as if all
the light began to vanish, as if a silver cloud rose from the
bottom. I kept up the words and rhythm of the incantation,
syllables soft and cadenced.

In the water, kaleidoscopic images swirled, cool greens
and warm creams, mellow shades of butter and amber and
the gold of sunlight on yellow roses. These were not the
rich shades of ruby and emerald I associated with Lolo. The
image began to sharpen into a sunlit room, walls painted
shades of sage, rosemary, and moss, with cream moldings.
A huge vase of flowers, roses and buttercups and freesia
against darker green fronds, sat atop a round inlaid wood
table. Over it a fan turned lazily, the air moving the flowers
in an artificial breeze.

Beside the table, reclining on a yellow chaise lounge that
was centered in a conjuring circle, was a woman. She stared
at me through the water and the miles, unsmiling, her face
giving away nothing except beauty and hauteur. Instantly
I felt like a bumbling country bumpkin in the presence of
royalty. She was elegant in gold silks and lace, her formal
mage-clothes embroidered in the leaves and flowers of her
gift. By her clothes I knew she was an earth mage with an
affinity for living things, one of the rarest and the most difficult to control mage-gifts. With it, one could heal or kill,
bring life or destroy it. She was staring at my scars, and
though her expression didn't change, I sensed her revulsion.

I fought the urge to raise my hand to cover my face and
throat. The visa throbbed with a rhythm of suggestions
and information and I recoiled. This was a consulate situation? *Seraph stones. Who had I contacted?* "I offer apolo-
gies for disturbing you," I said, following the visa's lead as
to proper protocol for a scrying mage. "I am Thorn, of the
litter of twins, licensed stone mage out of the New Orleans Clan, abiding in Mineral City in the mountains of the
Carolinas. Hail to Adonai. I was searching for the priestess
of Enclave."

"You found her," the woman said. She had a beautifully

modulated voice, mellow and serene. "And I know who you are. Speak."

"Forgive me. I searched for Lolo, the priestess of the New Orleans Enclave," I clarified, running over in my mind the words I had used in the calling. I hadn't mentioned Lolo's name, and I hadn't specified the New Orleans Enclave. I had screwed up again, calling for any priestess who liked music and lived by the sea.

The woman's voice grew hard as petrified wood. "You have found her," she said distinctly. "Speak."

Shock made my breathing speed up and my heart trip unevenly. "Lolo?" I whispered.

"The former priestess is in retirement." There was an edge of satisfaction in the words. I had no idea how to react to that but it seemed politic to ask after Lolo's health. When I did, the mage on the lounge flicked her manicured fingers as if tossing away something useless and said, "The old priestess is unwell. She suffered an apparent stroke during an unanticipated mage-heat rut." She turned her leaf-green eyes to mine, stroking honey-blond hair back behind her ears. She was about my age, maybe a bit younger, early twenties.

Unanticipated? Ruts were scheduled and planned, to prevent chaos and to keep bloodlines pure. An idea flickered in the back of my mind, but I didn't know how to ask my questions without getting burned. This mage was all sharp edges, like saw grass in a marsh, cutting and brittle. I said, "The date of this rut? Was it within the last three weeks?"

The priestess's pale brows lifted. "It was."

I took a deep breath, stabilizing my oxygen intake. "Was it caused by an unscheduled visitation by Barak, the Watcher, to Lolo?"

She reacted by the merest tightening of her lids. And I knew. I had freed Barak from his captivity and he had gone directly to Enclave, against all edicts of the Seraphic High Host, the ruling council of seraphs. Seraphs caused mages to go into heat. Mages had the same effect on seraphs. It could get ugly if it happened without proper precautions in place.

After an unnerving pause, she said, "Yes."

That was short and sweet. I tried another question. "Forgive my ignorance. I ask a point of clarification. Is Lolo also the one called Daria, the first mage to lie with a seraph and produce a litter of kylen?"

The priestess, who hadn't bothered to tell me her name, tilted her head, a small smile on her wide, coral-tinted mouth. "Old history. Barak has been chastised for his presence here. The Watcher claimed to have been prisoner of a Power of the Dark for many decades, and to be unaware of the edict against seraphs in Enclave." She lifted a negligent shoulder. "All know a Watcher has no need or coercion to speak the truth of the Most High. But the Watcher left willingly, when he saw the havoc he was creating, including Lolo's seizure."

Seizure? A coldness settled in my chest. Across the loft, my eye was caught by a faint green glow. Barak's flight feather, a talisman of great power, freely given, was shining with lustrous energies, reacting to something, but I didn't know what. The scrying? The conversation? His name? The presence of a charmed circle? I took it as a warning, though I didn't really need one. "He left willingly?" I asked. "So the seraphic council didn't imprison Barak for his visitation?"

"They did not. But they asked many questions when they scried us. They have uncovered a conspiracy by the former priestess," she said, a barely contained glee in her words, "one that jeopardized all Enclaves. It is believed that you are in the center of this intrigue."

Careful, the visa throbbed at me. *No kidding,* I thought back. This mage didn't like me. And she was Lolo's enemy. *Meekness,* the visa suggested. I could do meek. Unless I got riled; then my mouth tended to run away from me. "Me?" I asked. "How can I be involved in any Enclave plot? I am the least of my kind." This was true from several viewpoints, formal mage training uppermost, pecking order in any Enclave next, and consular assignments last, though I hated to sound so pathetic. Yet, the visa was right. Humility, even false humility, would help me most here, if I could keep my temper long enough to feign my way through it.

"True," she said. "You are from an abnormally small litter. Only twins. And all know that small litters often result in weak and unworthy offspring."

I wanted to slap the woman for the insult, but I kept

my face immobile. If she was testing me, I needed to show restraint. If she was really this stupid, I could learn more by curbing my temper than by giving in to it. And if she had reached the position of priestess at such a young age, she wasn't stupid. But I felt my back molars grind.

"However, though from an atypical litter, you *were* created by Lolo, who locked your parents together during a rut." She was watching my reaction to see if this was new information. It was, but for reasons I couldn't articulate, I didn't want her to know that. "There is evidence that the mating was against their desire, as both were paired with others at the time, and further evidence that they were brought together by a love incantation in the hopes of more litters."

I remembered seeing a love potion in the *Book of Workings. Blood and plagues.* What had Lolo done? Such crimes carried ghastly penalties. When I didn't speak, she went on.

"What do you know of her plans for her offspring? If you provide us with answers, you may be spared punishment when you return, after your visa runs out next year."

Return? I had no plans to— *Her offspring?* I thought back over the conversation. Had my parents been of Lolo's lineage? Daria had born both kylen and pure mage children. Were Rose and I of Daria's mage lineage? Yeah, that's what the smug little priestess was insinuating, and that opened up an entirely new strategy for this conversation. Because if I was of Lolo's line, I was genetically superior to the little twit baiting me from afar.

I let the idea settle into me. I had never looked up my genetic ancestry, though all mage family trees are carefully cataloged. Mage heat could cause mating too closely in a direct family line, so most mages have a thorough knowledge of their lineage, down to the human, Pre-Ap ancestors. I never expected to experience a rut so I hadn't bothered to learn my own. And even had I looked myself up, I hadn't known that Lolo and Daria were the same person, making it impossible to comprehend the connections.

The mage was still speaking and I dragged my awareness back to her. ". . . with a small cadre of seraphs to affect the course of developing mage powers and gifts. If you tell me all you know, I would be willing to stand for you before the mage council when you present your defense for leaving Enclave without authorization."

I had missed something, but I recognized the carrot and stick. I was being herded and I didn't like it. I put aside my qualms about speaking out of turn and said, "Priestess, what is your official title?"

The woman blinked. She had been rude and officious, and now the ugly, scarred, and provincial mage was calling her on it. A mage who had to outrank her. Had to. *So that's why she's all prickly.* The priestess sat up slowly in her chaise and stared at me through the surface of the mirrored water, trying to intimidate me with her influence and position.

I had been stared at by a Major Darkness. There wasn't much that a less powerful being could do to me. And that had to tick her off too. I raised my brows and allowed a bit of my own power to shine through the scrying. Her shoulders went back, and the pearly flesh beneath her silk lace blouse glistened. "Thorn of the twins, of the line of Daria, I am Élan, of the litter of seven, of the line of Eugene." She put peculiar emphasis on the name, as if he held some special importance. I had some research to do. "I am an earth mage and acting priestess of the New Orleans Enclave," she said, adding the last line almost unwillingly.

Acting priestess? I smiled at her. I didn't need a mirror to know it wasn't a pretty smile. Her face hardened like old wood, polished and smoothed. The gloves had just come off. Whatever this woman had against me, her antipathy had surfaced and multiplied. Lucky me. And so much for humility.

Lolo's line is preeminent, the visa confirmed, a tiny pulse of information.

Feeling myself on surer footing, I said, "Priestess Élan, I didn't leave Enclave without the consent of the council, I was drugged and smuggled out, banished by the former priestess when I was still a child. If there is sin, it wasn't mine, as all children are innocent." I was parroting mage law. Audric had prepared me for this accusation, knowing it would come once I was found out. "I am properly licensed," I continued, though there was a time when I hadn't been, which made it a sticky situation, "and my visa and GPS locator device were provided by the Angel of Punishment Cheriour himself"—which she well knew, as it had been reported on SNN. "They are both in working order and were presented when requested by the town fathers of Mineral City. There will be no trial," I said.

"Accusations have been made that you were in the human world for some time before the appearance of the angel, living without diplomatic sanction," she said, her tone laced with satisfaction. Yeah. She wasn't stupid. "Additional charges have been laid that you went to war against a Major Darkness without Enclave permission."

I needed permission to fight evil? "My champard will answer all charges when I am brought before the entire council," I said, with emphasis on the word "entire." Her lids flickered again. I refused to be judged by a small cadre of neomages. As a mage in the human world, it was my right to ask for a full ruling, and she knew it.

If Lolo's line was preeminent, then maybe that offered me another opening in the little battle of wills and knowledge. But it meant taking a chance. I raised my chin slightly and let my mouth soften. "I was not notified that Lolo was ill and that her duties had fallen to another. You are kind to take such onerous responsibility from my shoulders until I return."

Her eyes tightened and lips thinned. *Bingo!* Now I knew why she was so bitchy. That knowledge gave me more options and confidence. I wasn't powerless in this battle of wills and words. And it helped that she was a lot less beautiful when she was being backed into a corner.

"Should I decide to give up my place in succession to the position of priestess," I said, "I shall consider all your service at this difficult time." *Carrot and stick right back at you, you little witch.* They couldn't pay me enough to take that job, but she didn't have to know that.

While I had her off balance, I could take the chance and confirm my conclusions about who and what I was. I said, "It has been brought to my attention that Rose and I, while only lowly twins, were bred to be the first battle mages who could join mentally with seraphs, without physical mating, in the fight against evil. We would become a new weapon in the war against the Dark, a weapon that would provide new war strategies to the High Host. Surely the current council concurs with the historical record." Assuming there was one.

Reluctantly, Élan nodded, and I said, "Bred to fight, under the aegis of the previous council, I did not require the permission of the current council to fight Darkness. Especially when seraphs fought with me under mage-in-dire regulations."

For an instant, the priestess's expression blanched. And then she smiled, sweetly, cruelly, and I knew I was about to be sucker punched. "You are better versed in your history and purpose than we had supposed. But you are an orphan." The blow went home with breath-stealing force. *I am alone.* "You have no littermates, no parents, no litter of your own. No mage but our emissary with whom to mate, none but filthy humans with whom to breed powerless *mules*. You are unworthy to be priestess. You have no family to draw upon, no power base to support a claim on my position of command. You are *nothing*. And you are far away from Enclave."

Bruised at the truths she threw, I felt anger rise in me. Without thought to the consequences, I said, "All true. But I have bested a Major Darkness in mortal combat. I have fought shoulder to shoulder with seraphs. There are no reports of mages, *except for me*, fighting the Dark in more than a lifetime. You, like all the mages in captivity, are soft and weak and beautiful, but utterly useless at anything but being a pawn of seraphs or stronger mages." Her mouth opened in shock and I felt a brutal joy at her reaction. "I carry a seraph stone, freely given by Zadkiel, battle companion of the ArchSeraph Michael, and a flight feather gifted to me by the Watcher Barak." I leaned in while I had her off balance and said, very softly, very distinctly, "And I am linked to the wheels of one of the cherubim. If I want your pitiful little job, witch, it is mine." *And my sister is alive, curse you. A seraph said so.* But I didn't say it. I had that much self-control left to me.

Outside my conjuring circle, outside my loft, far up the Trine in the ice and snow, the lynx howled. The omen of danger. I flinched. What had I said? What had I just done?

Plagues and blood, I thought. I had just declared political war against the acting priestess of the New Orleans Enclave. *Me and my big mouth.*

"You are rude and untutored and coarse," she spat at me, her beautiful face twisted with malice. "A barbarian, ugly and scarred. I will challenge you to personal combat for this position should you ever be foolish enough to contest my right to it. And you will lose, no matter what seraph power you have in the human world." With cruel delight she said, "Seraph energies are barred from this place."

I tightened my hands in my lap. I had forgotten about that. *Stupid, stupid,* stupid.

"But because I am magnanimous and because the ruling council dictated there should be one year of active service before I am confirmed, one year before I am formally approved as priestess, I will share with you their advice. Do with it what you will, provincial as you are. *Trapping Darkness in Stone.*" With that enigmatic little phrase, she raised a hand and dropped something. The surface of my conjuring bowl went opaque.

Chapter 10

A sharp clap made me jerk. I swiveled on the now-warm tile and saw Audric sitting on the couch. He clapped again. And again. The rhythm was mocking and insulting. Knowing I had been an idiot, I broke the circle, the energy that powered it feeding back with a little snap and buzz along my limbs. Audric studied me, face impassive. When he didn't speak, I stood and began to put away the accoutrements of the conjure, my face burning with embarrassment.

I swept up the salt and dumped it in a large plastic bag labeled CONJURES, USED, put away the candles and stones. Finally I placed the *Book of Workings* on its shelf and carried the silver bowl to the kitchen sink, where I drained it. I laid the stones on the cabinet on a towel to dry, and polished the bowl with a soft rag. When I had nothing else to occupy my hands I forced my feet across the room to the rocking chair and sat. The chair seat was upholstered, wood arms carved in lion claws. And still my teacher said nothing. When I couldn't stand it any longer I said, "Two questions. How long were you listening? And just how bad did I screw up?"

"I entered as she was telling you about Lolo's state of health. And very badly. You were a fool."

I flinched again, ducking from his contempt. "I'm sorry. I let my mouth run away when she insulted me."

"And now the acting priestess knows your weakness:

pride. You have declared war on her and given her a weapon to use against you. You boasted away your greatest strength. The wheels. A strength you did not trust your champards with," he said sadly. Shame washed through me. After a pause, Audric said, "Have I misunderstood? Do you wish to be priestess?"

"Plagues and blood! No!" I exploded. I stood again and walked to the kitchen, to make a second pot of tea, to busy my hands. "Sit around all day in meetings and listen to self-important mages and humans conduct trade negotiations? Set policy for the Enclaves? Keep a circle open just so communication is available? Have to ride to the nearest human town to make a simple phone call or check the Internet? Mate where and when they tell me to? Spend all my time building political power? No way, Audric."

I heard him release a pent-up breath. "But you will have to return to Enclave someday. And now you will be forced to either make obeisance to Élan or fight her."

I put the kettle on the stove, braced my elbows, and hung my head. *Stupid, stupid, stupid.*

"It is time to begin protocol lessons. We will begin with dance. Come here."

I raised my head. "The town is sealed off from outside help. The Dragon is free, or almost free. I may have no choice but to call mage in dire again, and risk killing every human in town, and you want me to *dance*?"

"When emissaries reenter Enclave from the outside world, they are expected to enter correctly. Do you know the routine? Do you know the steps to properly approach the council? To approach the priestess? Can you perform a full court curtsy, head to the floor, hands up and out to the sides like wings, knees close together, body bent tight? And rise without aide? In a dress? You have declared war. I intend to give you the weapons." He stood and rolled the rug back from the living space. When he straightened, he said, "Come here."

I cursed. Audric laughed. And then he made me dance. For an hour he worked on foot placement, which, oddly enough, was a lot like the foot placement in fighting stances. He made me do hip slides and circles and a rhombus circle, which was a highly sexual move with a little belly cant and thrust, as if I was throwing a coin out of my belly button. He made me do camel hips, which was a joke, skinny as I am. He made me watch in mirrors as I did chest slides, and I looked like a monkey hit by a Tazer. The chest thrusts I tried were pitiful, as I had no boobs, and my chest circles were even worse. I couldn't do snake arms worth spit. But when the lesson was over, I felt looser and calmer and I could think better, my mind no longer fuzzy and mushy. As punishments for shooting off my mouth went, it was relatively painless. I thought I had gotten off well. Until Audric informed me I had to appear before the town fathers to plan for the defense of Mineral City. I had been summoned, and he hadn't bothered to tell me. Now I was late. Cheeky mule.

With my champard's help, I dressed in full battle dobok, all my weapons and amulets in place. When I let my neo-mage attributes blaze freely, Audric asked, "Are you sure you want to do that?"

"Yeah," I said, looking at myself in the mirrors of the armoires. "I'm tired of hiding my light under a bushel."

Snorting with amusement at the New Testament reference, Audric followed me down the stairs and across the street. The sun was setting, a bright red orb low in the sky, tinting the clouds pink and gold and fuchsia. The eastern sky was plum-colored, and long shadows striped the ground. The snow picked up the reds in the sky, and the town was rosy with reflected light. But my breath puffed, and even through my gloves, my fingers felt the cold. My feet, still tender, ached with every step on the icy street.

"Watch your big mouth in here," Audric said as he opened the door.

The smells of yeast, sugar, cinnamon, and fresh bread hit me in the face with a mingled scent that smelled like peace and calm and home. Not war. My mouth watered. Four elders—Shamus and Ernest Waldroup, Culpepper, and Jasper—were sitting at a table in the back corner of the bakery, drinking from chunky mugs. A loaf of bread rested on a bread tray with a serrated knife. A tub of butter sat to one side.

The most senior fathers were dressed in casual clothes,

gray and black tunics and leggings, their brown robes of
office thrown over the chair backs. Two of the men wore
visible bandages. Shamus, a thick slice of bread in one bony
paw, waved me over. Ignoring Culpepper's annoyed look,
Audric took up a place near the front windows, his back to
the side wall so he could see both the table and the street.

"I don't know what I'm doing here," I said as I hooked a
foot around a chair leg, pulled it from beneath the table and
sat, "but I'll help any way I can."

Without preamble, Shamus set aside his bread and began
clearing the table. He said, "As the sun sets, fires'll be lit at
every street corner. We'll have patrols on snow-el-mobiles
making circuits through the streets." He unrolled a map in
the cleared place and put their coffee cups on the edges to
hold it flat. "The fire truck's goin' here." He pointed to an
intersection at the top of a hill. "Every family with a wood
roof has been moved to the meetinghouse. The slate roof
and stone walls will provide fire protection. We got plenty
of ammunition. It came on the train with your mage friend,
and the EIH is busy loading a store of rounds with Dead Sea
salt. Double-aught buckshot and salt." At my raised brows,
he said, "We have a common goal. Survival. The kirk has
agreed to work with the heretics until this crisis is over."

"Then you'll go back to hunting them down and branding them on the cheeks?" I asked. So much for watching
my big mouth.

Culpepper reared back in his chair, disgust on his face. "I
told you she would be impossible to work with."

"She has a point," Ernest said. "And our hypocrisy and
lack of compassion for others' views will be addressed when
this is over, if we survive it. For now, let's look at the placement of snipers and sentries with radios. If anything un-
toward is sighted, word will be passed via radio and the kirk
bell will be rung as an alarm. No one will leave his post to
investigate; instead, men will come from the meetinghouse
to survey the problem. Jasper?"

The young elder supported himself on one elbow and
pointed to buildings on the map, indicating porches and sec-
ond-story roofs, detailing where everyone was positioned.
It all seemed pretty straightforward but I still didn't know
why they needed to talk to me. When I said so, the men

looked back and forth between themselves. After the silent decision, Jasper took the lead. "We know about the ward on your home. Can you, maybe with the help of that new mage, make one big enough to cover the town?"

"And how much would it cost?" Culpepper said scornfully.

I'd had enough scorn for one day. I boosted my attributes higher, making my skin glow with a fierce light. My voice cold as an ice cap, I said, "If I could protect the town I would have. For free, Elder Culpepper." The older man looked away, frowning. "But I can't. That kind of incantation takes a number of mages with synergistic and related gifts, or littermates who have found ways to meld their disparate gifts into a single function." I could tell they weren't understanding. "It takes more than two mages. Maybe seven or twelve working for several days. Cheran and I don't have gifts that would mesh or meld for any kind of working. But I do have these."

I pulled a dozen polished quartz stone rings off my necklace, each circular with a central hole. "I filled some illumination amulets. You can give these out to the sentries. I've charged them to activate at onset of full night. Have the guards tie them to long strings and hide them in a pocket so their night vision isn't compromised. If they need to see something at a distance, they can toss the amulet to the limits of the string and pull it back after."

I added twelve additional amulets to the pile, these made of various different stones, but none of them quartz, so that even the least familiar with minerals could tell them apart. "Healing amulets. You can give these to the fire and medic brigade."

"Not enough," Culpepper said. "We need protection for the entire town and you're holding out on us. How much do you want, mage?" He made the last word an insult. "What cost for your help? Our blood?" His face twisted with abhorrence. "Our young men?"

I stood, letting the chair legs scrape the floor, barely stopping myself from drawing a blade. The fathers froze at the faster-than-human movement and the screech of wood on wood, even Culpepper falling silent, realizing he had gone too far. Switching my gaze back and forth between the Waldroup brothers, I said, "I can't ward the whole town. I'm not powerful enough. No mage is. But I can fight. Do you want my champards and me in place for defense, or does working with former enemies not apply to mages?" I heard Audric sigh in exasperation, but I didn't care. I was beat up, used up, and worn out trying to keep this town safe, and the town fathers were bent on hatred.

"You are *our town mage*," Shamus said gently. "Just because some are trapped in the smallness of their own minds doesn't mean we don't need you." Culpepper had the grace to flush at the senior elder's soft reprimand. "We need you bad," Shamus said. "I believe it's why the seraphs gave you to Mineral City for a full year. You're part of the mercy of the Most High."

Suddenly I had no place for my hands. I balled them and stuffed them into my pockets. The Waldroup brothers and Jasper wore sober faces, and an underlayer of fear rode their souls. Culpepper stared at the far wall, not meeting my eyes, but at least his hostility was reined in. I let my attributes die away and retook my seat.

Shamus said, "We need all our fighters. We want you to rest until an attack. Experience says Darkness seldom attacks two nights running. No need for you to waste your-selves until the fighting starts again. And who knows? The army may find a way to get troops in here." Culpepper made a derisive noise in the back of his throat. I hated to agree with him, but I did.

"We do have one favor to ask," Shamus said. "Since you can't provide a ward for the entire town, would you be willing to allow the children to sleep in your shop until things return to normal?" I blinked and swallowed a reflexive refusal. "Parents can't fight when they're worried about their young."

Sweet Hail Mary. They're serious. "How many?" I asked, panicked by the petition, amazed that my voice didn't squeak like a trapped squirrel's. It was a reasonable request, but I couldn't imagine how we'd get all the town's children in the shop. It would be standing room only. It would be a madhouse. *Spawn balls.*

As if he couldn't see the terror blooming in my eyes, Sha-mus said, "Only those twelve and younger. About seventy indicated a desire to take advantage of the shelter."

Seventy kids under the age of twelve? I was pretty sure the shock showed on my face. I could hear Audric laughing under his breath.

"They'll provide their own cots and bedrolls," Shamus continued, "and the younger ones will double up, two or three to a cot. Some adults will stay over to care for them. I've seen your shop. It'll be tight, but they'll fit."

He had thought it through, and I didn't miss the verbs. Will, not might or could. Either he had known I'd say yes or he intended to insist. And clearly plans were already under way.

"I offer the shielded floor space in my storefront," Audric said from the door, not bothering to hide the humor in his voice. "There are also spaces in the stairwell at the top and the bottom of the stairs, though that area isn't heated. And there is room for more in the dress shop next to mine. Thorn's ward covers it as well, and I am certain the owner will allow the children to stay over. Together, we can easily accommodate seventy children." Audric laughed aloud. "It will be my mistrend's pleasure."

And then I understood. This was my punishment. And it would be ongoing. Seventy wild, unfettered, untamed kids running amok in my life. *Seraph stones. Death and plagues. Blood of the saints!* There weren't enough curses available for the horror. The men were still talking, this time about war, and now Audric was in the middle, offering suggestions as to tactics, weapons, and placement of prayer warriors for future battles. I just dropped my chin and sank into my misery. Seventy kids.

The sun was below the horizon, the sky deepening to plum and cerulean velvet when I crossed the street, Audric on my heels, and reentered Thorn's Gems. Bells clanged over the door and a roar blasted out. I stopped in the doorway. A fast scan showed me there were a couple dozen children and three adults in the display room, three toddlers chasing one another, arms outstretched, squealing. Bundles of supplies and bedrolls were tucked in the corners. Toys, dolls, stuffed animals, and cots lined the walls. Savory pork stew bubbled on the stove.

"Seraph stones," I whispered. They hadn't wasted any time. Audric chuckled under his breath and I resisted the urge to sink an elbow into whatever body part was closest. I managed a smile and a wave at Jasper's wife, Polly, who raced from the fireplace and enveloped me in a breath-stealing hug that rammed my head between her breasts. I felt myself flush with embarrassment even as I suffocated.

"Thank you, thank you, thank you," she said from over my head, rocking me back and forth, smothering me. "Thank you again and again and again."

Gently I pushed her away, filling my lungs, the grin I had faked becoming real. "You're welcome," I said. Okay. This wouldn't be so bad. I liked Polly. We could have tea. Visit. "The bathroom is in the back. It's clean. The floor isn't well insulated and gets cold, so keep the gas logs up high. Keep a kettle simmering so the air doesn't dry out too much. And keep the kids away from the hot stove."

"You sound like an old mother hen," she said, squeezing my shoulders.

My flush deepened and I patted her arm, turned, and looked right into the lens of a camera. I caught myself before I cursed on live TV, but it was a near thing. Romona Benson, camera on a shoulder, stuck a mike under my chin. "You found a way to provide mage protection over the two buildings here." Behind her, the door opened with a jaunty jangle and a stream of kids entered. I stared at Romona, who was blond, like Polly, though with the polish of the big city. "Can you tell us why you can't cover the whole town?"

I could feel my smile freezing into a semisnarl. Audric, sensing that I was about to make a blunder, stepped up beside me. "My mistrend is working at the full extent of her gift. A ward for an entire town requires many mages working together." Before she could ask, he said, "The two mages in Mineral City have gifts that do not meld well."

Another voice took up the narrative. "And so, Thorn St. Croix of Mineral City is offering Thorn's Gems, and Darlene Smythe is opening her dress shop next door, making available all the buildings that are protected by Thorn's ward," Rupert said, stepping between the camera and me. "The children and the elderly of the town may sleep in safety for as long as needed."

The elderly too? I fought the need to sit down fast. So much for being asked to provide space. Someone sneaky had planned all this behind my back and the town fathers had dumped it on me. Looking at Rupert, I had a good idea who.

"Her champards will be bunking in with her," Rupert continued. "I have offered my loft, also under protection, to accommodate the numbers." He swept out an arm and the camera followed the motion, Rupert leading Romona into the human clutter. My friend and partner was dressed in navy robes, the cut made popular by the seraph Uriel, when he visited the White House last fall. His eyes were ringed with navy and his hair was loose on his shoulders. He looked fully healed. And spectacular. And very dramatic as he stared into the camera, gesticulating, talking.

However, I smelled blood and knew his back was still a problem. He ought to sit down, but I wouldn't spoil his fifteen minutes of fame by pulling him to a chair. Instead, I used the opportunity to slip upstairs to my loft. There were humans in the stairwell, preteens using the relative privacy to huddle and giggle, and still more in Rupert's loft, adults dividing up space and laying out bedrolls. I nodded weakly to them, slid into the privacy of my own loft, and closed the door, sinking against it. This sucked Habbiel's pearly toes.

It wasn't quiet. The building was old and the walls were thin, and the muted roar of many voices, punctuated by the occasional high-pitched scream, made their way through. Even here it was chaos, Rupert's and Audric's things piled in front of the couch, weapons and clothes and what looked like Pre-Ap board games, Scrabble, Yahtzee, a pack of playing cards. "Blow it out Gabriel's horn," I said. "I'm in hell."

Feeling trapped in my own space, I draped the amulet necklace over a chair back, changed into jeans and a fuzzy sweater, opened the *Book of Workings,* and looked up Trapping Darkness in Stone. The *Book of Workings* was constructed of blackberry ink on handmade paper. The book itself wasn't a thing of power, not a book of spells or incantations, nothing so mundane, only a guide, a map of sorts, showing mages the path to our gifts. It was divided into thirds and the directions for the incantation were in the final third of the book, the section dedicated to warfare.

I seemed to be studying that part of the book often these days.

I had always believed that incantations seldom used blood for conjures, but had discovered that really difficult workings required either several mages or blood, though never on the full moon, which made it black magic. It was only the easy conjures, the daily incantations for cooking or heating bathwater or illumination that could be done with just the mind. If I had studied the book like Lolo had wanted for the ten years I was banished, I would have known that. There was so much I didn't know, so many misconceptions. I needed a teacher.

Cheran Jones came to mind, and I flipped through the sheaf of papers he had left. Nothing I could use. Mostly cryptic notes that hinted at solutions to several neat incantations, but nothing with a big arrow that said, "Do it this way!"

I could ask him, beg him, to teach me how to use the visa to call for seraphic help, but he hadn't done so himself last night, when his own life was in danger. Maybe there was some prohibition against calling for help, like the proscription from calling mage in dire unless a human innocent was near death, or a mage's life was threatened by humans or Darkness. Or maybe he was telling the truth. Maybe he was here to watch, judge, and teach me, but that didn't include saving humans in danger. There wasn't time now, but I would go to him in the morning and ask for his help. A small part of me insisted I didn't have to like him to let him teach me.

But for now, I had nothing, absolutely nothing, and a Dragon, a Prince of the underworld, was coming. Threads of true fear coiled under my skin, burning with cold. I stared at the incantation suggested by the new priestess.

Trapping Darkness in Stone was an incantation for seven mages. Big help there. It needed a lot of power. A *lot*. Power I didn't have. Unless I drew on the Trine again. Or on the wheels. Or commanded seraphs to help me. I closed the book.

If I drew on the Trine again—all that stored, polluted power, left there by the Darkness—it might warp me. Or it might bring the Darkness closer. I didn't know how often a mage could use Dark might before becoming Dark herself. If I drew on the wheels for a working this big, Amethyst would know. My guess is that she would kill me without a second thought. The only other way I could think of to perform the conjure was to command seraphs to help.

Cheran had drawn the conclusion in the battle in the street. I remembered his whispered word, *omega*. Something I didn't think about too much. I was an omega mage, among the most rare and dangerous of neomage traits, one that was poorly documented and scary as death and plagues and all the powers of Darkness combined. I could command seraphs in battle against Darkness. And I could command them in other ways too, if I didn't mind dying. Most omega mages died young when they overstepped the bounds of their gift and commanded seraphs in other things. And when mages died at the hands of seraphs, it was a bloody mess. Literally.

I wandered my loft, stopping at each window to stare out over the nighttime street. There were bonfires at each corner, the forms of men and women backlit by the flames. Snow-el-mobiles whizzed past, moving shadows. It occurred to me that I should remain dressed in the dobok so I could race to trouble, but I couldn't stay battle-ready twenty-four/ seven. Standing by, waiting, I hung my weapons, boots, and clothing on hangers on the open door of an armoire, within easy reach.

A knock sounded at the door at my back and without looking around, I called, "Come in." It opened and I saw Ciana, reflected in the armoire mirror, framed in the black space. She was wearing a pink shift and leggings, the seraph wings pin on her chest glistening with energies.

"Miss Polly thinks they're all here," she said. "You can set the ward."

I sighed and went to the bedside table, picked up the marble sphere that held the trigger. With a touch and a thought, the ward activated. Mage-sight blazed on and I felt, more than saw, the energies flow from the energy sink at my spring, through the ground and into the foundation. They rose over the first floor and up the walls to the roof. It was a powerful conjure, perhaps the most powerful I had ever tried. Ciana, who stood in the doorway, watching, glowed in mage-sight like a bright star. Not human. Not human at all anymore. My throat grew tight at the sight of her. She said, "Can I stay downstairs with the girls from school? I have a bedroll and extra blankets. And Uncle Rupert has a cot I can borrow."

"What did your uncle say? What did your father say?" Rote words. Important words. Lucas had divorced me. I was no longer her stepmother. My heart wrenched at the thought, as if it was squeezed in a huge hand. But if she heard what was in my mind, she didn't say so.

"Uncle Rupert said it was up to you. Daddy is out patrolling with the other men."

"Fine, then. But if you get cold, come back upstairs and get in bed with me."

"I'll be okay. Cissy can sleep with me. And they're going to roast marshmallows after supper." She cocked her head, a little-girl mannerism marred by world-weary eyes. "Will you be okay?"

I dredged up a smile for her. "I'll be fine." *Liar, liar, pants on fire.* I shielded my thoughts from her. She smiled so sweetly, the child of my heart. The tightness in my chest eased as she closed the door, leaving me alone. On its faint echo I thought, *I could use you. I could make you help me trap the Darkness in stone, you and that pin.* I crushed the thought, ground it to nothingness, and opened the fridge.

I had fresh green beans, rare and costly, and potatoes to add to the stew downstairs. I could pick the meat out of my bowl. I took the bag of beans from the crisper and with the other hand lifted the bag of potatoes from the countertop.

A sudden tightness gripped my belly, twisted up through my spine. A cloying heat touched my breasts and warmth flooded out into my limbs. Waves and waves of heat slammed into me, rolling over me. Mage-heat. My spine arched, throwing my head back. The bag of beans and potatoes fell to the tile and rolled as if drunken, ungainly wobbles that made me nauseous. My knees buckled and I hit the floor. I caught myself on my palms, the bright light of the fridge bathing me, throwing sharp shadows.

My side, punctured by the spur of Darkness, wrenched hard, as if all the muscles on that side contracted at once. As if the spur pierced me anew. I clapped a hand to my side

and rolled forward, to the floor, across the beans, crushing
them. My side was blazing hot, and the flesh deep inside
rippled and spasmed. I couldn't breathe. Agony and mage-
heat surged over me like an avalanche, exquisite and deadly.
Tears and blood, I *wanted*.

And then, as if someone pulled a plug, it reversed. My
back clenched and I flipped over on the floor, my whole
body contracting. With a shudder that wrenched the muscles in my back, the heat and the agony were gone. I managed to inhale. "Tears of Taharial," I groaned, focusing on
the rafters and crossbeams overhead. "What the heck was
that?"

Beneath me was a lump of beans, a potato was under my
thigh, but I didn't care. I quivered a final time in reaction
to the sensations that had seized me. Overhead, the fans
turned lazily, pushing warm air to the floor. Downstairs, a
horde of children squealed with excitement.

When I could draw breath easily, I crawled to my knees
and scooped up the bag of beans and chased potatoes until
I had them all. Laying the bags of food on the kitchen table,
I started to lift my sweater and paused, as my abdominal
muscles tightened. I realized I was afraid. And fear had
always made me angry.

Stubborn, I crossed the room and raised the sweater and
under-tee, activated mage-sight, and looked at my side. The
wound was worse. I had thought it was getting better, but
the wound site on my left side where the spur had punctured me in two realities—one I called the *otherness*, or
the here-not-here, and in this one—was worse. It was now
an irregular, raised black ring with a bloody red center. In
human sight it was more colorful, looking like an old bruise,
purple center ringed with purplish black, greens and yel-
lows swirling out. Like an eye, I thought. Like an eye from
hell, staring out at the world from my side.

I had been better. A lot better. But I had kept the spur,
opening myself up to reinjury and maybe even claiming
should the amulet fall into the wrong hands. *Stupid, stupid,
stupid*. I had kept a talisman of Darkness like some kind
of memento. Someone in the street battle had realized I
was under its control and had broken the spur, shattered it
with a single blow. Audric? I remembered the sight of a big

body, silhouetted in the light of a fire, raising up a weapon, two-handed, to the sky, and bringing it down. Smashing the amulet.

It had been nearly twenty-four hours since I was freed of its hold. Shouldn't the wound be healing? Unless . . . What had Audric done with the shards? I remembered the sight of the queen, dead or nearly so, broken down to dust and scooped up by the Dark tornado. Had Audric taken time to burn the splinters? Had he safeguarded the remains? Why had I just experienced both mage-heat and pain from the wound unless something seraphic— or not—had the spur?

I dropped my shirt and sweater and went back to the kitchen. I'd have to ask my champard just how much danger I was in now. I wondered if even he would know the answer.

Chapter 11

I t was dawn, and the sky in the east was a metallic gray. Darkness hadn't come. I was filled with relief, safety, a false sense of security brought on by the rising sun. It wasn't real, but it felt pretty good.

Outside, the footsteps of sentries crunched through old, crusted snow. A rooster crowed. Inside, the buildings were silent, almost a hundred humans finally asleep, no crying babies, no whining toddlers. No preteen girls giggling in the hallway.

I should've been asleep, but I was cramped and miserable. To one side, Rupert snored softly, little puffs of sound. He slept on his side, his healing back held clear from the mattress. I still smelled blood and worried about that, but he needed sleep more than he needed a pesky inquisitive mage poking around on him. To the other side, Audric lay like a dead man, breathing so shallowly his chest didn't seem to rise and fall, only his body heat proving him alive.

Though the dream of seraphs killing me hadn't intruded on my rest, I hadn't slept well with two big men in bed with me. Notwithstanding the rare mage fantasy, and my few months as a married woman aside, I liked sleeping alone. It had been different when I was injured, weak, too exhausted to roll over, too feeble to get to the bathroom alone. I had needed them then, and welcomed their combined warmth, but I had been really happy when they left me and returned to the loft apartment across the way. Now the bed was crowded, and the mingled scents of human, half-breed, and mage were strong, almost unpleasant. I wanted my bed to myself again. I wanted my life to myself again. If wishes were horses. . . . Yeah, right.

I sat up and crawled down the middle of the bed to the floor, and padded to the bathroom on bare feet. After I relieved myself, hidden behind a screen I had put in place the night before, I dressed in clean underwear and socks, yesterday's jeans and fuzzy sweater, my amulets around my neck. Audric and Rupert slept on.

Silent, I paced from window to window, watching the morning's activities in the street. Black rings had burned through the snow to the cracked asphalt beneath, and charred remains of logs still smoked. Men and women who had spent the night watching stretched and walked off night terrors and doldrums, exchanging words as they passed. I spotted Cheran Jones striding away in the distance, and an idea formed.

I left a note on the kitchen table for Audric to make a quick trip north if possible, and before I could change my mind, turned off the ward on the lofts and shops, grabbed boots and a jacket I hadn't worn in a while, and slipped out the door. Stepping over girls snuggled into a thin down mattress, around a woman on a cot, I went downstairs and into the frozen morning.

As I left the shop, I hung the Apache Tear over the doorknob and activated an identity glamour I had used before. To the world I looked like a middle-aged woman, plain, nondescript, unmemorable. The conjure was a two-parter, the glamour and a second conjure, less strong, less well defined. It simply made people forget they had seen me. Her. Whatever.

Miz Essie lived across the street and up a ways, in a small two-story house wedged in between two others of similar Post-Ap design. The house was at least fifty years old, constructed of sturdy rock and brick with functional solar panels lining the roof and white-painted trim. It had been built after the start of the ice age, and the front door was up ten steps, on a narrow stoop. A little more than ten feet separated the houses to either side, sloped lanes where snow and ice collected when it melted off the roof and ran down the hill behind, refreezing along the way.

Right now, because there had been no snow accumulation for two weeks, the collected ice was only a few feet deep, but it was slick and solid, and I could see fine cracks radiating through the foundations of all three houses from the constant varying pressure of ice.

I climbed up the front steps as if I belonged there and entered the house. I had never been in Miz Essie's home, and immediately I saw dozens of pictures hanging on the walls. Eli as a baby, as a toddler with two other children, as a young man, with a beautiful Cherokee girl, both laughing, the girl with black hair blowing in a spring wind, arms bare to the bright sunlight. Other children, some that looked like him, were in even more photographs. The stairway was also lined with prints, and as I climbed, I upgraded my estimate of the numbers of photos to hundreds. Every vertical square inch was covered. Where there weren't photos, there were embroidered plaques, cross-stitched homilies, and embroidered winter scenes, a dizzying panoply of images.

Voices and the smell of frying bacon brought back my mission and I hurried quietly up the stairs and paused at the top. I hadn't known for certain that I would be able to spot his room, but number two glowed weakly with mage power. I ran my hands over the jamb and spotted two telltales, little conjures that would keep humans out. I had never deactivated any conjure but my own, figured I didn't have time to try, and so I took a chance and opened the door. Nothing happened. The telltales appeared unchanged, and I slipped inside. I was a mage. He hadn't prepared a secondary conjure to keep mages out. I closed the door behind me.

"Ducky. Now what?" I asked myself. I stood in the unexceptional room, studying the multicolored handmade quilt and wrinkled sheets all rumpled on the old iron bedstead, the lumpy mattress beneath. There was a hooked rug that looked as if it had been made at the same time as the house, a small upholstered chair, ditto, a scarred table, a chest of drawers, and a closet. And a huge stack of luggage beneath the narrow window. I grinned at the sight, remembering Cheran's big plans to live in a consulate, waited on hand

and foot by adoring humans. I wondered if he had been forced to clean the toilet yet.

Indulging in the mental picture, I opened Cheran's closet and went through the hanging and folded clothes. Fancy court stuff was on one side, several tuxedoes in fashionable shades—teal, black, and an oxblood brown—ruffled shirts, highly polished lace-up leather shoes. On the other side was business clothing and day-to-day stuff—wool suits, dress slacks, tunics in muted shades, shoes with textured bottoms to make walking in snow easier. There were also two pair of jeans and hiking boots. Most of the casual clothes still had price tags on them, all from local shops. The mage had been busy spending money I didn't think he had.

I ran my hands under the mattress, looked under the bed, and went through the chest of drawers. I found clothes and personal items, nothing that would tell me more about the visiting mage emissary. I eyed the neatly stacked bags, matched luggage, heavy-duty stuff with tough leather exteriors and locks. All were black except one, which was scuffed, worn, and lockless.

Long, wide, and only a few inches deep, it bore a suspicious resemblance to my own weapons case, except it was larger, older, and constructed of better quality leather. I pulled the case to the bed and after a quick inspection with mage-sight, I opened it. It was filled with socks, underwear, and several really nice silk scarves, but like mine, the case had a false bottom. I set the clothes to the side and found the hidden catch. With an unobtrusive click, the case opened.

Blades gleamed inside, really beautiful mage-steel blades, the superstrong, amazingly elastic steel made by steel mages. The cutting edges were microns thick, the tips so sharp they would damage flesh before the eye could see them touch the surface.

There were two matched sets of blades, each set meant for very different purposes. While each weapon was made from a single length of mage-steel from pommel to tip, one set was made for battle, the other for a different kind of fighting.

The battle weapons had silverplated handles over steel tangs. These blades were set with faceted stones around the crossguards, and the pommels—the decorative piece below each grip—were single faceted nuggets. There was a sapphire on a kris, emeralds on four throwing knives, matched citrines on two tantos, and a smaller knife that was too large to be a dagger but too small to be a kogatana, even for a mage—weapons that would be long-bladed knives for a human were shortswords for a mage. There was a spear in two parts, with decorative green tourmaline accents.

A single pink quartz nugget was set in the pommel of the longsword. Each stone glittered with ancient energies, wild mage energy, the energies gathered and used by the first neomages, the teenage children of human parents. That made the weapons old, maybe as much as eighty years old, and they were downright gorgeous. They were the kind of weapons that were passed from generation to generation, showpiece battle weapons, shaped and forged for a warrior of small stature. A battle mage. I studied the cutting edges. They were clearly well used and cared for. One was nicked and blackened where demon-iron had impacted it. My hands ached to pick them up and try the balance but I didn't touch them.

The other group of blades was different in style, smaller, neater, more easily hidden in clothing or boots or even a hatband. I remembered the ostentatious hat Cheran had worn when he arrived in town, and the pile of weapons Audric had taken from him. Those blades had come from this set, and the mage was likely wearing them still. There were vacant slots. A shiver of warning slithered down my spine. I hoped it wasn't a premonition.

These weapons had handles—the grip part, molded around the tang—shaped to the same grip, as if formed from molten steel and fitted for a specific hand, Cheran's hand. Half were made of crosshatched steel for a firmer grip, the other half were smooth metal, to allow the blade to slide from his hand easily. Throwing blades.

This entire set appeared to be new, maybe only a few years old, and I had a mental picture of Cheran dressed in the heavy leather apron of the steel forger, armor maker, and swordsmaster, sweating over an anvil, shaping a length of steel to his own specifications and requirements. Wild mage energies building around him.

I closed the case and set it aside, pulling the next case to the bed and opening it. It wasn't locked, none of the cases seemed to be, and it held clothes. Cheran Jones had brought enough to last a decade, or enough to last a full year as an emissary in a consulate posting. In each piece of luggage were different types of dress, some formal, made of velvet or lace or silk, the outerwear of wool and cashmere, finely woven. His pajamas were silk, his socks of silk-blend, and most of his shirts were silk. His loose tunic-suits were nubby raw silk. Even his boxers were made of charmeuse, and I wondered how he could sit upright in them.

One case was heavier than the others, and it was locked. I thought about trying to pick the lock, but I had never done that before and assumed it was harder than the Pre-Ap TV shows indicated. I had an incantation that would work, but using it would destroy the locking mechanism. No way would Cheran miss the tampering and he would know I had been in his room. Regretfully, I set it aside.

The smallest case, about twenty inches long and deep, and maybe half that wide, opened like my armoires, two swinging front doors and a one-piece back. Opened out, it revealed deeply padded red velvet on the doors and back. In little hoops, snugged down tight, were unmarked vials, twenty of them, all containing liquid. I carried the satchel to the window, which offered only wan light because it looked into the wall of the next house. I tilted the case back and forth. Some of the vials held clear liquid, like water. One contained an oily, silver substance like mercury. One was a blue so dark it looked black. One was the red of cinnabar.

There were measuring spoons and a small Bunsen burner, a flint, and a tiny scale. There were powders too, in little glass jars with strange-shaped lids. A pair of rubber gloves were rolled into one corner. Along the edges of the case, in pockets held closed with snaps, were syringes, needles, a ring with an adjustable bezel but no stone, and little cabochons shaped to fit. The bezel was formed so that when the center stone was removed, a small needle was revealed.

I stared at my find, a cold dread beginning to grow. As my trepidation increased, I searched my pockets until I found a scarf left there who-knew-how-long-ago. With it, I wiped down the case of vials and all the other luggage I had touched, replacing everything just as I had found it. Just as carefully, I wiped the dresser, closet, and anything else I might have touched. My unplanned jaunt had resulted in consequences I didn't know how to gauge, but I knew enough to be worried about them.

Standing at the door, I inspected the room. Other than the two sets of weapons and a small case of liquids, there was nothing to indicate why Cheran was here or what he was here to do. Or rather, who he was here to kill. Because a mage who traveled with poisons was on assignment. Cheran was an assassin mage. The gift was rare—and deadly.

Unnerved, I made sure my guise was in place, then slipped out of the room and down the steps, confident that no one would remember me. I was in front of Thorn's Gems, stopped by a long line of children and parents leaving, chattering about the night in the mage's den, before I heard Cheran's thoughts. He was approaching from the east, talking to two humans, whom he despised, thinking them stupid and traitorous. They were Elder Culpepper and his son, Derek. While I couldn't hear their words, I was able to follow Cheran's mind. Father and son were planning something against the town and against me, hoping to enlist Cheran's help. Before I learned what it was, Murphy's Law stepped in and the men were interrupted.

Inside my shop, I lifted the Apache Tear and almost put it back over my head. Instead, I carried the talisman to the workroom and dug into a box of snowflake obsidian. I found a nugget of roughly the same dimensions and a tiny shard of black jasper.

Quickly, I did a down-and-dirty incantation, filling the jasper with a simple conjure for heating bathwater. I then wrapped and strung them together, the jasper hidden in a wire knot, so the Tear looked like the amulet prepared by the Enclave council. Unless he did a deep inspection, the new, fake one, with the jasper so close they touched, would look like the original to a metal mage's sight, the conjure in the jasper providing the radiance of power. I hung the phony on my necklace; the real Tear went into the drawer at my worktable.

As I strung the fake Tear on, I noticed that one of my amulets was glowing, a small citrine nugget shaped like

a pear with a nub of a stem and a small leaf, an amulet I
hadn't made but had purchased at a swap meet. It was one
of three wild mage-stones I owned, created in the time of
the first neomages. I still didn't know what they did, but I
had noticed that the citrine sometimes glowed when the
wheels of the cherub Amethyst were around. On a hunch,
I went to the metal boxes that stored the stone recovered
from the wheel's crash site midway up the Trine.

The boxes were in the stockroom, lined against the wall
in a short stack. I had been lazy about getting things in the
stockroom put away—my job in the business—and it had
been easier to simply push them aside than to find a logical
place for them. Where did one store shards from the wheels
of a cherub?

I hefted one of the boxes to the floor and opened its
keyed lock, peeled back the metal straps that held it
closed, and raised the lid. "Son of a seraph," I whispered,
swearing.

Inside were two double-fist-sized hunks of stone, vaguely
flame-shaped. The last time I looked at them, they had been
pale, nearly clear, and so empty of power that they could
have passed for midquality quartz. Now the crystals were
purple and lavender, rich shades of color swirling in vague
curves. As I watched, one mutated, revealing a grape-toned
iris and a pupil of deeper purple. The eye looked at me,
pupil contracting, focusing, and the stone seemed to vibrate,
a long, slow pulsation, half purr, half heartbeat.

Without thinking, I reached in and touched the stone.
A faint electric charge tingled against my fingertip. Mage-
sight came on with a snapping sensation and I jumped
back as a lavender serpent undulated up from the stone,
swaying in front of me. Its hood swelled open, cobralike,
and a tongue so deeply purple it looked black tasted the
air, menacing. Its body was composed of eyes, all watching
me. Its mouth opened, tissues within bloodless and deadly,
white fangs snapping down. I started to turn away.

The snake struck, demon fast, fangs buried in my throat,
stopping my breath. I tensed and clawed my throat. But
there was nothing tangible. Something—venom? poison?—
pulsed into me, hot and burning. *No, not demon fast. Seraph
fast.*

My heart beat, a single throb. Instantly, I was here, not here, eyes closed. Vertigo gripped me and I swayed on my feet, light-headed in both worlds as a whirlwind of voices filled my mind, singing a harmonious scale.

I opened my eyes to a place of dappled purple light. The world was shades of purples, but nothing in it made sense. The floor beneath my feet was a purple deeper, darker than wine grapes, to my sides were spiraling hues of lilac and violet, and overhead, a shade of delicate orchid. Even the air was a lavender mist, and if sound had a color, it too would have been purple. The note of the song changed, a dirge dying away, and I heard beneath it a crooning hum. I caught my balance and searched for a recognizable pattern in the purple world. My mind was free, floating, tethered to my body, which was still in the shop.

I had been in the *otherness*, a place not of Earth, before, and I knew how it worked, sort of. This was much like that place-no-place. A here-not-here. Time and reality were different. I could be wounded in one plane of reality and not in the other, time could be slower in one reality than the other, I could move faster than I could on Earth. But if I died in one reality, I was probably dead in both.

This place was different from the *otherness* I had visited before—a different *otherness* or a different location in the *otherness*, I didn't know which. More stuff I didn't know.

I breathed in and the soft air, slightly arid and tart, moved into my lungs, When I exhaled, the air was clear, moving through the lavender atmosphere like a pale stream before being absorbed.

My heart beat. It was a slow sound, like the slow-motion fall of a wave on the beach. I looked down and focused on myself. Though I had glanced at myself in the *otherness*, I had never found the time to study my spirit vision, as each time before, I had been in battle, dying. And I was . . . different. Very different.

I was still short and too slim, but here I wore scarlet armor and black chain mail, and boots that latched on with flat, black buckles. A full-sleeve, black chain-mail shirt lay against a scarlet silk knit tee. Warm on my skin, the mail was a heavy, pervasive weight that came to midthigh. An over-the-shoulder coif covered my shoulders, forehead, neck, and head, leaving only my face bare. Over it, buckled to my torso, I wore a scarlet cuirass shaped to my form, my amulet necklace strapped to the cuirass with links of black steel, arranged as if it was a decorative piece. Articulated gauntlets, leg armor, and a segmented girdle were scarlet metal as well, but my arms and shoulders were armor-free, sheathed in the black chain mail over heavy silk underclothes. The boots on my feet were soft bloodred leather, not steel. I carried a shield and two swords.

I was half armored for battle. No helmet, no mace, no spiked flail, no battle hammer or ax. Which was a weird thought as I had never practiced with the heavier weapons. In my belt was an eagle-headed Damascus blade dagger I had never seen before, my longsword in its walking-stick sheath, and the Flame-blessed tanto, weapons of Middle Eastern, English, and Japanese origins, at all odds with the medieval-style armor.

In my belt was a long, iridescent green flight feather. Barak's gift. My necklace of amulets glowed softly. The seraph stone on my necklace, a gift from Zadkiel when he healed me, was glowing bright. I lifted it and it tingled through the gauntlets, an electric charge. I dropped the stone.

Something moved in the lavender air and brushed my cheek, softer than the breeze, feather light. I caught it and held a pale lavender feather. I managed not to curse aloud in surprise. I knew where I was. *Saints' balls*. I was in Amethyst's wheels. The knowledge jolted me, and I caught my balance on the smooth floor, a floor made of the same substance as the crystals in the metal box back in the stockroom. Where I still was.

The deep mellow crooning of the wheels changed timbre and softened as they noted my recognition. *My heart beat*. I was pretty sure I had been here three heartbeats. Three pulses that carried the venom into my body. I lost sensation back in my own reality. Earth faded away. *Tears of Taharial*. What was happening to me?

"I will honor the promises of my Mistress," the words whispered into my mind. *"Her promises and obligations. I will not let her sin by forgetting you. By forgetting her Watcher."*

Nothing else ensued and I raised my eyes to see Amethyst, the feathered and many-winged cherub, sitting in a gold chair, facing away from me, staring out over a low wall. Cherubs are nothing like the chubby babies on Pre-Ap Valentine cards. Cherubs have four faces on one head and eyes in weird places, like under their multiple wings, and hands in even weirder places, under their wings and along the outer edges, covered by downy feathers. They jutted from shoulder blades and from calves, fingers fluttering and gripping and grasping. The seraph face was looking out, the eagle face was toward me, its eyes closed, as if sleeping. Her primary hands were in the proper place, at the bottom of human-looking arms, and they rested on the gilt arms of the chair, lightly clenched, long nails like golden talons curled around.

Leaning against her was a young man dressed in skin-tight lavender, his long black hair loose and flowing. Malashe-el. Older than when I last saw him, as if he had aged years in the past weeks, he was still lissome and his face in profile was touched with a faint smile. A black beard and goatee sculpted his already sharp features into severe planes and angles. Both mistress and son were intent on something beyond the ship.

Fear was building beneath my skin, threading its way across my flesh. I should get out of here before they saw me, but I didn't know how. I resisted the urge to draw the weapons I carried. It might not be the most politic thing to appear armed and ready to kill in the presence of a holy being.

Around me, the wheels were a glowing thing with a flat floor and low walls and protuberances everywhere. It was easier to see the oblong shape of the wheels from the inside, sitting in the innermost section of the ship, and it looked smaller somehow. Unlike the outside of the wheels, the inside had no eyes to blink and stare, but had an organic smoothness that threw back the light, like the surface of a pearl. And the entire ship pulsed. Like a rapid heartbeat, light emanated from one end and throbbed along it to the other end. With each pulse, something whipped by overhead, too fast to see, several somethings, some closer than others. Whatever they were they should have created a breeze or a vibration through the floor. They didn't.

A single note caroled. Together, the former daywalker and his mistress leaned in and opened their mouths, joining other voices, singing in a pleasing tenor and alto. It was a hymn I knew from my youth, from Psalm 98. "O sing unto the LORD a new song; for he hath done marvelous things: his right hand, and his holy arm, hath gotten him the victory."

Hundreds joined in, thousands, the singers out of view beyond the walls of the ship. A verse out of order from the scripture was sung as a chorus. "Make a joyful noise unto the LORD, all the earth: make a loud noise, and rejoice, and sing praise."

A strange euphoria gripped me, raced through me. If melody and harmony could exist in a dozen parts, twenty parts, all on perfect pitch, this was the sound of the singing. The reverberation rose and fell, notes like bells and harps and oboes, tones so rich and intense they raised prickles on my skin. My knees felt weak and I put out a hand to steady myself.

Walking over the last notes, a single voice, a rich baritone, took over. "The LORD hath made known his salvation. . . ." The one voice was so pure, so full, it throbbed through me, quaking in my bones. Tears gathered in my eyes and I leaned against the wall of the wheels, the amethyst smooth beneath my gauntleted hand. The lavender air I breathed changed odors, becoming the smell of honey and orange blossoms. The physical sensations of this place in the *otherness*, this here-not-here, were strong, overpowering. Mage-heat began to rise in me. The seraph stone on my necklace took on a brighter hue. The light from within it was a rainbow of colors, scintillating.

I realized that one of its uses was to stop mage-heat. I snatched the stone from the cuirass and pressed it against the bare skin of my cheek. Mage-heat died as if plucked away. Well, well, well. I dropped the stone down my shirt and the heat vanished entirely.

The choir sang, "Let the floods clap their hands: let the hills be joyful together."

I forced my knees to steady and eased around behind the walker, more toward the sleeping face of the eagle, edging so I could look over the wall—railing? gunwale?—and see out. Around me, the massive song continued, voices swelling, "With trumpets and sound of cornet, make a joyful noise before the LORD, the King!"

And I looked out over the site. My eyes were nearly blinded by a surging brightness in the center, directly below. Shielding my eyes, I looked to the sides. For a moment I couldn't make out the confusing scene. As it resolved itself, I nearly fell.

Seraphs. Countless hundreds of them. Thousands. Millions, covering a square of land that stretched out of sight. My knees buckled and I fell against the wall, supporting myself, trying to take it all in. Some seraphs were in winged form, others appeared as whirling lights. Minor Flames darted through the throng, bright balls leaving plasma trails. Bursts of light flickered through, like heat lightning.

At the four corners of the square were the cherubim, each in her wheel, each wheel seeming composed of different gems the size of football fields, the living, breathing, seeing ships of the cherubim. The wheels were shaped like gyroscopes, the exterior wheels spinning, the interior one a platform with a being at the gold navcone, the navigation cone, the origin of the pulsing light. One wheel was like a ruby, one like an emerald, one like a citrine. Amethyst made the fourth. And each ship had eyes only for the brightness in the center of the square.

I looked up, overhead, to see a dome of light, a coruscating prism of light that seemed to look out on the center of a galaxy, glistening like a billion stars. I looked back down, still protecting my eyes from the brightness in the center of the square, to see a grid laid out, a grid of glowing gold. Between each of the lines of the grid I saw rectangles, tall boxes, and domes and—

My mind interpreted the images. The grid was streets, lined with buildings.

The euphoria that washed through me became a flood, a wild, tumbling torrent of motion and emotion. I was in a ship of a cherub, in a Realm of Light. The crowd below shifted, revealing the floor on which they stood. It was clear, like the finest quartz, or maybe diamond, etched with symbols and shapes my mind couldn't interpret.

Visible through the floor was a plane of greens and

browns and gold, like spring and autumn blending into one time and place, life and death. The thought vanished like a dream as I saw what ran through the plane. In a brilliant golden sweep, raced the river of *time*. At one end was a waterfall that threw off a dancing, swirling spray of mist. At the other was a volcano that erupted with a spray of golden water. Both fed the river, as did tributaries and streams, and the river emptied into a crystal sea, so still and placid that it reflected back the light like the face of the full moon.

Above the river, the bright light in the center of the square rose, levitating, lifting between the four cherubs, which settled lower, closer to the crowd below, a dizzying disorientation of movement. Below the bright light was a sapphire, a single faceted gem that rippled with energy. The bright light in the center undulated with amber and rainbow radiance.

The voices rose higher in pitch as if following the lifting lights, and I covered my head with my arms to block out the light and the noise, which was wondrous and splendid, so grand that no words I knew could define or explain it. My eardrums thudded like drums from the decibels. Dizzy with the sound, I fell, resting on the lip of the wheels, bruising the undersides of my arms. I was crying, tears drenching my cheeks. The volume finally fell and the descant changed key as the hymn changed. "Holy, holy, holy," the throng sang, pianissimo.

I was in a Realm of Light. Or worse. I was in heaven.

The song faded away to the final strains, the notes so pure even the air shivered with the beauty of them. Amethyst swiveled in her ornate chair, bringing her human face around. She saw me. Her eyes opened in shock. For a long moment, we stared at one another.

A tremor ran through her, and all the eyes on her many wings opened and focused on me.

Holy Amethyst lifted her head and screamed. Her screech ripped into the tapestry of music. The voices faded away. The scream echoed from the four corners of paradise.

Chapter 12

At the sound of her shriek, the wheels dipped and spun, throwing me flat. I landed hard and my training took over. Instinctively, I rolled to my hands and knees, but the ship dipped again and one shoulder rammed the wall. My right arm was instantly numb; pain bit in at my elbow and along my gauntlet-covered hand. The wheels steadied and I looked up to see Holy Amethyst standing at her chair, keening like a banshee, her eagle face lifted to the dome overhead, her beak open in a warning cry. Anger lit her narrow, feathered face and crackled into the air.

Demon bones. This can't be good.

The singing stopped and Amethyst's cry fell away. Her wings unfurled, two sets shaped like butterfly wings, a third set sweeping away from her body to reveal a downy, many-breasted torso and hips swathed in white linen. I caught a glimpse of her feet, which were rounded and hooved, like horses', but shining like gold.

Above the railing, faces appeared. Faces of seraphs. I was in trouble.

Flames zipped into the ship and past me, trailing blue plasma so bright I closed my eyes, blinking hard. I rocked back on my heels and cradled my injured arm, my elbow brushing across my blades. The tanto sizzled with power, burning my flesh through the chain mail of my right arm, the blade issuing a high-pitched hum, a sensation like bees buzzing, crawling over me.

Rise, my mage visa said.

Not entirely certain that was a good idea, but not having any other ones, I stood. I had an instant to remember the serpent and the venom and wondered if it was still pumping into me. I no longer heard my heart beat. Perhaps I was dying. That seemed to happen a lot when I was in the *otherness,* the here-not-here. Hysterical laughter bubbled up between my lips and I swallowed it down hard, wiping away my tears.

Malashe-el, moving with the speed of its kind, was suddenly in front of me and caught me up in a hug that bruised my ribs. It smelled of brandy and lilacs, and its arms seemed to offer a measure of safety. Though we had once been mortal enemies, I clung to it.

The daywalker withdrew and brushed its fingers over the chain mail at my forehead, its labradorite eyes like blue-gray opals. It had been made of evil and holy matter, mixed and formed to follow its master's call, shaped and bred to be a killer. I had wondered in past days if it had been built to destroy a cherub, yet the daywalker, the being of legend, had decided against the Dark. Light brightened its odd eyes. Behind it, Amethyst screamed again, but when Malashe-el didn't flinch, neither did I.

"You are a warrior like your Raziel," it said, acknowledging the significance of the scarlet armor. That thought had been in the back of my mind, and I agreed, touching my breastplate with a clink of metal. The scarlet steel was the same shade as Raziel's flight feathers.

As seraphs gathered and hovered just beyond the rotating gyroscopic bands of the lavender wheels, the former daywalker lifted the seraph stone on my chest. Purple light played within, muted, but growing brighter. "Yet Zadkiel has placed you under his protection. He plays a dangerous game with divisive politics."

Malashe-el's tone made the words sound felonious and Holy Amethyst, Zadkiel's mate, screamed again, this time in agony. She fell again to the gilt chair and covered herself with her wings, rocking like a grieving child hiding from a painful world.

The seraphs beyond the wheel walls swept hard with their wings, maintaining position, but several had drawn swords and more were congregating by the second. Emotions were gathering like an electric charge on the air and I had a feeling my window of safety was closing. I had so much to ask, and no time at all. "How did I get to a Realm of Light?" I asked, voicing the most useless question of all. "Mages are mortal. And soulless."

"As am I. Yet, my place is here. And here there is no *time*."

"Give her to me!" Amethyst begged, her voice like an owl's. I had no idea who she spoke to, but whoever it was, it couldn't be good. "Though I did much for her, the little mage has defied the sanctity of my wheel. This is blasphemy."

I wondered what she had done for me, except ask dangerous favors that put my life at risk. At my thought, the cherub hissed and swiveled her lion face toward me. Exposing long fangs, she lifted black lips and growled like a jungle cat.

Mortal and soulless, mages can't call on the One True God, God the Victorious, for help. Prayer doesn't work for us. Theologians insist that the Most High doesn't hear us. Other theologians contend that if he doesn't hear an intelligent creature, it proves he isn't real and never was, but that was a theological argument for passionate believers and heretics. I was just in trouble, so I said a silent prayer, in case the One True God heard me. Just in case—the excuse for prayer when uttered by atheists and agnostics for millennia.

Malashe-el cocked its head almost as if hearing my prayer. *"It's not safe here,"* it thought at me, arms tightening like steel bands around my waist. As if he'd been invoked by a magical charm, her seraph now stood beside Amethyst, holding her human-looking arm, his deep purple wings half-furled, his beautiful face expressionless as a block of marble.

"Go," Malashe-el said. Ducking a shoulder, it rammed into my chest. Hard.

Not expecting the shove, my feet in improper position, I rocked back, hitting the wheel wall. Stunned, I plummeted over.

A moment of shock immobilized me and I tumbled

past the hull in open air, buffeted by the strong turbulence whipping off the rotors. I had a single jumbled glimpse of the wheels rotating at sickening speed. The city spread out below me. Empty. The streets were all empty.

My heart beat. Far away. And again as fear slammed into me. My right arm and ankle impacted the nearest wheel with quick, hard cracks, spinning me toward the next wheel. Pain shivered through me. Heart ramming my chest wall, I fell.

Crack the stone of ages, I'm going to die. Desperate, I drew on stone, on all my amulets.

Instantly I was back in my body. Vertigo knocked me backward. My head banged hard, nausea rose in my throat as the world spun about me. Light flashed overhead. I was sprawled on the floor in the stockroom. On my chest was a two-handed fist of amethyst. It was looking at me, which was way weird, and it was humming, a faint vibration through my palms. I had drawn on stone. This stone. I had drawn on the wheel, using it to—what?—save me from itself? Themselves? Scripture used "wheels" and "wheel" interchangeably, and no one knew if the living ships were singular or plural. Either way, Amethyst would kill me for that. Another blasphemy.

Using my left foot and arm, I scuffed my way against the floor and into a sitting position, back to the wall. When I inadvertently moved my right arm and ankle, pain jolted through my limbs and I hissed.

"Shhh. They'll find us," a voice whispered.

I jerked in surprise, which spiraled the pain higher and I bit down on a curse. To my left was a little girl, squatting down, arms tight around her knees. Mostly hidden under a shelf filled with racks of storage bins, she was little more than a shadow.

"Who are you?" I asked as I cradled my hand and pulled up my sleeve.

"Shhh," she said again. "Kimmer is It, and he's real good."

"Hide and seek?" I asked, lowering my voice. My wrist and forearm were purple, as if from a hard blow. I was almost afraid to stress it, but I flexed my fist closed. The pain increased, though not as badly as I had feared, and I opened and closed my hand several more times, feeling intense relief.

Mages have brittle bones and a single hard blow can shatter them. Our broken bones don't heal as quickly as humans', either, and a bad break can mean permanent disability, even with healing incantations. I had survived a ruined left hand only after seraphic intervention and what I suspected had been Lolo's far-reaching incantation.

"Hide, seek, and tag, and the winner gets a prize."

I flexed my right foot up and down, easing my jeans leg up to view the ankle. It was in even worse shape, but I curled my legs under me and stood, forcing the foot to carry weight. Pain shot through me, bringing another surge of nausea. I leaned over the boxes of stone and dropped my head into my arms. I was still holding the amethyst, and the crooning grew louder.

"You're the devil woman, aren't you?" she said. When I grimaced, more from pain than from her question, she confided, "My daddy says you're going to hell, but my mama says she'll take sanctuary from the Dark Lord himself if it means keeping us alive."

"Isn't that just peachy," I managed. I placed the fist of lavender stone back in its case. From the outer hallway, squeals erupted and feet slapped against the floor. "Tag! You're it!" a young voice shouted gleefully.

Beside me, the little girl duck-walked from under the shelf and stood up. I'm short, not quite five feet last time I stood against a ruler, and the girl came to my elbow, making her five years old or so. She was dressed in orthodox black. "I'm Estrella." She put out her hand and I took it in mine. She gave me a firm shake, well taught by her parents in that at least, and scampered away.

Another child, no more than two years old, ran through the workroom. Arms in the air, squealing like a baby piglet, she made a loop of the center storage area and ran back out, leaving my ears ringing. This child was dressed in summer-sky blue, and reminded me achingly of my twin. Though technically identical, Rose had hair a shade more blond than my own scarlet, and it was straighter than my sometimes kinky snarl. Just like the little girl.

Instinctively, I reached out for Rose, calling to her, needing her, feeling the loss of my sister as a deep wound never healed, far more painful than my ankle and wrist. It was nothing like the formal scrying I had tried before, no ritual to prime my mind, no carefully prepared incantation, not even a simple calling. This was a wordless plea, emotion only, the voice of loneliness, a bitter, aching need I seldom looked at, rarely acknowledged.

"Rose," I whispered.

Nothing answered. Not even the raucous, blaring demand of her mind that met mine when I first came into my gift and our minds touched with such power and intensity. Nothing. I sighed, the breath an admission of defeat.

"*Thorn?*"

I stilled, froze, the immobility of marble. "Rose?" I whispered. Quickly I stepped away from the wall and, with a thought, opened a narrow charmed circle. Inside the protected space, I gripped the amethyst. If I had to steal the power of the cherub's wheels to find my sister, I'd risk the consequences. "Rose?" I said louder, insistent, throwing my mind at the universe to find her.

She didn't answer. Yet, something had changed. Now, instead of the blackness of night or the blackness of nothingness, there was ... something ... a pulsation, a susurration. A soughing, like the soft roar one hears in an empty shell.

"Rose?" I closed my eyes and concentrated, steadying my breathing, drawing on the amethyst that purred beneath my hand. Behind my closed lids, I saw soft light, a confused blurred scene, and black strings, like vines that curled all in one direction, images that made my already queasy stomach roll. My heart pounded a painful tattoo against my chest. My breath was an aching rip of tissue. I gripped the amethyst so hard my bones ground.

I realized I was seeing through someone else's eyes, seeing eyelashes and the scene beyond, and it was another's sickness I was feeling. The eyes were crossed, perhaps, and ... she? Rose? ... blinked once, a slow and drugged movement. "Rose?"

The muzzy vision I saw through her eyes began to focus, a scene of wood and stone and brick arched over her head.

The roar increased, and I recognized a sound like the surf, like the ocean pounding nearby. Was Rose near the sea? In a stone building near a waterfall? She blinked once more and closed her eyes. All the sensations dimmed, the roar last to fade. And Rose was gone.

Was it my sister? Had I found her? Had I sensed her? Was she alive, just as the Darkness had asserted? Or had I focused in on a sleeping mage, my imagination and hope making her drugged or sleeping mind seem familiar? Terror and elation scoured through me, tears stinging my eyes. If I had found her once, I could find her again. If. If it was Rose.

I didn't pray often, but now I said a quick prayer of thanksgiving. For the first time in years, it was possible that I wasn't alone in the world of humans. It was possible I had found my sister. Maybe. I clicked off the charmed circle, put the stone away, closed the metal top that housed the amethyst, and secured the metal straps in place.

Rose had been a licensed mage in Atlanta, the largest city in what was left of the United States of America. The city had once taken up most of the state of Georgia, and even now was a sprawling megalopolis. It was also home to the largest number of mages outside of an Enclave. Rose had been one of many.

On a night of portents, a night of a bloodring, Lolo the priestess had called us both, warning us that danger was near. A bloodring was a ring of scarlet far out from a full moon, a ring caused by ice crystals that picked up only the red wavelength of light, and against the black sky, it foretold peril—general peril like earthquakes, personal peril for mages, danger to all and sundry of my kind. My sister had been getting ready for a diplomatic event when Lolo called. She had warned Rose, as she had warned me, to be careful, to go armed.

According to police sources, someone—or something—had crashed through Rose's door and attacked her. Neighbors had called the police when they heard screams. All that had been left of my twin had been a trashed room and a large pool of blood. Because the blood hadn't been sucked from the floor, and because Rose had been living under the largest mage-dome outside of an Enclave, the

cops had ruled out an attack of Darkness. At first. But when
no body turned up, when none of the other mages stationed
in Atlanta had been able to scry her, they had reluctantly
admitted that Darkness might have been involved. I had
always believed that. Now I knew it for truth. Darkness had
stolen my sister and kept her drugged—

My thought cut off. No Darkness would keep her above-
ground, where daylight might free her. *Aboveground.*
Because that was where she had to be. That was what
I had seen in the vision through her eyes, morning light.
And because it had been dawn light, not nighttime, that
meant she was somewhere on the eastern seaboard. Rose
was close by. Waking from whatever had been done to her.
Waking alone, to danger.

If it was Rose. Once I had seen into the mind of my twin
with perfect clarity. The glimpse just now had been too
brief, too clouded and confused, for me to be certain. But it
had felt familiar. It had.

Thoughtful, worried, so excited my stomach ached and
my heart rate wouldn't settle, I turned off the light and
locked the door to keep out other inquisitive children or
snooping adults. Limping, I made my way through Thorn's
Gems, my mind in a snarl, grateful that my ankle could support my weight, wanting to whap Malashe-el, wondering
why the daywalker had thrown me over the side, giddy with
success at possibly finding my sister. Worried that she was
in danger I couldn't fight. Especially if I couldn't find her,
get to her.

The shop was empty now, the nighttime visitors gone. The
place felt different this morning, more alive than before.
Warmer, from all the body heat and the logs that had blazed
all night long. Different. Better. And that surprised me. I
had expected to feel invaded, violated by the presence of so
many humans. Instead, even the room felt happier.

I had to be nuts. Rooms didn't feel happier; people and
mages did. And I was not happy because I had housed a
horde of humans under my roof, under the protection of my
gift, all night. No way. My feet echoing on the bare board of
the stairwell, I climbed to the second floor.

In the loft, Audric and Rupert were eating breakfast at
my table. They went silent, watching me as I limped in. I

kept my eyes down, thinking over the discoveries of the
morning as I dished up a bowl of hot oatmeal, added a bit
of my costly, hoarded sugar, and poured cold milk over it.
Sugar and cacao, unlike coffee and tea, were best grown in
warm weather, and so were hard to come by in a mini ice
age. Sweets and chocolate had become an indulgence of the
wealthy, but every now and then I treated myself. I figured
that visiting a Realm of Light, stealing a ride on a cherub's
wheel, and nearly getting killed were good enough reasons
for full-scale pampering.

I made an ice bag before I joined my champards at the
table, still not meeting their eyes. Propping my foot on a
chair, draping the ankle with the bag, I ate, ignoring the
way their eyes met, before they applied themselves to their
own breakfasts.

When I could no longer stand their speculative silence,
I told them what I had discovered. Most of it. But not all. I
kept the part about Rose to myself, hugging it to me like a
treasure.

After breakfast, Audric went downstairs, planning the best
way to get my errand done. Rupert washed dishes, standing
at my sink, his back to me. Once again I smelled blood, and
spotted a smudged, fresh mark on his shirt. "You're bleeding again, aren't you?" I said.

He stilled a moment, his hands in the water. When he
shrugged, his shoulders moved stiffly, and when he spoke,
his voice was carefully emotionless. "The wound keeps
opening up. Ciana tried twice to close it. Wore herself out
using that pin of hers." He rinsed the last bowl and washed
the mugs, the only sound in the loft the splash of water,
oddly silent after a night marked by the myriad sounds of
motley humans. When he had dried the last dish, he stood
unmoving, back to me, as if waiting for something.

Not knowing what to say, I asked, "What will it take
to heal you?"

"I don't know." When he didn't go on, I stood and went
to the sink to stand beside him. Rupert was a little taller
than the average human male, a little over six feet, so that
meant that the top of my head didn't reach his shoulder. I
leaned against his deltoid, wrapping my arms around his,

sliding my hand through his damp fingers. He seemed to take comfort from the touch and he said, "I had a dream."

I squeezed his hand, staring at the blank wall over the sink with him, wordlessly encouraging him to continue.

"There was this crowd of people in a stone building. You, me, Ciana, Lucas, Audric, Thadd, some others from town. And a bunch of seraphs were all around us, hovering in the air, beating the air with their wings. I knew three of them, Raziel, Zadkiel, and Cheriour. Three with black wings and black tunics."

I tightened my grip. Rupert was describing my own dream.

"And there was this green feathered one with silver hair," he said.

"Barak."

He shrugged. "They all looked different, like things do in dreams, sometimes, you know? The seraphs all had wings, swords, shields, but they looked angry. Evil. The green one had that thing Audric busted up in the street fight, that spur you were carrying in your pocket."

My breathing hitched a moment. Everything kept coming back to the spur.

"The walls were crawling with these huge snails, and it stank." He snorted softly, laughing through his nose. "I never knew you could smell in a dream, but these things reeked."

I tightened my hand on his, so tight my fingers ached. Rupert was right—dreams seldom contained odors. But visions? Visions were often fully sensual, with all five senses in play. And in his, Barak had the spur, which was different from my own dreams. I remembered the moment of mage-heat earlier, a heat that hit me like a huge fist, brought me to my knees and then vanished. If Barak had the spur, did that give him power over me? But I had his flight feather. Was control mutual? Did we each have a weapon over the other? I struggled to maintain calm, to keep my breathing steady and rhythmic. "Rupert—"

"It's storming outside," he said, without letting me comment, though I noted the tense change. "Rain is blowing in through the window openings. Most are broken out and the walls are dripping with slime.

"Anyway, this green seraph, he's yelling, 'Do it. Do it now. Do it or she'll die.' And you pull that green feather out. And you give it to me. And then you pull your sword, but it's not like your sword, you know?" he said. "This one has a pink quartz nugget on the pommel. And you stab me with it."

I flinched and closed my eyes. Rupert's flesh was warm against my hands, which were growing colder than snow-melt.

"I fall to my knees," he said, "and you pull out the sword. And you point at Barak—yeah, his name is Barak. I hear you say that. You point at him with the sword that's dripping with my blood. And he gives you the spur. You give him his feather. And I'm calling to you, begging you. But you don't hear. And I can't wake up."

My throat was so tight breathing was painful. I pressed the side of my face to his arm, as if assuring myself Rupert was real and alive.

"I see this girl, she's lying on an old oak table, and you help her sit up. She looks like you, but she's skinny and dirty, covered with scabs and old wounds, like she's been sick or held prisoner or something. You give her to Eli. And Thadd picks me up and puts me on the table. I'm dying," he said. "And it hurts. It hurts so bad that you killed me."

A single tear scalded a slow path down my cheek. I wouldn't. I would not give up Rupert for Rose. I wouldn't. This wasn't prophecy. This was a dream. Only a dream.

"All these women who look like you walk in. They make the seraphs go crazy, ripping off their clothes. Their wings disappear and they look like human men. Or like beasts with human faces. They start to have sex with the women.

"Barak laughs. And he says, 'Curiosity killed the cat.' And then Barak and Raziel start to fight. And blood goes everywhere. And I wake up." Rupert looked down at me. "Curiosity killed the cat. Isn't that a weird thing for him to say, Thorn? Some dumb old saying, when it should have been scripture. Not that it's any weirder than the rest of the dream."

Rupert pulled his arm away and tilted my face up to his. With a thumb, he wiped away my tears. "Don't cry, Thorn. It's only a dream."

I caught his hand, holding it away from my face. I didn't

want comfort from him, refused to accept comfort from my best friend, who had just predicted the unbelievable. Who had just foretold that I'd kill him, murder him, to get my sister back. Unthinkable. Unbearable.

The thought flitted in the back of my mind, quickly banished. Was his prediction a dream future, one possibility among many? Or was it true prophecy, the immutable future, set in stone, unchangeable and inflexible? No. No way. Not true prophecy. Only a dream. A prediction. I wouldn't consider anything else.

Without asking, I pushed him around and pulled up his tunic, lifting the cloth with cold, clumsy fingers, gathering up his T-shirt. As if to help me, he bent forward slightly and braced on the sink edge. Holding up the shirts, I exposed his back, his pale skin untouched by the sun. Beside his spine, taped to his skin, was an eight-inch-wide, ten-inch-long pad with fresh scar tissue showing at each end. The bandage was crusted around the edges with dried blood and was crimson-wet in the center.

Breath uneven, I peeled back the tape and raised one side of the bandage, not lifting the centermost section. I knew enough about battlefield wound dressings to know that platelets were collecting there, clotting the blood. The area I didn't inspect, the unhealed area, was about three inches long. Around the edge of the deepest wound was a raised ring, blackened, puffy, hot to the touch. I pressed my icy fingers against the flesh there, and it gave under my fingers. Rupert hissed softly with reaction.

I should have stopped, but I didn't and pressed harder, feeling the tissue beneath the toxic perimeter. "Thorn!" he said, cringing, his back arching. I stepped away, hands still holding the shirts high, staring at the wound. It was like mine, hard and ridged beneath. It was shaped in an oval, like a link. Seraph stones. We had both been marked. What in the name of the Most High did that mean? What had been done to us?

Rupert wasn't human. Neither was I. I had figured out that we were both part of some crazy conspiracy, but new bits of the puzzle kept appearing, skewing my interpretation, elements kept falling out of place, out of joint. I dropped his shirts.

I went to the bath area and dug out a box of bandages, a new addition since my life had become a constant battle. From my bowl of stones by the window I chose three healing amulets, two small, drilled nuggets and one slab of white marble about the size of my open hand. All were newly filled with power that wasn't mine to use. Might stolen from the wheels of the cherub Holy Amethyst.

In the way of longtime friends, Rupert watched me gather supplies, standing silent, not asking questions, but patiently waiting. When I returned to him, he faced away again and braced himself, unmoving against the sink. After rolling his shirt and tunic high on his back and pulling off the bloody outer bandage, I added a new layer of gauze over the center pad. On top of the clean wedge of outer dressing I pressed the slab, the two nuggets, and three shards from Amethyst's wheels, and taped it all in place. To secure the extra weight, I rolled some gauze wrappings around his torso. As I worked, I felt some of the tension go out of him as his pain lessened. His breathing evened out and he exhaled with relief. "Feel better?" I asked.

"Much. Thorn?"

"Don't say it," I said, stopping him, not knowing what he might say, but not able to hear it. Not just now. I wiped away a new, unexpected tear and placed my tear-damp hand over his wound, bowing my head. In my other hand, I gathered the seraph stone and my visa.

"I know you can't hear me," I said. "I know you don't care about mages, that we're less than nothing in your holy sight." Rupert stiffened under my hand when he realized I was praying. "But just in case they're wrong, I promise you this. In the name of the Most High, in the name of the unsayable God, I will give my own life in exchange for Rose's. I'll give my own life in exchange for Rupert's. I'll die by my own hand rather than kill one of those I guard. If I had a soul, I'd swear by it. Instead, I claim it by your unspeakable name. By your name, I do so vow."

I shuddered hard with the power of the hallowed words. Exhausted by the effort of speaking them, I rested against the body of my friend, the heat of my champard like a furnace against me. My forehead lay against Rupert's bare back, and a single tear ran down his skin, into the waistband of his jeans.

Mages didn't make vows easily or lightly. The one I had just made, calling on the unsayable God, was one of the most sacred among us. God the Victorious never heard the prayers of neomages, but if he ever bothered to hear us, it would be because of the passion of such an oath. Perhaps he would understand the weight of our words. Perhaps he would know that with such vows, we revered him. Perhaps he wouldn't judge us too harshly.

For a long moment we stood, unmoving, my head against his back beside the wound, my tears twin runnels on his skin, marking him. I could feel his breathing, feel the movement of his heart as it pulsed his blood. Blood that was no longer human.

"Did you think I believed the dream?" Rupert asked, his voice rumbling through his chest, soft and full of wonder. He turned and gathered me up in his arms, his mouth against my hair. When he spoke, the words vibrated against my skull like a benediction. "I would sooner believe you were the Dark Lord itself than that. I trust you with my life, with my heart, with my very soul, knowing you will treat them all with the same care as I would."

They were formal words, the pledge of a champard, and I recoiled at them, afraid, pulling back. I met his eyes, so wide they looked black in his pale face, seeing his trust. Fearing that trust more than anything. Because even with my claim and pledge to the contrary, I knew the might of a prediction dream. I knew that there was a chance I would break my vow to the Most High and follow the dictates of the divination. Dreams were like that. They showed only the final result, not the ultimate reasons for each action. And I feared it like my own death.

Chapter 13

I picked up the phone to call Miz Essie's boardinghouse. When there was no dial tone, I remembered the phone lines had been cut. Because avalanche or attack of Darkness could leave any town isolated, every mountain town had multiple means of reaching the outside world. There were underground telephone lines and a satellite dish that worked off one of the remaining geosynchronous satellites over the North American continent. And ham radios. Darkness had never before cut phone lines *and* damaged a town's dish. No way was it a lucky mistake.

I put down the useless phone and went out on the porch at the front of the loft. Looking over the street, I saw Jacey's eldest stepson, Zeddy, and waved to him. When he waved back, I cupped my mouth and shouted, "You know where the new mage is?"

"Watching the kirk bury the dead," he shouted back, "taking photographs." His tone added, *like a tourist with a camera,* but he didn't have to say the words.

"Tell him I need him. Now."

"Will do, Miss Thorn."

When I shut the door, Rupert asked, "What are you doing?"

"Making sure the dream stays only a nightmare. No. You stay right here," I said when he pushed away from the sink. "I want you to see this."

Without the real Apache Tear around my neck, I knew

when Cheran headed my way and curled my lips into a snarl as I heard/felt his reaction. It was loathing. *I'm not at the beck and call of anyone, and certainly not a brainless rock-head mage without her first heat.* And then . . . *She'll be gone soon, and good riddance.* From Cheran, I had a vision of my body stripped and flayed in the snow, brown robes gathered around. I didn't know what he had been planning, but I had a good idea who he had been planning it with.

Then I had a single image of Cheran himself, in a consulate of his own. Grasping his intent, I let my smile widen. Rupert took a fast step back. I'm pretty sure I looked vicious.

"Go ahead and make any plans you want," I said softly, aloud. "I'll outlive you if it's with my dying breath." At Rupert's uncertain alarm, I shook my head and let the expression dwindle away. "I've changed my mind. You know those clothes you and Audric wore when you were my champards in the town meeting? You get to wear them again. Go change." When he stood there, indecisive, I said, "Hurry," and made it a command.

Rupert left, shouting to Audric as the door closed. Back on the porch, I propped a hip on the railing and crossed my arms against the cold, putting together the elements of a plan based on the number of cases in Cheran's room. A bluff. If I was wrong, I'd feel like an idiot. The mage strode up the hill, his velvet cloak swinging, the stupid hat in place, feather bobbing. Zeddy and a small group of teenaged boys followed him, a good ten yards back. In the distance the blasted lynx growled, the sound like a cough and a roar combined, peculiar to its species. *Thanks for the warning,* I thought, *but I don't need it. For once I know I'm in danger.*

When Cheran was close enough to lock eyes, I called out to him, letting my voice carry through the visa. "I spoke to the priestess of the New Orleans Enclave." He slowed, mouth parted, a startled curse in his thoughts. Good. I wanted him stunned. "She sent you. She included appropriate gifts to support my consulate." This was the bluff part.

Cheran stopped in the street, a speculative look on his face. In his mind was the question, *What does she know?*

It wasn't so much what I knew as what I could read from

him and what I could guess. "I believe you have them in your possession," I said.

"I do." He cocked a hip, which opened the cloak, revealing a black suit with green satin lapels and matching cummerbund. I had seen the suit hanging in his closet, and the visa at my neck offered the information, *Court dress, appropriate for official sessions or functions.*

Yeah. He'd been plotting against me behind my back. If there was a need for formal display it should have been only in my presence. In an instant I drew on the visa and searched through possible proper actions on the part of a visiting mage. I quickly concluded that Cheran Jones thought I was stupid. He was about to be disabused of that quaint notion.

"And?" I asked, drawing the word out lazily.

"No moment has been appropriate to present you with the bequest."

I stared at him long enough for him to know I had caught him in a lie, letting my reaction fill my face. Long enough for the kids behind him to snicker, the sound bright on the frigid air. Long enough for passersby to slow and watch, and for Jasper to stop in the doorway of the furniture store, his black robe of office swaying in the cold wind. I realized the kirk elder had come from the mass funeral and knew I should have been there too. My shame at missing the funeral made my expression harder and Cheran's cheeks reddened with more than the cold. I should have been there; it was too late now. But it wasn't too late to deal with my visiting mage.

"Well," I said at last, mocking, at which Cheran tensed, his smile stiffening in place, "gifts from the priestess of the Enclave of my birth, for the Appalachian consulate. I reckon that means me," I drawled. When he didn't react except to raise his brows, I hardened my tone, stood, and looked down my nose at him. "Cheran Jones, you have my leave to approach me with everything that is mine or that is the property of this consulate."

His mouth opened and closed so fast it was like a camera shutter working. I smiled, all teeth and anger, using the expression that had made Rupert backstep fast. "I allow you ten minutes' leave to be in my court, downstairs, in Thorn's Gems. Ten minutes."

It was a public humiliation, and Cheran's eyes blazed hot in the instant before he bent and bowed. "At the consulate's command."

"Then you better boogie," Zeddy called from the protection of the bakery's display window. "'Cause she looks pissed." The other boys hooted with delight as Cheran stood straight and strode for the boardinghouse, moving with mage-speed, a blur that left the humans gawking.

I cocked my head at Zeddy and smiled my thanks. To Jasper, I said, "The first official meeting of the Mineral City consulate will convene in nine minutes. Do you think some of the town fathers would be interested in attending?"

"Oh, yes," he said fervently, "I do indeed." Moving quickly, he took off and rounded the building into an alley, cutting through, making the most of his limited time.

From the corner of my eye, I caught sight of Romona Benson standing at the intersection, camera on her shoulder. She was grinning fiercely, and I knew she had me framed in a close-up. I wanted to curse, but I raised my brows instead, as if permitting her to speak. She lowered the camera to point it at the street. "Is the press welcome?" she called.

"Film only, no direct uplink with that sat phone you've been using, and give me the opportunity to edit out what I want, and you're welcome to attend." When her face fell, I said, "I know it's not the way things are done with the press, but take it or leave it. And we'll schedule a televised personal interview for later this week." If I live that long, I thought.

"They'll fry me for this, but we have a deal," she said, and the reporter took off too, moving pretty fast for a human.

I had nearly nine minutes. An eternity for a mage at full speed. I pulled my mage finery from the armoire and set it aside. The silk and lace were not enough. Or were too much. This was to be the first meeting of a consulate I didn't want, but knew I had to protect if I wanted to survive, wanted to keep my friends alive. I pulled out my dobok. It hadn't been cleaned since the battle. It was bloody, aromatic, torn and sliced, and very well used. It looked deadly.

Moving fast, I pulled off my clothes and dressed, adding every weapon I owned. When they were in place, I braided my hair into a battle queue and pulled on battle boots. The mage-leather boots were still uncomfortable on my puffy and tender soles, but I had washed out the old blood, and I didn't intend to be standing much.

Grabbing my battle cloak, a silk scarf in a vibrant bloodred color, and the weapons I liked best—the Flame-blessed tanto and the walking-stick sword—I went down-stairs to set the stage for what I hoped would be a very public affirmation of my intent to remain the town mage of Mineral City as long as I had a visa or as long as I drew breath. And the onset of a plan to protect the ones I loved. I set my amulet necklace over my head and drew on the visa and my primes for strength. For a mage, it was tanta-mount to a prayer for wisdom and strength. I'd need both if I was going to succeed at this. And a mountain of luck bigger than the Trine.

One minute to go, I considered the stage I had set in the center of Thorn's Gems, my favorite wingback chair in the center of the room, my battle cloak open over it, the silk lin-ing exposed to the world, ripped and stained with my blood, a small footstool nearby so my short legs wouldn't dangle like a child's. My silver scrying bowl filled with salt water was tucked behind my chair in case Cheran came prepared to attack me with an article of Darkness. Once he was disa-bled, I could cleanse the taint. It would be very flashy; Rom-ona Benson would love it; it made me sick to think about the media attention. But to protect the ones I loved, I'd do a lot more than play to the camera. Of course, if he used poison, I was a lot more likely to die.

A table to the side near the stove was heaped with jew-elry I had made, including one piece with a fragment of amethyst from the cherub's wheels, a gift for the priestess that I hoped would leave her reeling. The other things were for the Enclave's mage council, and one bracelet was for Cheran, the visiting dignitary who, I was pretty sure, wanted my consulate seat, the little snark. Others were for the town fathers, sundry gifts I might be expected to bestow. I would be paying back Thorn's Gems for months, but it would be worth it if it kept the backstabbing—maybe literally—mage from usurping my place.

I added water to the kettle, placing teacups, loose tea, and silver out just in case I needed it, though the visa assured me it wouldn't be proper to serve tea.

Breathing fast, Audric and Rupert clattered down the stairs and stopped, standing beneath the prophecy of my birth. *A Rose by any Other Name will still draw Blood.* A foretelling by the woman who had set my life in motion. I didn't know what had happened to Lolo and answers to my questions weren't going to come easy. I was flying by the seat of my pants, my life motto.

I grinned at my champards in their warlike finery. Audric, his dark-skinned head reflecting back the lights, was dressed in black dobok with his scarlet master's belt knotted beside a battle sword I probably couldn't even lift. He wore a weapon harness strapped to his chest and looked like a walking death machine, bristling with sharp-edged steel. Rupert again wore his best navy tunic and pants. His newly named battle sword hung at his side.

"Nice getups, boys. Audric, this is now the formal consulate of Mineral City. The consular residence is above. We'll need guest residences asap. Think we can rent the store next door and turn it into apartments?"

"It'll take money," he said. "And you'll need more than two champards. I made some calls. But you're wearing the wrong clothes. You need—"

"I'll get the money. And this is a battle station, not a trade consulate. I won't be dancing." Audric looked uncertain, but the visa that held a repository of diplomatic information wasn't offering anything to the contrary so I was going with the idea that I had been putting together since leaning against Rupert. Then I heard his words. He made some calls?

The bells over the door jingled, announcing Romona Benson, who rushed in with a swirl of icy air, her blond flyaway hair whipping in the outside wind. "Am I late?" she asked, and stopped cold. She surveyed me, then my champards, and back to me before swinging up the camera and clicking on a button. A red light glowed on the front, and suddenly the reality of what I was doing hit home.

My smile and the adrenaline high drained away. If I messed this up, I might end up dead. And so might my champards. So might Jacey, Ciana . . . *Spawn balls, what am I doing?*

As if echoing my thoughts in a different key, Romona muttered, "I'm gonna win a bloody Pulitzer with all this.

"Consulate General St. Croix," she continued in a newsy tone, "you have eschewed the usual mode of dress for formal events in favor of a bloody and war-torn battle uniform. Can you tell us why?"

Consulate general? What the heck was that? Formulating an answer to her question, I walked to the wingback chair and sat, motioning Audric and Rupert into place behind me. Before I could figure out how to answer the reporter's question, the door opened again and Eli Walker strode in, dressed in his usual cowboy finery: jeans, a great-looking pair of embossed and tooled boots, a fringed jacket, and a buff-colored cowboy hat that shaded his amber eyes.

He flashed me a glance but strode to Audric. "I ain't done embassy stuff before," he said, turning on a lackadaisical charm. "Where does the most junior champard stand, anyway?"

I froze in the act of settling myself, knowing my expression was caught in the camera, and when this aired, it would be clear to the world that I was . . . nonplussed was close. Looking like I had been hit over the head with an ax was closer. Calls, Audric had said. How many? And to whom? I slowly sank into the seat while Audric directed Eli to my left and behind Rupert. All I could think, was, *Good. Three is an auspicious number.* On its heels was the thought, *Another one I may get killed.*

The door opened again, the bells over it ringing like a paean of joy. Cheran Jones, his face impassive, walked in, carrying three cases. Into the opening behind him walked three city fathers, Jasper and Shamus in brown robes and Ebenezer in work clothes, smelling of smoke, dirty, and fire-scorched. He had either been burning the last of Darkness from the battle or he had been cleaning up a burned building. Yet even with the filth that covered him he stood tall, his back unbowed, face serene. This man had sat in judgment over me not long ago. He hadn't been in my favor at the start of my trial, but he had listened, and he had suspended final judgment until after all the evidence was presented, unlike several other town fathers and elders.

Farther along the street, Elder Culpepper and his son, Derek, raced to get in on the action. I was pretty sure they wouldn't make it, and schooled my face against the satisfaction I was feeling. It didn't last long. Lucas and Ciana pushed through the crowd gathering outside and entered the shop, faces pale but similarly determined.

"Uncle Rupert?" Ciana said, pulling herself up to her full height and squaring her shoulders. She was in play clothes, jeans and scuffed boots, the seraph pin blazing on her chest. "I wanna support my stepmama. Where you want us to stand?"

Lucas focused on Eli, as if reading something in my newest champard's face. His eyes hardened before finding mine. He said, "Ciana was there when the call came in. She insisted. And I agree. Where do we go?"

Home, I wanted to say. But I didn't. I let Audric direct them into place at my left, near Eli, but to the side, out of the way of guns and steel. I was pretty sure Lucas and Ciana were standing in the place protocol dictated for my consort and child, marking them under protection, part of my household, and under the protection of the Enclave that licensed me. It was something I should have thought of, a way to protect Ciana from those who might someday want to take away her seraph pin. Only problem? The small technicality that the seraphs had licensed me, not the Enclave.

The visa hadn't offered anything useful about the difference that tiny detail made in diplomatic dealings. I didn't know if that meant the visa had nothing to offer because my situation was unique, or if it meant that when I offered my protection to my three champards and my consort—heaven help me, my consort—and his child, I was legally offering the protection of the High Host of the Seraphim. Could I bind the Host with my word? I had an awful lot of questions, not a single answer.

Blood of the saints. I had no idea what I was doing; neither did the visa. If we didn't know what I was doing, it was likely no one else did either. The thought made a titter rise in my throat and I swallowed it down hard, afraid that if it got out, I'd cackle like a madwoman.

The small crowd shuffled in, the town fathers to the front. The door closed behind them. Romona Benson eased around to the side behind a display cabinet, a position giving her camera maximum scope of the events I was probably about to botch.

Knowing I had reached the point of no return, I arranged the amulets on my chest so the visa and my circular prime were unobstructed, and set the prime amulet that was the handle of the walking-stick sword to the front, across my abdomen. I allowed my neomage attributes to blaze out, my skin glowing the pearly roseate hue of my kind, a glow of energy that even humans could see, and a badge of office of its own.

I looked back at Audric. "Secure the door," I said softly. I heard Cheran gasp, but ignored it, waiting for my champard to seal us in. As the lock clicked, someone tried to open the door, the latch rattling. I didn't look up, and because I paid it no attention, no one else looked either. A polite knock followed, then one less polite.

Ignoring it, I stood, waiting for Audric to return to my right side, *the proper place for my senior champard,* the visa chimed in. *Seraph stones.* This stuff was complicated.

When Audric was in place, I drew on the visa and paged through the instructions, ignoring the dance steps. No way was I attempting a formal diplomatic gavotte on camera. Neomage attributes blazing with all the force I possessed, I said, "Cheran Jones of the New Orleans Enclave, visiting cultural attaché, gold and steel mage . . . *assassin,*" I said pointedly, "welcome."

Cheran blanched.

Gotcha. I tilted my head a fraction to let him know I saw the reaction. "You have my leave to approach." And I sprawled in my chair as if I were a monarch and this, my throne.

Cheran approached, following my lead and walking like a human instead of dancing like a mage, and swept off his hat. The bow was deep, as protocol dictated, but something about the set of his shoulders was mocking when he rose, swishing the silly cape back. "The Louisiana Enclave wishes to establish relations with the Appalachian consulate," he said.

Audric replied, emphasizing the words, "*The Battle Station Consulate* welcomes you and is pleased to establish relations."

Cheran blinked at the title. I liked it. The name fit the description of the town and it gave me all sorts of leeway to handle this any way I wanted. This might work. Maybe.

"As this is a new seat," Cheran said, "it is appropriate for the Enclave of Thorn St. Croix's birth to present her with gifts." He knelt and laid out the three cases, snapping open each and laying back the lid of the first. I felt Audric tense beside me, but the cases held nothing dangerous. Well, not in the usual sense. The weapons I had found in Cheran's room were dangerous, but not while lying in the case.

The weapons that had lain in one side were missing, the indentations empty, leaving only the silvered battle blades. Still, there were a lot of sharp, shiny objects, and I schooled my face to mild surprise at the sight of them. Taking a chance that Cheran wouldn't notice a blended scan, I quickly blinked on mage-sight and then opened a skim, seeing what I had expected. Not the taint of Darkness, but something else. I felt the world surge beneath me and dropped the skim before I tossed my cookies on TV.

Rising to his full height, Cheran met my gaze and said with poorly concealed satisfaction, "The Enclave presents the weapons that would have belonged to Thorn St. Croix had she not left the Enclave . . . illegally."

Well, well, well. He wanted to play dirty in all sorts of ways. The best defense was a good offense, but the unexpected ploy had its points. I threw a leg over the chair arm, assuming the position of the warrior barbarian, in truth. I narrowed my eyes and stroked the prime amulet that was the hilt of my longsword. And I sighed.

Beside me, Audric laughed and spread his stance, cocky and negligent and rude. "My mistrend did not exit illegally. She was drugged and removed. You are misinformed and ill prepared, mage." Around me, the other champards took on aggressive postures.

Cheran's face tightened in surprise. I knew from the haze in his mind that he was truly surprised, meaning that he hadn't been in communication with Élan.

"We suggest you do a little research with Lolo, former priestess of the Enclave," Audric said, his voice silky. "Though it is possible my mistrend was *banished* illegally, she has since been given license by the High Council of the Seraphim to protect her from pillaging humans, as is the right of the High Host." He waved a hand, the gesture bored. "You may present the gifts."

Cheran bowed again, this time as much to hide his thoughts as for protocol. From the large flat case, he lifted the longsword, holding it with a velvet cloth, tilting it to show off the sword's beauty. The blade was tipped on the hilt with a large pink quartz nugget. Beside me, Rupert inhaled noisily. I glanced at him, his eyes riveted on the sword. The sword from his dream. The sword I killed him with.

"The longsword of Damocles," Cheran said, holding the sword to me, one hand beneath the hilt, one beneath the blade, balancing the deadly weapon, yet his skin safe from contact, protected by the velvet. "Damocles, named after a Pre-Ap hero, was from the litter six in the second generation, the child of two battle mages who destroyed the attacking human army. This blade was made with wild magic by his parents, and he became a battle mage of great renown."

I stood in a single fluid motion and extended my arms. Cheran met my eyes, holding them while he transferred the blade to me, sliding the velvet away in a fluid motion. As the weapon came down, I pressed my arms forward slightly, taking the gift on my wrists, on the heavy cloth of my dobok sleeves, rather than my bare palms. Some unnamed emotion skittered through his eyes, and deeper, in his thoughts. "The Sword of Damocles," he said. If I hadn't been deep in his thoughts, I'd have laughed at the whole hokey concept.

The mage glanced down as he stepped back, seeing the Apache Tear on my necklace. He didn't know how much I knew, or if I had done the motion by accident, and he was uncertain, off balance, out of step with the dance that I now led. I wanted to keep him that way.

Something warm and powerful heated my arms through the dobok from the weapon I held, and I recognized the tingle of wild magic, the unpredictable power of my forebears, snared in the steel. It would be a joy to fight with such a weapon, I thought. But I never would. I couldn't risk it.

Seeing my stance, Audric stepped forward and accepted

the gift from me, holding the blade as I did, on the arms of his dobok. The uniform was protected by the conjures of mage masters, impervious to acid, resistant to fire. I nodded to the gift table, the table holding my offerings and, puzzled, Audric placed it there.

One at a time, Cheran Jones gifted me with the weapons that would have been mine long years ago, had I not been cursed with my talent. There were a lot of weapons. Audric accepted them for me, setting them on an empty display cabinet, within view of the camera. When the weapons had all been given, each with its history, provenance, and name, Cheran produced a small, flat box tied with string. Inside was a new leather dobok, black, but with a teal sheen like the iridescence of peacock feathers, and with a teal leather belt that held all the tools of the trade of war. A belt like Audric's, full of throwing stars, small knives, vials for salt water and salt and other, more esoteric things.

I sighed with delight and lifted the dobok out, holding it up against me. It would fit, I was pretty sure. Beneath the uniform lay a pair of gloves and battle boots turned on their sides, the leather a dark teal glowing with recently applied energies of the masters who specialized in defensive warfare conjures. The gloves and boots looked of a size to fit me too.

"I'm more than honored," I said. "The gift of weapons and battle clothes are needed and very welcome." Handing the dobok and its box to Audric, I sat back down and Audric stepped forward, accepting a large satchel of proper clothing, diaphanous and silky—come-hither clothes—all sewn with stones and gold thread. He also accepted a gift of money, a nice heavy sack of clinking gold coin to establish my consulate. Cash money would have worked just as well, but the ceremony of gold was proper, according to the visa's whisperings. Too bad the gold was official, and not mine personally.

Letters of state were presented in a coil tied with scarlet ribbon; others were sealed in envelopes, reminding me that I would need a lawyer with experience in international law and in the relatively new field of mage law. People I would have to contract with and pay. Therefore I needed experienced banking and investment advice. *Seraph stones.*

The teeth of a licensed mage were beginning to eat away at me—I was losing my identity and my life one bite at a time. I sank back, making myself smaller, the reflex of a rabbit caught in a trap.

But no one seemed to notice, not even the blasted camera, which was thankfully focused on the next gift, a fur cloak from the skin of a single buffalo, which, Cheran assured me, had been caught in an ice floe and died. It was a statement for the camera to prove that mages were not violent beings who would slaughter a beast for its fur.

I forced a smile onto my face, as if I were not aware that my life now belonged to others, that it had been stolen from me and there was nothing I could do about it. I accepted the fur and Audric slipped it about my shoulders. I felt the tingle of wild magic and wanted to toss it aside until I could inspect it with mage-senses. That might be construed as an insult to the New Orleans Enclave so I simply folded it from me as if the room were too hot, and handed it to Eli.

His young face was intent and careful and he accepted the gift with something like reverence, clearly wanting to do the job properly. I warmed at the sight and wanted to stroke his hair, which was plastered to his head in the shape of his hat, the cowboy hat resting on the counter behind him. Eased for reasons I didn't understand, I turned back to Cheran Jones.

There were more gifts, additional money to furnish a consulate and guest quarters, offers of trade for the town, which had the town fathers grinning happily, the gift of a snow-el-mobile and the private train car Cheran had arrived in, for when I needed to travel. The loan of two legal and banking representatives, which I accepted immediately. The offer of additional attachés, which Cheran did not want me to accept. Out of spite, I welcomed all the help I could get, though I knew it was a moot point as no one could get in or out of the town until the snow was cleared or melted. I just felt like yanking his chain.

When Cheran was done, he said a pretty speech, which I gathered was written by a lawyer he detested. His thoughts were coming clearer the longer he was close, and I wished heartily for the real Apache Tear to block them. He was a petty man, full of self-indulgent opinions, prejudices, and judgments. And occasional sharp, focused images of the deaths of those around him, especially Audric, Rupert, and me. A homophobe who also wanted his own power base. Warped by the talent that made him an assassin? I had spoken rightly when I named his gifts. Cheran Jones was a walking death machine.

When he was done giving me gifts, I presented the gifts he would take back to the new priestess of the New Orleans Enclave, the necklace with the bit of Amethyst's wheels, several fine, faceted stones that could be set into rings or necklace pendants, a small statue, and twelve necklaces, one for each dignitary at the Enclave of my birth. Cheran received an arm cuff made of Rupert's Mokume Gane, beaten layers of different colors of gold. Cheran's eyes widened at the magnificent gift. Rupert said nothing, though I hadn't asked him for the piece. I could pay the shop back for the gifts with the sack of gold coins. Goody. I was marginally less broke. And the necessities of a public welcome to the visiting mage were out of the way.

The visa, after offering a dozen different ways I might approach the town fathers, fell curiously silent when I stood and knelt to them. I should have danced to the men before kneeling, but there was no way I was going to risk falling flat on my face on TV. I should have offered a lengthy flowery speech. I should have been dressed in see-through chiffon and gauze and looked like a sex machine. No way.

Face near the floor, I said, "Delegation from Mineral City, welcome to the sovereign territory of the Battle Station Consulate. This poor emissary warrior comes in peace to fight in your war against the Dark. Will you accept gifts and offers of trade from this consulate and this neomage, Thorn St. Croix?"

"We will," Shamus said, his tone portentous. "We are honored by your presence."

I stood, reached into a pocket of the battle cloak, and pulled out the bloodred silk scarf. I also palmed a fire-starting amulet, the one that I used to light my stove. Turning to Audric, I held out the scarf and jutted my chin at the longsword with the pink quartz nugget in the hilt. Perplexed but agreeable, Audric took the scarf and covered his palms before lifting the sword and offering it to me. Our skin was protected from the hilt and blade.

Cheran's cheek quivered at the careful handling of the weapon, and I smiled at him, all teeth. Turning my back to him, I looked pointedly at Rupert and then turned to the town fathers. As if I were polishing a prized possession, I wiped the entire longsword with the scarf, and thumbed on the fire-starter incantation. The silk darkened and smoked. It burst into flame.

Everything seemed to happen at once. Moving with the speed of our kind, Cheran stepped back, his head down, his hands moving to his waist. Audric muttered a single syllable that sounded like, "Bird." Rupert stuck out a foot, neatly tripping Cheran, the simple ploy using the mage's own speed against him. Eli caught the small mage and settled him to the floor, a semiautomatic gun under his chin. Rupert, moving with the fluid speed that training with a half-breed had provided him, rested a dagger just below Cheran's breastbone, angled to pierce the mage's heart, effectively stopping any attempt the mage might have made at escape. Audric slapped a gag in Cheran's mouth. I dropped the sword and burning scarf onto the stove. Lucas dumped the contents of the teakettle over the small fire. Ciana picked up the mage's hat and set it on a counter. I pocketed the amulet. All that in an instant. It looked practiced, choreographed, as if Cheran's treachery had been expected.

"Place your hands on the floor," Rupert said, his voice conversational, "over your head." With another nudge, he said, "Hands, one on top of the other, palms down." It was an uncomfortable pose and Rupert repositioned his blade, pressing the point on the back of Cheran's upper hand, depressing it enough to draw blood.

His face pale, Cheran took a shaky breath through his nose, knowing he was well and truly caught. But not knowing why the scarf on the sword had erupted in fire. His thoughts said quite clearly that the poison he had used wasn't supposed to do that.

"If you try to move," Rupert continued, "I'll push down on this knife. Hard. If I think you *might* want to move, or if you start a conjure when my mistrend pulls the gag out, I'll push down. I'll stake you to the floor. Nod if you understand." Cheran nodded once. "Even if you get away, you'll sever tendons. It'll be nasty. You won't use your hands again for a while, maybe a long while if the town fathers arrest you. Understand?"

When the mage didn't respond, Eli shoved his boot tip into the mage's side. "Answer my buddy champard here, or I'll think you need to be taught some manners, bucko."

"I unnerstan'," Cheran said through the gag.

His voice was a bit too calm for my comfort level so I bent over him and took off the fake Apache Tear, letting him see me drop it on the counter. It landed with a soft tink and the mage's eyes widened. Clearly he had been counting on my wearing the Tear constantly, even when it would be smarter not to. Which made me wonder if the charm in the real one was addictive. It would be a clever move if so. Then I wouldn't want to take it off. Ever.

"Surprise," I said softly as I placed my hand over his forehead to better feel his thoughts. "What poison is on the sword?" I said, louder.

All I got from his thoughts were words from a mage nursery rhyme learned in the cradle. "Blood and kin prevail. Blood and kin prevail." The words hid his thoughts.

"Well, that's just ducky," I said. "Pull up his shirt."

While my champards exposed Cheran's belly, I pulled down the cuffs of my dobok and lifted the poisoned weapon in protected hands. Reaching between my two protectors, I placed the booby-trapped sword tip against his skin. I applied pressure, deliberately breaking his skin. Cheran turned white and gasped.

"Take out the gag," I said. The gag was pulled from his mouth, and I said, "What poison and what antidote?" When he didn't answer fast enough, I pressed harder, slicing a quarter of an inch below the skin, delivering a greater dose. His flesh quivered with shock. "What poison and what antidote?" I asked again.

I could read his desire not to answer, and his fear. In mage-sight, his attributes changed from the roseate hue of well-cooked shrimp to a paler shade, beer yellow. Sickly. He licked his lips. The camera zoomed close. I waited patiently, knowing he would break. Dropping the sight and opening a mind-skim, I breathed in his scent, both the scent that humans and animals can smell and the underlying scent of mages.

A strange odor came from Cheran, sweat and fear and imminent death. I bent over the mage and smiled wider, placing my foot on his abdomen. Making up his mind, his thoughts cleared. "It's called spider blue," he said, his voice vibrating beneath my boot sole, his throat working. "In my breast pocket. White vial."

Audric joined us on the floor, going through the mage's clothes. I spotted the TV camera maneuvering for a better angle as sweat broke out on Cheran's face and soaked his shirt. Audric laid six vials on the floor, ones I remembered from the case of liquids in Cheran's room. Poisons. *Assassin.*

"Please," he said. "The antidote. The blue bottle. Two cc's, delivered IV push."

I hadn't a clue what that meant, but Audric did, and found a small syringe with a needle in the killer's cummerbund. Cheran was a traveling pharmacy. Audric drew up a small amount in the needle and shoved the mage's sleeve up.

"Not yet," I said. Cheran's eyes slipped to me, desperation lurking within. I said, "What other nasty tricks are on the blades? On the other gifts?"

"None," he said, quickly. "Nothing. I swear." When I cocked my head to the side and waited, he shouted, "I swear before the High Host." His thoughts were clear and certain. There was nothing else. Not today.

"How do I clean the sword of the contaminant?" I asked.

"Salt water."

I stepped away and nodded to my champards. Rupert stuck the gag back in. Audric didn't bother to clean the mage's skin, simply inserted the needle and pressed the plunger. Cheran hissed, but his thoughts were unambiguous. We were in time. He'd live. I wasn't sure I wanted him alive, but I figured that killing a visiting dignitary on TV, even if he had tried to poison me, wasn't such a good idea.

I stepped back and sat in my chair, still holding the sword, the tip coated with mage-blood, the scent familiar and crisp. The town fathers backed away fast, the sounds of their feet echoing in the tall-ceilinged room. "I hope you'll forgive me," I said to Shamus Waldroup. "An internal matter."

"So we see," Ebenezer said, eyes wide. "Is it safe to allow him the freedom of the streets?"

"I think so. Or it will be after my champards remove his weapons and poisons and leave him with only those things he's purchased in town."

"It'll be my pleasure," Audric said.

"Good," I said, without looking around. "For now, tie him up. Rope, not chain." I laid the sword across the stove, careful not to touch any cloth that would—or should—burst into flame.

I stepped behind my chair and lifted the silver bowl of salt water I had placed there, just in case I needed it against a Darkness. It had another use now. I placed the bowl on the floor in front of the camera and the town fathers. Gingerly, I dipped in the sword's sharp point. Nothing happened. No burst of dark smoke, no spit of electricity, but then this wasn't a conjure. It was a poison. Audric handed me the singed scarf to complete the cleansing and I wet it, squeezing the salt water out to rinse across the sword.

When I was finished with the symbolic act, I lifted my battle cloak and used it to raise the silvered blade. Facing the town fathers, I angled my head for the camera, playing to it, using it to send a message to the New Orleans Enclave. They had sent an assassin. They wanted to play dirty.

"A battle warrior has few gifts to offer, except the might of her arm and a token of peace. This gift comes from the Enclave of my birth. It was meant to destroy me, and through my death, would have harmed this town. Therefore, it symbolizes a link between us.

"The weapon is cleansed and no longer a danger. Let it be hung in a place of the town fathers' choosing." I transferred the sword, still in the cloak, just in case there were traces of the nasty poison on the sword, to Shamus Waldroup's arms. "A symbol of the pact between us," I said. And proof to Rupert that his dream was not, could not be, fact. Rupert's face softened and he rolled Cheran facedown, placing his foot on the mage's back.

I bowed deeply to the delegation, indicating that I was finished with my part of the official business. Audric surreptitiously moved the silver bowl. Probably afraid I'd trip on it.

Shamus, the senior father, set the sword to the side, gave me my cloak, stepped forward, and bowed as low as his creaky bones allowed. Like me, he turned slightly so the camera could see his face. I didn't know if he was playing to the audience, making political hay while he could, nurturing the image of the town for the rest of the world, or a mixture of motivations.

He stood upright, his bald, dark-skinned head catching the light just as Audric's did. "The town fathers of Mineral City welcome the neomage representative. We accept the gift of the sword and its symbol of harmony between consulate and town. We come bearing gifts and offers of peaceful trade, as well as asking the neomage assistance against this present Darkness."

"Trade will be considered, of course," I said, "but the defense of the town does indeed come first. Both passes to the town are blocked by avalanche, tons of snow and ice obstruct the Toe River, the train tracks, and all egress and entrance." As if he didn't know all this, but it had to be said for the camera, for the rest of the world.

"Darkness attacked night before last, fighting with new strategy, unlike methods devil spawn have historically used. They fought as if directed, as if led by a master of warfare. Dragonets came, and wreaked havoc. And at the end, a Dark tornado came out of the night and swept much away."

I remembered the feel of the Dark wind, the terror, and the way my heart beat in triple time, fueled by adrenaline and exhaustion. I let the memory show on my face. And I settled back in my chair for a long, boring rehashing. But Shamus surprised me. Cutting through all the layers of protocol suggested by the visa, he said, "The Mineral City emissaries know the consulate general will offer her protection as she is able. We depend on her generosity of spirit and the gifts of protection and warfare provided by God the Victorious when he sent her to us."

Okay. That was a shocker.

He stepped forward, holding out an old wooden box, the top upholstered in maroon velvet and centered with a finial that looked like pure gold. "Mineral City offers this token of our favor and appreciation to *our town mage*."

The words and title warmed me and I stood with a lighter heart, accepting the box. I raised my eyebrows at him, and

Shamus nodded, smiling and showing coffee brown teeth. Carefully, I lifted the lid. Inside, lying on a red velvet bed shaped to hold it secure, was a cross made of gold. In its center was set a faceted emerald the size of a hen's egg, the gem glowing with green light.

"It's said that Benaiah Stanhope, the Mole Man, carried this cross into battle against the Darkness," Jasper said softly. "That he carried it aloft when he gave his life to bind the Dragon. It's said that his blood still lines the crevices in the setting of the stone. We offer it to you, knowing it should be carried into battle again, in the grasp of the one who will rebind the evil."

I knew what an honor this was, to be offered the use of any of Mole Man's possessions, and understood that, like the sword I had given away, this wasn't a personal present, but more in the nature of a loan, to be returned when the need was over, or to be kept in perpetuity in the consulate. Opening my senses, I breathed in, catching the scent of old blood, human and something else. In mage-sight, the artifact glowed with blue light, but specks of Darkness were there too, and that was something I would have to consider later, when no camera was present.

I looked up at Shamus. "Mineral City honors me." I closed the box and handed it to Audric, who placed it on a display cabinet. Bending over the table, I lifted the wrapped bundle containing my formal gift to the town. It too was more like a tribute, a gift of state. And while it wasn't worth as much in monetary terms as the cross or the sword, it was valuable to me.

"I offer this small token to the town fathers." I set it in Shamus' hands, supporting them when he was surprised at the weight. "I carved it from the quartz crystal of the nearby hills," I said as I peeled back the layers of soft cloth to reveal a small statue. It was a seraph with wings held high over his head, tips touching. He wore battle armor and carried a sword braced across his body. The figure was only inches high, but it had taken me weeks of recuperation time after the last major battle beneath the Trine to carve it. It was hand polished, but only in sections. The face and feet were clear as lead crystal, the stone bending light. The wings were unpolished, giving them a ruffled texture. The body was partially smoothed, still fruzy, the matte finish of the shaped but unpolished, natural rock.

Shamus stared at the statuette in shock, snapping his mouth closed and swallowing before he could speak. "The consulate general of the Battle Station Consulate is far too generous. We are honored to accept this gift on behalf of the town."

The camera focused full screen on the carving for half a minute before Romona backed slowly away, taking in the fathers, the tied mage, me, and settling on Jasper as the man moved close to Shamus.

Jasper touched the seraph with a finger as if expecting it to be cold, carved from ice. When it was warm to his touch, he sucked in a breath and lifted his head. Closing his eyes, he said, "The gift is fitting. Battle Station Consulate was created by the High Host, licensed by the seraphim, and blessed by the visits of seraphs at a time when they so seldom leave their Realms of Light." His voice was low, deeper than his usual tone, meditative and resonant, and a frozen wind seemed to blow across my flesh, raising it into tight goose bumps at the tone.

"This place has been sanctified by the presence of two sigils, one in the consulate itself"—he opened his eyes and gestured to the sigil burned into the display case glass, his brown robe of office undulating with the movement as if a wind blew through the room—"and one in the street, that glowed when our mage received help from Minor Flames in the battle two nights ago." He lifted his other arm and pointed out the window to the street, leaving him with arms outstretched to either side.

My throat went dry, aching with tightness. A shiver raced over me at his expression. My entire body tightened as if to ward off a blow, and I had to fight to keep from drawing my weapons. Audric and Rupert stepped back. I wanted to sink into the chair, or run away and hide from the look in his black eyes, fervent glory illuminating them with the light of prophecy.

The ordinary, down-to-earth Jasper was no longer in the room. In this moment, he was truly an elder of the kirk, dedicated to the service of God the Victorious. I had never seen the presence of true prophecy before, had never seen holy ardor fall on a spokesman of the Almighty, but I knew that had happened to my old friend Jasper. As if uplifted by the hand of his God, his eyes glowed with divine zeal, with the presence of the Most High.

Beside him, Shamus and Elder Ebenezer dropped to their knees, moving with awe, their creaky bones grinding in the silence. Eli fell to his knees as well, and then bowed his face to the floor in obeisance. I slid to my knees, and my champards all followed. Romona knelt as well, filming, still filming, and I wanted to laugh, a witless titter aching in my throat. I heard her mutter into the mike, almost below the sound of human hearing, "And every knee shall bow."

"Battle Station Consulate is a new thing," Jasper said, no longer sounding quite human, but with the richness of otherworldly passions, his voice a low rumble of sound. He raised his hands high, his sleeves falling away to reveal a work shirt of faded brown cotton, but he might as well have been wearing cloth of gold, because his flesh was glowing through it, full of power.

He raised his face as if he could see through the second story and into the sky beyond. Closing his eyes in ecstasy, Jasper whispered, "The children of men are gathered." His voice rose and deepened, the resonance vibrating into my bones. "The Dragon breaks free. All the old things have passed away."

Jasper dropped his arms slowly to his sides. His head came down, bowing, eyes closed as if he slept. And he slid to the floor in a boneless heap.

Chapter 14

*T*he children of men are gathered. That had been the prophecy. The words had gone out to the world, Romona not waiting for my approval before she uploaded the entire diplomatic session on the cell phone. God the Victorious had spoken, superseding my request to review and cut footage.

The children of men are gathered. Did it, could it, mean what I thought? What I hoped?

I had never been to visit Thaddeus Bartholomew, had never been to his room in the town's one hotel, but I seemed to be making a habit of slinking my way into men's bedrooms. And to be the recipient of predictions and prophecy. Predictions could be thwarted and bypassed. Prophecy could not. I pushed away the thoughts. Later. I could deal with them later.

The kylen was asleep when I opened the door, his big body stretched out on the sagging mattress, a down coverlet pulled over him. The blinds were closed, throwing the room into murky shadows, turning the chair in the corner into a hulking monster, transposing the open armoire into a gateway from another realm.

Gloved hands moving clumsily, I closed the door behind me, the latch snicking softly. I took my first breath. Scents of caramel and vanilla, a hint of brown sugar, and beneath it all something peppery, like ginger, filled my head, rich and heated. The scent of kylen, part mage, part seraph, and part human. The smell of sex and need and desire.

Mage-heat slid over me and into me, tightening my breasts and weakening my knees. Desire pooled in my belly and breasts. I stared into the need, into myself, considering.

The Most High had done some strange things in his creation, and mage-heat was up there among the strangest, *If* the Most High had done it. *If* mage-heat was more than an accident, and was planned by the creator of the universe. *If* there was such a creator.

The thought was blasphemy, but the existence of the creator had been questioned by others, people a lot smarter than I. I had questioned it myself until today. But now I was beginning to have suspicions about my own doubt. Did the One True God exist? Had he created the universe and all that was in it? Did he give a flying flip that we were here? Did he bother with our paltry, petty lives? Had he really created the children of men—the mages, the kylen, the Stanhopes? And if so, what were we? The next evolutionary step of humankind?

It sounded so ludicrous, like a really bad Pre-Ap movie. *Attack of the Killer Tomatoes. Invasion of the Body Snatchers.* Or worse. The films about superheroes, Superman or the X-Men.

The children of men are gathered. The old things are passed away. Seraph stones. I drew on my amulets to control my rising heat. If I was right, then Lolo's quest for a soul had some merit. Maybe a lot of merit. If mages were indeed a branch of the children of men, those special, anticipated beings prophesied about for millennia, then God the Victorious *owed* us souls. Owed us the opportunity for immortality just like the humans had. Owed *us*. . . .

Thadd's breathing stuttered. Halted. Resumed at a faster rate.

He was awake.

Slowly he turned on the mattress, sheets swishing, and met my gaze across the room. "You shouldn't be here," he said, his voice a sleepy growl.

"Yes, I should." *I think.*

He rolled from the bed, his big body lithe and muscled in the half-light. He was naked. Aroused. Reddish hair, penny-bright, covered his legs and arms, redder than the hair on

his head, brighter than the scruff of beard that covered his
jaw. Brighter still was the hair at his groin, his manhood
rising in the middle of his body. I stared and licked my lips,
hungry for him. Wanting to feel his touch.

"You should go," he said as he crouched, a warrior's
stance. He was holding himself back, his control a fragile
silken rein, easily broken. Violence and passion were intertwined for mages and kylen, twin desires, too often overlapping.

His hands rose, half reaching, half gesturing me away. His
kylen ring was not on his finger—the ring that had hidden
the truth of his genetic heritage even from himself—the
reason why our heat was rising so fast. I glanced to his side
and saw the ring on the table. He had been fighting the
change ever since he discovered what he was. I wondered
why he had taken it off now, allowing the transformation
into pure kylen to proceed at the accelerated rate.

"Come here," he demanded.

My body softened, need pooling in me like magma, hot
and melting. Breath shallow and fast, I kept my place, feast-
ing on the sight of his body.

Wings, feathered with the two-tone plumage of a kylen
youth, stretched up behind his shoulders and along the
length of him, to his knees. He half spread them, the
lighter-than-air bones lifting to the sides, feathers rippling.
The wings had achieved their full length, useless for flight,
ornamental only, but with cardinal-crimson flight feathers,
darkest at the tips, lightening to white down beneath the
wings, speckling white and red at his shoulders.

Paeans of song darted through me, mage songs, about
the wonders of mating with kylen, the unbearable heat, the
taste and smell and touch of them. The feel of seraph-down
tickling along a stomach. . .

I forced my gloved hand into my pocket and around the
seraph stone there. In a single, fluid move, I pulled it from
my battle cloak and tossed it to him. "Catch," I said.

On instinct, faster than any human could have, Thadd
reached out and caught the stone. And the heat flaring
between us died. The need didn't fade away. The instant he
touched the stone with his bare hand, it was simply gone, as
if ripped away, as if a spear point had been yanked out of

flesh, leaving a gaping, empty wound. I closed my eyes hard against the loss and blinked away the tears that gathered.

"What—? What happened?" Thadd asked, looking around the room. Slowly his shoulders relaxed, wings folding tight against him, his bare feet long and lean on the floor. There was no doubt that his desire was gone, wilted away, so to speak. Grief and relief blended within me.

"What is it?" he asked, turning the stone over in his palm. Thadd was unconcerned at being naked in front of me, almost unaware of his state, of my regard, of the barren and aching space between us. I wanted to cry, and struggled for the nonchalance that seemed so very far away.

I fought to speak normally and pretty much succeeded, only a little waver giving me away. "It's the seraph stone Zadkiel gave me," I said. "I knew it had healed me, but I wasn't sure what else it could do. Until now."

"How does it work? Are there more of them?"

"I don't know, except it requires the touch of skin to make it most effective. I wore it on my amulet necklace in the battle and when you showed up I went into mage-heat. With it in my pocket, I felt mage-heat. In your hand, nada. Nothing. No mage-heat at all." Which hurt like plagues and death, but I was through whining.

"I was guessing it worked along the lines of battle dire and bloodlust. Both can reduce mage-heat to varying degrees. I thought the Host found a way, or was given a way, to bring it under control, maybe by stimulating the same chemicals that blank desire during near-death warfare. But now, after experiencing it—" I stopped myself and licked my lips again. They were full and swollen as if Thadd had kissed me. The sting of loss spread through me and I pushed it away, chasing my thread of thought until I found it. "The stone works too fast to be promoting a chemical reaction. I think it's something else, a conjure, maybe."

Thadd nodded and turned, picking up a pair of jeans, sliding into them, buttoning them on his hips, hiding his form beneath the conformity of clothes. I tried to ignore the sadness that settled into me at the loss of the vision of his naked body, like something Michelangelo would have carved, had he ever found such a magnificent model.

Moving the stone from hand to hand as he worked, Thadd pulled a modified shirt over his wings and his arms with an efficiency that proved he had been practicing, and buttoned it in place.

"What do you think it means," he asked, "that a seraph gave this to you?"

"'The children of men are gathered. The old things are passed away,'" I quoted. "I think it means that all the humans alive now, the human remnant, and all the mages, and all the kylen, are the children of men, the final result, the ultimate genetic pool of the humans who survived the Last War. I think the mages were the first to demonstrate the changes that are coming to all humans. I think the Stanhopes are another phase of that change. If so, it means that the last days are drawing to a close. The end is near."

He quirked a half smile at me, not concealing a gentle mockery. "That's pretty melodramatic."

I told him about the consulate meeting that was playing over and over again on SNN, creating a worldwide sensation. I quoted the entire prophecy. And then I told him about Rupert's vision of the old church and the huge snail-like things that crawled up the walls. I told him about Rose, captured and drugged and lying on an altar in Rupert's dream. About how I was supposed to murder Rupert, but that I had changed the tools available to fate, or to God the Victorious, to make the vision fail. I told him about the dreams I had been having, dreams that mirrored Rupert's in so many ways.

As I talked, his amusement fell away, leaving him introspective, reflecting. He turned the stone again, his eyes searching mine. "We can change predictions," Thadd said, repeating my own thoughts, "but we can't change prophecy. Was I there? In Rupert's dream?"

"I think so. You. Lucas. Eli."

"And the things that looked like you?"

"I think they were his dream-interpretation of the succubus larvae." I took a deep breath, wondering if he would laugh at me. I plunged on. "I think the mages and the kylen weren't an accident, that we were planned for and expected by someone. Maybe by the Most High."

The small smile spread. He was amused at me and not trying to hide it.

"I think that we're necessary to ending the war between the Light and the Dark that's been raging for so long. For eons."

He shook his head at my whimsy.

I smiled back and shrugged, tucking my hands into my cloak pockets. "I know how it sounds. But look at the evidence. Battle Station Consulate was established and licensed by the High Host, not by an existing enclave. That's the way Enclaves were originally created. We have two mages, one kylen, two sigils, a Flame-blessed blade, three foretellings, a seraph stone that stops mage-heat, a mountain with a hellhole and three peaks, and new forms of Darkness. A succubus queen has laid eggs that then were moved to a safe place, and that place became part of a predictive dream that showed my sister, battle, and seraphs in a killing heat. We have a Dark tornado and a Dragon, which may be the same thing. I could list more, but—"

"I get the picture. So what do you want with me?" he asked, still amused. Big tough man humoring the little woman. It made me want to sock him. So I did, verbally.

"I want you to go public."

His face hardened. "No."

I looked pointedly at his wings. "You can't hide it anymore. I want you to meet me at dusk on the street in the center of the sigil, and swear to become my champard. That puts you under the protection of Battle Station Consulate. Under my protection. And under the protection of the High Host."

I watched as the logic of the argument made a home for itself in his mind. His face changed slowly, the stubborn cast fading, deliberation and something like respect growing. And his amusement was back, broader and wider. He chuckled and ran a hand through his too-long red hair, leaving it in stiff peaks. "You came up with this all by yourself?"

"I think I did. I'm not really sure how much I'm figuring out and how much God the Victorious is feeding me."

"If he exists. And if he speaks to mages, against all the

theology of the kirk about the Most High speaking to soulless beings."

I didn't agree with the disclaimer, I simply watched him.

"If I'm under your protection," he said, "then I'm technically under the protection of the High Host."

"Provided we do it formally, with all the ceremony required. Then they can't take you away to a Realm of Light without asking my permission. If they want you, it becomes a catch-22. They can't take you unless I agree. And if I want to fight it, this battle station could technically be described as a Realm of Light."

"Mineral City?" he said, laughing. "A realm?"

I wasn't insulted. He had a point. But my concerns were elsewhere. I jutted my chin at the huge ring lying on his bedside table. "Why did you take off the ring?"

Thadd's face fell, all amusement draining away. He looked down, busying himself buttoning his shirt, not meeting my eyes. "I couldn't stand the pain anymore," he said after a moment. "I haven't slept in three weeks. Pain meds weren't touching it."

One hand reached back to stroke his feathers, fingers sliding through the down. As he moved, his scent expanded and filled the room, stronger, more demanding. Just the smell of him was intoxicating. "I decided to let it take me at a time of my choosing.

"I think I'm a third-generation kylen," he said, extending his wings. They were six feet on a side, looking ludicrously small in comparison to a seraph's twenty-three-foot wingspan. "Flightless. And besides"—he folded his wings and shrugged as seraphs shrug, wing-wrist bones touching together behind him—"though we have no idea what I can do, maybe if the transition is complete, I'll have something to offer when the Darkness returns. Something you can use."

I understood that he meant some power, some talent for manipulating creation energies. He meant that he would be willing to share his gift, whatever it was, in conjures that I would control. Seraph power was very different from mage power, and mages couldn't wield it. But if he gave me control over it, helped me to utilize it, things might be different.

It was an offer of unprecedented generosity. Kylen were

notoriously tightfisted when it came to their gifts, a power
that could be much greater than any single mage possessed.
In the case of a kylen who had not transformed in the womb,
but had been under the constraint of a restrictive conjure
his whole life, power of any kind was questionable. It might
mean Thadd possessed a volatile wild magic, unstable, powerful enough to wipe Mineral City off the map. It might
mean he possessed nothing. Or any amount in between. But
it was more than I'd had available to fight the Dragon a
moment ago.

Prompted by the visa, I lowered my head in a bow and
said, "This mage is honored at the offer of your might." I
raised my head and searched his eyes, in which amusement
still lurked. But now it was the devil-may-care mirth of the
soldier who faced insurmountable battle. "So, you'll meet
me? Just before sunset?" I asked.

"Why not," he said, laughing the words. "I gotta die
someday. But since I may bleed out all over the streets of
this misbegotten town in the next few hours, there's one
thing I want." He tossed the seraph stone to the mattress,
stepped to me, and opened my battle cloak. In a single
motion, he slid one arm around my waist, gripped my neck
in firm fingers, and jerked me close. His mouth found mine.
Heat flared between us.

I breathed into his mouth, the taste-smell-feel of him
waking my mage-senses. I closed my eyes, knowing this was
stupid, but needing him, wanting this so very much.

Behind my lids, I saw his aura flare brighter than any
human's, brighter than any mage's, shocking and intense,
an image like cinnamon on my tongue, the synesthesia of
kylen-mage melding so intense that I couldn't separate sight
from taste and smell. With his transformation so nearly
complete, the mind-bending merge was concentrated into
all the colors of the rainbow, all the scents of a candy store,
a bakery, all the textures of heated velvet.

I arched into him, pressing along his length, rising onto
my toes as he lifted me closer. I was dimly aware when my
cloak fell to the floor with a swish of sound and I relaxed
into the mattress beneath me, sheets cool and scented of
him. Thadd settled between my legs and pressed against the
center of me, needing me as much as I wanted him.

Mage-rut roared, a wild whitewater river of desire, my body preparing for him, belly quivering, breasts so tight they ached to be touched. Pain and pleasure.

A dobok isn't conducive to mating, hard to get into when standing, impossible to get out of while lying on my back, my legs wrapped around Thadd's waist. I pulled at my own clothes, mindless fingers at the fastenings. His hand found its way through an opening and stroked along my side. I hissed and clawed at him, raking his skin until my fingers touched the down at his back, beneath his wing. I pulled in a shuddering breath and stilled. Slowly I eased my hands into the cavities beneath his wings.

Heated, hotter by several degrees than my own body temperature, the nevus, the massed and coiled blood vessels that fed seraph wings in flight, pulsed against my hands. His down, softer than the finest fur, rubbed against my palms, warm and alluring. I heard myself groan as his wings lifted and fell around me, the movement creating a prism of light in the air.

His hand found my breast, stroking it into a tight point. Need raked its claws through me and I pulled at his jeans, whispering, "More. Now. Now!"

Thadd laughed, a low thrum of sound against me, his breath rapid as he worked the hooks, buttons, and Velcro straps of the dobok. I tore at his jeans, the buttonholes, the blasted buttonholes, too tight.

A polite knocking sounded.

Thadd grunted. The knock came again, louder.

"Thadd?" It was Lucas.

"Son of a seraph," Thadd grated, swearing.

"You are a son of a seraph," I said, giggling senselessly. "Which means you just swore by yourself."

Thadd chuckled with me, raising his weight off, to brace on his locked arms, hands to either side of my face. "That's your husband at my door," he said. "My cousin. And his timing either sucks or is as lucky as the plague survivors. Either way, I hate his guts."

"Ex-husband," I said as he shifted to the left, scrabbling in the sheets, spotting the stone above my shoulder, nested in a pool of pillows. I realized what he intended and said, "No!"

"Yes. This may hurt." Thadd picked up the seraph stone.

It did. Heat whipped from me. I cramped brutally, stomach muscles contracting, ovaries in a spasm as the hormonal impulse to ovulate stopped in an instant. I rolled from beneath him, curling into a ball, holding myself tight. "Tears of Taharial," I whispered, knowing it was foolish to curse aloud so close to the Trine, but not able to stop myself.

Thadd rotated in the sheets, pulling the top one to the floor as he stood. He bent over and supported himself on his knees, breathing slowly, his thigh muscles rippling beneath the denim fabric, his wings half-spread, plumage quivering.

The knocking came again, this time banging. Lucas had heard me. "Thorn! Open up!"

"Did you lock the door when you came in?" Thadd asked, his voice rough. He looked at me. "How'd you get in anyway?"

I sat up and rearranged my clothes, pulling the dobok in place. Thadd had moved everything around, finding my breast through a rent in the padded cloth. "I stole a key at the front desk. And no. He can get in any time he—"

The door slammed open, Lucas standing in the opening, his face twisted in righteous anger. He took in the tableau, me on the bed, fully clothed, even my boots still on. Yet, the bed was rumpled, sheets on the floor, and my hair was snarled in what the kind might call disarray, the way hair looked after a riotous romping. Thadd was standing, his shirt open, jeans partially unbuttoned, feet bare, his wings half-spread. *Sweet Hail Mary.* His wings were spread.

Behind Lucas, Eli appeared. His mouth opened in shock and he said, "Holy crap. He's a kylen."

We looked like something out of a decadent television series, one of the Pre-Ap shows they called soaps. Three men, only one of them fully human, and the woman they all claimed they wanted. Well, sort of.

Had Lucas followed me? How guilty and stupid would I feel if I asked? Better to ignore it. If I hadn't been in so much pain from the interrupted heat, I might have laughed. As it was, I groaned in misery and pushed to my feet. I hadn't felt this bad since the fight on the Trine.

I looked from Lucas and Eli to Thadd, to the stone in his hand, and chose my battles by picking the smallest and easiest—and the one that made me the most angry. The mage stone. "That was just pure mean," I said.

"It's not like I'm enjoying it either," Thadd said, his voice tense with pain. "Between the stone and your men friends, I may not survive this." Still holding himself rigid, he backed up as Lucas and Eli crowded in. "But if I live through it, you can beat me up."

"Count on it," I said.

I stalked out of the old hotel into the late afternoon light and turned uphill, trudging toward Upper Street, still adjusting the dobok, which had gotten turned against my skin. My lips were bruised, my cloak was loose over my shoulders and dragging on one side, and my hair was half up in a queue, half straggling down my back. My thoughts and feelings were just as snarled and tangled.

I was unable to separate the individual strands of thwarted desire, irritation with the three men still arguing in Thadd's hotel room, logical interpretation of consulate protocol and diplomatic law, prophecy and predictions, and blasphemy. My life was a shambles. I wanted three men and could have no sort of normal life with any of them. If I chose Thadd, I'd have litter after litter of fourth-generation kylen who would probably be taken from me the day they were born and raised in Realms of Light. I'd stay in heat year-round, which would feel great, but turn me into a sex and baby-making machine.

With Eli, I'd dance a lot and have kinky sex, making half-breed babies, the physically anomalous, sterile, second unforeseen, like Audric. Bred for battle, perpetually unhappy, and probably ticked off at me for birthing them. I'd have a litter every time a seraph came near.

And if I chose Lucas, he'd cheat on me before the year was out, breaking my heart again. A small voice whispered to me that I couldn't get my heart broken if I didn't care for him. I ignored it. What did I know?

I had a sudden vision of Thadd tossing the seraph stone onto the mattress. Within easy reach. Then he tossed me up beside it. "Stones and blood," I hissed below my breath. *The son of a seraph had experimented on me.* He had set up the heat, tested it with a full-body clinch, and then used the stone to make sure rut could be shut off at almost any stage. It had been a test. *A game.*

I wouldn't just beat him up. I'd kick him so hard he'd be singing soprano for a year.

I stomped onto Upper Street and passed Waldroup's Furniture Store, seeing my ridiculous reflection in the big windows. Smoothing my hair, I slowed, adjusted my cloak, and forced my steps into a normal walking pattern as I reined in the anger. In the window, beyond my image, was a desk and chair carved in rococo, an ornate Pre-Ap style.

Even through my pique, I liked the set. If I survived the next week, I would need to furnish the Battle Station Consulate/Realm of Light. The thought of something so mundane and normal as decorating brought tears to my eyes. I had lost the opportunity for anything in my life to be normal. Of my quiet, introspective life, working stone, making jewelry, having friends who depended on me to get out of bed each day and show up for work in a store, there was little left. Next to nothing, in fact. Nothing except the half-baked plan I had devised to keep us alive.

I stopped and moved closer to the window, splaying my hand open on the glass, not really seeing the rest of the furniture in the showroom. No matter what happened with my plan, it would result in suffering. My breath fogged the window and froze, creating a glazed circle, spreading with each exhale.

It was getting colder. The puffs of white breath were denser. Snow was coming. A lot of it.

I turned to the street, pulling my cloak tight around me, and surveyed the place I had called home for a decade. It bore only marginal resemblance to the Mineral City of my memory, burned, damaged, its populace decreased by war and Darkness. There were few people out and about. Only one snow-el-mobile churning along the street. Two horses and riders moved at a fast clip. Businesses were closed. Blood splashed the dirty snow. The sigil beneath the ice glowed softly in my mage-sight. A cloud of smoke raced between the buildings, carrying the scent of burned wood and the residual, rank smell of cremated spawn. Above the town, heavy clouds gathered on the western mountains, presaging a blizzard.

A cold breeze was coming off the Trine, its three peaks wreathed in mist and cloud, white caps on the summits visible occasionally through thinning gaps. To mage-sight, the left peak appeared yellow, shot through with black, the air itself hazy with Dark energies.

Oh, yeah. All I had left was the plan. The wind caught my loose hair and plucked it from the braid, blowing strands across my face. I twisted them all back into the queue in irritation. What a mess. What a horrid mess. People were going to die. People I loved. And it was going to be my fault.

Chapter 15

S top. Stop right there."
    Lucas. Drat. I heaved a deep breath, trying to cleanse away sudden nervous irritation, and turned to him. I would rather face down a dozen devil spawn than my ex when he was ticked off. Lucas was rounding the corner onto Upper Street, moving in a jerky, hurried motion that signified anger, ruffled feathers—No wait, that would be Thadd. I grinned and relaxed a bit, waiting for him.

"I don't think it's funny," he said long before he reached me.

The words rang down the street and I raised my brows at his tone. He was jealous. My lips widened as I watched my ex-husband approach. He was beautiful, black-haired, blue-eyed, limber and slender, with the musculature of the tested and well-practiced runner.

My heart turned over in my chest. *Seraph stones.* I still loved the cheat.

"What were you doing in his room?" he demanded.

"I'm pretty sure it was an experiment," I said.

Confused at what seemed an improbable answer, Lucas stopped, blowing puffy clouds of breath like mine. The clouds met between us and merged. I stepped back, not liking the symbolism. I might love him, but I'd never go back to him.

"What kind of experiment?"

"To see if mage-heat could be stopped by the amulet Zadkiel gave me."

"So? You had to *kiss* him?"

I let the smile grow. "Yeah. I did. And it worked. Mage-heat died."

"Meaning that you..." He stopped whatever he was about to say and shoved his hands into the pockets of his jacket. It was the frustrated action of a little boy, and I was certain he had no idea he looked so adorable. The smile left my face at the thought. Lucas Stanhope was not—*not*—adorable. He was a cheat and a heartbreaker.

"Meaning you didn't have sex with him?" he said, half question, half declaration.

"I didn't."

When I said nothing further, he moved up beside me and we resumed walking toward the store. And the consulate. *Criminy. The consulate. Can I make my life any more complicated?* A silence built between us broken only by the wind whistling through the town and higher in the mountains and by the crunch of our boots.

Lucas started to speak once and bit down on the words. I waited. "Where do I stand?" he asked at last. "With you?"

"What do you mean?"

"You put me in the position of consort in the consulate. That announced to the world that we have a relationship, that we share a child. But afterward you left and went to another man. Where does that leave me? Consort or not?"

I watched my boot toes as they emerged beneath the cloak with each step. Left, right, left. I might die tonight. Or he might. The whole town might. I owed him honesty at the least. Kindness at the best. "I love you, Lucas. I think I've loved you since the first time I saw you."

When he touched my arm I shook him off, fighting the bitterness that welled up in me, tightening my throat, making words difficult to speak. "But I can't trust you. Because you can't help but look at any and every female you pass. You can't help but come on to them, flirt with them, and make sure they fall in love with you." I heard the long-repressed hostility in my voice but was incapable of controlling it, and I held up my palm when he tried to interrupt. "It's your nature, Lucas. You'd seduce and sleep with my twin if she were around."

"You keep bringing up the past," he said. "I'm different now. I really am."

I looked at him, sadness welling up like water between the rocks of old anger. "I was pretty busy at the consulate meeting. A little overwhelmed. But I had a moment to notice you noticing Romona Benson."

Lucas had the grace to flush. But at least he didn't deny it. "Is that why you went and 'experimented' with my cousin? Who has wings, for crying out loud. *Wings.*" When I didn't answer, Lucas put out a hand again, touching only my cloak, turning me to him. He looked bewildered and, at the sight, I wanted to give in, wanted to bring him back and comfort him. I crossed my arms instead, knowing it was a protective gesture, knowing he would know that.

"I remember how you looked in his bedroom, in his bed. You looked all tousled and beautiful, the way you looked with me, when we were married. And I could have killed him." He held out his hands, flexing them into fists, and a fearful wonder touched his voice. "I wanted to kill him. My own cousin. With freaking wings."

My resentment eased, leaving my heart just a bit lighter in spite of all the danger and uncertainty in my life. "Yeah, well. That's what the experiment was for, I guess, to see if kylen and mages can be in the same place without causing mage-heat. It worked."

We stopped at the entrance to Thorn's Gems and I looked sidelong at him. In mage-sight, Lucas glowed with a nonhuman energy pattern, a bright blue aura. Beneath his skin, blood coursed in veins and arteries, blood that throbbed and flowed in a rich, royal blue configuration. Totally not human. I said, "He's going to be my champard. Thadd is."

Lucas' mouth turned down hard. "I've been reading about the duties of champards. They include sex."

"Sometimes," I agreed gently, "for some mages."

"And you're going to make *him* your champard?"

"At dusk. In the sigil in the street. But I'm not making him mine for mating. I'm making him a champard so he can be part of the plan I worked out. So I can protect him."

"And me? Us?"

I opened the door to the shop and stepped inside. The heat within blasted my face after the cold of the street, and I stopped in the doorway, my back to him. "You divorced me, Lucas. There is no us." I closed the door, closing him out of my life, closing him into the cold.

Standing in my tattered dobok, I stood with my back against the kitchen counter and ate a huge bowl of oatmeal, needing the carbs and the sugar. I usually hoarded the sugar, doling it out in drips and drabs, but this time I had put as much as I wanted on the hot cereal. If I died tonight, why leave a perfectly good sweet uneaten?

Spooning in the oatmeal, I stared at my loft, the one place in the world that was mine. I had bought and paid for the building. I had decorated the apartment to my tastes and mine only, surrounding myself with the greens and taupes and teals I liked best. I loved this place. I never wanted to leave it. But for weeks, it had seemed as if I might have to leave it at any moment. I was always saying good-bye to my life.

Full, I set the dishes in the sink, unwashed. Stripping, leaving my clothes in a pile on the loft floor, I filled the silver bowl with charged stones and dumped them onto the bed, dropped down, curled around them, and pulled the comforter over me. I fell into a dreamless sleep. When I woke, it was after four, a dull afternoon light glowing softly through the windows, predicting the storm brewing. I was refreshed in a way I hadn't been in a long time.

I rose and took a hot shower to loosen muscles that had stiffened in sleep, and added several drops of eucalyptus oil to a rag I draped over the rail. The medicinal scent in the warm, wet atmosphere cleared my head, and I inspected my body in the writhing steam. The soles of my feet were paler and thicker now, not the bright shade of thin, healing skin. My calves and shins were healed over, my knuckles and the backs of my hands were the bright white of scar tissue. My throat was one solid scar. Other scars crisscrossed my body. Ugly. My side, however, was worse—a black ring with a hot, red, central depression. It looked infected, though it didn't hurt. In mage-sight it was even darker, swirling a sickly mustard yellow.

I stretched in the steam, eyes closed, head down, water pouring over me. The shower door opened. I whipped into battle mode and struck out fast, flowing into the claw—

fingers curled and stiff. I aborted the savage-chi move, just as Audric caught my wrist in his big paw. "Audric?"

I tried to cover myself, grabbing the towel from the door and holding it over me. "Get out!" I said, my voice sharp in the confined space.

"No. Turn around."

"You're not welcome in my bathroom, champard," I said, retreating into formality.

"You are my mistrend. You face battle tonight. You are not up to your usual strength or speed. You need a massage to loosen your muscles. Turn around."

I stared at him, feeling the towel molding itself to my body as the shower wet it through. I backed into the stall corner, tile icy on my spine as he entered and closed the door, trapping me.

Audric was a big man, nearly seven feet tall, with skin the brown of his African ancestors, a bald head, and steady eyes. In one hand he held a bottle of oil, in the other was a loofah and a cloth. Clothed, the half-breed was intimidating. With a towel wrapped and tied around his waist, the fabric just as wet as mine, his hairless, naked chest streaming and his feet bare, he was even more daunting.

"I'm not really comfortable with this," I said stiffly, knowing that, if I had stayed in Enclave, such massages, and even casual nudity, would have been part of my daily life. My champards would have lived with me, sharing every detail of my day. But I had grown up in Mineral City, with its stern kirk and unyielding elders, its repressed sexuality and its unremitting cold. Naked skin was seen only on hands and faces and, very rarely, on arms and shins. Never in my shower except for Lucas. My face burned from more than the hot water.

Audric, standing patiently, being blasted by water, raised his brows in amusement. I was a spot of comic relief to everyone today, it seemed, and it stiffened my spine against the cold tile. "I am your champard. A *mule*," he said, enunciating the insulting term. "While I could break every bone in your body, I can't rape you. It's not physically possible."

I couldn't stop the glance at his midsection. "You could try," I said. And blushed a deeper shade when Audric's laugh rumbled through the hissing shower. "Meaning the broken-bone part," I clarified, mortified.

"Turn around." So far as I knew, Audric hadn't seen the wound on my side. And he'd never seen me naked. Well, except for the times he and Rupert had cared for me after my injuries. Which had taken days. Weeks. Okay. I was being stupid. And I hated that.

Audric held out the cloth in his hand. It was a pair of my undies. "You may put these on if it makes you feel better."

You could have told me that first, I thought. I took the soaked panties and made a little "turn around" motion with my finger. Audric laughed harder and turned around. I pulled them on and held the towel to my front again, as I faced the shower stall wall and leaned into it. "Okay," I said. And when I heard the grudging tone, I added, more politely, "I'm ready. Thank you."

Audric said nothing, but his big hands descended onto my shoulders, fingers and heels of his hands pressing into the tight flesh. My blush melted away like soft wax. I groaned, sounds of physical bliss that resembled sexual pleasure. Sounds that would have had Lucas charging in with battle-lust in his eyes. After a moment, I mumbled, "You can shower with me anytime."

"Move your hair," Audric said, still with the timbre of laughter in his words, and I gathered the long mass to one side, giving in to the relief of the massage. So much for the stern kirk elders. Pleasure—one point; rules and regs—zilch.

When the hot water part was over, Audric dried me off as if I were a child and carried me to the bed, where he finished my rubdown, his hands efficiently working my muscles, stretching my joints and tendons, and prying up under my shoulder blades. As he worked, he talked and I mumbled responses and the rare question. I learned a lot of things, some important, some not, but one that had been troubling me was resolved. Audric had never heard of a mage who could blend a skim and mage-sight into one scan. Until me. Lucky me.

When he was done, it was five, and night was falling fast. Feeling really good, better than I could remember, maybe ever, I plaited my hair into a battle braid and let Audric help dress me, strapping and binding me into the new dobok and fastening the teal belt across my chest. I hadn't noticed it earlier, but the belt was tooled and dyed with tiny scarlet leaves the color of my hair. The color of Raziel's wings.

"I've filled all the vials on the bottom of the belt with holy water," Audric said, tapping the four at my hip, "and all the ones on the top with salt. The throwing knives in the middle are positioned to be drawn with either hand, hilts turned for easy withdrawal. Drinking water is in your cloak, lower down, near the hem."

He spun me as he talked, rechecking the position of each blade, some of them my old ones, some the new ones gifted me by Cheran. "But it won't be like drawing weapons from your old dobok. The straps are new and stiff. I would prefer you had a few weeks to get used to fighting in it, but your old one is ruined. It needed to be replaced the first time you went below ground. Same with the new blades, but they're sharper and keener and better balanced than the old ones. I think you'll find them more than acceptable after a few passes.

"That's the good news. The bad news is that the military is delayed. They're putting down an incursion on the outskirts of Atlanta. A couple million spawn massed at sundown yesterday and attacked. They got through the mage-shield that protected the town."

If I had been building any confidence at all, those words knocked it out of me. My plan had depended on the army and the EIH showing up to kill spawn by the thousands. Audric patted my shoulder awkwardly. With the exception of the massage, he was better at killing things than offering comfort.

"Where's Cheran?" I asked, as Audric knelt and held out socks for my feet. I let him slide them on and then inserted my feet into the boots he steadied, stepping forward to force them on as we talked.

"He's in the city jail, his visa, amulets, and papers piled up on the desk nearby but out of reach. He's tied up with anti-mage shackles left by Durbarge and the Administration of the ArchSeraph Investigators. The witch-catcher effectively stopped him from using his conjures, and the manacles are holding him tight."

A witch-catcher was a mask with rods that inserted into the mouth to stop a mage from speaking a conjure. They were said to be quite uncomfortable. Guilt flared at the thought of the mage's discomfort, but then—he *had* tried to kill me.

"Metal rods?" I asked.

"Replaced with wood," Audric said, as if I'd insulted him. Which I had, by not relying on my champard to do all that was necessary for my protection. But the pique didn't last. He grinned. "He's getting splinters."

I laughed with him and after a moment, he added, "Eli found the shackles and offered them to us."

I absorbed that. "Eli did? Not the town fathers?"

"Eli," Audric repeated. "If it should be proved that the man who would swear fealty to you is an assey, undercover for the AAS, I will kill him."

"Yeah. Well. Let's try not to kill any of our friends until after we bind the Dragon, okay?"

"Step down, harder," he directed, eyes on my boots. "And, yes, I will endeavor to obey my mistrend's commands." There was amused sarcasm in his words.

The new boots molded to my feet, supporting my ankles and instep, but leaving enough toe room to splay for balance and for fighting. I loved them instantly, and turned my ankles to see them better.

"Stop," Audric said, applying his strength to hold my feet in place so he could strap the new boots tightly. He was taking seriously the duties of a champard.

I put my fingertips on his shoulder, which was even with my own though he was kneeling. "Audric?" When he looked up I said, "You don't really have to do this, you know."

His eyes softened, and when he spoke, it was with all the formality of his kind. "For as long as the seraph who bound me will allow, I am yours to call, in wind and hail, in storm and lightning, in injury and healing, in this life, for as long as you will have me," he said.

Tears misted my eyes. I had never heard the swearing of fealty phrased like that before and I wasn't wearing my visa to prompt me how to respond. So I dropped to my knees in front of him, looked up, and said simply, "I accept your pledge and your faith, and will hold them both in honor and love and friendship for as long as I live, or until the seraph calls you to battle dire or you ask for freedom from servitude."

Audric bent and placed his forehead against mine, our faces so close I couldn't quite focus on him. "Thank you," he said. "I will hold you in the highest regard, and I will serve you and train you to the best of my ability. I will dress you for battle, and should you die by the sword, I will dress you for burial with all honor. All that, I swear."

He cuffed my shoulder, lightening the moment. "But if you get yourself killed, all bets are off. I'll kick you to the moon and back and beat you black and blue."

I nodded, moving my head against his. "If I get myself killed I promise not to complain at the treatment. I'll deserve it."

"Indeed you will," he said, easing back to rest on his heels. "I forbid you to die."

"I will endeavor to comply with that command," I said, as stilted as any half-breed.

"Good. I have the things you had me collect from the Trine."

I was blank a moment, but he pulled a canvas satchel over and opened it, reminding me of the errand that I had sent him on. Inside were stones that looked like black opals to my human sight, but when I viewed them with mage-sight, knowing what to expect, I saw Dark and Light in one conjure. They were amulets originally built by Forcas and meant to work like a bomb.

Holy Amethyst, the Mistress, the cherub who owned the wheels that had claimed me, wheels I had bound, had somehow gotten a quantity after she crashed on Earth, and altered them for her own needs. The conjure had protected her wheels when she was captured by Forcas. Thin blue wirelike strands of her conjure overlaid and enwrapped the Dark amulet-bombs, changing them to suit her needs.

They had been left on the Trine. And now they were mine.

Audric closed them up and stood, hanging the satchel over his shoulder. "Hurry. I understand you have a kylen to meet in the street and it's almost dusk."

My champards had been gossiping about me. That was good. I think. I stood and let Audric finish decking me out for war. While he dressed me, I told him my plan. I had the feeling he didn't like it, but other than offering a few

additions, he didn't demand any changes. He was letting
me have my head. That should have made me happy, for my
teacher to be so agreeable. Instead it scared the dickens out
of me that he didn't restructure my battle strategy.

I inspected myself in the mirrors of the armoires. Of the
new blades, one was in the spine sheath at the back of my
head, shielding my neck. Others were in loops and secured
in my belt, in the cuffs of my new boots, and strapped to
my thighs. The new blades were powerful and really spiffy
looking, but I settled the old swords at each hip, the walking-stick longsword and the Flame-blessed tanto. I wanted
the comfort of familiar blades just now, nicked and scarred
as they were. I dropped my amulets over my head and stuck
Barak's feather into my belt, as Audric disappeared into the
loft across the way. As a last addition, I stuck Mole Man's
cross into my belt, and secured it with loops so it wouldn't
come loose.

Satisfied, I made several phone calls and, moments later,
went down the stairs to face the night. Ringing in my ears
was Audric's promise. *Should you die by the sword, I will
dress you for burial.* Maybe not the best thought to take
with me into what might be the beginning of the last battle
of the Last War.

Standing in the street, in the center of the sigil left by the
seraph Cheriour, the Angel of Punishment, I watched as
Romona Benson raced up from the hotel, camera on her
shoulder, her blond hair flying. From across the street, Shamus and his brother emerged from the bakery, tying their
kirk robes. From farther down the street Jasper and Polly
appeared, pulling on their cloaks. Around me, parents and
children slowed, sensing something. They were on their
way to the shop to spend the night under the safety of the
shield, more than two hundred people this time. And they
all slowed to a crawl and came to a halt. I had chosen the
moment for the most witnesses possible.

Eli stepped from the jail, dragging Cheran. The mage was
white-faced with shock and wore no coat, only his shirtsleeves. Even from a distance, I saw him shiver. The witch-
catcher was secured around his head and into his mouth,
the ultimate degrading of a captive mage. The Culpeppers

raced from a side street, father and son skidding to a halt at the sight of Eli and Cheran.

Lucas and Ciana walked from the other direction, holding hands, Ciana so excited she was dancing and skipping. Rupert and Audric stepped up behind me, Audric taking the place of senior champard. Eli and his prisoner came to the right, and Lucas and Ciana went to my left.

The town fathers ringed me as if they knew where to stand, and maybe they did. Audric was surreptitiously pointing, directing everyone where he wanted them. Romona stood dead center, camera focused on me in my blood-stained, slashed, and worn battle cloak, folded back like seraph wings to reveal me in the new dobok, weapons bristling. My hair wasn't completely dry, and my head was cold. Dumb. But there hadn't been time to finish everything. I appeared to the camera as human, skin blanked, as I had worn it for so many years to hide who and what I was. Except for the clothes and my small stature, I looked like a regular human.

When the entire crew of town fathers was in place, I looked at Ciana and said softly, "Okay. Now." We had spoken on the phone, and the little girl had assured me that she could make the sigil glow, like she did the other night, but without bleeding. In keeping with her claim, she reached inside her coat. In mage-sight, I saw her touch the seraph pin she wore. She closed her eyes as if praying. Seconds passed. Nothing happened. I had hoped to use my stepdaughter to call the seraphs without my having to call mage in dire. Without my having to fight. Hopefully without anyone having to die.

Seraph stones. I'd have to go to plan B.

Chapter 16

Below my feet, I felt a faint trembling in the ground. *Dragon.* Fear quivered through me. *Crack the stone of ages,* the beast was early. The children...

I widened my stance, pulling two blades, stepping forward, feeling Audric and Rupert do the same at my sides. Battle-lust, half fear, half fury, flashed through me, and my mage-vision came on, my human glamour falling away. The vibration was metronomic, too regular to be an earthquake. The sigil around us began to glow, a barely perceptible sweep of energy.

The crowd sighed, and I realized the vision we made, the earth quaking, the sigil brightening, my mage-attributes flashing as I drew swords, my skin glowing with the terrible power of a mage in battle. The Flame-blessed blade was shining with holy energy. My champards stood to each side in battle stance. As an opening gambit, it was way more than I had planned. I had intended to ease into this thing. The best-laid plans of mice...

I allowed the glow of my skin to fade a bit and held my arms out to the sides, blades pointing to the heavens. What else could I do? I had drawn them, after all.

I addressed the camera. "People of Mineral City, children of men, remnant of the apocalypse," I said, drawing on the visa to imbue my words with power, making them ring up and down the street. "Tonight, we believe that battle dire will be fought in the name of the Most High, in the name of

God the Victorious," I said, reminding the people watching that the Most High had won once already.

"Battle Station Consulate was established by the seraphs themselves, accepted by a delegation of the town fathers, and introduced to the world today via SNN. This battle station and this town have already been challenged and attacked by Darkness. Have already been bloodied, lost young and old to evil, and battled minions not seen since the start of the Last War. This station stands between the earth and the rising Dark. And we stand without the help of the United States military, who battle elsewhere. We stand alone.

"Yet, the seraphs themselves provided the gifts and protection and the beings and weapons we need to fight and bind the evil that has been loosed on the earth. Tonight, I will discharge the second"—*and maybe my last*, but I didn't say that—"of my official duties and acts. Tonight, I will name my champards, accept public fealty from them, and carry out judgment on one who attacked me in my consulate, in full view of the watching world. And show the world proof of seraphic approval."

My plan had already been changed by the vibration in the earth, and now it felt full of holes, patched together by glue and baling wire, but it was all I had. I took a calming breath. I had been taking a lot of those lately, and they weren't working well at all.

I sheathed my swords. "Audric Cooper, second unforeseen, dead-miner, warrior, protector, teacher and friend, master of savage-chi and savage-blade, bound servant of the seraph Raziel, assigned to me by that seraph to assist in the fight against the Dark," I said, naming him in his full identity. It was a way to both claim him and to protect him, offering the half-breed the shelter not just of myself, but of the Battle Station Consulate, and through that naming, setting in motion the half-baked plan I had come up with when I lay against Rupert's back after his prediction. "I name you my first and senior champard."

Audric sheathed his weapons and stepped around me. He drew back his battle cloak and knelt in the snow. A large snowflake fell, landing on my cheek with a faint ping of discomfort. Another touched down on Audric's dark-skinned head. Others followed, falling slowly, drifting down on the still air, wide, flat discs of lacy white. To my back, the sun rested on top of the western mountains. Clouds thinned for a moment, throwing the world into golden tints of light.

Bathed in that light, the snowflakes caught the sunbeams, falling like coins of golden lace. My own body was thrown into momentary silhouette. Before the light faded, I said, "Rupert Stanhope, more than human, progeny of Mole Man, seer of visions, swordsman, metal worker, wise in the ways of the earth and of men, fighter against the words of man and the slings and arrows of the Dark, companion of my youth, I name you second champard."

Rupert sheathed his weapon and knelt bedside Audric.

"Eli Walker, aptly named, as you walk between two worlds, the world of the Earth Invasion Heretics and the world of the Administration of the ArchSeraph." The crowd murmured at the claim that outed the spy. "Tracker, miner, dancer, one who brings me laughter, I name you my third champard. Come. Kneel. Bring your prisoner."

Eli dragged Cheran with him, both men slight, delicate, but Eli with the greater human muscle mass, the mage's powers effectively constrained. Eli tripped the mage to the snow and knelt on top of him. Cheran grunted and thrashed his feet, boots grinding into the ice, trying to get away, until Eli casually cuffed him.

"Lucas Stanhope, former husband," I said, enunciating the word "former," "progeny of Mole Man, feaster on manna, sought by the Dark for the perfection of your blood, father of the child of my heart, I name you fourth champard."

Lucas left Ciana at my side and stood beside Eli. His eyes begged, asking me to relent and name him more. His back to the camera, his lips shaped the word, questioning, "Consort?" I shook my head no. Lucas glanced at Eli and then down to the street, not kneeling, as if making a decision. Seconds dragged by measured as heartbeats. Slowly, he dropped to his knees. A pent breath escaped, hurting my chest. I took in the frigid air and went on.

"Ciana Stanhope, child of my heart, progeny of Mole Man, braver than the fiercest warrior, seeker of truth, speaker to seraphs, caller of Flames, holder of the seraph wings," I said, giving away all her secrets in the hope of keeping her safe should I die tonight. If the world knew what she was, then the AAS would have a hard time making her just disappear. "I name you my fifth champard. As you are too young to accept, I ask Lucas Stanhope. Will you allow your daughter to accept my protection and favor?"

"In the name of her mother, Marla Stanhope, and in the name of the Mole Man, I will," Lucas said. He gestured Ciana and she raced to his side, kneeling on the frozen, iced street.

She was wearing the bloodstone cat I had carved for her, on a silver chain around her neck, and she grinned, showing me her teeth. She had lost another tooth, leaving a wide black hole. In case I missed it, she pointed at the hole and mouthed, "I lost a tooth."

I nodded and winked and felt my heart lift at the excitement in her eyes. For Ciana this was the height of fun. For me it was terrifying. Now came the dangerous part, the part not listed in the library of information or history stored in the interactive visa. This was the part I was making up. This was the part that could bring down on me the ferocity and might of the High Host.

I gripped the visa, drawing on the gift of volume it offered, and raised my voice. "Thaddeus Bartholomew, Hand of the Law, investigator for the Carolina State Police, progeny of Mole Man, friend, kylen . . ." The crowd gasped; Romona nearly dropped her camera. "I name you my sixth champard and emissary from the Realm of Light to the Battle Station Consulate."

Thadd, standing at the edge of the sigil, threw off the cloak he wore. His wings lifted, feathers trembling. Slowly he spread them, the wingspan catching golden snowflakes, the light of dusk riming his bright red plumage in gold. The crowd stepped back from him as he walked forward, crossing over the edge of the sigil in the street.

He came toward me, eyes locked on mine, fear and trust in them, waiting for the ruling of the High Host. They could appear and carry him off. Or they might, just might, offer their approval. In too many ways to count, I had stepped beyond the limits of my powers as consulate general. In others, well, there had never been a consulate general of a

battle station who was also an omega mage. I was blazing
new ground. Lucky me.

The light dimmed as clouds once again draped the sun.
A pall of gray, all the darker for the falling snow, settled on
us. Still holding my eyes, Thadd folded his wings and went
to his knees, the wingtips feathering out around him. He
tucked something into a pocket on the leg of my dobok and
folded the flap back down to keep it inside. The action was
furtive, and he looked up at me and raised his eyebrows. I
nodded and he shifted his weight back on his knees.

He was wearing the suit and overcoat I had first seen
him in, now slashed open along the back for the wings.
Thadd would need a new wardrobe. As my champard, I'd
have to outfit him. The irrelevant thought was the useless
kind of thing that flits through one's head at inappropriate
times, like now, when we were poised on the knife edge of
death and life and seraphic judgment. It pulled a smile at
my lips.

The sigil seemed to glow brighter for a moment, but perhaps that was just my eyes adapting to the falling night.
When nothing else happened, I took the breath I had feared
to draw and addressed the champards, speaking words of
my own choosing, words based on Audric's to me earlier,
rather than the more proper, official words the visa had suggested.

"You who would be champards, I offer you my protection,
such as a battle station in the midst of a war with Darkness
can proffer: safe haven, healing after battle, and a home
where you will be valued and loved." I lifted the necklace
of amulets from my neck and held the visa high.

"I am yours to call, in wind and hail, in storm and lightning, in injury and healing, in this life, for as long as you will
have me. I will meet your needs, dress your wounds, and
when you die at the end of a long and glorious life, I will
dress you for battle and send you to the Most High for his
blessing and reward. Will you have me?"

"We will," they answered, the words not quite in unison,
unrehearsed and unprepared.

Audric stood and said, "I am yours to call."

The others stood and repeated after him, and it was clear
that Audric had coached them at least a bit. Tears gathered

in my eyes as a feeling close to joy welled up and overflowed in me. I held Audric's gaze with my own, letting him
see my reaction, this gratitude and happiness, and some
unnameable emotion, as intense as ecstasy.

"In wind and hail, in storm and lightning," he said, and
the others repeated the refrain. "In injury and healing, in
this life"—the words in the uneven litany echoed up and
down the street—"for as long as you will have me." The
champards repeated the final line, their voices falling into a
common cadence at the last few words.

"Amen," a voice chimed from the side. I recognized
Jasper.

Unexpectedly, the crowd joined in, as if merging with
the ceremony, repeating, "Amen." The word was full and
deep, echoing off the buildings. The two syllables seemed to
gather up and hang on the air, to fall and settle on the earth
as slowly as the snowflakes. Jasper's eyes widened. Clearly
he hadn't expected the liturgical response. It made the town
more than witnesses; it made them participants.

The sigil around us brightened perceptibly. I took it as an
omen and would have been satisfied, had not the lynx taken
that moment to roar its warning across the mountains. Not
good.

With mage-sight, I found Shamus in the crowd and said,
"Get the children and anyone else who wants protection
into the shop." On my last word, the sun fell behind the
western mountain, darkening the whole city, and long shadows draped across the ground.

A sound like whispers built as sleet joined the snowflakes.
My skin seemed to burn from the snowmelt, something I
hadn't felt in years, though only a little had fallen on me.
The lynx cried again, a deep growl-scream that held warning, danger. "Hurry!" I shouted.

Shamus raised his voice, rushing the noncombatants into
Thorn's Gems. I saw him lift a toddler and toss her to Jasper, who placed her inside. Polly, Jasper's wife, stood in the
shop, and she shoved the girl across the room to an elderly
woman. There was a sudden rush for the door and children
were pushed, shoved, and dragged inside by their parents
and grandparents.

One woman, her belly big with child, her face lost in

shadow, called out to me, fear in her voice, "Is it tonight? Are they coming tonight?"

"I think so," I said, as the certainty of attack clamped down on my bones. "Yes."

"I'll pray for you," she shouted, and she ducked inside Thorn's Gems with the throng. The lights of the shop brightened; heads were bobbing everywhere. The dress shop next door was lit as well, and it looked as if the whole town were in one place, families jostling for position, for a bit of floor space, the elderly sheltering the young while parents rushed about.

Faster than I thought possible, the street was empty, but it looked like standing room only in the shops. I heard something fall and crash, and a chorus of "Oh no"s followed. This was going to be an expensive night for my partners and me. If we survived.

I looked around. Warriors raced along the street, lighting bonfires of scavenged wood. Other fires burned in old fifty-five-gallon drums. Armed men and women appeared, standing in small groups, legs braced, weapons ready.

Audric said to the new champards, "Prepare for war." As most of the champards raced away, he said to Eli, "You hold the mage." I shivered at his tone.

Lucas paused at my side and placed his hand on Ciana's head, like a blessing or a benediction. "See her safe," he mouthed to me. And he dove into the night.

There wasn't much more to do but wait. Except deal with Ciana.

I touched her on the head and when she turned to me, there were tears in her eyes. "I want to stay with you," she said. "I want to be a real champard."

I knelt at her feet and took her in my arms. Her bones were fragile and delicate as a butterfly pressed to my chest, her heart beating fast, her life and my weapons so close. I eased her away and wiped her tears. "I need you to be just what you are right now. Not a fighter, but the one who holds the seraph wing pin. I need you to help protect the townspeople in the shop." I placed the marble oval that activated the shield in her hand and closed her fingers around it. "I know you can make this work."

She sobbed once and threw her arms around my neck. I

cradled her close and rocked her, fighting my own tears. If I failed tonight, Ciana might die. We all might. And selfishly, I hoped that if Ciana died, I'd already have bled my life into the snow, because I didn't think I could live knowing I had failed her.

I sniffed and hugged her tightly. "Did I ever tell you how much I love you?" I asked, rocking her. "You are the child of my heart. And I love you with all my heart and mind and might. And if I had a soul, I'd love you with that."

"I love you too." I heard the tears in her voice, thick with pain. Her arms tightened so that my breath was stopped, and I nuzzled her hair, turning so I could breathe, drawing in her scent. To remember.

When I realized she wasn't going to let go, I reached around and pulled her arms from my neck. "Go inside," I whispered. "See if you can activate the shield. Go on." I pushed her toward Lucas, who had reappeared. He hugged her and whispered into her ear. With a final touch, he sent her on, leaving his outstretched arm empty. Kneeling in the street, the ice freezing my knees, I watched as Ciana walked into Thorn's Gems and reappeared in the display window.

She stared into the night and splayed open one hand on the glass like a benediction, her long Stanhope fingers oddly shaped. Her mouth moved, soundless in the distance, and energies rose in the foundation, lifting through the walls to the roof. The loft blazed with power, glowing with an energy pattern that looked like oily scales and dripping water. The shield was in place.

I took a frozen breath, inhaling air so cold it hurt my lungs, feeling raw on my scarred throat. The two-story shop and the building beside it weren't invincible, but they were now danged hard to damage. Satisfied, I rose from my knees and studied my champards as they began to return, armed to the teeth. They were checking weapons, looking toward the Trine, the three peaks lost in the night, sharing a word or two, but mostly they were silent. They were ready, or as ready as one can ever be to face death.

Eli was still waiting, and when my eyes met his, he stood and picked up Cheran. With a wrench of his shoulders, he dumped the mage at my feet. Cheran's face was white with frostbite where his cheek had rested against the ice, and his

eyes were slit, anger and humiliation spitting from them.
He was in shirtsleeves, shivering, wrists tied with rope at
the small of his back, the witch-catcher strapped around his
head, rods inserted in his mouth, holding his lips apart, his
tongue depressed. Unable to keep his mouth closed, spittle
had dried and frozen on his face. His ankles were snugged
together with leather straps over his boots.

I inspected him with mage-sight, seeing the energy patterns like lacework over his body. "Take off his boots," I
instructed.

At the words, Cheran bucked up and Rupert promptly
sat on his back. The small mage whuffed out a breath at
the weight.

"I always get the nasty jobs," Eli complained to no one in
particular. Giving the mage a halfhearted kick, he bent down,
saying, "Hope you ain't got smelly feet, bro." Eli grabbed a
boot and pulled, as the mage kicked and fought, both of them
grunting for breath. A moment later Eli said, "He's got his
ankles locked." With a wicked grin, he added, "Want me to
cut 'em off?"

"Yes," Audric said.

Cheran made a strangled noise and relaxed his ankles.
Quickly, Eli slid the boots off. Conversationally, he said, "I
meant the boots, not your feet, bro. But whatever works."

Cheran struggled again, mumbling what sounded like
"uck ooo," and Eli chuckled. "Now, now. Watch your mouth.
We got kirk elders nearby. Wouldn't want to get branded,
and scar up that pretty face. Hey, senior champard," he said
to Audric, holding up the boots, "I really like these. Mother,
may I?"

"Spoils of war," Audric said.

Eli wasn't much larger than the mage, and as he pulled
off his own boots, replacing them with the nearly priceless
mage-boots, I knelt in the snow and peeled down Cheran's
right sock. Against his skin was a circlet of gold and copper,
the wires braided and wrapped and shaped to fit his leg
without chafing. It fit him so perfectly there were no marks,
no blisters. Mage-work had gone into both the creation of
the conjure and fitting it to his limb.

"Mamma mia. That looks nasty," Eli said of the twisted
wire.

"It is," I said. "Very nasty." Cheran bucked and writhed. Rupert rode the struggles like riding an untrained horse. I worried about his back, but smelled no fresh blood on the air and hoped the healing stones I had bound there were working. When Cheran wore himself out, I rested a knee on his calf and inspected the amulet.

There were many kinds of conjures, from the simple ones I usually employed—incantations to heat bathwater or to spark the flame on my gas stove—to complex conjures that moved storms over places of drought or shielded entire cities. This amulet contained a complex conjure. It glowed with peculiar energies, and as I studied it, I decided my first impression was right. This thing had dangerous mojo.

Careful not to touch the wires, I nudged Cheran's foot over. The talisman was imbued with curious patterns, in colors I associated with Darkness, though it smelled of mage energies, not brimstone. Because I had made the marble egg, I recognized the amulet was a relay, a switch to draw on stored power. It was a link to a formidable energy sink, more potent than the energy sink that powered the shield over the loft and shop. The sink activated by this talisman had to be ten times bigger, and because Cheran was a metal mage, it had to be stored in metal, tons of metal dedicated to one conjure. Metal was rare and growing more scarce. I had no idea where sufficient unclaimed metal could be found, but wherever it was, it was primed for activation.

The talisman controlled way too much power to carry around safely, proving that Cheran had great control. Without it, he could go blooey, a very messy way to die indeed, scattering bits and pieces of himself as he took out half the town. Or half of the state where the sink was.

I wondered why he needed so much power, and doubted that the entire neomage council that licensed and sent him knew about it. If not, this was proof of something sinister in the ranks of the Enclave council. A shadow council? I should tread carefully here. Should but wouldn't.

I pulled the Flame-blessed blade and held it over the coil of metal. Softly, addressing the blue plasma minor seraphic being who had inhabited my tanto, I said, "I am omega mage, yet I do not demand or command. I merely ask and seek." The blade hummed against my hand, warm even through my glove. The vibration was almost like a purr, rhythmic and soothing.

"I am a stone mage, unable to access a metal conjure, yet I need the strength in this metal amulet." At the words, Cheran screamed a wordless cry, spittle landing on the snow and freezing instantly. Rupert slammed his fist against the back of the mage's head, knocking him into the ice. He fell silent, only his breathing giving away that he was still alive.

"Is it possible for a Flame to follow and comprehend the incantation and the mathematics of a mage conjure?" I asked the blade. It grew warmer in my palm, as if excited. I took that as a yes. "Will you interpret this conjure, show me its workings, and give it over to me?"

The purring grew louder, the heat against my hand hotter. A sizzle, like static electricity, tickled my palm, a sensation close to pain. In mage-sight, the blade grew bright, a small, thin sun, and I turned my eyes to the side to protect them, seeing only with peripheral vision. The blade pulled down toward Cheran's ankle and I allowed the point to drop.

It hovered over the amulet. The braided wire absorbed the presence of the Flame, warming. The anklet began to glow, quickly heating red hot, burning Cheran's flesh. The mage began to scream. I almost pulled the blade away when I realized what was happening. But I didn't know if that would be worse. I had a vision of Cheran's foot severed from his leg. I steeled myself against the sound of his screams. Against what I was doing.

With mage-sight, I watched the action of the Flame as it revealed the incantation buried in the wires, seeing it as it expanded and divulged itself. Neomages—and it had to be a group working together, as no single mage could fashion so complex and deadly an incantation—had created a weapon of mass destruction, a bomb drawing on the creation energy of luxons. Not an atom bomb. Something far more deadly. Something for which I had no name.

Cheran was screaming in cadenced bursts with each breath, strangled grunts. The stench of scorched mage-flesh and the hot smell of metal rose on the air. In mage-sight, I followed the incantation, feeling my way through the math by instinct, teasing apart the differing strands of equations, but I was unable to hold them all in my mind. Settling myself to sit on the icy street, I opened a mind-skim as well, blending the two scans.

Nausea rose like a cresting wave, a sour taste in the back of my throat. Holding the sword in one hand, I put the other on the street for balance. When the queasiness decreased enough for me to be fairly certain I wouldn't toss my cookies, I looked again at the amulet.

The relay and trigger were woven together in the anklet. They were built into the amulet, twisted wire forming two knots, one on either side of his ankle. They both sang with potential, dual notes of devastation. I blocked out both the destructive notes and Cheran's screams and followed the leading of the Flame.

Metal magery was a conjuring so far from stone magery that I could barely follow it. But both used heat, intense, unimaginable heat, to store and generate power. Both used luxons. With the prompting of the Flame, I followed the pathway of light particles through the incantation. South. To the place where the energy sink was stored.

"Well, kiss Habbiel's pearly toes," I said, so surprised I uttered the small swear.

"What?" several voices asked.

"It's underground. It's stone and metal combined." I leaned in and let my eyes trace the smooth lines of power that slid from the anklet, seamlessly south, far south, beneath the ground. Toward an iron ore deposit deep in the earth. "Rupert. You saw his papers. Did his train stop in Birmingham?" I asked.

"For several days," Rupert said, his voice sounding far away.

Birmingham. Yeah. The sink was in an undiscovered iron ore deposit near Birmingham. I studied the conjure as the stench of burned flesh grew. I spotted the hand of four mages: two metal mages, one stone mage, and one earth mage. And I would bet my pants that the earth mage was Élan, the acting priestess of New Orleans Enclave.

"Thorn?" Rupert called, his voice still sounding far away. "Unless you want him permanently maimed, you might better stop."

"Sure. Okay," I said, surprised when my lips didn't seem

to be working. I smacked them once and they felt numb. Shivers wracked my body. I opened my eyes to find it was full night. *Tears of Taharial*, how long had I been working?

Blinking, I pulled back to see the mage's ankle. Shock sparked its way through me. Cheran had stopped screaming, passed out from the pain of the glowing amulet. *Feathers and Fire*, what had I done? My mouth went dry. The wires had burned into Cheran's tendons and bones, leaving blackened flesh around the amulet and raw, bleeding flesh above and below. I leaned in closer and someone provided a flashlight. In its beam Cheran's toes were still pink, so I hadn't severed the circulation. Yet.

I lifted a healing amulet from my necklace and snapped the string that held it in place. Working on instinct, I placed the amulet on the mage's exposed and blackened anklebone and touched it with the tip of the mage-steel point. Instantly the Flame blazed again, and new skin sprang out from the edges of the mage's healthy flesh. The bone snapped as charred areas fell away to litter the snow. Fresh bone filled in and rounded out, and Cheran's muscles quaked and seized at the rearrangement of calcium and protein molecules. He groaned, coming awake, his voice sounding scratchy and strained. And still the healing continued as tendons swelled and stretched into place and skin seemed to crawl out of the blistered edges and seal it up.

"Angel snot," Eli said. "Would you look at that."

I managed a smile at his words. Minor Flames had healed humans after the battle against spawn. That had seemed nearly miraculous, but this was even more so. Healing in fast-forward. And the Flame wasn't drained by it. I was still using the blended scan and watched the Flame pull energy through the anklet from the iron ore deposit as it healed, using whatever power source was most handy. And it did so without triggering the bomb, though I hadn't told it to.

And the really cool part? I understood how to do that now too. Both how to use the energies without triggering the bomb and how to trigger it at will. Using the Flame-blessed steel blade, I knew how to steal the power from a metal mage's incantation. And if I could steal the power, I could also redirect it.

I sheathed the tanto and found the clasp that held the

amulet on Cheran's ankle. With cold-clumsy fingers, I unlatched the wire and lifted it away. The metal was still hot, but no longer dangerously so, and I slipped the wire around my left wrist beneath the glove. It clicked softly and shaped itself to my wrist bones.

Now that's a really cool amulet.

I had made impromptu plans for the coming battle. Not delicate, intricate strategy, but simple tactics along the lines of "Kill the Darkness any way we can." Now I might—maybe—have a way to make it all work. If I didn't blow up the town and half the state of Alabama along the way. Carefully, I eased back from Cheran.

Deep night had fallen while I worked, and the large flakes of snow had disappeared, leaving only sleet and smaller, irregular flakes that stung as they landed. My hair was wet beneath my cloak hood, which someone had belatedly pulled up. My primes were both warm, activated to protect me from the melt, but they had done nothing for my hands and feet, which were aching with cold. My muscles had stiffened where I had been sitting for so long.

On the wind, I smelled brimstone. Sulfur. Rot. Darkness was coming.

Chapter 17

I made it to my feet and stretched, hearing the creak of bones. I needed a hot soaking bath, though I wasn't going to get one anytime soon. Closing off the scan, but leaving mage-sight open, I looked up and down the street, checking the town's preparations. Sleet peppered down with a steady shush, settling into ruts and crevices in the ice, making footing treacherous. The temperature was falling. It was a dark night, with a heavy overcast. Not the best fighting conditions. Okay. The worst fighting conditions. But I was pretty sure there were ways to use the cold and the falling ice in battle. If I couldn't find them, Audric could.

My champards were gathered close, bright energy patterns in the night. This was the time when I was supposed to say something significant, something important, some rabble-rousing pep talk. And I had no idea what to say. Not a single one. I stared at the men, bracing my thumbs in my belt, the battle cloak pushed back. I cleared my throat.

One by one they all looked up and came to something like attention. It was almost funny. I was less than five feet tall and maybe a hundred pounds dripping wet. What in heck was I supposed to say to them, this bunch of brawny, battle-hardened men, armed to the teeth and waiting on me to lead them. This was stupid. *Stupid!*

I opened my mouth and words fell out. "Let's kick some butt." *Seraph stones. Can I be any more idiotic?*

But the guys laughed and seemed to relax, so maybe it wasn't so bad. Audric shook his head with a "What am I going to do with you?" look, a not-quite smile quirking his full lips.

I shrugged back. "Take Cheran back to the jail. Take off the witch-catcher and make sure he's awake. Tie him up but loose enough so he can get free if he tries hard. The iron bars should provide enough metal to protect him from attack."

I had expected Eli to take the mage and was surprised to see Gloria Stein and her husband kneel beside him. Together, they hoisted Cheran and carried him into the night.

Around us, the sigil brightened, lighting the street, and a downdraft of air spiraled about, smelling of cinnamon and vanilla, fresh-baked bread, mint, and pepper. It was a mélange of scents that set my knees to quivering, and I looked up, into the falling ice. Above the town, seraphs descended and hovered, wings beating slowly. There were six of them, just as in my dream, just as in Rupert's vision, and they drifted high above the street, bright in the blended scan. Though I tensed, expecting to be thrown into mindless mage-heat, it didn't bloom. Maybe when fear and worry reached hurricane levels, they were substitutes for battle-lust. Or maybe the purple snake and its venom had something to do with it. I'd had a lot of contact with the wheels.

Crimson Raziel, purple and lavender Zadkiel, and teal-plumed Cheriour hovered with three strangers, all winged warriors with raven black wings and black armor, and carrying blackened-steel swords sheathed at their waists. Six. Not a common seraphic number. They usually appeared in twos, threes, or in groups of seven. Six was not a goodly portent, but then I was seeing evil omens in everything just now.

"Give the kylen to us," one of the interchangeable three called, his voice like bells across the night sky.

Okay, this time the evil portent was accurate. They had come to cause trouble. My muscles quivered with panic and my breath came fast.

"He is ours," another dark-winged seraph said, higher tones pealing.

The three seraphs I knew said nothing, their faces unyielding, giving little away, but it was clear they weren't here to help me. On the wind, the stench of sulfur and brimstone grew, the scents of evil blowing off the Trine. I was running out of time.

I forced down the fear and gripped the visa for advice. *Formality in all things*, it said. Well, duh. Big help there. But maybe ... Before I could chicken out, I shouted, "Battle Station Consulate, the only battle station sanctioned by the High Host of the Seraphim, welcomes its first seraphic visitors. My champards, those under *my* protection, welcome you as well."

"No kylen may live among the mages," the first night-winged seraph said, answering my claim, his voice ringing like brass gongs, indescribably beautiful.

"Why not?" I challenged, forcing my voice to settle into the tones of debate. "Why may no kylen live among humans or mages? We are all the children of men."

"Mages and kylen are forbidden to cohabit due to their licentious and dissolute pursuits and the numbers of kylen that are born," the same seraph said. I named him Raven One. "The earth will no longer support the numbers of beings who once raped the planet. You may not breed indiscriminately. It is forbidden."

There was a lot in that speech, from sinfulness to overpopulation to the health of the earth, which had been damaged by humans, devastated almost to the point of destruction. Hence the seraphs annihilating nearly six billion people in the plagues of the apocalypse, and plunging the earth into war. And the ice age. The judgment of the Most High. Followed by the attacks of Darkness and planetwide war. Saving the earth from us? Or taking it from us?

I took a deep breath and chanced what I believed, what I hoped, speaking as formally as I could. "Mage-heat no longer runs wild among us." *Liar, liar, pants on fire.* "Sinfulness is controlled by the stone gifted to me by Zadkiel." *Partial truth.* "There will be no immoral rutting between the kylen and this mage." *Full truth. I hope.* "There will be no population growth. There will be no danger to the earth."

I added what I had once garnered from Raziel's obtuse comments in that place of *otherness* where spiritual warfare takes place. "There will be only the joining in battle against the Dark, as the Most High intended, mind to mind, purpose to purpose." *Assuming that mages were intended at all. How many lies and half lies can a mage tell before seraphs kill her off?*

The smells drifting down from the seraphs changed, growing sharper, less sweet. Their scents altered with their emotions, and I had hoped for something a bit more positive, like lots of chocolate and caramel. Instead, I thought of wood smoke, candle smoke, the reek of heated copper, and the salt spray of ocean waves. The new combination of odors slowed the building of mage-heat and that part was good, as long as it didn't also mean I was about to die.

I looked at Zadkiel and fell into the most formal speech pattern I could manage. "You blessed me with the stone, O mighty warrior. You gave me the power to override the heat that would rage between seraph or kylen and mage. Will you not provide more of the stones? Will you not offer that protection to the seraphs with you, that you might all join us in the fight against the evil that comes?"

"The Most High tests you, little mage," Raven One said.

"The children of men are gathered," Raven Three said, echoing Jasper's prophecy.

Crap. Frustration filled me like a raging fire. Formality be damned. "And who are you?" I shouted back, pulling the Flame-blessed blade. It sizzled brightly and sang a note of welcome to the sky. The note vibrated my hand and up my arm into my heart. "Who are you who comes to the Battle Station Consulate without proper greetings? Without proper protocol?"

"You draw a weapon against us?" Raven One demanded. "We are messengers from the Most High."

"We are his peacemakers. The long arm of his holy will," Raven Two said.

"We bring death and destruction to the human world," the third Raven said.

"And did the Most High tell you to let humans bleed and die today?" I shouted.

"There is yet no blood," Raven One said. "No mage in dire."

"No danger," Raven Two said.

"We watch," Zadkiel said. As one, their wings beat and they climbed higher in the sky.

I whirled and found Audric in the night. "They sent six," I hissed. "Six seraphs. Why six? Not three or seven or some propitious number."

Eli answered for him. "Because our winged wonder here makes seven. They intended to make up their number with one of us and you threw a monkey wrench into their plans."

"Eyes sharp. We got company," Audric said. My champards spread out around me, leaving enough room for blades to swing freely.

From the alleyway on the north side of town, spawn appeared, their stench and chittering carried on the wind, wiping away the smells of holiness and sex. Mage-heat curled up and died. The wind shrieked, piercing cold, its frozen claws throwing back my cloak like Thadd's wings.

I pulled the longsword from its walking-stick sheath, the bloodstone prime amulet that comprised its pommel hot in my palm. The tanto blazed again, as bright as it had in welcome of the seraphs, but now with a note that rang of war, deep and coarse and full of menace, a growl of warning that stirred my blood. The spawn moved in, walking in awkward rows.

"This looks bad," Lucas said.

He was right. Spawn didn't walk; they swarmed. They raced in like mindless beasts to feast. They ate their own injured while they were still screaming. They were clawed and fanged monsters who healed from almost any wound as long as their friends didn't eat them first.

They didn't come in disciplined rows. They didn't march. They didn't follow orders. They just didn't. Not ever. Yet, these were clearly under the control of someone—something.

Rows of demon spawn scampered slowly along the street, keeping pace with one another, reddish bodies black in the night, eyes the glowing red of Darkness to my mage-vision. In the midst of their ranks walked Dark half-breeds and humans. At the back of the troop strode a Dark mage, his skin pearly bright, but banded, a pattern of snake-skin in mage-sight. I was glad I was wearing the Apache Tear; I didn't want to know the mind of this one, not for a moment.

Along the street, many of the humans had created barricades and fortifications I hadn't noticed, with my attention on champards, Cheran, and the seraphs. The blockades offered protection, but boxed the humans in. Voices tense and shrill, they passed information along the street and through handheld radios. Other humans stood in small groups, loose and rangy, tattered clothes visible even in the night. The EIH. And the newfangled big-ass gun was in the middle of the street, pointing west. There was a new gun pointing the other way, a bigger gun with a longer barrel. It was mounted on an old automobile chassis and had a white tank on one side. It looked like a propane tank, which was really weird.

"They're carrying guns," Audric said, sending the champards out around me. Heads ducked, bodies crouched, making smaller targets. Spawn were too stupid to fire guns, but their humans and mages could. "I count six rifles," he said, softer.

Spawn scuttled, moving in jerky, disorderly rows, assuming positions at both ends of the street and at every intersection. They stayed well back of the fortified positions of the humans, and farther away from the EIH. And they didn't attack. Spawn squirmed and shuffled foot to foot, their three-clawed feet clacking on the ice, reddish bodies twitching. Once they found what looked like prearranged positions, they stopped, they waited.

Overhead, the wind was still moving; in mage-sight, I saw it curl, forming a twisting, sinuous snake that ran down the length of Upper Street. It wasn't much in terms of a tornado, but there was no doubt about its shape. As I watched, its tail dropped toward the earth. In arid desert places it would have been a dirt devil; here it was a snow devil. The swirling cone began to pick up speed, gathering falling snow and spewing a reek of sulfur and rot.

The Dragon was here. *Sweet mother of God.* We were in trouble. Guns to cut us down at long range, spawn to attack in close. Until now, they hadn't brought guns into the town to attack, though I had seen them use modern weaponry in the past.

In an instinct as old as the cave, I raised both swords. Every sphincter in my body tightened as thousands of scarlet eyes focused on me. The wind began to howl. I saw the champards adjust weapons, putting some away and checking others. Eli turned a gauge on his handheld flamethrower and slung it around to ride his back. With both hands, he drew handguns and checked the ammo. After holstering them, he pulled a rifle around and sighted along the barrel. I heard him mumbling, something that sounded like, "Come to mama, you big bad ugly."

Audric put away his wakizashi and swung two katanas, the longswords whispering as they cut the air. Rupert tested the heft of his bastard sword, both hands on the hilt for strength. He looked at Audric and the men held the glance a long moment. A good-bye in their eyes. Which gave me the willies.

Thadd lifted his wings, the feathers ruffling in the wind. His eyes were on the seraph ring on a thong about his neck. It glowed with a faint blue light and the etched and shaped seraph wings seemed to move as if flying, but that was surely just my imagination. He hefted a cutlass and an old Pre-Ap army knife. I hadn't seen him fight with blades, but he handled them as if he knew them well. Two guns were holstered at his waist.

Lucas turned to me. "Take care of Ciana. And remember that I love you." Without waiting for a reply, he ratcheted a shotgun and strode in front of me, a human shield.

Tears sprang to my eyes and I couldn't force words through my tight throat. Guns. No seraphic help. This was bad. This was very bad. I wiped my face, the tears freezing on my cheeks and cracking away. I had to do something. I could not let them die. I would not. I looked into the sky, seeing a faint blush through the clouds, six spots of pale light—the seraphs, standing watch, far enough away that their own heat wouldn't spike. *Cowards.* I drew a breath and forced panic down.

The seraphs wouldn't help. Not yet, and maybe not ever, no matter what happened. It wouldn't be the first time that holy messengers watched and did nothing as humans died. But maybe…maybe the Watchers would help. Or maybe I could force one to.

I sheathed the swords and pulled off a glove. I didn't have time to draw a circle of protection or pour a salt ring. But in a pinch I figured the seraph sigil in the street might work. If it didn't blow me up first. Quickly telling Audric what I planned, I fingered the necklace and located the carved, carnelian scarab amulet with numb fingers, my flesh feeling colder than it had any right to, short of a blizzard. Audric shouted instructions to the men and the champards raced to the far side of the glowing sigil. I placed a thumb on the conjure stored in the scarab, ready to open an inverted shield of protection. A mage cage to hold a seraph prisoner.

Power hummed through my boots as I stood and drew Barak's feather. Its deep green iridescence caught the night and threw it back like a dark rainbow, the downy points ruffling in the rising wind. Improvising conjures wasn't the smartest thing in the world, but I was between the hard place of that stupidity and ten thousand or so rocks with teeth and claws. And a battle plan. And a commander still in hiding. I prepared myself for a sudden flush of mage-heat. Taking refuge in verse, I shouted to the night, over the roar of the tornado that was poised overhead.

"A feather for flight and a silver sword, exchanged in battle dire. Gift for gift and life for life, blood for blood and freedom freely given. I call Barak, Barak, once the winged warrior Baraqyal. I call you by your true name. Baraqyal, come!"

For a long moment, nothing happened, and then I was thrown hard, hitting the ground and skidding into a snarl of my cloak. Mage-fast, I flung the cloak open and swiveled to one knee, the feather in one hand, tanto in the other.

Barak stood before me, wings out, half-spread, his flight feathers held taut and predatory, his silver hair in a long braid down his back, and his green leaf sigil on a chain around his neck, resting on his breast. He was dressed in pitted and scorched emerald steel battle armor, his shield

dented and scarred. But the silver shortsword I had given
him was bright, its steel blade now nearly four feet in length
and glowing like seraph steel, the wicked-sharp edges
bright. It wasn't the gift as it had been, and yet it was the
same, hilt tipped with garnets I had mounted.

Barak held the sword backhanded, turned away from
me. I started to smile in welcome but he flipped the sword
and cut at me. Seraph fast. Faster than I could parry. I
leaped back, the blade tip passing through the down of
the gifted flight feather. Barak screamed in agony and
wrenched back, the sword blackened along the edge where
it passed through the feather.

I thumbed on the inverted shield. The sigil flashed like
lightning, powering the dome of protection over us. Electricity shocked through me, the release of energy batter-
ing. With the extra energy of the sigil in the street to draw
from, the dome was visible even to human vision, appearing as overlapping feathers, glittering with energy. It had
once been purple feathered, visible only in mage-sight, the
construct the color of the amethyst in the storeroom. Now,
powered by the sigil, it was the teal of Cheriour's plumage.
I had drawn on seraph energies. Was this the first step on
the road to damnation for an omega mage? I pushed aside
the thought.

Overhead, the snow-devil tornado weakened, swirled
once, and fell apart. Outside the shield, the spawn swarmed,
breaking ranks, and fighting free of the control that held
them. My champards screamed with battle glee and attacked.
Gunfire erupted, almost obscuring the dull thunk of swords
biting into flesh.

I regained my balance and met Barak's eyes. Aqua rings
with a slit black pupil stared at me from across the shield.
Not Barak's silver eyes, not Barak who gazed back. And
the battle outside had changed totally when I imprisoned
it—whatever it was—in here. Cold slithered up my spine.
The Fallen Watcher had been possessed by a Major Darkness, the commander of the spawn. The Dragon? Crap. The
Dragon. And I had it trapped in the shield with me.

I was toast. Nothing was going according to plan.

I attacked, pulling the longsword at the same instant,

moving into the lion resting, rising, and rampant, the Watcher's flight feather waving beside the long blade in distraction. I saw what it did to the Watcher's sword—a seraph gift freely given, damaging a mage gift, freely given.

Barak—the Dragon—didn't dare parry or block the feather with the sword. The Dark in Barak danced back, drawing a shortsword of demon-iron, the steel black and icy, lethal if it cut me deeply. As a possessed Watcher, I figured the Beast could use demon-iron, mage-steel, *and* seraph-steel, could call on Dark energies *and* use the Light. It was the perfect fighting combo. I was so toast. Barak found its footing after its unanticipated transportation. A wing shot out and brushed by me as I jumped back. Thank heavens there wasn't room in the shield for it to fly.

Beyond the teal dome, my champards fought mindless spawn. Blood splattered, sizzling against the shield. All my amulets blazed with light, and I moved into the crab, the flight feather and longsword swiping against Barak's thighs, cutting and burning as I backed the beast against the dome wall. It was bleeding. My swords flashed, meeting the blade of demon-iron, clanging odd notes when the holy Flame blade met the cold iron. A strange scent wisped from Barak's wounds, thin dissipating clouds that caught the reflection of the shield overhead and glowed with aqua light. The stench of burned meat and the smell of Barak's blood— spring flowers overlaid with some other, new scent—filled the shield, dissipating through the air-permeable dome.

Bloodlust rose and I beat the Watcher back, considering the odds. It wasn't possible to kill a Watcher, an immortal being. I was unlikely to win one-on-one against a Dragon. If I lowered the shield, I would free it to destroy the town. Yep. No options at all. I was gonna die.

Dragon-Barak went on the attack, blocking my tanto with the demon-iron blade and cutting at me with seraph-steel. In moments I was bleeding from a nick on my collarbone and a surface wound on my arm. He struck so fast, so hard, I was winded instantly, my arms tiring. But twice, as the silvered blade passed through the feather, Barak grunted and his—its—steel darkened. In mage-sight, Dark and Light crackled through the blade; it was growing brittle. Had the beast known that would happen? Did it know that Barak had freely given me one of his feathers? From the fury on its face, I didn't think so.

The same battle between differing elements was taking place inside Barak as the Watcher fought against his attacker, his possessor, the fight visible with mage-sight, though the Watcher was only a small blue spark fighting against a black, orange, and teal tsunami of possession.

Unbidden, my battle cry came to my lips. "Jehovah saba-oth!" And scripture followed, as if placed in my mind by the One True God, the words cadenced with the fight. "And *David* put his *hand* in his *bag*, and *took* thence a *stone*, and *slang* it, and *smote* the *Philistine* in his *forehead*," I shouted, the rhythms of battle settling into me, "that the *stone sunk* into his *forehead*; and he *fell* upon his *face* to the *earth*." With each accented syllable, the blade cut Barak, spilling blood.

The Dragon roared, the bell-like sound of the Watcher's voice now like broken brass and thunder. I shortened the verse and again set a sword cut to each prominent syllable. "And *David* took a *stone*, and *slang* it, and *smote* the *Phil-is-tine. Smote* the *Phil-is-tine. Smote* him."

Barak's responses slowed at the holy words and my blades leaped under his/its guard, hitting true on thighs, across his torso. Blood fell in runnels as the Dragon and its host bled from a dozen deep cuts, the prayer and scripture adding spiritual power to my blade and Barak's internal fight. The scent of seraph blood and Darkness grew on the air as I cut and chanted, smelling like the stench of hot solder and overheated copper and the chemicals that Rupert used to pickle worked metal. Outside, blood splattered onto the shield, sizzling.

I had divided my attention and Barak thrust at me, his blade slicing by my face as I whipped to the side. The beast in Barak roared and thrust again. Curling my body, I rolled to the side, coming to my feet in the opening move of the cat, for the moment beating back a blade that moved so much faster than I. Light from the Flame flashed on my wrist. I remembered that I had the trigger of a big ol' bomb strapped around me.

Seraph stones. A bomb that big might kill this sucker.

It would kill me too, and destroy the entire town, but it might work. I liked having options, even a last-ditch one. But, instead of destroying the town in an attempt to kill the Dragon, I could try to dispossess it from Barak. Then I could ask Barak if he wanted to help me kill the beast that had possessed him. Like he'd jump on that. A witless titter tickled in the back of my throat.

Dancing through the swordplay, I dredged up from memory an exorcism incantation mages could use. All I wanted to do was cast out a Major Power, if it could be done without calling on the name of the Most High. Yeah. Easy. I had no idea if the power Mutuol had set aside for exorcism would work on a Dark this powerful, but I didn't have much in the way of options at the moment.

He cut at me, moving so fast I didn't see the path of the demon-iron blade. I dove hard to the side, feeling something stretch and strain in my knee as my balance shifted improperly. The beast whirled his blade and cut downward, through my cloak, shearing through the leather and piercing my thigh. It had altered its fighting technique to minimize dependence on the silver blade. A second cut went through the toe of my new right boot as if it was made of butter.

"Mutuol," I shouted, "cleanse this Watcher, by the power of the Most High. Transform him and bind the Darkness."

Barak's eyes blazed silver for a moment and he went to one knee. Instantly, he said, "Free me from this hell." His eyes glinted red but he sucked in a breath, straining to force down the beast within. "End this," he whispered.

It was a plea for his own death. No ambivalence. I whirled, extending the Flame-blessed blade, cutting the Watcher's throat with a backhand cut. I followed it up forehand, dragging the feather through the Watcher's torn flesh, calling on Mutuol. Blood pulsed out in a torrent. Barak gurgled, locking eyes with mine. Doing as he wished meant acting without preparation, flying by the seat of my pants. *Tears of Taharial,* would I never learn?

A cloud, an aqua mist sparkling with black motes, pulsed from the wound with the Watcher's seraph blood. *Aqua?* But there wasn't time to consider that. Blood, freely given in sacrifice, is powerful, even over Major Darkness.

The feather was part of Barak's power and gave me the

right to draw on the Watcher's personal energy. Using it in a
fight against him was dirty pool. But the Watcher raised his
head, tendons in his cut neck visible in the gushing blood,
arms and wings outspread, feathered tips nearly touching
the shield to either side. He dropped his weapons to the
ice.

"Hurry," he whispered, spitting blood with the word. "I
cannot hold it back." As he spoke, his neck began to reknit
as if sewn with aqua light, a seam of energy, making him
whole.

Why aqua threads, not black? Something was wrong. With
a silent prayer for forgiveness, one I knew would never be
heard, I said aloud, "Mutuol. Seraph of the Most High God,
cleanse this Watcher. Transform him. Bind the Darkness by
the power of the Most High."

With the words, and a last look for absolution, I stepped
back and set my feet for the scissors. In the space of a heartbeat, I lifted the blades and spread my arms wide. Time
slowed. Solidified. In a single move, I stepped forward on
the ball of my right foot, focused on Barak's offered neck.
And brought the swords together in a killing V of steel.

Both blades caught the teal light of the shield. And cut
into the healing flesh of the Watcher's neck. Pain shot up
my arms, numbing, paralyzing. But the swords flew true. The
blades thunked into Barak's spine and lodged there, hung
in the cervical bones. Blood fountained over me, crimson
overlaid with black lightning. Barak's eyes still sealed to
mine, he smiled, a single word formed on his lips. "Daria."

In mage-sight, Barak's energy patterns changed, growing
denser, thicker, brighter, as if mage energies flowed over
his own, a golden shimmer tinged with ruby. I wavered an
instant and Barak lifted a hand, caressing the aura. "Daria,"
he mouthed again. "My love."

Seraph stones. What am I doing? Who am I killing? Lolo?
But it was too late to change course now. With another
grunt, I forced the tanto over, severing Barak's spine just
above his shoulders. His head toppled. Blood erupted from
the stump, gushing, spattering up to the shield, where it
hissed. The green flight feather swished through the spraying blood. Barak crumpled toward the stained snow. I
danced back, wiping blood from my eyes.

Barak had just bet his remaining time before the final judgment that his blood, given in willing sacrifice, had power over evil. Even over a Major Darkness.

Time snapped into fast-forward. All I could think was, now what?

Aqua mist gushed out with Barak's blood, swirling together across the snow, draining him, bringing him close to the state that left seraphs empty until the final judgment. The golden and ruby aura of mage energies reshaped into an arrowhead of power. And it pierced the aqua mist, driving into the spreading pool of Barak's blood.

A flash of heat drove me back. The blood boiled. Fire and Light shimmered. The aqua fog covered the corpse of the Watcher, which twitched in a horrible spasm. The mage energies of a conjure I had never heard of, never dreamed of, spread out and formed spikes, like the roof of a cavern, stalactites sharpened into daggers. It dropped onto the mist. Where it touched, the aqua fog withdrew, jerking away as if in pain.

Barak's eyes opened and found mine. Shock shot through me. His lips formed silent commands. "Sigil. Take it. Touch it to me."

Lying in his own blood was the green leaf circlet that Barak had worn on a chain around his neck. I had to get really close to the twitching body and the battling energies to do it. *Ah, man.* Stepping through the gore, I speared Barak's sigil with the Flame-blessed tanto.

The blade sizzled as it came into contact with the Watcher's blood. I flipped the sigil on its chain from around the stump of Barak's neck, up into the air, and caught it. The green leaves were shaped in a ring, curling as if fresh picked, the veins of the leaves lit with inner fire, glittering as if stars danced through them. The sigil was alive. I was almost sure of it.

I held the bloody sigil in the fingers of my right hand, but I hesitated. I understood what Barak wanted, but I had no idea what this would do.

Against the outside edge of the shield, not touching the overlapping energy patterns, a purple mist winked into existence and formed a coil, a coil that was full of eyes, millions of eyes, all staring at me with love, the wheels in their

snake form. It began to grow, pulling energy from its source.
The snake had once pulled itself through a charmed circle.
Horror filled me. Surely it wouldn't ... Its tongue darted
out and tasted the shield. Light exploded at it and the snake
withdrew in a long sinuous slither. *Good. Be smart. Keep
away,* I thought at it.

I said, "And David put his hand in his bag, and took
thence a stone, and slang it, and smote the Philistine in his
forehead, that the stone sunk into his forehead; and he fell
upon his face to the earth." Bending, I touched the prime
stone of my walking stick and the sigil to Barak's forehead.
A shock of power slammed up my arm and into my heart,
which stuttered painfully. The light left Barak's eyes in a
rush, leaving them empty. His pupils flashed once with red
light. The sigil grew warm. The leaves curled, browning.

The golden and ruby aura coalesced and formed a vaguely
human shape, female. She looked at me. Lolo. . . . She smiled
at me and tears filled my eyes. "No," I said. "Please." She
extended a ruby hand and placed it on the sigil.

Barak's body burst into flame. I sprang back, slipping in
the Watcher's blood, wrenching my leg. I went down, right
into the aqua cloud, which had grown while my attention
was diverted. Outside, the snake of wheel-mist raised its
head, hood flaring, fangs white and glistening. The fire
cremating Barak's body rose up, blistering hot, absorbing
Lolo's shape into itself. Smokeless flames so bright they
roasted my skin.

I pulled my cloak over my face for protection and tried
to stand. Aqua smog swirled up my thighs to my waist,
filling the dome of the shield in a shallow pool. My feet
wouldn't move. Through a crack in the protective leather, I
saw the purple serpent slither high just beyond the dome, a
huge amethyst snake with deep-as-night eyes, all filled with
alarm. Its tongue tasted the air and it reared back, its hood
flaring wide, fangs unhinging, white as the sun.

The cloud trapped in the dome with me undulated, shadowy aqua where Barak burned, diaphanous around me. It
rose as I struggled to stand. Where the black-light motes
touched me, they brightened, like small explosions. I went
numb below the waist as the mist covered my chest. *Seraph stones. It's trying to possess* me! My heart slammed in

my chest. I tried to reach for the amulet to deactivate the shield. My arms were heavy, fingers clumsy.

I glimpsed the snake as it reared back, preparing to strike. Which would make the shield and me go blooey. No matter what happened, I was so toast. The mist covered my head.

I went cold. And I fell into the cloud of Darkness.

Chapter 18

I woke staring into the cloud-cast night sky, my face scorched. I lifted a hand to see the tanto, the blade bright with power. I forced open my fingers, which were frozen into a tight grip around the hilt, and laid the shortsword on my chest. I pulled off a glove and touched my face. My eyebrows were burned off. Again. But I was alive, and alone inside my own body. Which surprised me. I rolled to my side and looked around me.

The shield was gone, and with it the serpent and the aqua cloud. *Dragon?* An aqua Darkness? I wasn't sure what it had been. I sat up, pulling the battle glove back on to protect my hand from the icy cold. In mage-sight I could see that the battle was still taking place, the human combatants in tight groups surrounded by spawn. The numbers didn't favor the humans.

Eli, wearing night-vision goggles, backed toward me, facing the street so he could see both east and west. I could see his mouth move and knew he was speaking.

My ears were ringing with the effect of the explosion and my hands and feet felt tingly. Maybe the result of being tossed on my backside and banging my head multiple times already today. I jerked on Eli's pants leg and he looked down at me. I touched my ear and shook my head. His mouth moved again and I was pretty sure he said, "Only you, woman." He was still talking as he walked around me, guns drawn, guarding me until I could get myself together.

Certain that I wasn't in imminent peril, I crawled to my knees and took stock of my surroundings. The flight feather was gone. Near me was a charred spot, the ice melted away, the asphalt beneath blistered and scorched. Centered in the spot was a pile of ash and blackened bones. *Angel bones.* The truth behind the curse words.

At the heart of the pile was a curved thing like a talon. I brushed away angel ashes to reveal the amulet spur. The wounded place on my side gave a twinge of pain. Though the amulet no longer looked as it had, I knew it was the spur of my binding. It had been remade.

I lifted the spur and angled it to the light of a nearby window. In human sight it had once looked like horn, but now it was darker, almost black, its surface like the crackled finish of very old furniture. In mage-sight, it had once glowed with unhealthy pallor, but now it sparkled with black-light motes of power. My fingers, still feeling thick and numb, tingled where I touched it.

I knew better than to keep it. It would only fall into the hands of Darkness once again. But I had no idea how to destroy it. The spur had survived being smashed to smithereens by Audric. Had survived the near-death flames of a seraph-being as it was drained. Had survived the explosion that resulted from the convergence of the power of a cherub's wheels, the energy of a shield that was driven and supported by a seraph's sigil, and the mist of a—a Darkness?

An aqua Darkness. Yeah. Which bothered me. I poked the bones. *Near death. Sure looks like* dead *to me.* The spur sparkled brighter for a moment before dulling down again. Proximity to the bones? I didn't know. Why was there always so much I didn't freaking know?

I sniffed the air. While in the dome, I hadn't smelled the scent of spawn, of brimstone and sulfur and acid that burned my nasal passages. I had smelled the spring flowers of Barak's scent, overlaid with ... something. Something clean-smelling and subtle that I couldn't place now. Mixed seraph scent, no reek of the Dark. And I was mightily confused.

I tucked the spur into my dobok, under the waistband where the cloth folded over several times to create a secure, hidden pouch. As an afterthought, I gathered up the bones and wrapped them into my cloak. It had stopped snowing and sleeting, but a cold wind was blowing, and the air scudded past, carrying the reek of spawn and burning things and the clean smell of promised snow. Lots of snow. Blizzard coming.

I stood, looking around. Where do you hide the bones of a fallen Watcher seraph who had looked for absolution? They would be a powerful talisman. Bones any mage would be tempted to conjure with, though it was strictly proscribed. Bones that would give a Dark Mage untold power. And I had a lot of them. Two femurs complete with hip plates. Parts of both humeri. His skull, which looked at me through huge blackened orbits, and grinned as if at a great joke. And there was one nevus bone, the mass of bone where wing and shoulder met to create an underarm. I gathered up the charred bits I couldn't identify.

Not having anything better, I stepped away from Cheriour's sigil and dumped all but one of the bones under a porch, where I'd once had a terrific make-out session with a kylen. Over them, I opened a tiny shield. If the Darkness saw them, it could eventually get them, but removing the shield might sting.

If the Dragon had been the aqua mist that had inhabited Barak, had the color been a glamour? That sounded possible. Not very likely, but possible. And—what now?

Eli tapped me on the shoulder. This time when he spoke I could hear most of it. "If you're finished trying to blow up the entire town and yourself with it, how about you tell me what we're doing next?"

While I thought, I slung the battle cloak back around me and checked my amulets. They hadn't suffered much in the short fight with Barak. In fact they looked fully charged, which made me wonder what I had drawn on. The wheels? The Trine? Cheriour's sigil?

"Thorn?"

"I'm thinking," I said. I walked along the edges of the sigil, still glowing faintly through the snow. Eli followed. When I was across from Thorn's Gems I looked up and into Ciana's eyes. She was still standing as I had last seen her, hand splayed open on the glass. Her face was intent,

eyes wide. She was scared. For me. I had a feeling that she
knew what I was planning. Ciana nodded slowly.

I sighed. Angel bones. A curse. And a weapon of great
power. Barak had sacrificed himself, had been drained unto
near death to give me this. I rotated the femur, studying
it. The head of the femur looked like a club. I swung the
long bone for balance and heft. I stared at the street, up
and down, and at the sigil. On a hunch, I unsheathed the
tanto and spoke to it. "O Flame," I said formally, addressing a member of the High Host, "can you call others of
your ilk?"

"Ilk?" Eli said. "*Ilk?* Crap, woman. We got spawn bearing
down on us. Just ask it what you want."

The Flame on the blade hummed against my hand, a sizzling, ringing tone oddly like laughter. If bells could be rung
by lightning, they might sound like this.

Two Flames appeared in the air, hovering over the
blade, trailing twin blue plasma tails that burned my
retinas. I closed my eyes and reopened them, looking far
to the side. Making sure my feet were properly placed
and I was perfectly balanced, I opened a mind-skim and
blended the two senses. Nausea rose in a frightening wave,
tasting of burned metal. I swallowed hard, forcing it back
down, not looking at the *otherness* that beckoned just out
of reach. "Once, I cared for two Flames when they were
injured by Forcas," I said. "Are you those two?"

They dipped and swirled. "I'm taking that as a yes. Your
brothers, the seraphs, watch overhead. They will not assist in
a battle against a Dragon. Will you? Will other Flames?"

The Flames zipped away, straight up into the cloud cover.
And they vanished. A long moment went by. Then another.
I dropped the skim and the sight, and nearly fell. A hand
caught me, steadying me on my feet.

"I'd take that as a no," Eli said, breathing hard, night-
vision goggles hanging around his neck. At his feet lay five
crispy spawn, their scorched meat stink heavy on the air. He
had killed them with his flamethrower while I wasted time
parlaying with members of the High Host.

Still thinking, I beheaded the spawn, finishing them off so
they wouldn't heal and rejoin the battle. Down the street,

near the old Central Baptist Church/town hall, Audric and
Rupert stood back-to-back, fighting a dragonet flying overhead. Further on, the Elders Waldroup were kneeling, praying aloud, quoting from Psalms. The Steins were firing into
a line of spawn, chanting in Hebrew, while only feet away,
other spawn broke free of the battle lines and swarmed
inside one of the barricades. I heard screams and knew that
what they ate was still alive. Bodies lay unmoving on the
street, well chewed.

I didn't know what to do. I was fresh out of ideas and I—
From overhead came the telltale *whump, whump, whump*
sound of a helicopter. Eli let out a screech of triumph. "The
Special Forces are here!" he shouted into his mouthpiece.

The Steins raised their fists into the air. Ragged cheers
went up, echoing through the town. Three EIH soldiers
raced toward us, their makeshift shoes sliding on the ice.
They carried torches. "Set up the LZ at the intersection
of Upper and Crystal Streets," Eli said. I looked at him
blankly. "Landing zone," he explained.

"Ah," I said, looking up into the clouds. The Flames didn't
return. The Host wouldn't help. Fine. So be it. The Special
Forces could and would fight spawn. But when the Dragon
returned, I'd be on my own. And it would be back. As soon
as it got itself together.

Even as the thought formed, a purple snake slithered
around the corner of the shop. In mage-sight, it was nearly
twenty feet long and at least two feet in circumference at its
widest point. Eli whirled with his flamethrower, but I caught
the dancer's arm. "She's with me."

"That thing's a she?"

"I think so."

Eli jerked his arm free. "It caused the explosion in the
street. I saw it bite the shield."

"Yeah. I think it—she—did it to save my life. To get rid
of a cloud of Darkness that was trying to kill me." *Possess
me? I'd rather be dead.*

"If you say so. We're getting our asses beat. What say we
go give a hand?"

"You go," I said. "I'm going to call the Dragon into the
circle again."

Eli ran a hand through his hair, chuckling softly. "Crap."

I wondered what he'd done with his hat. He looked up and down the street and then overhead, where a helicopter transport was dropping through the clouds. "You got a death wish, woman? Or are you just plain nuts?"

"All appearances to the contrary, no."

Eli slung his odd-shaped weapon to his back and grabbed me around the waist with his free arm. His mouth landed on mine, lips cold and hard, his arm firm on my back. For an instant I stiffened, resisting, but I could feel him laughing into my mouth. *Laughing.* I felt my lips curl into a real smile against his. The tanto blazed up bright as I wrapped my arms about him and kissed him with abandon.

The cross of Mole Man, secured in my belt, blazed between us, the energies nipping my flesh through my clothes. Eli jumped back, laughing aloud, as the sizzle caught him too.

"That happened once before, in another battle," he said, meeting my eyes, "crosses gathering power. Funny how that happens when we're together, huh? Maybe we should talk about that sometime. Over tea and crumpets. Or better yet, beer and pretzels."

"Consider it a date," I said.

"Remember the saddle. Don't spoil my plans and get yourself killed." Eli whirled and raced to the far side of the sigil.

The snake glided to my feet and coiled itself into a snake-heap, raising its head up even with mine, its tongue tasting the air, its eyes so dark they were black in the night. "Your mistress will be royally ticked off if she figures out what you're doing," I warned.

"Yoursss," the snake hissed, spreading its hood, cobralike. "Bound to you."

"Fine. I need all the help I can get." A bright light burned the night in front of me. Reflexively, I ducked my head and stepped to the side. Then I realized. Flames. The Flames were back. Several of them, dancing in the air, a complicated Celtic knot of motion. Tears washed my eyes, and my breath stuttered with laughter.

The snake tsked an admonishment. It whipped out its tongue and touched one of the Flames, humming. They all hummed back at it, a minor-key chorus that made me think of violins tuning up. I counted seven Flames. Eight heavenly helpers counting the snake. The Host as a whole wasn't agreeable to helping me. But these members of the Host were. Seven Flames and a conscious, self-aware fragment of a cherub's wheels. While six seraphs in judgment watched from overhead. *Habbiel's pearly, scabrous, stinking toes . . . !*

Was I fomenting rebellion in the heavens? Was I about to be killed for overstepping the amorphous boundaries of an omega mage? The thoughts started an itch between my shoulder blades. I wasn't commanding anything or anyone, only asking. Could the watching seraphs tell the difference? Was there a difference for an omega mage?

Two Flames zipped up to hover at my shoulders. My two, for real, or only my hopeful interpretation of a flight maneuver? I figured I would never know. I took a deep breath. I was about to summon a Dragon. And fight it. Alone. Locked in an inverted shield of protection so it couldn't get out. Ducky. And dumber than dirt. Well, at least I wouldn't die alone.

I took another calming breath. Again, I found the carved carnelian scarab and touched it, getting ready. In the other hand, I took up the cross. The gold cross with Mole Man's blood in it. And the Dragon's. A cold wind shot down the street, whipping my hair from its braid.

In mage-sight, the cross's blood glowed with hostile shades, the pure blue of Mole Man's sacrifice and the orange glow of Darkness. Not aqua. Was the aqua cloud Azazel? Was Azazel the Dragon? Was I making a big mistake? Oh, yeah. I was pretty sure I was.

I put my finger on a dried spatter of blood and said, "Come. Darkness, I command you. Dragon, I demand of you. Come."

The tanto blazed brightly. Overhead, the clouds grew lighter. I could almost feel the seraphs descending. Drawing their swords to skewer me. And then kill the whole town.

I gathered my focus and stared at the crusted blood on the gold cross. "Come!" I shouted into the growing wind. My battle cloak blew out around me like black wings. It was so cold my teeth ached. I took a chance and shouted, "Azazel, come! Come! Leader of the battle, come."

Nothing happened. I looked up and back into Ciana's eyes. She was crying. My heart wrenched and I started toward her, knowing she needed my comfort.

A blinding light shattered the night. Something hard slammed me across the chest with the force of a bomb going off. Breathless, my whole body contracting, I landed on the icy street and skidded into the depression left by Barak's passing. My battle glove–covered knuckles and the cross skittered on the asphalt. I forced a breath, the pain wrenching through my ribs and lungs. I thumbed on the conjure stored in the scarab. The inverted shield snapped into place. I caught my balance. Drew my weapons.

I looked up into the eyes of the most stunning seraph I had ever seen. He lifted his wings, their plumage the shades of the rising sun, peach and fuchsia and the color of ripe melons. Persimmon flight feathers, deepening to almost black at the tips, fluttered, while beneath his arm the nevus was a delicate aqua. His eyes were a deeper tint, the color of rich amazonite, but full of opaline fire. His flesh was reddish, like a Native American's, contrasting with sea green hair, worn loose and flowing, falling over his shoulders.

Leader of the battle, I'd said. Crap. I'd called the wrong side. I'd called a seraph.

I stepped back. The tanto buzzed hard, the scars that covered my entire hand blazing so bright they pierced through the seams of the battle glove. *A warning.* Yeah, I got it. I was in trouble. This wasn't the Dragon, wasn't Azazel in his big bad ugly self, but a great seraph. A Prince of Light. Bigger and more powerful than Zadkiel. I had used my omega mage gift by accident. *Seraph stones.* They'd kill me. And a death at seraphic hands would be far worse than anything I could imagine.

As if it had heard my thought, the snake surged in front of me, coiling and lifting its head, hissing. Its hood was open, chest high to me, undulating, the motion mesmeric. I stepped around the snake, toward the seraph, and the snake slithered protectively in front of me.

Unlike winged warriors, the seraph wore flowing clothes

instead of armor, his under-tunic white, over-robe aqua, arms bare. He wore a silver chain about his neck threaded through an oval metal sigil. He carried no sword, his beautiful hands and long delicate fingers empty.

I took a sniff, pulling in the air and the ambient energies in a mind-skim. It smelled of charcoal and the earth. A reborn earth, moist and newly turned, planted for spring. There was no mage-heat; my bloodstream was too full of endorphins and adrenaline.

"Little mage," the seraph said, his voice like a harp and bells and the soughing of the wind. "Omega mage. You have called one of the Host. What do you wish of me?"

"I expected a Dragon," I blurted out. And I felt myself flush.

He smiled, his face gentle. "Evil? Horns and scales? A forked tail? A Darkness with burned, leathery wings and cloven hooves? A Lord of the Dark as humans have so foolishly depicted?" His smile widened, revealing blunt teeth that looked almost human. His eyes were full of laughter and compassion.

Foolishly?

The seraph's smile grew more gentle, if that were possible. "You have heard of me in the old tales." I shook my head and he said, "Where wast thou when I laid the foundations of the earth . . . When the morning stars sang together, and all the sons of God shouted for joy?"

I couldn't place the scriptural reference, but I knew the passage. I breathed the words, "Morning Star." The snake hissed, wrapping itself about my right leg and up to my waist, holding me in place, batting my shoulder with its head.

Scripture was mostly mute on the Stars of the Morning. There weren't many, and they had stood to the sides of the throne of God the Victorious, singing during creation.

The visa whispered explanation. *Two Stars of the Morning did battle in the heavens. One was the victor and was set upon a throne. One was defeated and cast out. The defeated took many of the stars of heaven with him.*

I kept my eyes on the seraph in front of me as my visa dredged up bits and pieces from the Revelation of John and apocryphal works. *And the great dragon was cast out,*

*that old serpent, called the Devil, and Satan ... he was cast
out into the earth, and his angels ... with him ... Woe to the
inhabiters of the earth ... for the devil is come down unto
you, having great wrath, because he ... hath but a short
time...*

I had called one of the primary combatants of the war in
the heavens. *Seraph stones.*

Chapter 19

A s if he could hear the voice of the visa, the seraph's eyes bore down, raking me from head to boot tips. Black motes flashed in his irises, and every pore on my body tightened. The seraph said, "It has been said among men: History is written by the victor. As above, so below. As below, so above. They are a reflection of each other."

Tears of Taharial. Is this a victor or one of the losers? And which one would be more dangerous? The seraph's eyes flashed again, dark with amusement. Hearing my thoughts? I drew on the visa. What I got back was, *Caution.* Big help there. The snake tasted the air beside my face, its forked tongue quivering. Its body tightened painfully on my thigh and my waist.

The seraph's wings lifted slightly, flight feathers ruffling as if finding a breeze. Outside, a fierce wind was blowing, catching up snow that struck the sides of the dome of shielding and sizzled. A broken branch hit with a thud and a spit of energy. Where had the wind come from? No time for distraction. The visa prompted, this time forcefully, and I said, "In the beginning, God created the heaven and the earth."

I could have sworn I saw something glisten at his lip but he smiled again. "I have power over all the earth," the seraph said, opening his fists, showing me his palms, the universal gesture of peace that even the seraphs utilized. His wings settled with a snap. "Without me, nothing was made that was made. Nothing."

Something odd about his phrasing made my heart race. Flight or fight. It wasn't a perfect quote but it was close to the King James words, "All things were made by him; and without him was not any thing made that was made."

The visa whispered to me, *Close but no potatoes*, which made a hysterical titter quiver in the back of my throat.

"You have nothing to fear from me, little mage," the seraph said. "I have long worked to bring the prophecy to pass."

"Prophecy?" *The one hanging over my door? A Rose by any Other Name will still draw Blood? That prophecy?* Or the one Jasper had uttered—"*The children of men are gathered. The dragon breaks free. All the old things have passed away.*" No, not a new prophecy. The seraph's words indicated that this one had been around a while.

So, maybe it was the one in my dreams about a certain mage, one the seraphs foretold. "*A mage, one of the foretold ones. . . . She is near.*" Foretold mages. No such thing. Except in my dreams.

Lucky me. Lots of foretellings, no explanations. The snake spread its hood, its mouth open to reveal a black tongue and white fangs that snapped down from the roof of its mouth, the action so much like the daywalker's that it shot a singular spark of fear through me.

"The prophecy among the Host," the seraph said, "that a mage, a child of man, the result of seraphic purpose, would someday be born." He tilted his head, his hair moving like a spray of aqua silk over his shoulder, resting on his wing. "History is written by the victors," he repeated, holding out his hand in entreaty. "Join with me."

I stared at the hand, skimming hard. It didn't smell like the Dark. This was a member of the Host. Beautiful, lovely, his hands shaped to create. Shaped to pray. To help. Not a Dragon. Hadn't Eli questioned me about why the big bad uglies appeared as they did? Hadn't he suggested that an incantation or curse might have deprived them of their beauty?

The snake was warning me. Opening both senses together, I blended the skim and the sight into the new sense I as yet had no name for. Vertigo rocked me. Nausea rose again in the back of my throat, sour and acidic. I braced my knees, trying desperately not to fall or throw up. I breathed him in, the wonderful scent of seraph.

"Join," he said, his voice a mournful bell. "Together we will retake what was mine and was lost. Together we will rule. The Most High will never share his throne with another. Even the Bright and Morning Star sits to his side. I offer you the throne itself, to rule with me. Beside me. Together we will heal the earth and restore the heavens. We will make right what was ruined by war and hatred and selfishness."

As he spoke I parsed the fragrance into its disparate components. I caught first his own unique seraph scent—charcoal and spring earth—and recognized them as the odors I had detected beneath Barak's own sweet flower aroma. But beneath his seraph scent were fragments of others, like pepper and mint, like honey and chocolate, like sweets and sex and spring flowers.

"I will free the mages," he said, "that they no longer live in gilded cages, free them to rule the earth; over the humans who fear them, who have killed them. And I will give them the souls they crave, that they may attain immortality."

Souls. To banish forever the fear and permanence of death. To have what humans had. But what had I seen when Barak died? Lolo's soul? The Flames spun around me, seven Flames, plasma trails bluing the light. They weren't attacking, as they had any Darkness that came near. They were hanging back. This wasn't a glamour. This *was* a seraph.

In the blended scan, the seraph's face was utterly beautiful, glowing with the light of heaven, energies like a halo around him, an aura of holiness. On the silver chain around his neck, his sigil glowed with the sunset colors of burned persimmon, shrimp, and fuchsia. Motes of black-light sparkled through it, like the light of a million black holes in space.

I stepped toward the seraph. *The Star of the Morning. The angel.* I took another breath, hearing my heart beat, a slow resonance as the *otherness* took me up. My mind continued to isolate the odors. Mint, pepper, honey, chocolate, spring flowers.

The scents in the blended scan were like ... Zadkiel. Raziel. Barak. Yes. Barak smelled of spring flowers. I blinked, stopped, and looked down. My glove rested on the ice at my feet. My hand was bare, scars whiter than burning linen, palm outstretched. In it was the prime ring I wore on my chest. A bit of black chain mail dangled from it. I had pulled the prime free.

Overhead, light broke through the clouds, a half dozen seraphs intoning, "Omega mage!" Their voices were slowed, tolling like the bells of war. "Destroy her!"

Smells. Raziel and Zadkiel and Barak. All seraphs who had been at war in the Trine with me. All who had given their blood in battle against evil. Fear and the beginning of comprehension spidered up my spine. The hair on the back of my neck rose. The wheels/snake reared back, bulking in height, tightening on my leg and waist, stealing my breath.

With a snap, the seraph snapped free the oval ring around his neck and extended it toward me. It was metallic, pulsing with lavalike energies, a sigil of great power. "Join with me," he said, the tone gentle but with a hint of steel in it. "We shall rule."

I understood. I had gotten what I asked for when I called it to me. The ring was the link made of Mole Man's blood. The link that freed the Dragon, Azazel. He could take it off, but he couldn't get rid of it. Unless someone else helped. Accepted its curse? And the Dragon had me, the only living omega mage, in a shield of protection. Offering my prime amulet to him.

I drew on the *otherness*; time slowed to the consistency of honey. The light overhead expanded to noonday brightness. Huge brass bells were ringing, tones angry. The Flames buzzed around me, a slow circlet of lightning. Ozone lifted the hair all over my body in a painful electric charge. Nausea rose in a wave. My hands felt tingly and numb.

Mage-fast, I pocketed my prime. I pulled the cross from its loop, the cross stained with Mole Man's blood. And the blood of the beast that Benaiah Stanhope had chained with his sacrifice. The beast that was Leviathan, Azazel, and looked nothing like a Dragon, but surely was one. My hands blurred with speed even as Azazel reacted, fingers closing on the link. Faster than I could see, I speared the end of the gold cross through the link the Dragon held.

As if coupled to my mind, moving in tandem with my

hand, the snake struck. *Seraph fast.* It buried its fangs in the back of my rebuilt left hand, driving deep into my bones. And through the cross and link, into the hand of the True Fallen seraph beneath it.

Overhead, the light exploded.

I never lost consciousness. I never closed my eyes. I never turned off the blended scan and its enhanced awareness. As if I stood outside myself, I saw my body as I flew above an empty plain, arms and legs pinwheeling. I heard *my heart beat*, assuring me I was in the place of time-no-time, place-no-place.

As in my last vision of myself, when I stood on the deck of Holy Amethyst's wheels, I wore scarlet armor over black chain mail and silk, and bloodred boots. I carried a shield on my arm and a sword in each hand. Here, both glittered with the light of Flames.

I was represented as a battle mage. A battle knight. In my belt I carried a long bone, the femur of Barak. In this reality, it glowed with peculiar light. If a rain cloud could glow, it would look like the femur. In my left hand with the hilt of the tanto I carried the cross-speared Dragon's sigil. The gold cross sparkled with Light and Dark, the blood of the combatants in Mole Man's sacrifice. The sigil was cold and a strange aqua mist was rising from it.

Blinking, I moved my feet under me to land. In that instant, I was back on Earth, falling into a tangle toward the snow. The seraph lifted his head, opened his mouth. He bellowed with fury, raising wings and arms toward the teal shield. And he changed. His skin blazed with aqua light, as if his very atoms softened, separated, and caught fire. He exploded into a fine mist and . . . transmogrified. A true transmogrification. A reshaping of atoms and luxons into a different form.

That which is Fallen cannot transmogrify, the visa whispered. If a device could experience shock, I'd have said the visa was stunned. The seraph was no longer the winged beauty, but rather, was becoming something else.

In the Earth reality I slammed into the snow. Again. Breath was knocked out of me. My head impacted the ice. I lost consciousness. My vision of Earth vanished.

In the *otherness*, I landed hard, skidded along the ground on thigh and foot, sliding into the flow of the river of *time*. Rocks and boulders protruded above the river's surface and one of the rocks had three humps, like the Trine. Raziel had named them "rocks in the river of *time* for me." Whatever that meant. I was in the same place as before, but it was subtly different. I turned, my battle boots *shushing* through the river-lava, the heat growing uncomfortable but not burning me.

Off in the distance were small humps I took to be mountains. In the other direction were skyscrapers, like the skyline of New York City, back when humans had lived there, before it was a Realm of Light. *Seraph stones.* I was near a Realm of Light. Again.

The city drifted closer, buildings rising up out of the plain, windows shining with Light. A strange buzzing, like the sound of electricity in old wiring, or the sound of a million bees, filled the air. I spotted the grid of streets above me, streets I had seen below me while standing in Amethyst's wheels. Realities stacked like coins, one atop the other? Off to one side was the remembered bright spot, like the sun but more diffuse, and with a square, flashing, sapphire light beneath it. The sky was getting closer, falling toward me.

I heard myself groan. Back in the reality of Earth I was about to wake up. I had a feeling that was gonna hurt. Bad.

The lava-water boiled, a geyser of light that fountained up and rained down, creating a shining mist. In the center of it, a bulge rose from the river straight above the surface. *Blood and plagues. . .*

At first my eyes couldn't grasp a structure, seeing coral and green bands, swirls, and diamond configurations. My hackles rose and I tightened my grip on the talismans. The bulge became a body. Arms lifted out to the sides, giving it form. Webbed fingers separated, revealing long razored talons. Its back to me, the beast stood on muscular legs, skin banded green. No. It was aqua. The seraph, the Dragon, had followed me into the here-not-here in a way that I hadn't seen before.

When the Fallen were kicked out of heaven, they lost the ability to transmogrify and were denied access to the river of *time*. They had been stranded on Earth, bound by time as humans were. When Forcas fought the Light on Earth, it had been visible here, reflected in the *otherness*. But the Dragon had found a way to access the river itself. And in a completely different form. I had a feeling this was very, very bad. Hands sweating, I regripped the swords.

The Dragon shook itself free of golden droplets, flinging them away like a dog caught in the rain. A crest snapped open, running from the base of its spine up over the top of its head. An aqua tail rose above the river, muscular and smooth-skinned. Around its neck, the Dragon wore a chain, the silver burning into its neck and crest, blackened flesh hanging in tatters.

The silver chain was broken, but still in place. Mole Man's chain. Broken by the link I held skewered through with the cross.

The beast turned toward me, a Dragon with a seraphic face, the utterly beautiful face. And aqua eyes. Not the red Dragon of the Revelation, but another. An aqua Dragon, stunning and awful and beautiful to look upon.

Azazel, the visa whispered.

"Yeah. I figured that out a while ago," I said, backing out of the river, along the shore.

The beast whipped its head and golden light ripped out, a shining sun of energies. I blinked and the Dragon was gone. Standing in the water was Azazel, the seraph. He could transmogrify. He could access the river of *time*. That might mean he could also return to heaven.

Azazel saw the link and the cross. He threw back his head and roared again. Fangs and sharp, barbed teeth caught the light of the city overhead. The shape of his head changed, a liquid movement throwing off sparks of energy before it solidified again into the beautiful mien. On Earth, my body took a blow or was thrown. Pain spiked through me.

The aqua mist given off by the link in my hand steamed thicker. The chain glowed red and his flesh around it smoked, the smell of charred, rotting meat scenting the air for an instant.

It had taken all of us to make the link that broke the chain binding Azazel. He had broken it, but he hadn't gotten the chain off. No matter what it looked like, the Dragon, this fallen seraph, wasn't completely free. It was still bound by something. *My heart beat.* It had been a long time since I heard it. Either time was slowing down here or I was dying there. If I died in one reality I would die in the other. I had no soul, so for me, dead was dead.

I raced from the river, choosing a level place to make my stand. The flight feather was burned to ash. I had no idea how my amulets would react to being activated here, if they would work at all, or explode and kill me, or have some other reaction. I hooked the link to my necklace. It clinked against the prime and the visa, throwing black-light sparks. I tucked the cross inside my hauberk, the metal warm.

I held the swords, the cross, and Barak's femur. The back of my hand was still punctured, the purple mist of energy was flowing into me through the puncture marks, energies from the wheels. The energy was a potent weapon, if I could use it without letting Amethyst know I was siphoning it. Or, maybe, now, it no longer mattered if she knew.

Seven globes of light blazed up through the river and whirled around my head. A purple snake slithered out behind them and coiled into a writhing mass. It opened its mouth in a parody of a smile and tasted the air. The purple mist flowing into my hand came from its mouth.

Azazel in pure seraphic form waded from the river, golden drops splattering. Yet, when I blinked, I saw it as the beast, and it hissed, its tongue stabbing out fast as a blade. Its right hand hung to the side, useless, skin blackened, fingers curled in protectively. Blood dripped from two puncture sites, and reddish streaks ran up its arm as if infected.

The vision shuttered closed and Azazel the seraph stood before me, his face gentle, his wings spread, flight feathers lifting and settling. The shadow of his wings stretched out on the ground and spread to cover my feet. I resisted the urge to step back, into the light.

"Give me the link," he said, his voice like silver bells and the sound of distant violins. "Give it to me, and I will spare your sister."

The words were a cold spear driven into my heart.

"Fear not, little mage. She is safe. My queen guards her. But the succubus hungers. She will not wait long to feast on mage-flesh." He smiled compassionately. Spreading his wings, Azazel shook golden water from his plumage. The vision of him flickered on—featherless leather wings flourished, the tint of cooked shrimp. They would make a great coat and boots. At the thought I grinned, showing teeth. Bloodlust simmered beneath my skin, making me itchy. "Liar. Father of lies."

"Not I. But I am the father of many things. War, which you love. Riotous sex that humans, in their foolishness, call sin." When I didn't respond, he said, "I will offer you a gift in good faith, to show my generosity." He gestured with his uninjured arm.

The world tilted, vertigo hitting me with the force of an avalanche. Retching, I stumbled and caught myself on the body of the purple snake, my hands on its scaled skin. Where I touched, the scales separated and eyes looked up at me.

"Thorn?"

I had an image of the night sky. Lashes blinked over the vision.

Hope and shock cleared my head. I knew this mind. "Rose," I breathed.

A foul smell filled my head with my next breath, but it was Rose's sensation, Rose's breath, Rose's lungs that expanded her chest. The smell was stagnant water and dead lilies. And the stench of spawn. A face bent over her. The succubus queen, teeth razor sharp. Rose cried out. The vision dimmed. She was gone.

I caught a glimpse of my earthly self, dressed in dobok and cloak. And then the knightly me returned, overlaying the earthly. What had just happened?

"Rose is safe. She has always been safe. If I rule the heavens, she will be safe forever."

Temptation. Ruling the world had no appeal for me. But getting Rose back. . .

Over my head, the Flames slowed again, appearing as long, overlapping trails of light. They dropped down, humming in a minor key. "Ssssacrifissse," they buzzed.

"Yeah," I said, hope dying and grief resting heavy on my heart. "Gotcha." Azazel offered me a way to save Rose, but the others I loved would die. Tears stung my eyes, my decision made long before this day. Moving slowly, so Azazel would follow the misdirection and wouldn't realize what

I was doing, I wiped my eyes with my glowing left hand, tanto bright. The longsword making me clumsy, I released two anticonjure amulets and thumbed them on with a whispered word. I tossed them at the Dragon.

Faster than they could fly through the air, I flipped the tanto and sheathed the longsword. Took up Barak's femur bone. And I attacked.

Chapter 20

Drawing on the energies that filled me through the puncture marks, I raced at Azazel. The anticonjures hit him, both striking his chest midcenter. They exploded, throwing the seraph back, hard. He landed deep in the river of *time*. Golden water gushed up around him.

He vanished underwater. I stopped, staring at the river, my boot toes in the lapping stream. I wasn't wet. The river wasn't really composed of water. I knew that, but it was disconcerting. It's weird, the things you think about when you've just refused to make a deal with the devil. When you've just killed your twin. Sorrow welled up in me. I shoved my grief deep inside, holding on only to the rage.

Misery a solid knot in my chest, I watched for Azazel. Time passed. My heart beat in the slow pace I associated with the passage of time on Earth. Had the anticonjures thrown Azazel back to Earth? My arms drooped, weapon points falling toward the ground.

The snake slid closer, hissing. When I glanced down, my hand and the bone caught my attention. The stream of purple energy that filled me with power was stronger, heavier, but it had divided, a small part flowing along my gauntleted fingers to encircle Barak's femur.

The snake licked the bone, its tongue a flash of movement. "I honor my Mistressss's promissse," the snake hissed. "I will not allow her to ssssin."

I remembered the words the purple wheels had spoken to me, mind to mind, when I was on the deck. *"I will honor the promises of my Mistress,"* the words had whispered into my mind. *"Her promises and her obligations. I will not let her sin by forgetting you. By forgetting her Watcher."* Holy Amethyst owed favors to more than just me, and wasn't of a mind to fulfill them. The lavender mist seeped into the surface of the bone and vanished. Did she owe promises to Barak?

The Dragon burst from the surface. I raced a half dozen steps back from the river in shock and lifted my blades. Throwing water in a huge spray, the beast leaped at an angle into the sky, leathern wings unfurling, to fly. The angle of flight brought it directly over me, one arm curled protectively against its chest, talons closed in pain.

Time did one of those strange shifts, where it seems to slow, and where every eyeblink takes long moments, and every sensation is intense and crisp.

I flipped the blade, bent my legs, and jumped with all my might, straight up, shouting from the book of Judges, "And he found a new jawbone of an ass . . . and slew a thousand men therewith!"

As I leaped, the Dragon swerved, bringing its healthy arm down. Razor talons reached for me. I scored a long cut across the top of its healthy forearm and brought the femur down, my aim filled with the growing fury of Rose's loss. Barak's sacrificial leg bone impacted the beast's wounded right hand with a solid thwack. Tears thick in my throat, I shouted, quoting Samson, "With the jawbone of an ass . . . have I slain . . ."

The Dragon howled and tucked its wings, tumbling away from me, its right hand tight against its chest. The claws of its good hand scraped along my cuirass as I twisted in the air.

I landed with a jar, rolling, hearing a second and third splash. I caught myself against a boulder and rocked to my feet.

Out of the river flew Raziel and Zadkiel, their scents filling the air with honey, chocolate, mint, and pepper. Golden river water rained down from their bodies and wings, their plumage catching the light in a dazzling rainbow burst. They shouted battle cries, notes of true sound, gongs of challenge in a language I couldn't understand.

Raziel's ruby irises were alight with the joy of battle. He checked his flight, crimson wings twisting and pulling in to stall his momentum. With two massive sweeps, he hovered, the wind of his flight buffeting me. "You did not join him?"

"No," I said, the question a barbed pain, rage for my twin filling me. "Why?" I shouted. "Why does it matter?"

He shook his head as if I were a curiosity. According to traditional wisdom, seraphs are curious about nothing, yet I had seen them surprised, puzzled, and even inquisitive. Bastards.

Raziel held out his hand to me; he spotted the snake. His face underwent a series of changes, too fast, too complex for me to follow, ending with shock. The snake uncoiled from its mound, slithered up my leg and around my waist as if protecting me. Or claiming me. Or maybe it was hungry and had decided I was dinner. It spat at Raziel.

The seraph swept his wings down hard and returned to the chase. "There will be a reckoning," he shouted back. "I have chosen you."

"Mine," the snake hissed. "*My* mage."

Ducky. I was a point of contention between a seraph and the wheels belonging to another seraph's mate, a cherub who hated me. The snake undulated and fell away from my body. It looked up, recoiling fast.

I started to pivot and was hit. Hard. My body slung forward, then was caught around the waist, limbs jack-knifing. I was pulled underwater. A current buffeted me. A large fist clamped down on my waist when I struggled. I looked up into the eyes of the Dragon, goat-slitted aqua eyes, in a featherless snake face. It opened its mouth and hissed at me, fangs flashing.

Shock made me inhale, and my lungs filled with the golden river water. I gagged, alarmed at the fluid in my lungs more than the touch of the Dragon. But I didn't drown. I coughed and again inhaled.

I twisted around to find Raziel and Zadkiel swimming—flying?—after me, wings pushing them through the water at great speed. They were gaining. The Dragon looked back.

I tightened my fist on Barak's femur and lifted it high. Once again I brought the bone down hard on the beast's wounded hand. With the tanto, I stabbed underhanded into its chest. No finesse, no delicacy of form, just a hard thrust with the Flame-blessed blade. It struck the Dragon's side, burning, scorching, cauterizing even as it sliced deep. I shoved it in, the thin crossguard bumping against the beast, its blood pulsing out to cover my gauntlet and spew up my armor, coating me with crimson and the smell of seraph.

The Dragon crushed me to its body, squeezing the breath of river water from my lungs. A rib cracked, the pain like a stab into my chest. I was sure that I was injured here in the river of the *otherness* and on Earth as well. Nausea filled my mouth, a taste of bile. I twisted the tanto and forced it up at a sharp angle, cutting the beast in a swath of destruction. Azazel roared with pain, the sound like broken bells rung under the ocean, long peals of off-key notes.

My sense of vertigo worsened. The Dragon's skin was hotter than a human's or mage's, smooth on its sides, but formed into scales like a reptile's over its joints, tiny scales that caught the pellucid light of the river. Wrenching the tanto out of the beast's side, I shoved the femur bone into the wound, shouting underwater, "With the jawbone of an ass . . . have I slain . . ."

The Dragon howled and shook me, my spine cracking and joints bowing in directions nature never intended. I caught myself on the chin with my own knee and white lights whirled through my vision. The nausea was back, but felt different now. Concussion, maybe. I took another breath of the river water. I heard *my heart beat* on Earth. I exhaled, feeling sick, wanting to throw up. I shoved the bone in deeper.

We broke out of the river of *time*, flying through the black of night, clouds overhead, not the strange sky of the *otherness*, but the winter temps of home. The world spun and my stomach emptied in a violent rush, water gushing from my mouth. I coughed hard, cleansing my lungs. *Seraph stones.* I was no longer in the *otherness.* I had made a physical transition from a spiritual place. I had flown through the river of *time*, clutched in the fist of a Dragon.

Looking down, I affirmed that we were in the Appala-

chian Mountains. Tiny lights and fires glinted below, showing me the shape of Mineral City, the Toe River gorge a
black stripe through the middle and the black form of the
Trine to the north. My battle cloak flapped around my
calves, my dobok was black leather. My clothes and hair
were dry. My boots were the new boots gifted me by the
Enclave of my birth, but the slice in the boot toe was gone,
the leather smooth. My rib was still broken, the femur bone
was still buried in the Dragon's side, and its blood poured
over my hand, slicking the leather of my gloves. *How weird
is that?*

Azazel folded his wings and dropped dizzyingly fast
toward Upper Street, to touch down with an ungainly lurch.
The shop was still protected by the shield, but Ciana was no
longer centered in the darkened display window. New snow
lay heavy on the earth. Smoke, rancid and thick, filled frozen air. I glimpsed shops down the street, windows blackened, walls crumbled, brick smoke-stained. Bodies were
snow-crusted humps. The big-ass gun was a blasted hulk.

Shock tightened my chest, sending a spiral of pain through
me. I had flown through the river of *time*. How long had I
been away?

Above us in the night sky, flying in close formation, were
three seraphs, their bodies bright with the energies of the
High Host. Their wings, hair, and armor were black, and
they carried glittering black swords. Ravens. I didn't know if
they were here to kill me, help me, or study me. I had never
heard of Ravens, or whatever they were really called, but
they looked liked winged warriors—troops, not princes or
battle leaders. They altered their angle, diving for us, pulling
swords. I was about to become collateral damage.

The Dragon leaped again into the sky. I was ready for
the shift this time and braced myself for increased g's. But
Azazel crushed down on me and I heard more of my ribs
break. My breath was a painful catch and I was able to
inhale only in a quick, shallow draft. It could have crushed
me dead—mages have brittle bones—but it didn't kill me.
It wanted me for something. Which scared me silly.

I shoved the femur deep in the Dragon's side, releasing it to
pull my longsword. At such close quarters it was handy only
for slaughter work. I slid the point into the wound beside the

femur and shoved the blade in. I heard the beast grunt with pain, its breath stuttering. I pulled the sword out halfway and altered the angle, stabbing deep, grazing the femur bone in passing. A sizzle of electric energy quivered up my arm. The Dragon gasped and dove.

I sawed into it again and again. Blood spattered over me.

I caught a hint of succubus and spawn. The bones of a half-destroyed building resolved out of the night, its outer walls standing, roof gone, fire shooting up in places within, and smoke curling in lazy streaks. A shield sparkled over it, a shield unlike any I had ever seen, the energies a cascade of aqua and black-light motes, like Azazel's eyes. The beast said a word in a language I didn't understand, like the ringing of bells, shivering the air. The shield snapped off, revealing a desecrated church. Orange and sickly yellow energies emanated from it, rising on the air in spirals, reaching for us. Layered conjures were contained in the walls.

I recognized the building, though it was vastly changed. The Central Baptist Church, Mineral City's town hall, had been destroyed. *Stones and blood.* What had happened to the town? How long had Azazel kept me away from the fight?

Fear warred with pain and anger inside me. Fury won out, numbing the pain for a moment. "How long did you keep me away, you bastard?" With the blade, I ripped deep into the Dragon, twirling the sword and cutting, cutting, cutting, speaking scripture in spiritual warfare, not able to shout for the pain in my chest, my words rasping, "With the jawbone of an ass . . . have I slain . . . With the jawbone of an ass have I slain." I felt the sword nick something inside, the density of an organ slowing the blade.

Azazel roared. Blood covered me and I withdrew the longsword to dash it from my face, the motion grinding broken ribs. Its blood didn't stink or burn. The blood of Darkness was always foul and acidic. Doubt filled me, but it was way too late to rethink my choices. I redoubled my attack on its side. "With the jawbone of an ass have I slain."

The conjures snapped off below us. With a swoop and a shift of its wings that jarred my bones and nearly pulled my shoulders from their sockets, Azazel braked and dropped through the rafters of the church. It—he—landed with a thump that made us both hiss. I had a feeling its landings were usually a lot more graceful. I had hurt it. Good. Because it had hurt me. Blackness hovered in my vision as I took small breaths, agony tripping through me.

I smelled succubus. Still held in the beast's grip, I looked around at the walls, vastly changed. Days had passed. Surely days. The walls were glowing with strange, spiky energy patterns, the colors jaundiced and sickly. Silvery trails wound up and over everything, coating walls and floor and piles of rubbish with a shimmery substance. Snail tails. Huge, immense mama snail trails, a foot wide.

Crawling through the slime were *things*, four feet long and bulbous. I had never seen them before but I knew what they were. The smell alone told me. Succubus larvae. Lots of them. I regripped the bloodied weapons, ready for another attack, but the white-bodied pupae with strange, jointed bodies and blunt, black snouts didn't attack.

The Dragon threw me. I crashed against a wall, cracking my elbow, grinding my ribs. I lost my blade. The femur bone cracked the wall beside me, thrown by the beast. I slithered through gunk collected at the base of the wall. It was a long moment before the haze of pain thinned and I was able to breathe.

I looked around, trying to orient myself. I was at the front entry of the destroyed church; with mage-sight, the sanctuary was alive with Darkness, larvae everywhere, but no Azazel.

Fear crawled around in my chest on its little spider legs, a feeling I was coming to hate. Above me, the shields snapped back in place, overlapping bubbles of power. The awful smells vanished. Poof. I remembered the overlapping conjures I had seen from the air, looking down on the church. Reality had changed while I was in the river of *time*. I had been gone longer than I thought. How long? And where was the beast?

In mage-sight, I spotted the glowing energies of the tanto and retrieved the blade, wiping slippery gunk off it and off my hands, gooing up the edge of my cloak. Having the blade made me feel immeasurably better. I sheathed the tanto and gripped my side gently, supporting the loose and grinding ribs.

"Thorn?"

A distinct mind opened to me, clinging, thoughts that smelled of roses in spring and the salt smell of the sea. "Rose?" I whispered, holding my side.

"Help. Help me!" she called, her mental voice a weak echo full of static and dark energies, as if she were far away. Her mind was a well of panic, fear like a storm blowing through it, lightning spiking. I couldn't place her direction. I ripped at my amulets and held the Apache Tear away from me. I found the remembered mind. Close by. Very close. *"Thorn!"*

She was alive. "Rose!" I screamed, the sound croaking as agony speared me.

I turned, searching for her. Though I couldn't smell it, I spotted the succubus queen. It was sitting on a pile of rock and brick, staring down at me, protected from me, separated from me by black motes of energy in a small circle of power, hiding behind a shield. The queen was once again in its human form, not Gramma, but the form of Jane Hilton, Lucas' lady love, blond and green-eyed, so utterly beautiful she—no, *it*—should have been a seraph. It stared at me, hunger in its eyes, its hands on a body supine beside it.

"Thorn . . ." My thoughts were sucked beneath a wave of Rose's pain. Unthinking, I dropped the Tear. Rose's mind closed to me.

Blood coated the queen's perfect jaw. Mage-blood. Rose's blood. Jane licked its lips and bowed its head, its tongue flicking. It was drinking her blood.

Rage roared up. I pulled a throwing blade and stabbed the shield. Black sparks flew, but it was like hitting a diamond. My blade slid off. I couldn't get in. I couldn't get to Rose. I sobbed, my broken ribs grinding. Throwing back my head, I screamed in rage, the shattered edges of my ribs stabbing together in torment, the agony slicing. Pain brought me back and dropped me breathless to my knees in the slime. Some still-sane part of me found and pressed the Apache Tear against my neck. Calm settled on me, and I took two shallow breaths, fumbling with the amulets in

my necklace, searching for a weapon to get me through
the shield.

I shoved an anticonjure amulet against the shield-wall,
holding it against the energies. The scorched smell of burned
leather rose from my gloves. The scent cleared the last of
Rose's panic from me. Resting in the icy slime, I pressed the
Tear close as shame threaded through me.

Rose's head rotated to me and her eyes met mine. Horror and panic were mirrored there, and her body quivered in
minute waves of terror. Tears flowed through the grime on my
twin's face. "Thorn," she mouthed at me, her words silenced
behind the shield that was more than protection, stopping air
flow and sound as well. I was a coward, but I couldn't put away
the Apache Tear again. I couldn't bear Rose's fear inside me.
The succubus had her mouth at my twin's neck, sucking. And
there was nothing I could do to stop it.

Flames blinked into sight over me, dropping over my
head, spinning in a fiery circle, stealing my night vision.
They hissed words as they raced around me, plasma trails
in the night. "Omega maggge," they said. "Foretold one.
Omega maggge."

I crawled to my feet and stepped away from them, focusing on Rose. "If I'm so great a mage, then why can't I conjure me some help?" I whispered, my feet slick on the snail
trails.

A brilliant light snapped into space overhead, bathing the
church in a dazzling radiance. The concussive movement of
air from its arrival slammed against the shield and should
have thrown me to my knees, but the Dark energies protected me. There was only one thing I knew that displaced
that much air on arrival. A wheels. No way had there been
time for it to answer my plea. Someone else had brought it
here. Not good.

The Flames swirled in a climbing spiral, toward the
wheels overhead. A shaft of light pierced the shield above
me and the Flames swept through. The lights went out, the
world going black, though there was no massive boom. I
waited a beat, but the Flames didn't return.

Feeling unaccountably betrayed, I drew the kris and the
tanto, holding them ready. Stepping in a circle, I placed my
feet carefully in the slime, trying to isolate various noises:

my footsteps, rustling, a soughing that might be a distant
wind. To compensate for my ruined night vision, I opened
both mage-sight and a mind-skim. When I caught my balance and the resulting nausea settled, I looked around. The
church glowed weirdly in the blended scan.

Out of the night, a voice groaned, saying, "Crap. That
hurts."

I closed my eyes as joy blossomed in me. I inhaled to call
him and pain thrust deep, broken ribs stealing my breath,
but I didn't care. I wasn't alone. Eli was just beyond a pile
of rubble.

Chapter 21

L ouder, Eli shouted, "What? No 'Beam me up, Scotty'?
Just drop me ten feet into a slime pit and take off?
What's the matter with you, you big, ugly, feathered
fiend! You trying to kill us?"

"That's a cherub, you young pup," another voice said,
creaky and strained. "We just got picked up and dumped in
the church. Shut your yapper or it'll blow us to electrons."

For a moment, I couldn't place the voice, but I remembered Ernest Waldroup, the senior elder from Atlanta.

"Tears of Taharial, that hurts," Thadd swore. "I broke a
freaking wing."

"What is this, old home week?" Rupert asked. "Audric?"

"Here. What happened?"

"Patience, brothers," Shamus said. "When we rushed
inside the sigil to take Thorn from the seraph, the wheels
descended. And they took us up."

"Like Elijah," Jasper said, awe in his voice. "'Behold,
there appeared a chariot of fire, and horses of fire,'" he
said, quoting from the second book of Kings, "'and parted
them both asunder; and Elijah went up by a whirlwind into
heaven.'"

"We didn't go very far for this to be heaven," Rupert
said.

"And if this is heaven, we've got to talk to the cleaning
crew," Eli said. "Room fresheners, a little dusting, and a
good vacuuming would do wonders."

I couldn't help my smile. I think if I were dying, Eli could make me smile. Come to think of it ... I set the death thoughts aside. "How many of you are there?" I asked, my voice scratchy.

"Thorn?" Eli asked.

"Yeah."

"Hot *damn*," he said, fervently. "Where are you? You sound like crap. Are you hurt?" Limping, holding my side, I rounded the rubble and saw them in the scan, their bodies bright in the night, smoldering energies that had texture and smell. Joy danced at the edges of the scan, a synesthesia similar to mage-heat that I hadn't noticed before.

Eli and Lucas stood near Thadd, who held one wing close to his body, the other half-furled. The two Waldroup brothers, Jasper, Rupert, and Audric were in a loose circle, weapons drawn. Five of my six champards, three elders of the kirk. They all looked worn to the bone, faces smeared with grime, body odors rank. They were beat. I could smell exhaustion on them, and old blood, and the reek of death.

I stopped as another spear of agony stabbed me. I touched my side where the spur had pierced. The worst of the broken ribs were just above it, and the pain of the two wounds seemed to mingle and consolidate, becoming more than the sum of the two. I was really hurt.

"Thorn? What's wrong?" There was worry in Eli's voice, and it warmed me.

I pulled off a healing amulet and two pain-relieving ones, thumbing them on and sliding them into a dobok pocket over the wounds. "Broken ribs."

"How bad—"

"Later," I interrupted. "Did you smell a reek when you landed? Something awful?" Eli nodded. "That smell is succubus larvae, and the queen is here."

I saw their auras spark with sharp colors, and heard the steel-on-steel scritch of more blades being drawn. Afraid they would kill one another by accident, I pulled three illumination amulets, thumbed them on, and tossed them in a circle around the men. I should have done it sooner, but I wasn't thinking clearly. And the Flames had burned out my human vision, which was only now returning. The level of pain in my chest subsided marginally as the amulets went to work, and I managed a single breath. I handed another healing amulet to Thadd, who held it against his wing as Audric fashioned a crude splint.

"That's what those things are on the walls," I continued. "There are overlapping conjures here. I have no idea how many or what kind. But as long as the smell is contained, and no seraphs land, we should be okay." A tickle started in the back of my throat, a dangerous cough that would hurt. I breathed shallowly, hoping to stifle it. "How long was I gone?" I asked.

"Too damn long," Eli said, touching my shoulder as if to reassure himself I was alive.

"Forty-eight hours," Audric said over his shoulder, reporting as he bound Thadd's wing. "The seraphs watched as the town was attacked. We defended ourselves, but we lost many. The Special Forces were decimated in the first twelve hours, as if the spawn knew the greatest threat and targeted them specially. But the children and elderly are still safe behind your shield."

Lucas stepped close, smelling of blood, crusted and old, but his sweat was sweet with the scent of manna. He reached out and touched my face, stroking my scars, wordless. I felt his relief. He had thought I was dead. I touched a crusted place on his hand. He shrugged my concern away.

Thadd sat down on a pile of rubble, rocking, holding his wing. One hand turned the seraph ring he wore on a chain around his neck. His plumage was caked with dried blood. It wasn't his. A human had died in his arms.

To the side, I saw a shift of movement in the scan. Cheran was glamoured and hiding. I was surprised, as he was supposed to be in jail. I didn't believe in luck or coincidence anymore; ergo, several things: someone important wanted him free, his liberator didn't have to be one of the guys on my side, and Cheran wanted to remain hidden. He didn't know about the blended scan, didn't know I could see him. I decided to keep his presence quiet, but the scan wasn't helping my light-headedness, so I dropped the skim and felt marginally better.

The Flames again blinked into sight overhead and spiraled back down. They passed through the shield with spits of energy, to circle behind me, saving my vision but holding back. Which I didn't like at all.

A light illuminated the old church and the Ravens touched down in a back-to-back triangle, swords drawn. Their mouths opened and it was clear they were shouting, though there was no sound. And they didn't see us. Interesting.

"Speak of the devil," Eli muttered, hate in his tone.

Up close, I could tell these were crack troops, holy beings who lived to fight. They furled their wings tight, as if they intended to stay. The Ravens searched the night with glowing eyes.

Seraphs with swords. A succubus queen. Larvae. Not good at all. We were one heartbeat from judgment and death, a second heartbeat away from forcing the seraphs into heat. I had seen that happen when a seraph came upon a succubus. It hadn't been pretty.

I shouted to the Ravens. They didn't look my way. I stepped toward them and smacked into the shield, a barrier that brought me up short, a hot electric charge sizzling up my arm. This shield was a lot stronger than the one the queen was behind.

Azazel was luring seraphs here. The wheels had brought my champards—Amethyst in a rage, helping the Dragon, or the wheels bringing me assistance? And it sent them through the shield. I had a feeling that was unusual, even for a wheel. Whatever forces were working, it was Rupert's dream. I needed my longsword, its prime amulet, and the femur bone.

Overhead, I caught sight of three more seraphs spiraling down, Zadkiel, Raziel, and Cheriour. But the wheels were nowhere in sight. Glamoured? Gone?

My threatening cough was growing more insistent, my breath harder to catch. I feared I had punctured a lung and it was filling with blood. But I had a battle to fight. I could die later.

To the Flames, I composed a formal request, saying, "Omega mage, I have been called. Omega mage, so be it. Yet, I ask, not demand. I beg, not command. Will you help this battle?"

"Yourssss to command," they said, the words like the explosion of gases, the hum of electricity, and the ringing of heavy brass.

"The queen is protected by a conjure. Kill it," I said. "Protect the other mage."

"We cannot break the ssshhhield," one said.

Despair filled me as they spun slowly away in a snaking line to hover over the queen's shield. I followed them. The queen was crouched beside a pile of broken stones and brick on the cracked, burned floor. Rose was stretched out at her feet. I was in no condition to fight the succubus one-on-one. I wasn't in condition to fight off a preschooler armed with a toy club. I reached out and touched the shield. It shocked me to my toes and I eased back.

On impulse, I stabbed into the shield with the Flame-blessed tanto. The blade slid in with a grinding sound like metal on stones. Deep purple-black embers sparkled around the insertion point. I shoved down on the blade, but it didn't give. And now the tanto was stuck. *Seraph stones.* I couldn't do anything right. I braced a foot on the shield, ignoring the electric shocks through my boot and the agony of my chest, and pulled. Slowly, with a sound like rocks in a tumbler, the blade slid free, leaving a thin slice. The stink of succubus wafted out.

I considered the small hole, and touched a throwing knife blade to the tanto. The touch created a tiny spark, like a minuscule sun, startling me, bringing a smile to my face. With a flick of my wrist, I threw the knife at the queen. So fast I couldn't follow, the knife pierced the shield with a spit of sound, fine cracks shattering through the protective conjure at the impact point, centered around an elongated hole, like glass hit by a bullet. "Yes," I yelled, exultant.

Beyond, the blade quivered in the succubus's lower abdomen. Its scream filtered through the two holes. Eli threw a fist in the air. "You did it!" Sometimes flying by the seat of my pants paid off.

The queen screeched, bouncing away from my twin, beating around the wound in pain. It was a horrid vision, the human-looking woman beating herself, a knife sticking from her. Black blood trickled out around the blade. I hardened myself to the image as a tiny blaze of hope ignited in my chest. If the Dragon stayed gone we might. . .

If. I knew better than to think Murphy's Law would keep its ugly paws off. Yet, the Flames formed into two arrows. Both shot forward, through the small holes, hitting the succubus at the wound site and disappearing inside. Eli cheered again and the other champards gathered close, Lucas at my back. Within the shield, Rose looked around, as if trying to find the source of the screeching. Her head bobbed on her neck like a bloom on a broken stem, drunken, and she seemed to fall asleep before she ever found me beyond the shield. She lay on the floor of the church as Jane danced around her, kicking her once in her pain.

I had to figure out how to get *me* through the shield. I touched another blade to the tanto, this time prepared for the spark, squinting my eyes. I threw it. Off balance from the pain of my ribs, my aim not sure, it sliced through the protective barrier and sliced the queen beneath the arm, to skitter away.

Cheran appeared beside me. "We need to work on your aim." My champards flinched, weapons ready. Cheran held out six blades, wordlessly asking permission to touch the tanto.

"You try it with broken ribs," I said, breathless. I waved off the champards and offered the Flame blade. He touched them to my weapon, making sparks each time. Faster than I could see, he threw them. All six struck the queen, five penetrating joints, one piercing over her heart. If the beast had a heart. Her screams rose in pitch, tinny through the broken shield. Black smoke came from her wounds. Her flesh began to darken. In her rage, she kicked Rose hard, in the ribs. My twin twitched on the floor, retching. My vision darkened in rage, but there was nothing I could do. The pain in my own side stabbed hard, stealing my breath.

"What's the plan?" Cheran asked, patting his pockets, pulling more blades.

"Last time there was a fight, you ran away," I said, sounding puny and hating it. I offered the tanto again, and he touched three small, palm-sized blades to the Flame.

"That was last time. Let's just say I had some bad advice,"

Cheran said, face tight. He slapped a metal amulet into my pocket. My pain level dropped dramatically. "That should help with the broken ribs. You breathing okay?"

"No," I said, trying unsuccessfully for a clean, deep breath. "I'm not." His conjure was a lot more powerful than mine. Maybe I should have let him teach me. Then again, thinking about his poisons, maybe not.

"Cough? Hemo or pneumo-thorax?"

I was pretty sure he was asking me if I had blood or air in my lungs. "Fighting it, and maybe." I didn't know if Cheran was regretting not fighting before or rebelling against orders not to fight now, but it didn't matter. I gestured with the tanto to the descending seraphs. "Soon as the last one lands, I figure the conjure containing the scents will be disrupted and the succubi will drive the seraphs insane. Rupert had a prediction, a partially prophetic dream about this. It didn't end well," I said.

"Partially?"

"Yeah. I gave away the sword that was part of the dream." I looked again at Rose. She was on her side, facing away from me. I hoped she was unconscious.

"Dang, woman," Eli said from the side, checking his flame-thrower and handguns, shadows making arcs on the stone wall behind him. "You're tellin' an awful lot to a chicken-ass stranger." Cheran ignored him and Eli shook his head. "Not much fuel left. Only a couple extra clips of our special ammo. I can't use a sword worth spit. And even over the conjure that's keeping down the stink, I smell spawn."

Twice, I too had scented devil-spawn. I looked at the Ravens. The winged warriors had spread out, moving bent-kneed in widening arcs, sniffing the air. Something was getting through to them. "Think you can pierce *that* shield?" I asked Cheran, offering the tanto for blessing again. He tried, but the throwing knife bounced away and spun into the night. Cheran shrugged.

The seraphs overhead were still descending, but their flight was measured. They seemed to be moving through a veil of black-light sparkles, in slow motion. The Dragon was slowing them. That was probably another of the things it wasn't supposed to be able to do, like transmogrify and take a bath in the river of *time*. If Azazel could manipulate seraphs in flight, then he could do almost anything. We were so toast.

We could be here a month, a day, or an hour. Maybe our air would hold out beneath the conjures. Maybe we would all die of suffocation. Maybe we could roast a couple of succubus snails for dinner. Chuckling at my own morbid whimsy, I pulled a bottle of water from a low pocket on my cloak and drank while I had the chance. Beside me, Eli did the same.

I figured Azazel was off somewhere, sometime, healing his wounds, so he could fight his little war healthy. It looked like the Dark Prince had planned for all contingencies, even his own wounding. I screwed the top back on and tucked the bottle into my cloak.

"Cheran, can you still kill spawn at a distance, burning them the way you did before?"

"Oh yeah. Of course I could do it better if you gave me back my anklet."

"Not gonna happen, mage boy," Eli said for me.

"I figured." The mage flipped two knives, blades flashing in the light of the illumination amulets. He caught them deftly, a cocky grin reshaping his face. "We need weapons, Consulate General."

"No shit," Eli said.

I had pulled the longsword when I landed against the wall, and Azazel had thrown the femur. I checked the position of the succubus, arms flailing at the Flames, the form of Jane shrieking like a fishwife. My sister lay nearby on the church's burned, scarred floor, still breathing, but drugged or unconscious. Blood coated Rose's neck where the queen had fed.

I couldn't tell if my twin still had her amulets. Rose was an earth mage, like the new acting priestess of Enclave. She needed something alive, or once alive, to cast a conjure. Or an amulet made of something that lived or once lived. I had a few thoughts about that, but anything I could figure out had to be a last-ditch effort to destroy the Dragon because they were drastic measures and we were all going to go blooey. A bloody messy way to die.

I walked, mostly upright, to the spot where I had first landed. A dim glow showed me my longsword, deep under the muck of slime. "Ducky," I said, and plunged my hand into the glop. I pulled the sword free and, wishing for wash water, cleaned it off on my cloak.

"You might think that slime would be acidic," Cheran said conversationally.

Eli, who had moved with us, said, "You'd think."

"Eli, are you guarding me?" I asked.

"Just followin' orders, ma'am." He rested his hands, fingers hanging loosely, on his gun butts. "Your head champard suggested it might be wise."

"Mmmm." It wasn't much of a response but it was all I had. "Cheran, you want to help? Open up your mage-sight and look around. You see a big bone? A femur bone of a seraph."

"You mean like this one?" He toed the tip of the bone with his foot. He had been standing on it, and no way did I think he hadn't known. Best bet, he had spotted it in mage-sight and was planning on claiming it for himself, though his face looked bland and innocent.

I pushed him away and fished Barak's bone from between two rocks. It still retained a lavender glow from the snake-wheels. I now had my swords, one Flame-blessed, one with my bloodstone prime amulet, and a seraph bone given in sacrifice; I still had the Dragon's link; and my pain was receding. With a flash of thought, I felt around in my dobok for the cross, not finding it. Beneath a particularly deep glop of muck, I spotted it. I cleaned the cross in the wan light. "Yeah," I said softly. "Okay." I was ready to get my sister back from a succubus bitch.

"Audric," I called, now able to shout. When the big man looked up I said, "Remember that errand I sent you on? Do you still have them with you?"

"Yes, mistrend. I do."

Ignoring the formal word, I said, "I'd like them now, please."

Audric came forward and knelt at my feet. Shock flashed through me. I was about to order him to get up when I realized he was on the ground so he could open a canvas satchel.

I swallowed back the command. *Seraph stones. Can I be any more stupid? Audric knelt at my feet to swear fealty, not*

as a matter of habit. He might kneel for me if he screwed up
and drew my blood while practicing. Or not. Audric flipped
back the top of the satchel.

Inside were stones that looked like black opals to my
human sight, but when viewed with mage-sight, appeared as
Dark and Light in one conjure. Thin, blue, wirelike strands
of Light overlaid and enwrapped the Dark amulet-bombs.

Audric said, "Things are going to get interesting shortly."
Eli snorted at Audric's word choice, but the big half-breed
went on. "Throw these, or use them as land mines?"

I considered the playing field and the number of the
opals. Someone could lose a hand throwing them. "Set them
up as mines." Audric nodded his approval.

I experimented with a deep breath. My lungs ached
and creaked like rubber folded over and rubbing against
itself. The rib bones were sharp and grinding, but Cheran's
handy-dandy amulet was working. I swung my blades, the
motion painful but not debilitating. I checked the position
of my weapons and tucked the femur into my belt, the cross
looped through beside it.

The Waldroup brothers shuffled closer, exhaustion
clear in their postures. Ernest touched the shield separating us from the Ravens and jerked back when it shocked
him. "One question," Shamus said, blinking into the night,
steadying his brother when the old man wavered on his
feet. "Why didn't the Dragon attack us in small groups?
Why do all this?"

"I think it wants the flying wonders to mate with the succubus queen," Eli said in disgust. "I think it set this up so
seraphs will sin, so they'll be forced to join the Dark against
the Host. That Final Battle humans fought a hundred years
ago? It ain't over. That's what I think."

"They been taking a breather for a hundred years?" Shamus asked me, incredulous.

I looked up, shrugging. The seraphs had tilted and tucked
their wings to land. The Ravens seemed to see them for
the first time, their motions slowing to match the dimin-
ished speed of the descending three, as if caught in the time
change. "I agree with Eli," I said.

"And your twin?"

"I'm going after her. Forcas and the Dragon took her

and kept her alive for some reason. We get her back and we mess up some part of the plan."

"We need to be fighting before the seraphs land," Cheran said. At Eli's blank look he said, "Mage-heat. I'm already feeling it, thanks to our winged friend here. It's going to get worse when the conjure that's keeping the smells down is canceled and the seraphs and you humans smell the succubus and larvae. It's going to be a mating orgy in the middle of a bloodbath. If we're fighting, Thorn and I won't be affected and we can stop it." After a slight pause he added, "Maybe."

I didn't trust Cheran any more than I could throw him, uphill, over my shoulder. But he was right. Pulling three amulets off of my necklace, I said, "We need to get through the queen's shield. I have anticonjure amulets, which may work now that it's damaged, but they kind of explode." I was just glad they hadn't gone off when I pressed them into the shield. How stupid could I get?

Eli laughed. "More than just kinda explode. They'll rock your world." He raised his voice. "Down, everybody. Thorn's going inside."

Chapter 22

My champards ringed me. Audric said, "Land mines are in place around the dais and the outer perimeter. I marked a pathway if we need to regroup. Champards, to arms."

I hadn't thought about a place to regroup but it was a dandy idea. I squatted behind a low pile of roof rubble, and steadied myself with a hand. Beneath my palm, beneath a layer of ash, I felt thin slate slabs, roof tiles, burned and fallen in. I turned one over, looking at it in mage-sight.

I couldn't use stone for conjuring if it had been open to the elements, and had unconsciously disregarded the stone of the old church, the inside and outside walls of which were exposed and damaged by the Dark. But the church had been burned, then protected from the elements under a conjure. The rocks in this pile had gotten so hot, they'd burned free of wind and rain contaminants, and the shields had kept them that way. They were slime free. I looked around, reconsidering. There was plenty of stone and some of it glowed with pure creation energies. I bet Azazel hadn't thought about that. And when it dropped its conjures from the church, all the stone was going to be available to me.

I also once used the contaminated Trine. I banished the thought. *No. Not again.*

Feeling a bit more secure, I aimed at the damaged shield, tossed an anticonjure, and covered my head. The concussion threw me to my hip, and I rolled, catching myself on closed fists. I pushed up in the same instant, pulled swords, and raced toward the succubus, toward Jane Hilton. I opened with the dolphin, nicking its thighs and forcing it away from Rose, who rolled her head groggily. I cut Jane deeply. Screaming, she—no, it—began to bleed.

A conjure sparkled over and she raised her arms defensively, begging, "Stop! Stop!"

Human blood gushed and splattered. Human blood drenched Jane's pink dress. Pink! Shock roiled through me and I moved back, lowering my blades. This wasn't the succubus! I was killing a human. Seraph stones. I had attacked a human. . . .

The scent of succubus rose all around and I heard Thadd groan with want. Thadd who had the seraph stone, but who couldn't fight because of his wing. If he was having mage-heat difficulty, the seraphs were in deep trouble. Audric urged him to fight, to stimulate battle-lust.

Eli danced up beside me and hit Jane with a blast of the holy oil he used in his gun. The scent of eucalyptus and conifers filled the air, mixing with succubus scent and her pitiful screams. When she was drenched, oil and blood mixing, he reset his weapon and said, "Throw one-a them exploding things at her. Let's see what she's got under that skin."

I started to argue, but he fired again. This time a flame shot out, hitting Lucas' lady love in her bleeding chest. The scream that followed was nothing like human; it cleared the conjure from my head. I tossed another anticonjure into the midst of the inferno. Jane exploded.

Or rather, the glamour of Jane exploded away and the queen rose up from the center of her, burning and raging, all claws and teeth. "There she is," Eli sang out, laughing, flamethrower to the side. "Miss America!"

The fear staying my hand, the fear of killing a human, was stripped away with the sight of the queen as her big, bad, ugly self. Walking-stick blade held to the side, perpendicular to the ground, tanto low, at my thigh, I attacked. I cut, letting the weight of the longsword do the work. Flames zipped through the wounds, burning, leaving hideous gaping holes. The reek of succubus gagged me and I forced down the sour taste. I cut and cut, splattered by acidic blood, not human blood. Foul Darkness. My champards fought at my side, even Thadd, hounded into action by Audric.

To my right, I heard the prayers of the elders begin, "I will love thee, O LORD, my strength. The LORD is my rock, and my fortress, and my deliverer; my God, my strength, in whom I will trust; my buckler, and the horn of my salvation, and my high tower. . . ."

Shocked, I danced back. They were quoting the Eighteenth Psalm, one I had particular fondness for, as it claimed victory over Darkness and called the Most High a rock. It was a psalm for stone mages, a specific and distinct sign of approval and support. I saluted them with the tanto and returned to the attack in the ugly forms of the crab. The sounds of battle were bright in the night. Battle-lust began to rise in me, my heart pounding, wounds forgotten.

An icy wind blew, circling through the broken walls and through the arched windows. The winter air was frigid, freezing the slime and blood pooled on the broken, burned floor into a slushy mess. Footing was precarious. Nearby, the seraphs were inches from the church floor.

I swung backhanded with the longsword and caught the blade in the queen's shoulder joint, jarring me to the spine, ripping me from battle-lust. I yanked to free it. The succubus clawed me, catching my chest and ripping aside the battle cloak, scoring my skin beneath in its claws. Three knives landed with hard thunks in the beast, distracting it from me.

I wished the champards had saved the big-ass gun. We could use it about now. I gave a final hard wrench. I felt a snap and I fell back, taking the hilt with me.

Beyond it, there was a three-inch length of steel and a cleanly broken blade. Shock and alarm shuddered through me, trailed by the pain of loss. I loved that sword.

I tucked the amuleted hilt into my dobok and pulled the kris, now holding only short blades. This wouldn't do. I resheathed it and lifted out the war ax, sliding my hand through the loop at the base before gripping the handle. Its head was smaller than a human's war ax, but with a wider flange at the cutting edge. I swung, finding its balance. I didn't like it. Not at all. Like I had a choice.

Tanto in one hand, ax in the other, I leaped back to the

fighting. Rupert moved in on one side of me, watching me with tight eyes, fighting with his named blade. He knew where we were. He had recognized his death dream. "I won't," I said to him. "No matter what. I refuse."

The elders were chanting verse six: "... and my cry came before him, even into his ears. Then the earth shook and trembled; the foundations also of the hills moved and were shaken, because he was wroth."

The earth beneath our feet began to tremble. "Crap," Eli said, appearing at my elbow. "The big bad mojo is back."

"Thorn?" Rose said. Beneath the conjure of the Apache Tear, her mind touched mine, static-filled visions of horror, things she had seen. Things that had been done to her. I faltered.

Rupert, as if he knew what had happened, shouldered me back. "We've got it here. Take care of the girl."

I sheathed my blade and secured the ax, kneeling at Rose's side. I gathered her up, easing her from the cold church floor to a slab of blackened wood in the corner, under a patch of the roof that was protected from the wind. She was cold, shivering, and I pulled off my battle cloak, wrapping it around her. Rose was little more than skin and bones. Azazel and his minions may have kept her alive, but they hadn't fed her much. She was filthy, her hair in loose clumps, bald scalp beneath, her clothes rotted.

"You can be near me?" Rose whispered. "Without going crazy?"

"Yes." I tapped the Apache Tear hanging around my neck. "A conjure to keep my mind separate."

Rose's fingers brushed the Tear, and her touch overrode the conjure. I glimpsed a dark place, a cave, and a seraph face close above hers, a face I had seen before—Forcas, in his glamoured state. Too close. Too intimate. She shivered again and forced the vision away as she focused on me. We hadn't been together in ten years, since I was spirited away from Enclave for my own sanity's sake. We shared a moment of gladness, a burst of joy and relief that I— we—felt to our toes. Rose laughed softly and the laughter brought on a coughing spell.

I showed her where in the cloak pockets I kept bottled

water, and opened one for her. "You haven't eaten in a while," I said. "Take it slow."

She took three sips, her throat working as if it hurt to drink. "How many weeks have I been gone?" she asked. At my blank look, she said, "I was taken on Monday the twelfth. What day is it? How long have I been prisoner?"

"Rose," I breathed. "Rose, you've been gone four years."

She held the bottle away in horror, her eyes, so like my own, wide. "Four years?" she whispered. She shook her head. Her gazed tightened on my cheek scars and my remade throat, glowing white in the night. She reached out and touched them, her fingertips cold as death.

"Yes," I said, my throat clogging.

Beneath the conjure that kept us separate and me sane, I felt her mind as it tried to grasp the concept. Her thoughts were muddy, disjointed, her pulse faster than my own and thready. "Did it find you?" she asked, her tone full of shame.

"Find me?"

"Forcas. It was looking for you. I never told it where you were. I swear."

I knew what the Darkness had done to her. I could see it in her mind. And if Forcas had been standing before me I would have killed it dead with my bare fists.

Rose stroked my jaw. "It's okay, Thorny. It's okay. I didn't get pregnant and bear a litter of . . . *things*. There was enough earth and life nearby for me to draw on to keep it away after that one time. I survived it. And I'll keep on surviving it."

"Why did it want us?" I asked, an answer I had waited for, for what seemed like forever.

"It said we had a weapon that could burn its master unto death. A great Prince of Darkness."

"Azaz?" I whispered, truncating the name so it would not be a true calling and bring the beast here.

"Yes," she breathed, her mind clearing more with the name.

"And if we could kill Azaz, then we could be used to kill seraphs of the Most High." I looked at my twin, pulled off a glove, and brushed away dried blood from her chin. She swallowed painfully and touched her neck where punctures still dribbled blood. "We could be a weapon to use against the High Host, if he could convert us." Rose closed her eyes and turned away. I wondered how close she had come to breaking. How close she still was.

"Azaz is free," I said, stroking her arm when she cringed. "And the only thing I learned about a weapon was about us. I think that we, together, are supposed to be the weapon."

The elders had reached the tenth verse and were speaking of God. Their sonorous voices incanted, "And he rode upon a cherub, and did fly: yea, he did fly upon the wings of the wind."

As if it had been called—which it had, called by scripture—the sky brightened, throwing a lavender brilliance into the church. Overhead, the wheels hovered, rotating like a gyroscope on its side, whirring softly. Over the gunwale leaned the cherub, her lion face staring down. I didn't think it an accident that the cherub chose to watch us with the mien of a man-eater.

Rose ducked her head, shading her eyes, her mouth parted. "What is that?"

"It's a cherub," I said, pulling on my battle glove. "And she's pretty pissed off at me."

"Thorn," she chided.

I chuckled. My twin *would* scold me for coarse language, even during a battle. "Rosie, that weapon Forcas was looking for? I think it's us. Mind to mind. And joined to seraphs."

Her lips parted, startled, making her look like a baby bird, hungry. "Oh," she said.

"I did it once, joined to a seraph's mind. Not its body," I said, reading her thoughts, "just its mind. And we were…" I took a breath at the remembered power. "We were almost invincible."

"Theoretically it's possible. In school—"

A concussive force threw us across the rubble. I rolled over Rosie, protecting her with my body, tucking her into a crevice of debris. Shaken, I spun on a knee to see that the seraphs had touched down. The conjures holding back time had blasted away. Azazel stood in the midst of the stunned seraphs. He was glowing with might, with intense seraphic power, shining with aqua- and peach-toned energies, a small sun of power. His sunrise-tinted wings half lifted, taut for battle, his eyes bright with aqua light and black sparks of might. He was dressed in battle armor—overlapping discs of aqua light, fine as scales. So much for any wound I had given him.

The six seraphs, dull by comparison to the sparkling Dark, attacked. Instantly Azazel threw lightning, blasting against the seraph shields and the walls of the church. The sound of battle was so loud it beat against my eardrums, a physical sensation.

Rose quivered, delight and horror on her face. "Seraphs. They're fighting each other. The EIH were right all along?" she asked, confusion growing.

I gripped her chin and jerked her gaze to me. "I don't know. But the beautiful one? That's a Dragon. A Darkness. Not a seraph."

"Forcas' Lord," she whispered, understanding. Helpless tears pooled in her eyes, spilling down her cheeks, washing clean trails through the accumulated filth. I pushed her behind a pile of rubble, burned pews and stained glass from the church windows, and stone from the walls. Stone I could use. Wood Rose could use. I placed a spar in her hand, turning her face to me, away from the battle. "Rose," I shouted over the screams and the sound of thunder, "you can fight. You're a gifted and well-trained mage. *You can fight.*"

Her fingers clamped down on the wood, her eyes raking the pile of rubble. In an achingly familiar gesture, she dashed away the tears with a wrist. She took a calming breath, and I could hear her mind settle with the childhood chant, "*Stone and fire, water and air, blood and kin prevail. Wings and shield, dagger and sword, blood and kin prevail.*"

My mind cleared with hers and, remembering the Apache Tear, I pressed it close. I loved my sister, but it was hard to think with her in my thoughts.

"Yes, it is," she said. And I chuckled again.

The elders were chanting, "Yea, he sent out his arrows, and scattered them; and he shot out lightnings, and discomfited them." From the elders emanated strange energies, the power of spiritual warfare. Not human, mage, or seraph. Something else entirely. The men were kneeling, facing a

large shadow at the front of the church. The inner walls had
burned away, revealing that a cross had once hung there.
Now it was a cross-shaped scar on the stone.

Rose sat up and began to inspect the wood pile, her gaze
intent, her skeletal fingers touching this piece of wood then
that, pulling some to her, simply noting the positions of others. I stood and drew my ax, standing between her and Azazel, searching out my friends.

Chapter 23

Two champards were hacking at the succubus. The beast was on the floor of the old church, bleeding into a pool. Rupert was using his bastard sword to behead it. The others had raced for cover when the seraphs attacked, and I found them safe behind rubble, in a semicircle between me and the fight taking place.

Over us, Amethyst stared down at the fight, hate for me on her feline face. Swords flashing, the seraphs hemmed Azazel, lightning bursting from their hands, the energies shattering long before they harmed him. Their own shields took the brunt of dark lightning, bolts of black-light flashing into the air to strike at them. One Raven took a hit and fell, screaming, burning, to the church floor.

In mage-sight, I saw a conjure take shape. The flames on the burning Raven went out. Cheran ducked from cover to pull the seraph to safety. Nifty use for the fire-snuffing incantation I hadn't bothered to learn. A second Raven fell. And so did Zadkiel, in a gout of flame that lit the church, rising in the night with his screams. Amethyst shrieked with him, a howl of grief.

In silhouette, I saw my champards shield their faces. The elders fell to the ground and scrambled for cover. The flames snuffed quickly, but I could see that the Raven and Zadkiel, the right hand of Michael the ArchSeraph, were badly wounded. Battle-lust shot through me in a burst of adrenaline and fear. We had to drain the Dragon. I needed the wheels.

Lights appeared in the wheels' eyes at the front bow, near the golden navcone. Amethyst had fired up her weapons. She was going to help us! Triumph filled me and I stood, ax and tanto held in the air, my eyes full of tears. A single laser-like beam fired, a pencil-thin lavender light. It struck the beast. Azazel cringed, his fingers shifting as if to strengthen a shield. "Yes!" I shouted.

Amethyst stared down at me, raging, "No! The wheels are mine! You have no right!"

I lowered my weapons. She thought I had done that? "Not me," I shouted back. Guessing, I yelled, "The wheels themselves! Do they act alone?"

Her human face turned to me in shock and disbelief. She brought down a fist on the side of the wheels, anger so strong the ship jolted. The weapon stopped firing. The wheels' eyes closed. The gyroscopic rotors slowed. She had powered down her ship.

"Ask them!" I screamed. Amethyst glared at me, her demi-wings fluttering.

Desperate, I turned back to the fight. Azazel had a feath-erless score along one wing where the beam had hit, but no other sign of injury.

It looked bad, now three to one. Raziel had been burned by a glancing bolt of black energies. His battle armor on one side and one wing were scorched, the smell of burned feathers foul on the air. The third Raven knelt in a pool of blood. Cheriour was bleeding, one arm gone, amputated at the elbow, his teal plumage splattered with his own gore. The Dragon looked just dandy. We were going to lose this fight unless we could do something.

"Audric?" I shouted, spotting him kicking something, sending it flying. Jane's head.

He whirled to me and screamed, "To war!" Bloodlust sparked through me like lightning.

My champards raced in, firing weapons and cutting at Azazel. I followed at the seraph's side, weapons raised, the war ax whirling slowly. The Dragon laughed and took a sin-gle sweep with one wing. An arc of black energy sent us all flying. I caught the backlash and hit the floor, skidding, bowling into a pile of debris. Something jabbed me hard,

slicing through my new dobok, and I pulled out a long sliver
of wood tipped with my blood.

My ribs grated as I sat up, trying to find my breath through
the pain. I smelled human blood, fresh and deadly. Dread
filled me. They would die. All of them. Because of me.

I crawled across the heap of broken pews to Rose. "Do
you have your prime or your visa?" I asked her.

"No. But I have this." She held a cross she had formed
from a bit of wire and two long splinters of ancient wood.
We had been raised Christian. Rose had never wandered
from the faith as I had. For her, the cross was an icon of
great power. "I just have to fill it."

The seraphs dashed in, wings sweeping. Thunder rocked
the floor beneath my feet. Champards followed, moving as
a team, holy oil, smoke, and ozone adding to the sensory
miasma. But they were two short. Dread filled me. I swept
the church with my eyes, spotting them in a shadow just as
Audric shouted, "Thorn! Rupert's hurt."

"Rupert," I whispered. *His dream. His damn dream.*

"Take me to Thorn," Rupert said, his voice barely heard
over the fighting.

Audric shouldered him, carrying him around the back
wall of the church, as far from the battle as he could get,
weaving through the detritus. I smelled bowel and blood.
A lot of it.

Audric settled beside Rose and me, easing Rupert to the
floor between us. An avulsion separated his entire left side,
a slab of tissue hanging out. I saw intestines and something
that had to be his liver. Rupert was nearly gone.

I fell to my knees. Hands shaking, I ripped off every healing amulet I had, mine and Cheran's, and dumped them
into his wound. Gloves blood-slicked, I tried to force the
huge slab of flesh back in place, trying to close the wound.
I heard a shaky litany, "No, no, no, no, no, no"—my own
voice, shocked and breathless. I held up the tanto, but the
flame sizzled and I knew it hadn't enough power to heal the
fearful wound.

There was little bleeding; most had bled out. Audric
was drenched in Rupert's blood. More spread in a small
pool at my knees.

Rupert was dying. Unless ... Unless I could get a stasis shield, the shields that can keep a human alive long enough to be healed. Raziel had given one to Ciana in the pin she wore.

"Raziel," I shouted, rising. "To me!" My seraph met my eyes, his alight with the joy of war. He saw Rose at my side and his eyes widened. He touched Cheriour and started to us.

Azazel swept once with his left wing, a long arc. The energies of a conjure fell away like black dust. The smell hit them. The scent of succubus. Everything went still.

Slowly, Zadkiel raised his burned head. The seared Ravens scrabbled, trying to rise, rattling charred arms and wing bones, metatarsals like long sticks against the floor. Raziel turned from me, hunger on his face. An icy wind blew straight down into the church, whipping the scent of succubus high.

Azazel chuckled, the sound like gongs and bells, angelic. Horrific.

"No. No!" I screamed.

To one side, the last Raven standing began to pant, his eyes bulging, his hands tearing at his clothes. An aqua light washed over him, a wave of bright mist that coated all the seraphs. Raziel stepped away from me as if I no longer existed.

"No," I gasped, whipping my eyes to Rupert. His mouth opened, trying for breath, but only a whisper of air passed.

The visa, silent for so long, informed me what was happening. *The seraphs are losing their heavenly bodies, not in transmogrification, but in a baser transfiguration. They acquire sublunary bodies, just as did the fallen Watchers when they joined with the daughters of men.*

Sublunary bodies meant they were stripping themselves of power. *"How do I stop it?"* I asked. But the visa had no comment. "Answer me!" I shouted to it, my mouth dry, my skin hot with fear. In the nave, explosions went off, the small land mines planted by Audric triggered by converging snails. I covered my face against shrapnel, deafened by the sound.

The elders had started over on the psalm. They reached a verse that said, "He brought me forth also into a large place; he delivered me, because he delighted in me."

God. They were talking about God the Victorious. About his willingness to deliver humans out of the hand of death. About his care and love. The love of God. The same God who was allowing this to happen.

Fury rose up in me, hotter than magma, the fury of years lost, of lives lost. I rose straight and shouted at the sky, "You claim you care! If you love, if you love at *all*, then fix Rupert! Fix him!" I raised the tanto and screamed at the sky, *"Fix him!"*

A hand brushed my boot. "Too late," Rupert whispered, his voice rustling like paper. "Use me. Like Mole Man. To bind the Dragon. The dream. The pink quartz sword," he coughed, blood bubbling up his throat. He was drowning in his own blood. His image wavered in my tears, his energies stuttering in mage-sight like a flickering candle.

"We will not sacrifice you," Audric said fiercely. He shifted Rupert more upright, so he could inhale, and Rupert made an awful sound, wet and thick and tortured. "Help him," he demanded of me.

"He's dying," Rose said, her voice dreamy, her eyes on the wound.

I felt all the blood drain from my limbs. Rose. She was an earth mage. The rarest, most generous, the best of healers. And, if not controlled, the most deadly of all mages. Earth mages could heal from the brink of death. And they could steal the life of another for the power it gave them. I remembered the prophecy at our birth. *A Rose by any Other Name will still draw Blood.* The prophecy that claimed Rose and I together would become a weapon. Or perhaps, if I let her use me, a killer.

A killer, like in Rupert's dream. The sword tipped with a pink quartz nugget wasn't Rupert's prophesized murderer. Rose was. Rose, who had always been associated in my mind with rose quartz. I should have figured it out. I should have understood.

"I could have saved him if I had drawn power. But it's too late. He's . . . almost . . . ." She smiled, breathing in his scent in a mind-skim, and finished, ". . . lost."

"Take me," Rupert said, his voice a breath. "Use me." He lifted a finger as if to reach for her, a plea in his eyes.

Rose inched across the icy floor and took his hand. "As

you will, so mote it be," she said. Rupert took a breath, wet and sucking, his mouth working. Agonal. Dying. And Rose dipped the wooden cross she held into his wound.

"No." Audric said, his grip tightening on his lover. But I could see the knowledge of death in Audric's face, a desperate pain.

"No," I repeated. But I was paralyzed. Watching.

Shrieks and pain-filled cries echoed off the stone church walls. Lightning threw the scene into sharp relief and dark shadows. Rupert's blood glistened in a huge pool, reflecting the lightning. Thunder rumbled.

Power filled Rose fast, flowing from Rupert into the cross, into her hand, into her core. Her body began to glow with mage energies. She threw back her head and laughed, a reckless sound, full of glee and joy and power. Rupert's mouth fell slack. His pupils widened. His life force being sucked away. On his last breath, he whispered, "Audric . . ."

My sister laughed, the sound echoing off the church walls, joyous and blissful. Laughed as she killed my best friend.

And Rupert died.

His spirit, his energy, filled Rose. And the cross became a weapon.

With a wordless cry, Audric fell across Rupert, fists bunched, his grief like a hot iron charring into my heart.

Rupert was gone. My tears fell, ignored, burning my face, dripping onto my dobok.

I looked up at the church, taking in the scene in a dazed sweep. The six seraphs were in the process of transfiguration into something less than seraphic. Light blasted from their eyes and from between their joints as power left them to swirl around Azazel in a rainbow hue of force. Their armor disappeared, leaving them clothed only in sharp, mottled energy patterns, not human energy patterns, not seraphic. Something between. In defiance of the edicts of the Most High, they were becoming the lesser, sublunary beings that were Watchers. Cursed.

Around us, the succubus larvae had abandoned the walls and were crawling closer. White pupae, the bloodless color of Rupert's skin, hundreds of them. Another touched a land mine and exploded. I was so shaken, I didn't even cringe.

Above us, Amethyst was screaming, a wail of horror. But she wasn't fighting. *She doesn't know how,* the visa informed me, the mental voice didactic and unemotional. *In battle, a cherub depends upon her seraph-mate to direct the energy and weapons of her wheels. They are true mates, joined mentally and spiritually, much less powerful when separate.*

Zadkiel wasn't fused mind to mind with Amethyst. He had broken their merge. I sobbed, the sound desperate, frantic, full of the hoarse tones of fury and failure and wild grief.

Lucas was holding back Thadd, who was ripping off his clothes, shrieking to be let go, needing to mate, caught in rut like an animal. But he had been fighting. He had the seraph stone. Or ... I put my hand on the pocket he had touched eons earlier. The seraph stone rested there, warm against my skin. He had given it back to me. So that if something attacked us with the rut, I would be spared. *Stupid kylen.* All my champards were giving up so much. Were giving up *too* much. For me.

Cheran was standing, his entire body quivering. I could read his need at a distance, his mind filled with desire, stimulated by the seraphs. When Azazel dropped the conjure, it had allowed all the scents to merge. Cheran turned, his face filled with lust, and focused on Rose and me. There was danger in his need. I didn't want to have to kill him.

I looked at my twin, glowing and powerful, full of the force of life and death. I touched the pink quartz amulet carved into a rose that I carried on my necklace and jerked my fingers away when it burned.

From the pouchlike folds of my dobok, I pulled the spur of binding, the spur that could be used to make me a slave to Darkness. It had been a part of Darkness, part of a dragonet. It was composed of life, a tool for an earth mage. My cloak, lying forgotten in a torn and bloody heap at Rose's feet, was splattered with Azazel's blood and the slime of succubus larvae. I bent and wiped the spur across it, then smeared it into the pool of Rupert's blood at my feet.

"Can you use this?" I asked her.

Rose, bright with the energies of sacrifice, took the spur and stood, bracing her feet, the cross in one hand, the spur in the other. She whispered to me, leashed power in her voice, her eyes shining of the might of death, "Are we the weapon? The two of us together?"

"Yes," I said, my voice low, clogged with tears. Hating it. Hating it all. "We are."

"No," Audric said.

"You want his death to be for nothing?" Rose asked, her voice fierce. She threw back her head, glowing with death. "I have Rupert's life force within me. I hold his spirit, if not his very soul. He wanted this. He wanted his death to mean something." Her face took on a sly cant. "Would you take that away from him before he finds the Light? Would you waste his death, waste his life?"

Audric looked at the body of his partner for a long moment. With a slow hand he reached out, hesitated, his fingers a hairsbreadth from Rupert's face. I heard his breath hitch in his chest. I bent and placed my fingers over his. Together, we closed Rupert's eyes. I sensed Audric's mouth moving, his words silent, the warrior's prayer for the dying. My tears fell on Rupert's ashen face, mixing with the blood and gore there. And I knew what I had to do.

"Burn the larvae," I whispered to Rose. "All of them."

"As they die, their energies will fill me," she said. "I can't protect you."

"Don't worry about me," I said. I reached out with my mind, with my hate, and touched the pile of stone near me. I had never lifted anything so massive, but I understood the physics of gravity and mass and my mind did the equations with an ease I'd never experienced before. Without a qualm, I summoned the purple snake. It slithered from beneath a pile of charred stone, as if it had been waiting for the call. It coiled around itself, hissing with glee and warning. I put my hand on the snake and spoke a single word. "Rise." I felt the snake tense, taking weight and mass into itself, as we lifted the pile of stone. It was so easy. So simple.

The stone rose. Holding it five feet off the floor, I shouted, "Get under here!" When they were all in place, Rupert's body pulled into the very center, cradled in Audric's arms, Lucas holding his brother's hand, Thadd and Cheran fighting, held down by Eli and Jasper and the elders, I opened a protective shield around the champards and elders, pulling the power to maintain it from the snake. Overhead, Amethyst shrieked as if she were dying. Her ship—my ship—had powered back up.

"Hurry," Rose said, still standing outside the levitating stone. She laughed and closed her eyes. Instantly, heat gathered around her body in a tube of power, a ring of might, like a prime amulet, but large enough to encircle her. Her own shield, powered by Rupert's death force.

My heart cold as stone, I glanced at the scene taking place on the church floor, the powerful Azazel, the changing seraphs. I focused on the snake, gazing into its myriad dark purple eyes, all watching me adoringly. The snake's body and tail rippled, forming a perfect ring around me, and power surged through it, a charmed circle. If I'd not been dead inside, I might have laughed. I eased my hand away from the levitating stone.

The seraphs would destroy me after I saved them, and would attempt to kill all under my protection. I would do what I could to protect the ones still living. I had betrayed Rupert. I had failed him. I'd rather die than fail another. I drew on the gifts of omega mage, pulling in energies, sucking them through the snake.

Feeding.

The energies were a wild, almost feral mixture of stone from the church, magma from the center of the earth, and the might of the wheels. When I was glowing, my mage-attributes flaring like a torch, as bright as my twin's, I pulled the Flame-blessed blade and held it, point down, over the wire amulet on my wrist. The amulet opened with a faint click and slid from my hand. I laid the tanto blade along the length of the snake's neck, added Mole Man's cross, and held them all together. With my other hand, I dropped the wire amulet over the snake's head, sliding it over the tanto blade and cross. I secured the amulet to the snake, tanto, and cross, making a bizarre and deadly necklace. Flying by the seat of my pants. Becoming the prophecy that hung over my door. *A Rose by any Other Name will still draw Blood.*

"Hurry," my twin whispered, her voice a full-throated rasp of desire. "Oh, God, hurry."

The snake and the tanto began to hum, a strange disharmony at first that softened and smoothed and changed key until they were singing a minor-key variation of three notes. In mage-sight, they shared similar energy patterns, a soft violet aura of compatibility. They had merged, the Flame and the wheels, the amulet and its iron ore bomb in Alabama, into a single weapon. And the gold cross blazed with light. No ... with *Light*.

From the Fallen, lightning shot into the night, black lightning, burning the sky with Darkness. Thunder boomed all about us, shaking the floor, the walls, sending rocks sliding, except where I had them levitated.

About Azazel, energies churned, swirls of Light, painfully bright, throwing out heat like a small star, and clouds of blackness, darker than the reaches of space, colder than the farthest reaches of hell. A storm of hot wind and icy currents built in the center of the old church.

I closed my human eyes and blended the mind-skim into mage-sight. I was too empty to feel the usual nausea. Too empty and too full of power. I reached out with my mind, into the *otherness* of light and heat and the glowing river of *time*.

Time slowed. *My heart beat.*

The flesh of my face burned, blistered, my eyes watering in a slow-motion flush of protective tears that scalded down my cheeks. And I heard the Waldroup brothers praying the Lord's Prayer. "Our father, who art in heaven, hallowed be thy name...."

I took the snake into my hands, allowing it to wrap about me, undulating coils of muscle. Moving faster than the gathering energies that were Azazel, I slid Mole Man's link, the link of binding, over the blade and followed it with my own prime, the four-inch stone ring. I held the snake's head and the tanto toward the swirling maelstrom of energies that was Azazel.

The suggestions for Trapping Darkness in Stone came to mind, but I discarded the incantation for something more complex, and yet far more straightforward. Something that used the elements in my current possession. The math swirled through my mind, clicking into place with solid mental snaps.

I said simply, "Stone and iron, Flame and steel. Consume."

Purple light raced at me through the earth, forging channels through rock and stone and earth and deep water, gathering power as it moved, ripping energy from the iron ore deposit in Alabama, from minerals and stone and unmined ores as it passed, faster than light. The snake's and tanto's hum rose in pitch, merged perfectly, a duet of death.

The energies slammed into me through the bottoms of my feet. Shot out from my palms where they gripped the snake and the tanto and the wire amulet. Blasted their way through my prime and the link that had once bound Azazel, the Fallen, Leviathan, the Dragon, who blazed in glory. Pure white Light ripped into the Dark seraph with concussive force, rocking me back.

Motes of black light detonated from him, shot out, whipped into the maelstrom. Azazel roared and turned to me. Fierce aqua eyes stabbed me. And he laughed, huge golden gongs of amusement and hatred mixed together in an unholy new emotion. He reached out a hand to me. I saw the black lightning gathering in his fingers, a ball of Darkness, a small black hole of chaos. But he moved slowly, outside of the singularity of time I had become. Rose turned to me, her eyes slowly focusing, her mouth opening in a time-lapse O of surprise.

"Wheels. Now," I said to the snake.

Light stabbed down from the living ship. It hit Azazel with the destructive power of a Pre-Ap nuclear bomb. In a slow, sinuous movement of luxons, the Fallen caught fire.

Black motes shifted out from Azazel, realigning into slow-moving rivers of energies. With a thought, I slowed time again, into a honey-thick construct that I moved through with the ease of heated steel. *My heart beat*, a sluggish susurration, beginning to speed, but still so slow.

Faster than the explosion, I opened the charmed circle of coiled snake and backed toward the shield. Snapped it off and eased beneath the stone, pulling the snake with me. I reactivated the shield. The explosion hit. Time readjusted in a flash of changing energies.

Even beneath the shield protection, we were thrown to our knees as if a huge hand had swatted us down. Scuttling,

my champards and the elders cringed together under the
levitating pile of broken rock, fear turning their auras into
spikes of green and red gold.

Azazel whirled like a dervish, flaming, burning, silent
but for an electric hum that hurt my ears. Lightning flew,
hitting the walls, exploding through them, sending some
tumbling to the ground. Black-light motes sizzled and
popped. The stench of burning seraph altered, tainted by
the reek of brimstone. Azazel's form was a black core,
deeper than Darkness. More than night, Darker than
eternity. Black-light swirling with chaotic energies older
than time.

Rose turned away from me. Protected by her shield, she
extended her arm, holding up the bare wood cross. Heat
exploded from it in a ball of flame, expanding, rolling out
from her, a conflagration. Fire rolled over the seraphs and
into the larvae, a wave of destruction, scorching the bloodless succubi to ash as it moved. The new things, the crea-
tions of the Dragon, died. The flash of fire was so intense,
nothing unprotected could survive it. The fire slammed,
surging like a tsunami against the church walls.

The flame climbed the stone, cleansing it, heating the
remaining walls red hot. Shattering the rock with the
sudden heat transfer. Flames coiled up and over like a
wave of fire. Recoiled. Reversed. Unbidden, time again
thickened.

Rose looked at me, smiling, burning mage-bright, standing in a ring of power, a cross in her hand. In that instant, I
hated my twin. Hated her. And I knew she saw it in my face.
Her smile faltered. The flames rushed at us.

I released the pile of stones. With a roar, they fell over
the shield, providing insulation from the heat that was ric-
ocheting back. In the endless instant as they descended, I
saw the seraphs.

Standing in the midst of the fire was Raziel, Rose's death
fire whipping away the spell of lust that had crippled him.
Beside him knelt Cheriour and four other forms, each flaming, not with destructive fire, but with its own power. Trans-
mogrifying. Wings spreading for flight.

And Azazel. In a single instant of *time*, his energies

imploded like a black star, scintillating, dying. Surely dying. . . .

Untouched by it all was my twin, her face full of shock and horror, perhaps realizing only in that instant of time-no-time what she had become, shining with death and sacrifice. The stone of the earth closed over us.

Chapter 24

We sat, my champards and I, and the kirk elders, buried under a dome of rock, slate tiles, and detritus, tons of it pressing against the shield. The fire was so intense that it heated the stone, heated the air inside with us, carrying smoke. The silence was broken only by a rare cough and groan of pain I couldn't dispel. I had used all my healing amulets on Rupert. I was drained of power. I couldn't even ease my own pain, the broken ribs stabbing me with each breath.

When the smoke and heat grew too intense, I touched the snake, which lay coiled loosely around my right leg, eyes on me in the dark of the artificial cavern. Its tongue tasted my hand, much as a dog might lick its master. Wordless, I asked it to give us breathable air. Immediately a stream blew in through a crack in the rock, cool and fresh. The mélange of smells, human, kylen, half-breed, and me, all dirty, bloody, wounded, and full of despair, decreased.

In mage-sight I watched them, trapped in the dome with me, their body language saying so much more than the silence. Lucas sat crouched in the far corner, as far from me as he could get. Thadd cradled his broken wing, his face turned, as if he could see me in the dark if he looked my way. The elders Waldroup sat back-to-back, heads nodding with exhaustion. Jasper stared at me through the dark, his eyes blazing with prophetic power and zeal. Audric sat beside Rupert, his back to me, silent, unmoving.

Tears trickled down my cheeks at the sight of my teacher and the body of my friend. Cheran slept. I had chained the Dragon. And my twin had destroyed its minions, the larvae of the succubus. And it had cost me a life I held dear.

Of them all, only Eli lay close, supine, staring into the dark above him, as if he could see the domed rock above. One hand curled around my ankle, as if securing me there, near him.

An hour passed before I could no longer bear the silence. I set aside the Apache Tear. And waited.

A tapping came, at long last, Rose, assuring me that the heat was dispelled enough for humans to survive it. I recognized my sister's mind. I was frightened of what I saw there. But I had no choice, and no time to deliberate, decide, and choose a course of action. With a word, I let go of the stone. The rock slid and fell with a crash, forming a three-foot-high, ring-shaped pile on the floor of the church. I felt the floor give and shudder with the action, but the ancient wood held.

I smelled seraph on the icy wind, rich scents of vanilla and pepper and wonderful things. But mage-heat didn't flare, not even a little, killed by the endorphins of battle-lust and the horror of death. When the dust settled, I clambered over the stone to stand in the night, the snake slithering after me and retaking its position on my leg. More slowly, my champards followed, all but Audric.

Beside a Raven, my twin sat on a pile of old pews in front of a huge hole in the floor. The wood edges were scarred, scorched, and brittle, leaving floor space only around what was left of the outer walls of the old church—which were mostly gone. Only the front wall with the door openings still stood, staring out at the night. The dais was burned away.

The wind blowing in was frigid and I shivered: I had lost my battle cloak, seeing it last in a puddle of Rupert's blood. The floor creaked again. The whole place was about to go. And I couldn't have cared less.

Eli moved slowly to my left and waited. Thadd limped to my right. Some small, sane part of me noted that it wasn't the proper positions for them, but I pushed the thought away. Nothing mattered now. I looked overhead, to see a cloud-thickened night sky, and the first hint of snowflakes. Two fell in lazy spirals, chunky and wet, to plop on the still-warm floor and melt. The wheels were nowhere to be seen. As if it heard my thought, the snake licked my face, a single touch of its tongue.

Ignoring the snake, ignoring the seraph, I studied my twin. Twin, not just littermate. We shared the same genetic structure. The same blood. She looked at me, her face gaunt, smeared with filth and blood, her eyes fearful and guilty. "I'm sorry," she whispered.

My voice rasping, impassive, I said, "Death mages always are." Rose flinched in the silence that followed my words. "The spur?" I asked, not knowing why, except that I couldn't ask the harder questions.

Fingers fumbling, she pulled a thong from beneath the frayed dress she wore. On it dangled two amulets, one the spur, black-light motes dancing through it. She touched the spur. "I bound it to me," she said. "I took it as my prime."

I hadn't known that was possible, but I didn't quibble. The other amulet was a seraph stone. I had no reaction to that either. I wasn't certain I'd have an emotional reaction ever again. Finally, I looked at the Raven. It was Raven One. I wondered if he had a name.

In lieu of greeting, I said to him, "Stone and fire, water and air, blood and kin prevail."

The Raven answered back, his voice like bells chiming in a high tower. "Wings and shield, dagger and sword, blood and kin prevail." He snapped his wings open and closed, the sound like a hand clap. "The Most High is pleased with you."

"Well, isn't that just ducky," I said, hearing my vicious undertone.

Rock and debris scattered and shifted and I felt Audric join me, his body heat like a furnace at my frozen back. He said, "If the omega mage has earned the pleasure of the Most High, then offer her a boon." There was something formal about Audric's voice, the tones of a mage's legal counsel. I wanted to glance around, but suddenly this had become something other than a chance for me to be spiteful to a seraph who had survived, when the most important one in my life was dead. I kept my eyes front and center.

The Raven closed his eyes a moment, turning his beautiful face to the night sky. When he reopened them, he said, "A blessing is acceptable. Raziel comes."

The night sky brightened and my seraph circled the church, scarlet wings outspread, shining the clear ruby light of seraphic energies. With a dip and curl of wings, he dropped down and landed, toes pointing. He was wearing a white tunic and a crimson robe, the exact shade of his plumage. His ruby eyes reminded me of the gold and ruby aura that had hovered over Barak. *Lolo? Another one I lost.*

Raziel looked at me, took in the stances of my champards, and something in his expression flickered. "What would she have?" he asked Audric, his voice beautiful and serene.

"Bless her by bringing back Rupert," he said.

Hope, which I had thought buried and dead, shot through me.

"That is forbidden," Raziel said, flicking his eyes to me and away. The hope died, settling like ash in my heart.

"His sacrifice was a gift of great power in the heavens," Raziel said. "But I will save the lives of the mortals my mage cares for, and restore them, heal them. I will bring her additional seraph stones that she may share and use as she will, that others of her choosing may be part of us. And we will fight together, my mage and I and the wheels." Turning to me, he said, "You are blessed. A boon you may ask at a time of your choosing. Blessed, blessed indeed."

Blessed. The thought was a curse in my heart. Tears, long cried out, gathered in my eyes, making the seraphs waver. Making Rose look soft and innocent, her matted hair and tattered dress fluttering. She glowed with mage energies, and I noted the conjure she used to keep warm. Noted it and hated it because it was torn from Rupert's life.

A third unarmored seraph touched down behind Raziel, his approach not noted until he landed. It was Barak, but a changed Barak. Shock scudded through me, my heart thumping painfully. *They'll bring one of their own back, but not one of mine?* A spike of fury stabbed deep. The snake tightened on my leg in commiseration or warning. If I let go of the anger I held in check, I would bring down destruction, boon or no boon.

Barak stepped around Raziel, toward me, pale green

robes flowing, his wings tightly furled, hands empty as he knelt at my feet. The seraph was glowing with white light, his hair falling shimmering over his shoulder. Dark green feathers were bright with radiance, an iridescence that came from within more than reflected from without. His silver-flecked gray eyes lit on mine, his face smiling and peaceful.

"He fell among the Watchers," Raziel said. "He was punished. He suffered in the prison of the Dark."

Barak lifted his face. "You set me free," he said, "you and Daria, who gave her life for mine." I felt my heart crack at the words. Mages always gave too much when seraphs were involved. Gave the ultimate.

"Now, you must judge him," Raziel said, ruby irises sparkling like gems.

"Me?" my voice broke, ugly against the backdrop of seraphic tones.

"Child of man. Omega mage," Barak said. At the titles, the seraphs stood.

"You saved us from temptation. You judged the Dragon," Raziel said, "a Prince of the Fallen. You must also judge the Watcher."

I remembered Jasper's prophecy: *The children of men are gathered. The dragon breaks free. All the old things have passed away.* I licked my lips. I couldn't bring Rupert back. I couldn't exact revenge for his death by killing my twin. My hands clenched, reaching for swords I no longer carried. I took a breath of the frigid air and blinked away the useless tears. There was so much I couldn't do. But I *could* help the Watcher.

I cleared my throat, wishing for water that was long gone. "Barak gave up his life to destroy the Dragon. He gave his bones to be burned," I said. That sounded like scripture, but I couldn't have said which one. "He gave himself in the fight against Darkness. Against"—I tested the word before I spoke it—"against chaos." That felt right. The snake turned away from me and stared at the seraphs.

I drew on the visa for advice and considered the scripture it gave me, Genesis 1. God, in the original creation story, was always plural, the singular names for him appearing only later, as he began to interact with humans—and after the Fall. So I quoted the scripture, using the plural Hebrew word for God that was in the creation texts. And I did so to let the holy ones know that I understood about the Stars of the Morning and the group effort it had taken for creation. A group effort that may have included Azazel . . . "'At the creation of the universe, the Elohim said, "Let there be light": and there was light.'"

The seraphs didn't look away, expressionless faces seemingly patient. Raziel finished the quote, "'And Elohim saw the light, that it was good: and Elohim divided the Light from the Darkness.'" He nodded once, as if in agreement.

"Barak stood in the balance, between Light and Dark," I said. "He chose Light and order. He gave his body to be burned. I say let him be restored to the Host."

Wordless, Barak fell to the ground at my feet. At first, I wasn't certain that I had said the right thing, but when he opened his eyes, he was crying and smiling, ecstasy so strong on his face that I closed my eyes.

Raziel knelt beside him and said, "Welcome, brother. You are home."

The seraphs threw their arms around one another, clasping one another close, wings lifting and flight feathers intermingling. Barak and Raziel stood together, the ruby and the . . . the emerald.

Oh no. No.

"Damn. He used you," Eli muttered.

It was clear, clearer than the moon on a cloudless night. Raziel and Barak were more than brother warriors, they were brothers indeed.

"Yeah. He did," I said. Raziel had pushed and herded me toward Barak. From the very beginning, as had Daria, my Lolo. A seraph of the Light can't help a Fallen, not even a Watcher. But he could make sure someone else did.

My seraph? If I'd had a blade, I'd have skewered Raziel where he stood.

Epilogue

I woke feeling warm and safe, surrounded by the smells of human, kylen, and, more distant, half-breed. Eli's arm was around my waist, my body cradled against his. Lucas slept facing me, his head on my outstretched arm, his breath soft and scented with the anise aroma of manna. Across the foot of the bed, Thadd slept, his healed wings draped over his body, plaid flannel pajamas peeking through the plumage, my crocheted afghan twisted around him.

They weren't sleeping with me following multiple-partner sexual antics. Well, not yet, anyway. They were here because there was no other place to sleep. There hadn't been much of the town left standing. Mineral City, with the exception of the shielded lofts, dress shop, and Thorn's Gems, had been a smoking ruin.

Downstairs and in the landing outside my door, I heard the soft susurration of breathing and the muted footfalls of someone going to the bathroom. Seventy people still routinely slept here, though more moved out of the shop each day, as they began to accept that the danger had passed, that safety had been restored to the hills.

I raised up on an elbow to see Audric, his big body sprawled across the leather couch that had once been in Rupert's apartment. It was one of the few things he had claimed from Rupert's estate. No one had gainsaid him. Not even the orthodox, who had looked a bit dazed when we walked out of the night, trailed by three seraphs, and shouted for Ciana to open the shield. The seraphs had been singing, voices like bells and oboes. It was weird. I wasn't able to understand a single word they sang, but I was pretty sure it was a song about me. About the prophecy they were so sure I had fulfilled.

Rose slept on my old couch, pushed into the corner of the room. Away from the rest of us. So far, all my champards had shown a distinct disinclination for being around her. I made it a point to look at her with only human vision, so I didn't have to see the strange aura she now carried, pale rose spiked with green. It wasn't a healthy mage pattern. Rather, the one time I had looked at her, it had been ragged, as if chewed at the edges. Ugly.

Eli mumbled and pulled me to him, but I eased away and draped the covers to keep him warm. I didn't want him to wake with me snuggled close. The day before had been uncomfortable enough, with proof of his interest pressed against me. For the last few weeks, several of my champards had been silently urging me to take one—or more—of them as bed partner, but I was resisting.

Unsurprisingly, Eli had brought the silent tug-of-war into the open, boldly suggesting I take all of them, together. He'd been serious, or as serious as he ever was, offering to have an orgy-sized saddle specially made for us.

Though she had to know she was an outcast of sorts, Rose had looked interested. But I had been raised in Mineral City, under the hand of the orthodoxy. Lucas and I had both looked away at his suggestion. Thadd had laughed and released kylen pheromones, reminding me he could give me something none of the others could offer. And I knew I wasn't ready. I may never be ready to either choose between them or take more than one.

I was undecided about a lot of things. Like, what now? What was I going to do? Stick around and help finish rebuilding Mineral City? The reconstruction had been moving fast, with Rose, Cheran, and me helping move and transport stone for buildings. It was tiring work, but we had found a way to meld our disparate gifts in a useful way. It was the only time I could stand to be around the other two, and even the useful work left a sick taste in my mouth.

Or I could head back to the New Orleans Enclave. They

had issued an invitation to join a research group on the nature of the Most High.

Me. In a research group. Eli had laughed at that one too. Audric had pronounced it a ruse to get me back there and dissect me. Especially the angry black ring that marked my side, like a tattoo of the link that had chained Azazel. The fact that they knew about the ring was evidence that Cheran had been in communication with them. Needless to say, the mage had been ousted to sleep elsewhere, crowded among an adoring gaggle of human females.

My greatest fear, however, was for Ciana. Fear that the mages really wanted her and were using me to get her close enough to take her. I had no idea if they would honor my jurisdiction over her as mistrend.

I crawled out of the bed and gathered up a tunic, T-shirt, and jeans and moved on bare feet to the front of the loft. Outside, I heard the drips, tinks, and pings of water, the gurgle of runnels, the splash of melted snow. Spring was coming early, the sun rising each day to reveal more of the green earth budding out.

Dressing in the gray light at the front window that overlooked the ruins of Shamus Waldroup's bakery, I looked down, straight down to the Toe River. Everything between it and the loft was gone but for a few old stone buildings. Only three new ones had been rebuilt so far.

As for the river, it was flowing again. As if the snake knew what was needed, the wheels had appeared in the second week after the battle that chained Azazel, and cleared the avalanche debris from both ends, melting the tons of snow, burning splintered trees, and restoring the river of water. Amethyst had said nothing, sitting like a marble statue in the navcone of her living ship, eyes closed. I knew I had made an enemy. I hadn't seen the snake or the ship since, but the citrine pear hanging on my amulet necklace now had an eye in its center. A purple eye that never closed. It was more than disconcerting.

I could hear the Toe River over the sounds of the loft as I pulled on my socks and shoes. It was roaring, the way it did in spring when the winter's accumulation of ice and snow began to melt. And far down the mountain, I heard the sound of a train whistle.

Read on for a preview of another
Rogue Mage novel by Faith Hunter,

SKINWALKER

Available from Roc.

I wheeled my bike down Decatur Street and eased deeper into the French Quarter, the bike's engine puttering. My shotgun was slung over my back, a Benelli M4 Super 90, loaded for vamp with hand-packed silver fléchette rounds. I carried a selection of silver crosses in my belt, hidden under my leather jacket, and stakes were secured in loops on my jeans-clad thighs. The saddlebags on my bike were filled with my meager travel belongings—clothes in one side, tools of the trade in the other. As a vamp killer for hire, I travel light.

I'd need to put the vamp hunting tools out of sight for my interview. My hostess might be offended. Not a good thing when said hostess held my next paycheck in her hands and possessed a set of fangs of her own.

A guy, a good-looking Joe, standing in a doorway, turned to follow my progress as I motored past. A dark-haired local, he wore leather boots, a jacket, and jeans, like me, though his hair was short and mine was down to my hips. His eyes followed me down the street. A Kawasaki motorbike leaned on a stand nearby. I didn't like his interest, but he wasn't hunting. He didn't prick my predatory or territorial instincts. Maybe just a guy looking for a quick lay. In this city, anything was possible.

I maneuvered the bike down St. Louis and then onto Dauphine, weaving between shop workers heading home for the evening and early revelers out for fun. I spotted the address in the fading light. Katie's Ladies was the oldest continually operating whorehouse in the Quarter, in business since 1845, though at various locations, depending on hurricane, flood, rent, and the agreeable nature of local law. I parked, set the kickstand and unwound my long legs from my bike.

I had found two bikes in a junkyard in Charlotte, North Carolina, bodies rusted, rubber rotted. They were in bad shape. But Jacob, a river rat and restoration expert living along the Catawba River, took my money, fixed one up, and used the other for parts, ordering whatever else he needed over the Net. It took six months.

During that time I'd hunted for him—keeping his wife and four kids supplied with venison, rabbit, turkey (whatever I could catch, as maimed as I was)—restocked supplies from the city with my hoarded money, and rehabbed my damaged body back into shape. It was the best I could do for the months it took me to heal. Even someone with my rapidly healing body and variable metabolism takes a long while to totally mend from a near beheading.

Now that I'd healed, I needed work. My best bet was a job killing off a rogue vampire who was hunting in the City of Jazz. It was taking down as many as three tourists a night and had left a squad of cops, drained and smiling, dead where it dropped them. The scuttlebutt was that it held all the men in thrall while it feasted. It hadn't been satisfied with just their blood. It had eaten their livers and a few other internal organs. All of which suggested the rogue was an old, powerful, deadly, wacked-out vamp. The nutty ones were always the worst.

Just last week, Katherine "Katie" Fonteneau, the titular head lady of Katie's Ladies, had e-mailed me. According to my Web site, I had successfully taken down an entire blood-family in the mountains near Asheville. And I had. No lies on the Web site or in the media reports—not bald-faced ones anyway. Truth is, I'd nearly died, but I'd done the job, made a rep for myself, and then taken off a few months to spend and invest my legitimately gotten gains. Or to heal, but spin is everything. A lengthy vacation sounded better than the complete truth.

I took off my helmet and the clip that held my hair, pulling my braids out of my jacket collar and letting them fall around me, beads clicking. I adjusted the braids, rearranging them to hang smoothly, with no lumps or bulges. I used the motion and the time to assure my safety through the upcoming interview. To take in the city. And to try to relax. I was nervous, and being nervous around a vamp was just plain dumb.

The sun was setting, casting a red glow on the horizon, limning the ancient buildings, shuttered windows, and wrought-iron balconies in fuchsia. It was pretty in a purely human way. I opened my senses and let my beast taste the world. It liked the smells and wanted to prowl. *Later,* I promised it.

Soon. Predators usually growl when irritated. As it was, she sent mental claws into my soul, kneading. It was uncomfortable, but the claw pricks kept me alert, which I'd need for the interview. I had never met a civilized vamp, certainly never done business with one. So far as I knew, vamps and skinwalkers had never met. This could get interesting.

I clipped my sunglasses onto my collar, lenses hanging out. Cool is good, but most vamps like it dark and I didn't want to limit my senses. I glanced at the witchy-locks on my saddlebags and, satisfied, walked to the narrow red door. The man inside was definitely human, but big enough to be something else. Professional wrestler or troll. Both, maybe. The thought made me smile. He blocked the door, standing with arms loose and ready. "Something funny?" he asked, voice like a horse-hoof rasp on stone.

"Not really. Tell Katie that Jane Yellowrock is here." Tough always works best on first acquaintance. That my knees were knocking wasn't a consideration.

"Card?" Troll asked. A man of few words. I liked him already. My new best pal. With two gloved fingers, I unzipped my leather jacket, fished a business card from an inside chest pocket, and extended it to him. Troll took the card and closed the door in my face. I might have to teach my new pal a few manners. But that was nearly axiomatic for all the men of my acquaintance.

I heard a bike two blocks away. It wasn't a Harley. Maybe a Kawasaki, like the bright red crotch rocket I had seen earlier. I wasn't surprised when it came into view and was the

Joe from Decatur Street. He pulled his bike up beside mine, powered down, and sat there, eyes hidden behind glasses so much like mine that we could have ordered them from the same online site. He had a toothpick in his mouth, and it twitched once as he pulled off his helmet.

The Joe was a looker. A little taller than my six feet even, he had olive skin, black hair, black brows. Black jacket and jeans. Black boots. Bit of overkill with all the black, but he made it work, with muscular legs wrapped around the red bike.

No silver in sight. No shotgun, but a suspicious bulge beneath his right arm. Made him a leftie. Something glinted in the back of his collar. A knife. Maybe more than one. There were scuffs on his boots—Western, like mine—not Harley butt stompers. But his were Frye's and mine were ostrich-skin Lucchese's. I pulled in scents, my nostrils widening. His boots smelled of horse manure, fresh. Local boy then, or one who had been in town long enough to find a mount. I smelled horse sweat and hay, a clean blend of scents. And cigar. It was the cigar that made me like him. The taint of steel, gun oil, and silver made me fall in love. Well, sorta. My beast thought he was kinda cute, and maybe tough enough to be worthy of us. There was a faint scent of something deeper on the man, hidden beneath the surface smells, that made me wary.

The silence had lasted longer than I expected, since he had been the one to pull up to me, but silence didn't bother me. Clearly, it bothered the Joe. His cheek jumped. I let a half grin curl my lip. He smiled back and eased off his bike. Behind me, I heard footsteps inside Katie's. I maneuvered so that the Joe and the doorway were both visible. No way could I do it and be subtle, but I lifted a shoulder to show I had no hard feelings. Just playing it smart. Even for a pretty boy.

Troll opened the door and jerked his head to the side. I took it as the invitation it was and stepped inside, leaving the Joe outside. "You got interesting taste in friends," Troll said as the door closed on the sight of the pretty boy.

"Never met him. Where you want the weapons?" Always better to offer than to have them removed. Power plays work all kinds of ways.

Troll opened an armoire. I unbuckled the shotgun holster

and set it inside, pulling crosses from my belt and thighs and from beneath my coat until there was a nice pile. Silver. Thirteen of them—excessive—but the number drew attention away from my backup weapons. Next came the wooden stakes and silver stakes. Thirteen of each. And the silver vial of holy water. One vial. If I carried thirteen, I'd slosh. Small joke. One I made from time to time when I was trying to be ingratiating. Or cute. I don't do cute well. It takes effort.

I hung the leather jacket on the hanger inside the armoire and tucked the sunglasses in the inside pocket with the cell phone. I closed the armoire door and assumed the position so Troll could search me. He grunted as if surprised but pleased, and did a thorough job. To give him credit, he didn't seem to be enjoying it overmuch—used only the backs of his hands, no fingers, didn't linger or stroke where he shouldn't. Breathing didn't speed up. Heart rate stayed regular. Things I can sense if it's quiet enough. After a thorough search inside the tops of my boots, he said, "This way."

I followed him down a narrow hallway that made two crooked turns toward the back of the house. We walked over old Persian carpets, past oils and watercolors done by famous and not-so-famous artists. The hallway was well lit with stained-glass Lalique sconces every few feet. They looked real, not like reproductions. The walls were newly painted a soft butter color that worked with the light to illuminate the paintings. Classy joint for a whorehouse. The Christian children's home schoolgirl in me was both appalled and intrigued.

When Troll paused outside the red door at the hallway's end, I stumbled, catching my foot on the carpet. He caught me with one hand, and I pushed off him with just a little body contact. I managed to look embarrassed when he shook his head. He knocked. I braced myself and palmed the one cross he had missed. And the tiny two-shot derringer, both hidden against my skull on the crown of my head, and covered by my braids, which men never, ever searched, as opposed to my Lucchese's, which men always had to stick their fingers in. It was a partial excuse for the faux stumble and having my hands high.

He opened the door and stood aside. The room was neat

and Spartan, but each of the pieces within looked Spanish. Old Spanish. Like Queen Isabella and Christopher Columbus old. The woman, wearing a teal dress and soft slippers, standing beside the desk, could have passed for twenty until you looked in her eyes. Then she might have passed for said Queen's older sister. Old, old, *old* eyes. Peaceful as she stepped toward me. Until she caught my scent.

In a single instant her eyes bled red, pupils went wide and black, and her fangs snapped down. She leaped. I dodged her, sliding under her leap to the far wall as I pulled the cross and ripped the derringer from my hair. The cross was for the vamp, the gun for Troll. She hissed at me, fangs fully extended. Her claws were bone white and two inches long. The second I'd started moving, Troll had pulled a gun too. A big gun. Men and their pissing contests. *Crap.* Why can't they ever just let me be the only one with a gun?

"I'm not human," I said, my voice steady. "That's what you smell." I couldn't do anything about the tripping heart rate, which I knew would drive her further over the edge. But I'm an animal. Biological factors always kick in. So much for trying not to be nervous.

"Predator," she hissed. Vamp pheromones filled the air, bitter as wormwood. The cross in my hand glowed with a cold white light, and Katie, if that was her original name, tucked her head, shielding her eyes.

"Katie?" Troll asked.

"I'm not human," I repeated. "I'll really hate shooting your troll here, to bleed all over your rugs, but I will."

"Troll?" Katie asked. Her body froze with that inhuman stillness they possess when thinking or resting or whatever else they do when they aren't hunting, eating, or killing. Her shoulders dropped and her fangs clicked back into the roof of her mouth with a sudden spurt of humor. Vampires can't laugh and go vampy at the same time. It's two distinctive parts of them—one part still human, one part rabid hunter. Well, that's likely insulting, but then this was the first so-called civilized vamp I'd ever met. All the others I'd had personal contact with were sick, twisted killers. And then dead. Really dead.

Troll's eyes narrowed behind the .45 he had aimed my

way. I figured he didn't like being compared to the bad guy in a children's nursery tale. I was better at fighting, but I'd try negotiation. "Tell him to back off. Let me talk." I nudged it a bit. "Or I'll take you down and he'll never get a shot off." Unless he noticed that I had set the safety on his gun when I fell against him. Then I'd have to shoot him. And I wasn't betting on my twenty-twos stopping him unless I got an eye shot. Chest hits wouldn't even slow him down. In fact they'd likely just make him mad, so I *really* didn't want to shoot him.

When neither attacked, I said, "I'm not here to stake you. I'm who I said I am. I'm here to do a job, to take out a rogue vamp that your own council declared outlaw. But I don't smell human, so I take precautions. One cross, one stake, one two-shot derringer." The word stake didn't elude her. Or him. He'd missed three weapons. No Christmastime bonus for Troll.

"What are you?" she asked.

"You tell me where you sleep during the day and I'll tell you what I am. Otherwise, we can agree to do business. Or I can leave."

Telling the location of a lair—where a vamp sleeps—is information for lovers, dearest friends, or family. Katie chuckled. It was one of the silky laughs that her kind can do, low and erotic, like vocal sex. My beast purred. It liked the sound.

"Are you offering to be my toy for a while, little nonhuman female?" When I didn't answer, she slid closer, despite the glowing cross, and said, "You are interesting. Tall, slender, young." She leaned in and breathed in my scent. "Or not so young. What are you?" she pressed, her voice heavy with fascination. Her eyes had gone back to their natural color, a sort of grayish hazel, but blood blush still marred her cheeks, so I knew she was still primed for violence. That violence being my death.

"Secretive," she murmured, her voice taking on that tone they use to enthrall, a deep vibration that seems to stroke every gland. "Intriguing scent. Likely tasty. Perhaps your blood would be worth the trade. Would you come to my bed if I offered?"

"No," I said. No inflection in my voice. No interest, no revulsion, no irritation, nothing. Nothing to tick off the vamp or her servant.

"Pity. Put down the gun, Tom. Get our guest something to drink."

I didn't wait for Tommy Troll to lower his weapon; I dropped mine. Beast wasn't happy, but she understood. I was the intruder in Katie's territory. While I couldn't show submission, I could show manners. Tom lowered his gun and his attitude at the same time and holstered the weapon as he moved into the room toward a well-stocked bar.

"Tom?" I said. "Uncheck your safety." He stopped mid-stride. "I set it when I fell against you in the hallway."

"Couldn't happen," he said.

"I'm fast. It's why your employer sent for a job interview."

He inspected his .45 and nodded at his boss. Though why anyone would want to go around with a holstered .45 with the safety off is beyond me. It smacks of either stupid or quiet desperation, and Katie had lived too long to be stupid. I was guessing that the rogue had made her truly apprehensive. I tucked the cross inside the leather belt holding up my Levi's, in a little lead foil–lined pocket, and eased the small gun in beside it, strapping it down. There was a safety, but on such a small gun, it was easy to knock the safety off with an accidental brush of my arm.

"Is that were you hid the weapons?" Katie asked. When I just looked at her, she shrugged as if my answer were unimportant and said, "Impressive. You are impressive."

Katie was one of those dark ash blondes with long, straight hair so thick it whispered when she moved, falling across the teal silk that fit her like a second skin. She stood five feet and a smidge, but height was no measure of power in her kind. She could move as fast as I could and kill in an eyeblink. She had buffed nails that were short when she wasn't in killing mode, pale skin, and she wore exotic makeup with an Egyptian flair around the eyes. Some kind of glitter. Not the kind of look I'd ever had the guts to try. I'd rather face down a grizzly than try to achieve a *look*.

"What'll it be, Miz Yellowrock?" Tom asked.

"Cola's fine. No diet."

He popped the top on a Coke and poured it over ice so cold it crackled and split when the liquid hit it. Placed a wedge of lime on the rim and handed it to me. His employer got a tall fluted glass of something milky that smelled sharp, toxic, and alcoholic. Well, at least it wasn't blood on ice.

"Thank you for coming such a distance," Katie said, taking one of two chairs and indicating the other for me. Both chairs were situated with backs to the door, which I didn't like, but I sat as she continued. "We never made proper introductions, and the In-ter-net," she said, separating the syllables, as if the term were strange to her, "is no substitute for formal and proper introductions. I am Katherine Fonteneau." She offered the tips of her fingers, and I took them for a moment in my own before dropping them. I had never liked handling cold meat.

"Jane Yellowrock," I said. She sipped; I sipped. I figured that was enough etiquette. "Do I get the job?" I asked.

Katie waved away my impertinence. "I like to know the people with whom I do business. Tell me about yourself."

Cripes. The sun was down. I needed to be tooling around town, getting the smell and the feel of the place. I had errands to run, rocks to inspect, meat to buy. "You've been to my Web site, no doubt read my bio. It's all there in black and white." Well, in full-color graphics, but that was a mouthful.

Katie's brows raised politely. "Your bio is dull and uninformative. For instance, there is no mention that you appeared out of the forest at age twelve, a feral child raised by wolves, without even the rudiments of human behavior. That you were placed in a children's home, where you spent the next six years. And that you again vanished until you reappeared two years ago and started killing my kind."

My hackles started to rise, but I forced them down. I'd been baited by a roomful of teenaged girls before I even learned to speak English. After that, nothing was too painful. Instead I grinned and threw a leg over the chair arm. Which took Katie, of the elegant attack, aback. "I wasn't raised by wolves. At least I don't think so. I don't feel an urge to howl at the moon. I have no memories of my first twelve years of life, so I can't answer you about them. Yes, I was raised in a Christian children's home in the mountains of South Carolina. I left when I was eighteen, traveled around a while, and took up an apprenticeship with a security firm for two years. Then I hung out my shingle, and eventually drifted into the vamp hunting business.

"What about you? You going to share all your own deep, dark secrets, Katie of Katie's Ladies? Who is known to the world as Katherine Fonteneau, aka Katherine Louisa Dupre, Katherine Pearl Duplantis, and Katherine Vuillemont, among others I uncovered. Who renewed her liquor license in February, is a registered Republican, votes religiously, pardon the term, sits on the local vampiric council, has numerous offshore accounts in various names, a half interest in two local hotels, at least three restaurants and several bars, and has enough money to buy and sell this entire city if you wanted to."

"We have both done our research, I see."

I had a feeling Katie found me amusing. Must be hard to live a few centuries and find yourself in a modern world where everyone knows what you are and is either infatuated with you or scared silly of you. I was neither, which she liked, if the small smile was any indication. "So. Do I have the job?" I asked.

About the Author

A native of Louisiana, **Faith Hunter** spent her early years on the bayou and rivers, learning survival skills and the womanly arts. She liked horses, dogs, fishing, and crabbing much better than girly things. She still does.

In grade school, she fell in love with fantasy and science fiction, reading five books a week and wishing she "could write that great stuff." Faith now shares her life with her Renaissance Man and their dogs in an Enclave of their own. Faith is working on another book and a role-playing game, called The Rogue Mage, based on Thorn.

To find out more, go to www.faithhunter.net.